Sailor of Liberty

J. D. Davies is the prolific author of historical naval adventures. He is also one of the foremost authorities on the seventeenth-century navy, which brings a high level of historical detail to his fiction, namely his Matthew Quinton series. He has written widely on the subject, most recently *Kings of the Sea: Charles II, James II and the Royal Navy*, and won the Samuel Pepys Award in 2009 with *Pepys's Navy: Ships, Men and Warfare, 1649-1689.*

Also by J. D. Davies

The Matthew Quinton Journals

Gentleman Captain
The Mountain of Gold
The Blast that Tears the Skies
The Lion of Midnight
The Battle of All The Ages
The Rage of Fortune
Death's Bright Angel
The Devil Upon the Wave
Ensign Royal

Jack Stannard of the Navy Royal

Destiny's Tide
Battle's Flood
Armada's Wake

The Philippe Kermorvant Thrillers

Sailor of Liberty

J. D. DAVIES

Sailor of
LIBERTY

CANELO

First published in the United Kingdom in 2023 by

Canelo
Unit 9, 5th Floor
Cargo Works, 1-2 Hatfields
London SE1 9PG
United Kingdom

A CIP catalogue record for this book is available from the British Library.

Print ISBN 978 1 80436 087 3
Ebook ISBN 978 1 80436 086 6

Cover design by Patrick Knowles

Look for more great books at www.canelo.co

Printed and bound in Great Britain by Clays Ltd, Elcograf S.p.A.

1

MIX
Paper from
responsible sources
FSC
www.fsc.org   FSC® C018072

For Wendy, for twenty glorious years!

Hep stourm ne vezer ket trec'h

(There's no victory without fighting)

Old Breton proverb

AUTHOR'S NOTE

Throughout this book, the French characters use the words 'English' and 'British' interchangeably, as French people (and, of course, many other nationalities) often do to this day. Some of the names and words used by characters to describe different nationalities and races reflect the common, and in some cases universal, attitudes of both educated and uneducated people in the Western world in the 1790s.

Before the introduction of metric weights and measures in 1799, France had a byzantine and bewildering system of measurements with perhaps a quarter of a million different units in everyday use across the country. Derived from the system introduced by Emperor Charlemagne and loosely equivalent to that used in Britain, matters were complicated by the existence of (in some cases) several hundred names for the same unit across the different regions of France, while the amounts represented by the name of one unit might be wildly different between one province and another. Fortunately, the main units had names roughly similar to their English equivalents, and in most cases represented broadly similar weights, areas or distances: the *pied*, foot, was closer to thirteen inches than twelve, the *toise*, fathom, consisted of six *pieds*, the *pouce* was the equivalent of an inch, the *livre*, consisting of sixteen *onces*, was equivalent to a pound weight (but with many local variations), and so on. An exception was the *pinte*, which, confusingly, was more nearly equivalent to an English quart. There was nothing even roughly close to the English gallon, so I have used the French word *velte*, which corresponded to roughly 1.7 imperial gallons.

Characters

(Real historical personages are indicated by an asterisk)

The French

Philippe Kermorvant

In Saint-Malo and on the road west

Didier Larsonneur, seaman of the privateer *Le Quatorze Juillet*

Andre Defargues, innkeeper

Jean-Baptiste Carrier*, *représentant en mission* (representative on a mission) of the National Convention of the French Republic at Saint-Malo and then at Nantes

Etienne Pennec, old seaman

Gaspard Anquetil, lieutenant in the republican (Blue) army

Serge Retaillou, sergeant in the Blue army

At the Chateau de Brechelean and, later, in Paris

Alexandre Kermorvant, Philippe's illegitimate half-brother

Leonore, Alexandre's wife

Jacques Penhouet, steward of the estate

Martha, his wife, housekeeper of the chateau

Roland Quedeville, revolutionary

Madame Guitard, widow from Amiens

In Brest

Jeanbon Saint-André*, *représentant en mission* of the Committee of Public Safety at Brest

Justin Bonaventure Morard de Galles* , admiral commanding the French Atlantic Fleet in 1793

Valentine Hauchard, prisoner

Olivier and Roman, child beggars

Aboard the frigate Le Zéphyr

Martin Roissel, *lieutenant de vaisseau*, first lieutenant

Juan Ugarte, *enseigne de vaisseau*, second lieutenant

Claude-Marie Fingal, *enseigne de vaisseau*, third lieutenant

Jerome de Machault, lieutenant of Marines

Yves Guillaumin, *maître d'equipage*, sailing master

Marcel Garrigues, Marine sergeant and master gunner

Guy Payen, boatswain

Guillaume Fouroux, master carpenter

Valery Saint-Jacques, steward (purser)

Fabian Vaquin, *aspirant* (midshipman)

Jean-Jacques Lievremont, *aspirant* (midshipman)

Armand Carabignac, *aspirant* (midshipman)

Max Driaux, valet

Pierric Korbell, seaman

Arnaud Lucas, seaman

Morgan Launay, seaman

Gaston Mougenot, caulker

Paul Herbin, Marine

PART ONE

CHAPTER ONE

To whichever high, eminent and no doubt virtuous, etcetera, dignitaries of the new-fangled French Republic who read (or, indeed, are able to read) these words, this letter serves to introduce Captain Philippe Kermorvant, and to recommend him for a command in your navy. By birth he is a man of honour, by upbringing a mongrel who somehow fetched up in Reval and then Saint Petersburg some years ago in the wake of that eminent and famous sailor, Admiral John Paul Jones. I understand that Kermorvant's father has something of a name in your country as a 'philosopher', an odd trade, which I believe carries more weight in France than here in Russia. Thus his often strange opinions are apparently in accord with those of your republic, namely liberty, etcetera, equality, etcetera, etcetera, and he has an unaccountable urge to serve the cause of what he describes as his fatherland, especially since the unimaginable tragedy that I am sure he will relate to you. I have now sailed with him and fought with him for several years. He is a fine seaman, etcetera. A gallant warrior, etcetera. A loyal and dependable friend, etcetera, etcetera. You will not regret it if you employ him, for he is a good fellow despite not being Russian. If you reject him, though, I beg you to remember that he owes me money and implore you not to employ your fascinating new beheading machine to cut off his head.

Yours, etcetera, etcetera, etcetera,

Dmitri Ivanovich Kharabadze

Captain of the 110-gun line-of-battle ship Pyotr Velikiy in the service of Catherine, Empress of All the Russias, whom God and the archangels preserve

A lucky shot.

It could be nothing else. In such a fog not even the finest gun crew on Jones's old *Bonhomme Richard*, nor even on 'Black Dick' Howe's flagship far to the west, could ever have aimed blind and made such a devastating hit. A carronade, probably, one of the lethal smashers that were utterly deadly at close range. But even at point blank, such carnage could only have been achieved by a lucky shot.

The quarterdeck of the privateer *Le Quatorze Juillet*, six days out of Gothenburg and no more than six hours away from her home port of Saint-Malo, was an abattoir. Philippe saw the remains of Caradec, the captain, propped against the mizzen mast as though he were asleep. But the left side of his torso was gone, his organs oozing through the shattered remains of his ribcage. The remnants of his other watchkeeping officers and the helmsman were strewn across the deck. Somewhere astern, towards the hostile shore of Jersey, was the ship that had fired the devastating shot, hidden within the impenetrable bank of dense summer fog. A fellow privateer most probably, a corsair running out of Guernsey or Jersey to try to mop up any merchantmen that dared to run inshore, close to the Cotentin. Unlikely to be a ship of the British Royal Navy, Philippe thought. The *rosbifs* were hardly going to risk even a ketch so close to the shore of France.

Philippe knelt down by the body of young Morvan, a lively, carrot-headed fellow who had been keen to hear Philippe's tales of battles in strange navies and faraway seas. There were still signs of life, notably a barely audible groan from his lips, but as he turned Morvan over he could see the large oak splinter protruding from the lad's neck. Morvan's eyes seemed to settle upon him and recognise him, but the next moment they were fixed and unblinking. Morvan's body was the closest to the ship's wheel, which was, miraculously, intact; the enemy shot might easily have destroyed it, or the mizzen, or both. But Caradec had evidently taken the full force of the shot, albeit only after it had torn through enough planking to pour forth a deadly timber cloud of large shards and splinters.

Satisfied that the enemy was, for the moment, out of range and invisible, Philippe continued to survey the slaughter before him. Even through the deck above his head, moments before, he had heard Caradec's sudden cry of 'Alarm!' Other urgent voices screamed that a hull had suddenly appeared out of the fog, very close on the starboard quarter. Then there was the unmistakeable sound of a gun firing, quite a large one, not a swivel, followed by screams, followed by silence.

The silence was the strangest thing. He had been in several sea-fights during the last sixteen of his twenty-nine years – the preliminaries, the engagement itself, the aftermath – but there had always been noise. The sounds of commands being issued, men hauling on ropes and singing songs of defiance, trumpets blaring, drums beating, guns being hauled into position, the gunfire itself, the splintering of wood, the pitiful cries of the wounded and dying; all these were as familiar to him as breathing. Here, though, there was only the lapping of the water on the hull as it moved slowly through the fogbound waters of *La Manche* (or, as the enemy arrogantly termed it, the English Channel), the gentle creaking of the hull and the rustling of the sails, the murmuring of the men behind him in the waist of the privateer. Barely audible were the identical sounds from the enemy ship, invisible somewhere in the enshrouding fog. Silence. Or at any rate, as close to silence as one ever got at sea.

Philippe stood, turned and looked for'ard. Until a few moments before he had been reading in his tiny cabin below decks. This was not his ship and not his fight. There had to be one officer left, someone with the experience and the competence to take command of *Le Quatorze Juillet*. She was undermanned and underofficered, thanks to the unexpected haul of Dutch merchantmen they'd encountered off Texel and the generous prize crews Caradec had allocated to take them into Dunkirk, but surely there had to be one man left who could take acting command, fight off the enemy ship if it came to it, and give the necessary orders to see them all home to Saint-Malo. Surely not every single man capable of standing a watch could have been on the quarterdeck when the enemy opened fire?

Yet all he saw were lubbers or ordinary *matelots*. In turn, they would have seen a man of slightly above average height who looked older than his twenty-nine years and wore his long chestnut hair knotted behind his head, as many of his old shipmates had been wont to do. A few of the braver men were inching towards the unspeakable slaughterhouse on the quarterdeck, but most hung back, their expressions utterly terrified.

An old and very short *loup de mer*, a veteran sailor with skin like a lobster who must have been fifty if he was a day, had evidently been elected as the crew's spokesman. He took two steps forward.

'We heard tell that you're a seaman,' said the oldster with surprising boldness, his atrocious French overlain with a thick Breton accent that had become slightly more intelligible to Philippe during the course of the voyage. 'We heard tell that you're a captain.'

'I'm just a passenger,' said Philippe, speaking slowly to ensure his French, still slightly inferior to his English despite everything, was absolutely precise. 'I only took a berth with you because Captain Caradec agreed to give me a swift passage from Gothenburg.'

'We know,' said the old man, 'but like I say, Captain Caradec said you were a captain, too. That you'd been captain of a man-o'-war. So we're begging you… *Captain*. Take command. Get us away from those bastard English. Get us home to our wives and our children.'

Philippe cursed the fourth bottle of wine he had agreed to share with Caradec on the third night of the voyage. The Breton captain was an amiable man, and Philippe must have revealed more than he intended to. At the very least he had forgotten the old seamen's adage that nothing aboard a ship was private and everything was overheard.

He did not want this. He had hoped that his arrival in France would be unobtrusive, the better to ease his passage through the watchful troops and functionaries of the new republic. Caradec had assured him that he could buy the silence of the right people, ensure that eyes were turned away at the appropriate moments. But Caradec's shattered body was about to be bundled into a tarpaulin and his crew were asking Philippe to take command of his ship. No unobtrusive landing, then. Whether Philippe took command or not, *Le Quatorze Juillet* might be destroyed by the enemy somewhere out there in the fog bank, or she might be forced to surrender, in which case the delights of a pestilential English prison awaited the survivors. There was one alternative, though, and the more Philippe thought on it as he scanned the nervous faces and fearful eyes of the men before him, the more sense that alternative made.

'Very well,' said Philippe, laying his misgivings to one side. 'You all swear to obey my commands without dispute or hesitation?'

He saw four score of nodding heads, and heard nearly the same number of mumbled *Ouis* or Breton *Yas*. Still he remained silent, assessing this crew and this situation. He thought of other ships, of other men, many of them now dead. He thought of one woman… now dead. Finally he nodded almost imperceptibly to himself.

'Then I have the ship,' said Captain Philippe Kermorvant.

'So what are your orders, Cap'n?' said the oldster, exhaling with relief. 'Put on sail and try to outrun them? Wear away for Granville?'

Philippe considered the wind direction again, the probable position of the enemy, the state of the sails, the thickness of the fog. The likelihood was that the enemy had no idea what they had done, otherwise why would they have veered away after just one shot? The distant shape he had glimpsed through the fog seemed smaller than *Le Quatorze Juillet*, but it might well be nimbler, and her captain would certainly know these waters better than he did. He thought upon all these things, then came to his decision.

'*Non,*' he said, looking up at the only sails *Le Quatorze Juillet* bore aloft; staysails and topsails reefed to ensure they navigated the treacherous waters with utmost caution. Many a good ship had perished on the Chausey Isles, or so Caradec had said. '*Diminuer les voiles!*'

The French commands were still unfamiliar to Philippe, but he had to make the effort. After all, there would be no point in addressing this crew in Russian, or even the English of the Virginia tidewater. 'Take in all sail, but in absolute silence, you hear me? A dozen men to cover the officers' bodies, take them below and stow them on the orlop. With dignity, mind – with respect! Then all hands to your stations and await further orders.'

The old man assigned the detail that would attend to the dead. The rest of the crew dispersed to their stations, their definition of 'absolute silence' involving low murmuring and nods towards the strangely spoken unknown quantity whom they had just elected to the command of the privateer. His order to take in all sail, effectively taking all headway off the ship, had evidently caused consternation. If the enemy vessel had an entire battery of carronades, then surely *Le Quatorze Juillet* would now be a sitting target.

Only the old man was left in front of him. He had a few wisps of white hair left to him, roughly equal in number to the few teeth remaining in his mouth.

'You know these waters?' said Philippe.

'Been out in 'em since I were six,' said the oldster proudly. 'First fishing with my old *père* and my big brothers, then on privateers or men-o'-war. Sailed with De Grasse back in the day, too, on the old *Ville de Paris* before she was lost. Came home after the American war finished.'

Philippe had once been under the lee of the huge *Ville de Paris* when she lay at anchor off Cape Henry, so he and this old Breton had probably been only a few feet from each other all those years before. But this was no time for reminiscences.

'You can read a chart?'

'A chart, *ya*, but don't ask me to read a book, Cap'n. Sorry, Citizen Captain.'

The etiquette of the infant republic was still new. The former captain had paid lip service to it, but Philippe suspected that in his heart Caradec had been a secret royalist and not a *sans-culotte*, a term whose literal meaning – a man who wore rough trousers rather than the more dignified *culottes* – had somehow come to be applied to the truest, most diehard revolutionaries, the politicised peasants and artisans intent on driving the Republic's leaders to more and more extreme policies. There had been much amusement in Saint Petersburg at the news that the fledgling French Republic had named one of its largest warships the *Sans-Culotte*.

'And your name, *monsieur*?' said Philippe.

'Larsonneur, Citizen Captain. Didier Larsonneur.'

'Very well, Citizen Didier Larsonneur, you are now the *maître d'equipage* of *Le Quatorze Juillet*.'

The old man seemed unimpressed with his elevation to the usually exalted rank of sailing master.

'So that's more pay?'

'Yes, *Maître*, that's more pay.'

'Good, the old woman will be pleased.' The old man's leathery features creased as though he was suddenly in pain. 'Pardon me for saying so, Cap'n, but...'

'Yes, Citizen?'

'You talk funny. Perfect French and decent Breton, which is rare in a man of your breeding, I'd reckon, but it's like you're from somewhere else. You sound your words all strange, whichever language you're talking in. Like a foreigner, only your name is Breton. Why's that, then?'

'That, *Maître*, is a *very* long story.'

Then Philippe saw the indistinct blur of a dark shape emerging very slowly from the fog, a vengeful ghost ship vacating the underworld and edging once again towards the starboard quarter. The enemy had caught them.

CHAPTER TWO

From the rough log of the privateer Duke of Dorset, Captain Peter Guilbert, three days out of Saint Helier:

Winds SSW but very light, swirling fog banks. 11:15, briefly sighted unknown ship, believed to be French, nine miles by dead reckoning SSE of La Rocque. Fired one broadside at point blank, damage to enemy (if enemy she be) unknown. 11:20, lost sight of enemy. 11:50, sighted enemy again and now closing her. God willing, she will surrender without further bloodshed and will prove to be a lawful prize.

Philippe gave his orders to Larsonneur and the other senior hands in a low voice, then despatched them to all parts of the ship to pass on the commands to the men. Larsonneur raised an eyebrow at his new captain's orders but made no complaint. Philippe smiled. The old fisherman was more compliant than he himself had been when faced with such orders. But old Chichagov, the ancient, skeletal and affectedly Anglophile admiral who had commanded Philippe in the bloody Reval and Vyborg fights against the Swedes always used to say that an enemy's strategy depended chiefly upon their opponent – upon *you* – doing something. Preferably something stupid, but anything would do. That being the case, nothing proved more confusing than an adversary who resolutely refused to act. Philippe had been sceptical at the time, as had all of Chichagov's other officers. Yet the old man had been proved right.

His commands issued, Philippe placed his hands on the rail and watched the enemy vessel emerge slowly through the fog. Very soon, Philippe would learn whether his reasoning about his opponent was flawed and whether Chichagov's dictum did not apply in this instance. If it was, then he had already condemned the men of *Le Quatorze Juillet* to death, and he would shortly join poor Caradec to sail the celestial ocean for ever.

9

Courage, mon brave. The only plausible reason why the enemy would have veered away after firing just one shot was that they had no idea what or whom they had fired upon. Perhaps a junior officer had excitedly ordered a warning shot to be fired and disastrously bungled it – surely no captain would fire indiscriminately into the stern of a ship whose identity he did not know. Whatever the reason, the enemy could not have been close enough for long enough to be certain. Perhaps the enemy captain thought *Le Quatorze Juillet* might turn out to be a friendly ship, a fellow Englishman, maybe even a warship, in which case he would surely be destined for the gallows. But Philippe was banking on greed winning out in his enemy's calculations. The steadily but cautiously closing Jerseyman, if that's what it was, would see a stationary ship making no effort to get away, surely not what a man-of-war would be doing. The temptation to see whether it might be a rich French merchantman, and thus a fair prize, was proving irresistible, as Philippe hoped it would. And if it was a neutral instead? Well, that was surely the question the enemy captain was asking himself. In one sense it hardly mattered, for a neutral could be seized on suspicion that it was carrying goods bound for the enemy. There would be tortuous legal battles in the English Admiralty courts but it might be worth the risk, depending on what flag the neutral flew. Some neutrals, after all, carried rather more weight than others.

The idea had come to him from Caradec. During one of their pleasant dinners together, the corsair skipper had told Philippe of the time when he was sailing out of Civitavecchia and managed by distinctly underhand means to procure a most unusual trophy. A cardinal's whore had featured somewhere in the tale, but Philippe could not quite remember how.

The enemy ship was almost entirely visible now. In truth she was little more than a large cutter, certainly no more than two hundred tons, seemingly cut for only five great guns on each side. Almost certainly a uniform battery of carronades only. Fast, for sure, and more manoeuvrable than *Le Quatorze Juillet*, but much smaller than Philippe had expected, which was to the good. But the carronades had to be at least twelve-pounders, and that meant yet more serious, perhaps fatal, damage if they were permitted to make a sustained bombardment. Philippe could see the individual shapes of men in her fo'c's'le and in her tops. A large boarding party was forming in her waist, armed and ready to take possession of their quarry. Yes, they would be wondering exactly what the strange, silent ship before them might be. Time to enlighten them, then, although Philippe had precisely the opposite of enlightenment in mind.

He gave his signal to the man who was already in position at the foot of the mizzen shrouds, and the fellow nimbly ran up the chosen colours. The strange flag unfurled enough in the negligible breeze to reveal its device: an image of Saint Peter upon a white ground. The colours of the papal navy.

Philippe saw men on the enemy deck pointing at *Le Quatorze Juillet*. He could almost see his opposite number ordering his signal book brought up from his cabin and then thumbing frantically through the pages displaying the flags of every known nation on earth. Perhaps his finger was finally landing on the papal colours, and even a good Protestant would surely baulk at attacking a ship that might, just might, belong to the man who claimed to be the successor of Saint Peter himself.

The British ship was very close to the starboard quarter of *Le Quatorze Juillet*, but its bows were beginning to swing away, reflecting its captain's uncertainty. Even so, the existing momentum of the enemy hull was bringing it inexorably onto the broadside of the Breton corsair, and at point-blank range.

'Now!' cried Philippe, drawing his sword. 'Colours aloft! Run out your guns!'

The papal colours came down and the *Tricolore* of the infant republic broke out in their place. The men who had been in hiding in the tops and behind the rails stood up and levelled their muskets. Gunports snapped open, and the main armament of the French ship was run out.

The enemy captain now knew his mistake for certain. Philippe could hear him ordering all sail set and his carronades run out ready to open fire. But it was too late, the Jerseyman was too close, and the French ship's armament of six-pounders was much heavier.

'*Feu!*' Philippe ordered, the French words for the command coming to him from somewhere in the depths of his memory. '*Feu roulant!*'

A brisk fire. The Breton gun crews responded well, even the first two or three shots striking their target. Their enemy got off about the same number of shots from his carronades. One struck *Le Quatorze Juillet* forward, but low down, causing nothing like the havoc that had slaughtered Caradec, Morvan and the others. By contrast, the French battery was sweeping the deck of the much lower enemy vessel with grapeshot and chain shot. Philippe saw bodies torn to pieces by his men's fire. Disembodied limbs and heads appeared to swim through the air before falling to the deck or into the sea. Men screamed pitifully. Timbers, sails, shrouds and stays were shattered and shredded. Small fires broke out in several places on the enemy hull. The enemy continued to turn away, but this could only be a mistake, Philippe thought. The greater the range, the less effective the Englishman's carronades would be, and the more deadly the battery of *Le Quatorze Juillet*. The enemy captain had a chance if he came in close and duelled it out at point blank. He now knew that Philippe had greater firepower, but even if there were fewer of them, the carronades were short-range smashers and a fight at close quarters might yield another catastrophic shot like the one that had done for Caradec and his officers. Yet such a fight came with the risk that the guns of *Le Quatorze Juillet*, firing so much higher and now loaded with bar shot, might entirely destroy the Englishman's masts and rigging, making it impossible for her to run for Jersey or Guernsey.

Philippe did what a captain was expected to do. Waving his sword at the enemy, he strode up and down the deck, shouting encouragement at his men.

'*Vive la Republique! Vive la France! Vive la Bretagne!*'

The answering shout for Brittany was significantly louder and more enthusiastic than those for the Republic or France.

The Breton gun crews reloaded with the speed and zeal of a man-of-war's complement. Caradec, who had served in the navy back in the American war, had boasted that he was a stickler for gunnery and claimed his men were the best gun crews of any corsair on the Atlantic coast of France. Philippe had been sceptical at the time. The Bretons were not quite up to the standard of the tough New Englanders who had largely crewed the old *Lexington*, but they at least matched the erstwhile Russian peasants he had commanded on *Strela*. Second shots were pounding the hull of the enemy ship, now with no response from the English carronades. The captain must have transferred most of his men to the sails and the pumps in a desperate attempt to get away.

'A pursuit, *mon capitaine*?' asked Larsonneur, who was bathed in sweat.

Philippe turned to survey the scene all around *Le Quatorze Juillet*. As he did so, he felt a sudden pull and a stab of pain from the old wound in his side, inflicted by an Ottoman scimitar in the second Battle of the Liman. It always seemed to afflict him in combat, as if reminding him how close he had once been to death and how fortunate he was to fight another day.

'No, *Maître* Larsonneur,' he said, grimacing as he did so. 'He might easily lose us in the fog, and even if we caught and took him, what sort of prize crew could we muster after all the others that Captain Caradec assigned?'

One other thought crossed Philippe's mind, but he did not air it. If they captured the English ship, they would have to escort it into Saint-Malo. As it was, his arrival into the port was going to be far more public than he had wished for, but it might still be possible to get ashore, past the inevitable sentries, and away to his destination, without too many questions being asked. Bringing in a prize, though, would focus the full attention of every man, woman and child in the town on the victorious heroes of *Le Quatorze Juillet*, and that would mean immediate dealings with both the civil and naval authorities, followed by weeks, if not months, of paperwork, depositions, and all sorts of other legal niceties that Philippe would rather avoid.

'You don't want some prize money, then?' probed Larsonneur.

Philippe watched the shattered hull of the English corsair disappear back into the enveloping fog, the Breton crew jeering and bawling obscene insults at her wake.

'I can live without it, Citizen, just this once, but I'm sorry to deprive you and the men of it.'

Larsonneur shrugged. 'Truth to tell, Captain, we've all made enough for this cruise from all those hulls Captain Caradec took off Texel. Besides, who can say that the *rosbif* wouldn't just lure us into a trap? Some big frigate out of Saint Helier, or maybe the whole of Black Dick Howe's fleet. No, we all just want to go home, Captain, an' that's the truth.'

'Amen to that, Citizen Larsonneur.'

—

Le Quatorze Juillet left the rocky isle of Cézembre to starboard as it ran in towards the mouth of the River Rance. Philippe studied the ramparts and buildings of Saint-Malo, their destination, on the east bank of the estuary. It was a formidable place that reminded him a little of Kronstadt, for some reason, although they looked nothing alike. It was virtually an island but for a narrow strip of land connecting it to the mainland. There were batteries and fortifications galore, a chateau from earlier times off to the east, a newer, larger fort on a peninsula projecting into the harbour to the south, and a tall church spire towering above everything, making a superb seamark. The walls enclosed a densely packed town full of high, relatively modern houses, with warehouses nearer to the water. The harbour was packed with shipping of all sizes: large Indiamen, by the looks of them, moored side by side with corsairs, fishing boats, barges, coasters and foreign craft, the colours of Denmark, Sweden, Hamburg and other neutral nations apparent among them. Philippe looked for vessels bearing the familiar stars and stripes, but saw none. Huge Tricolours, the new national flag of the French Republic, flew from the ramparts surrounding the town. Philippe felt a schoolboy's excitement. Here was proof that this was the France he had dreamed of: a new-born republic devoted to liberty, equality and fraternity, the better, more perfect France that his father had worked for all his life.

'Good to be home, eh, Citizen Captain?' said Larsonneur.

'I've never been here before in my life,' said Philippe, looking out at the strange shore before him, barely registering the words he was saying.

'What, never been to Saint-Malo? Even though you speak Breton and have a Breton name?'

'Never to Saint-Malo, never to Brittany, never to France itself. This will be my first time on French soil, *Maître* Larsonneur. The first time in my life.'

'Bugger me. How's that, Captain, if you don't mind me asking, like?'

Philippe Kermorvant smiled. 'That, *Maître*, is another very long story.'

Larsonneur shook his head. He was a strange one all right, this Captain Kermorvant.

CHAPTER THREE

To the Minister of Marine of the French Republic or those who act on his behalf

...in short, I commanded Kermorvant, then only a lieutenant, for a short time before Alliance was paid off at the end of the war, but I was much impressed by his conduct in the fight off Cape Canaveral in March 1783 when we traded broadsides with the British frigate Sybil. This, of course, was the last action at sea in the whole of that mighty war, where the soldiers and sailors of France did so much to help us to our liberty. Kermorvant commanded the gun crews in the fo'c's'le and displayed exemplary bravery throughout the engagement, encouraging the men by his fearless example. This, you will note, was when he was still no more than eighteen years of age and should by rights not have been a lieutenant in any navy, even such a ragtag force as our United States then possessed. If he has matured as I hoped he would and not been corrupted by the malignant ways of the merchant trades and the Russian navy, then I have no doubt that he is now a formidable seaman who will be entirely worthy of a command under the flag of the French Republic.

I remain, sir, your most obedient servant,

James Barry

Sometime captain in the Continental Navy of the United States of America

After exchanging salutes with the fortress to the south and being towed, then warped, to her berth, *Le Quatorze Juillet* came to an anchor within the mole of Saint-Malo. Philippe left the ship in Larsonneur's care.

When all was said and done he held no commission as its captain, had no responsibility to its owners, and as far as he was concerned he had discharged any responsibilities he had to the crew simply by bringing them home alive. He said a perfunctory farewell to Larsonneur, but the old man's thoughts already seemed to be fixed upon buying a bottle or three in the bar nearest to their berth before wending an unsteady path back to his wife. Philippe, too, wished to get ashore as quickly as possible, but for rather different reasons. He wanted to get out of Saint-Malo, but this imperative clashed to a degree with the pressing needs to obtain up-to-date intelligence of the state of affairs in the town and the wider countryside. Caradec and his crew had been cruising for weeks, and the information he had gleaned from them was bound to be redundant by now. Philippe also needed to make enquiries about the best way of continuing his journey overland. Reluctantly, then, he made for the inn that Larsonneur had recommended, leaving the sea-chest that contained most of his worldly goods to be brought across later by some men from the ship.

The mood in Saint-Malo was feverish. Youths and small boys were running through the streets, deliberately hitting passers-by and screaming oaths in favour of the Republic. Every street corner and doorway seemed to have at least one beggar, their ages varying from ancient – maimed men with badly written placards proclaiming them to be veterans of wars long ago – to mere children, the most poignant being a girl of no more than six who had only one leg. Troops, many of them little older than the youths, patrolled up and down, their eyes glancing nervously towards alleyways and upper floor windows. Philippe picked up a copy of one of the ubiquitous newssheets, *L'Auditeur National*, which told of the successive and gloriously inevitable victories of the Republic's armies against the invading forces of the mighty coalition arrayed against France. But Philippe had read enough bullshit of this sort in his time and could read between the lines, regardless of whether those lines were published by the Americans, the British, the Russians or the French. The forces of the Prince of Coburg and the Duke of York still had Valenciennes under siege, no matter what the newssheet writers said; or rather, were being paid not to say. If Valenciennes fell, as it was sure to do, the road to Paris would be open for the advance of the avenging coalition of enemy monarchies, all outraged by the execution of King Louis a few months earlier.

The inn to which Philippe had been directed by Larsonneur lay close to the chateau in the north-east quarter of the town, and his route from the harbour brought him suddenly into the square before the small cathedral, built from the ubiquitous granite that dominated the architecture of the town. The space was packed with noisy, impatient people of all ranks and conditions, all looking eagerly towards the strange wooden structure in the centre of the square and talking about little else. The deadly blade that it was built to serve glinted in the sunlight, just out of the shade cast by the cathedral. Philippe had heard of the guillotine; by now, every man, woman and child in the world must have heard of France's notorious killing machine. But until he saw it for himself, Philippe had not grasped the chilling, relentless efficiency of the device. The erstwhile king had been executed on it a few months earlier, and now the guillotine was being deployed across the country to dispose of the enemies, real and alleged, of the fledgling republic. Philippe could make no progress through the crowd, but by chance most of those in front of him were women or relatively short men, giving him a clear view of the device, the executioner, and the victims. Several heads had already been lopped off, judging by the amount of blood around the scaffold, but the first execution Philippe witnessed was that of a willowy red-haired young woman in her early twenties. She was pale, beautiful, defiant to the end, and reminded him a little of his lost Natasha. Philippe did not want to watch but was unable to draw his eyes away from the spectacle. The blade fell, severing the head with dreadful efficiency. The remainder of her corpse, still tied to the bascule, seemed to twitch for a fleeting moment before it was roughly removed and bundled onto the common cart. A small black dog – perhaps the woman's, Philippe thought – threw back its head and howled. A young man turned white, opened his mouth to form a silent scream, and took a step or two towards the scaffold, but he was held back by two others, perhaps friends of his, and none of the soldiers forming a defensive ring around the guillotine moved towards him. A few of the hundreds of other onlookers looked away or groaned, but most of them, even some of the youngest children, cheered, raised their fists, and called out for more heads. The next victim, a boy of fourteen or so dressed in a torn, grubby silk shirt, was already being jostled onto the scaffold, even before the executioner had turned round after lifting the dead woman's head from the basket by the red hair, displaying it to all corners of the cathedral square of Saint-Malo and shouting '*Vive la Republique!*' to the baying audience.

Shivering and weeping, the boy was strapped to the bascule by the executioner's six assistants and his head placed within the lunette to await the fall of the blade. As the deadly halter closed around his neck, the boy screamed for mercy.

Philippe had seen bodies blown apart, had even seen the head of his closest friend, Ben Dawkins, shot directly off his shoulders aboard the old *Lexington* off Cape Charles, but that was *war*. What he was witnessing now was dressed up as the justice of the new republic, of the new age of liberty, equality and fraternity. The justice that was the will of the sovereign people of France, or so the likes of Citizen Robespierre proclaimed. But this was slaughter, plain and simple. The slaughter of innocents.

The next victim was an elderly man, an *aristo* who, according to the excited talk Phillippe heard around him, had once been a colonel of the Royal Musketeers. The fellow held his head high and attempted to deliver a speech, but those nearest to the guillotine jeered loudly and drowned him out. The rest of the crowd displayed less ambivalence about his death and cheered wildly when the executioner lifted the severed head. Even the most ardent revolutionary might baulk at the killing of women and the young, but someone who had seen a goodly number of years and might once have been in personal attendance on the deposed and despised former king, Louis Capet, was fair game.

It was the speed of it that astonished and alarmed Philippe the most. His crumpled edition of *L'Auditeur National* reported gleefully that recently in Paris, a particularly efficient team had guillotined sixteen people in fourteen minutes. It seemed as though Saint-Malo wished to compete for this macabre prize, for Philippe witnessed the execution of a dozen people in what could have been barely a quarter of an hour. He had seen many executions in his time, in places as far apart as New York and Kiev, and all such occasions had been attended by at least a degree of solemnity and the allowance of a certain dignity to the victims. Not so in republican France, where the whole process had been reduced to something akin to a butcher chopping a string of sausages on a platter.

Philippe turned away, having witnessed enough of this horror. He should be safe from such a fate, he thought to himself. He had sent letters to those he knew he could rely upon in France from Saint

Petersburg, others from Gothenburg, and he would send more from Saint-Malo that very day. He had his testimonials, assiduously collected over several years against the day when he might have to seek new employment, never anticipating the horror that had torn his life apart and brought him to France. He also had safe conducts under multiple hands in his sea-chest. He had a passport that ought to guarantee his immunity anywhere in the world. Yet what he saw in the square before the cathedral shook him to his core, although he could not really understand why. He believed in the glorious dream of a free republic of the people, as had his father so famously before him, and there were bound to be casualties in the making of that republic, as there had been in America. But those who fell in America, including his father, had done so in open warfare. Both the army of that new republic and its adversaries had worn uniforms, were composed of grown men bearing arms, and proceeded according to the universally acknowledged laws of war. In what way though had that young woman and that mere boy been such inveterate enemies of the French Republic that it was necessary to cut off their heads? Was this the vision that his father had been exiled for, and that Philippe had come to France to serve?

These thoughts were still troubling him when he found the inn, an ancient, narrow and rambling four-storey building with a steeply sloping roof named the Duguay Trouin after Saint-Malo's, indeed France's, greatest corsair. The principal room was thick with smoke, much of it, if Captain Caradec was to be believed, coming from tobacco smuggled in from Jersey in defiance of the French state's monopoly. The denizens of the room glanced at Philippe, looked him up and down, then returned to their drunken conversations. As in every port town in the world, even the most exotic creature attracted next to no attention if he was obviously a mariner. The innkeeper of the Duguay Trouin, one Defargues, was a huge, greasy fellow with hands like shovels and a thick Parisian accent. Philippe received a *pinte* of bad wine from him and explained his requirements, but as he did so Defargues tilted his head to one side, a quizzical expression on his broad face.

'American?' he asked when Philippe had finished.

'Breton, by way of America.'

Defargues shrugged. 'Plenty of Yankee ships come in here, but not many of the men on 'em can speak French as well as you, I'll give you that. An American Breton, you say? Who'd have thought it. Hang on a minute – you're the fellow who brought in Caradec's ship?' Philippe nodded. 'Well damn me! He was a good customer, Captain Caradec. Killed so close to home, too. But word of what you did is all over town, my friend, so it'll be an honour to have you staying here. In fact, you can have the first night on the house. Least I can do for the man who saved the old *Quatorze Juillet.*'

Philippe was uncomfortably aware that many eyes were now on him and the landlord. Defargues had a remarkably loud voice and the Duguay Trouin Inn had a very low roof, so pretty well all those present now knew exactly who Philippe was. So much for the discreet arrival he had sought and the customary anonymity of a port town, where men from every nation in the world could usually go unnoticed among those who had seen all sorts and were accustomed to asking no questions.

Defargues took him up to his room, a surprisingly spacious and relatively clean affair on the second floor, and promised that Philippe would not have to share it unless there was an unexpected influx of guests.

'Not that it's likely,' said the large innkeeper. 'Everyone's convinced the English are going to try to capture Saint-Malo, and pretty damn soon at that – or else they'll bombard it to rubble again, just like they did a hundred years back. Those who've got family inland have already left town, and I can't blame them. People are steering well clear of Brittany anyway because of the Chouans, though most of those bastards are well off to the south and west. Then there's the *représentant*. Came with quite a reputation, he did, and he's certainly living up to it. Those executions earlier? His doing. A great enthusiast for the guillotine is Citizen Carrier.'

'Carrier?' said Philippe. 'What's he the representative of?'

'The Committee of Public Safety, which these days is the government, to all intents and purposes. Acting on behalf of the National Convention, although all that seems to do is talk.' Defargues sniffed loudly and at length, evidently thinking this a more satisfactory way of clearing his nose than blowing it. 'More of a mouthful than "king", which is about the only thing the old Bourbons had in their favour. Nice short word, "king". Committee of Public Safety, though, that's a hell of a mouthful, that is.'

Philippe's heart sank. He had known of the royalist Chouan revolt in Brittany well before he left Russia and had been told more by

Caradec, but the presence in Saint-Malo of a powerful representative of Robespierre, Danton and the rest of the Jacobin leadership was an unwelcome addition to the pot. It gave greater urgency to his letter writing, so, after thanking Defargues and finding out from him the best way of continuing his journey, Philippe settled down at the small table beneath the grimy window that allowed a tiny glimpse of the sea. He remembered how he used to write almost daily to Natasha in either his rudimentary Russian or her negligible French, then dismissed the thought. Tasha lay alongside their son, beneath the earth of her beloved Mother Russia, now and for ever, put there by another's resentment of his love for her, and that terrible truth had driven Philippe Kermorvant to leave her land and seek a new future for himself here in France, his father's country. For good or ill, that die was cast.

Philippe wrote three letters, although whether any would reach their destinations – or reach them in time – was in the lap of the gods, if it was still acceptable to use such a metaphor in an atheist republic. Then he went back down to the main room of the Duguay Trouin, arranged with Defargues for the posting of the letters, and settled down to a meal of *cotriade*, the Breton fish stew that his father had attempted with little success to teach the cooks on their Virginia estate to make for him. As he ate, Philippe was aware of watching eyes, and heard whispering that was undoubtedly about him. One very old man in the far corner of the room stared at him for minutes on end as though he recognised him, but that was surely impossible. Saint-Malo was far to the east of the lands the Kermorvants called home, and it was unlikely that any man in the Duguay Trouin that day had heard of Philippe's father, let alone read any of his works. Yet still the ancient fellow kept up his scrutiny, until at last he stood up stiffly and shuffled across the room to where Philippe sat.

'Can I assist you, Citizen?' said Philippe.

'You look like him,' said the old man, slowly and warily, 'but you don't talk like him, that's for certain. But I heard your name from some of the boys off of *Quatorze Juillet*. Kermorvant. You're him, aren't you? Admiral Saint-Victor's son? I served under the admiral when he hoisted his flag in the old *Royal Louis*, must be fifty years ago almost to the very day...'

Philippe's first instinct was to deny the old man's words as senile ramblings, but the fellow was still as sharp as a pin and was obviously well known to Defargues and the other denizens of the Duguay Trouin. Besides, Philippe could hardly deny his own name.

'That was my grandfather.'

'I knew it!' cried the old man. 'His grandson! Damn me, that I should have lived so long to see the day!'

Philippe gestured to Defargues, took out a couple of coins, and handed them to the ancient creature.

'It's an honour to buy a drink for a man who sailed with my grandfather. I never knew him – he died long before I was born. Will you tell me what you remember of him, Citizen?'

Before the man could answer, however, the door of the inn was opened forcefully. Half a dozen men in the blue and red uniforms of the National Guard entered, holding their muskets at the ready. They scanned the room purposefully but a little fearfully, too, as if they expected an imminent attack from a regiment of Chouans. The man at their head, wearing the uniform of a junior officer, looked to be no more than fifteen, but surely had to be somewhere in his twenties. His eyes settled upon Philippe, and he stepped forward to stand before him. The old man retreated back to the corner, lowered his eyes and took a long swig of his drink.

'Citizen Philippe Kermorvant?' said the officer, his accent betraying origins far away from Brittany.

'I am he.'

As with the old man, how could Philippe possibly deny it?

'Citizen Carrier's orders. You are to accompany me to an interview. Maurier, Lalande, search this man's room – innkeeper, show my men the way. Look sharp now or else we'll take you in, too! Citizen Kermorvant, if you please.'

Philippe nodded and stood. What else could he do? As he left the inn, he saw the looks in the eyes of the drinkers and the expression on the face of the old man who had served with his grandfather. The unanimous opinion of those who watched him being escorted out of the Duguay Trouin, an opinion that did not need to be spoken aloud, was that Philippe Kermorvant was unquestionably bound for the guillotine.

CHAPTER FOUR

Paris, undated but summer 1793

To the senior representative of the Republic in Saint-Malo

I write on behalf of Philippe Kermorvant, who by his recent letter to me reports that he is newly arrived in your town aboard a privateer. I knew him quite well when he was a boy and I was often in the company of his father, whose name and reputation, I trust, require no reminder from me. That most worthy gentleman was the first to extol and promote my little pamphlet called Common Sense, and I have no doubt that had he lived, he would have been entirely in accord with my more recent work, Rights of Man. I know his son to be firm in the same principles. You may think it strange that a man of his origins might seek to serve the Republic by taking a command in its navy, yet I beg you to remember that here am I, born an Englishman, by choice an American, a man who speaks no French, yet who sits as a member of the National Convention of the Republic. All of us who treasure liberty, equality and fraternity should rejoice that a man like Philippe Kermorvant seeks to draw his sword for our new France and the new world we seek.

I remain your respectful colleague and friend,

Thomas Paine

Jean-Baptiste Carrier had been in Brittany for no more than a few short weeks, but it already felt like an eternity. He had been given the best rooms in the old chateau, as befitted his status as the *représentant en mission* of the Committee of Public Safety, but his windows were almost entirely west or north facing, which meant he could see the sea. Carrier had developed an immediate and profound hatred for this previously unknown and utterly inexplicable environment. The sea brought weather that seemed to change every few minutes. Even now, in the season that was alleged to be summer, there could be bright sunshine one minute and driving hail the next. Great storms lashed his windows, threatening to break in and sweep him away, but an hour later he was subjected to baking heat even more intolerable than that of Paris in August. The sea might be a flat calm, its colour a deep and benign blue, but before he could drain his wine it might be a ferment of mountainous black waves topped by angry white storm-spray. In short, the sea, and thus Brittany as a whole, was not conducive to Jean-Baptiste Carrier's peace of mind; and that was without even considering the enormity of the responsibility that the committee had placed upon his shoulders in this momentous time, Year Two of the French Republic, one and indivisible, which the priests, the ignorant and other recidivists persisted in calling 1793.

Brittany was far from being an easy assignment in a quiet backwater. Oh, quite the opposite: speaking on behalf of the committee as a whole, Citizen Robespierre had made it clear to Carrier that this distant, rocky province in the back of beyond, peopled by oafs who spoke an incomprehensible tongue, was almost as great a threat to the survival of the Republic as the rebellious Vendée, just to the south. The Bretons still clung to priestcraft and superstition, some of it reportedly not even Christian. They saw demons and spirits everywhere, especially in the thick black woods that stretched over so much of the land and which unsettled even a rational man like Jean-Baptiste Carrier. Oh, but Bretons could be rational enough when they wanted to be, if slyness, cunning and disregard for the Republic's laws and the unity of France could be deemed as such. At every opportunity they declaimed loudly about their special privileges, granted by one of the tyrant kings when Brittany was finally united with France. Oh, Citizen Carrier, the Treaty of Union of 1532 means we don't have to pay the salt tax, which means we can smuggle it into the rest of France at an obscene profit! Oh, Citizen Carrier, the Treaty of Union of 1532 means the general conscription doesn't apply here! Oh, Citizen Carrier, we must keep our own legal code and our own language! Worse, many of the ungrateful inbreds still adhered to the fallen House of Bourbon, proclaiming the guillotined Louis Capet's son as their 'King Louis the Seventeenth' even though the sickly boy they so revered was locked away in the

Temple prison. They were in open rebellion against the Republic, taking the name of Chouans, organising themselves into what passed for proper armies, and marching proudly under the hated white flag of the monarchy and the sacred heart of superstitious priestcraft.

But not even that was the limit of Carrier's difficulty. By its position and geography, Brittany was particularly vulnerable to attacks, perhaps even full-scale invasions, from France's perfidious and eternal enemy across the water. Saint-Malo, where Carrier now sat, was threatened by the nearby presence of Jersey, Guernsey and the other islands that swore allegiance to the fat, mad farmer, George Wettin, the so-called King George the Third. It was an abiding mystery, and a mute testimony to their betrayal of the French people over many centuries, that the Bourbon kings and all the preceding crowned leeches had permitted such an intolerable state of affairs to continue. But there it was. Carrier knew he could not stop the English landing their murderous legions of foul-smelling bloodsuckers on the Breton coast. Aside from anything else, the regular troops here in the west were overstretched because the Army of the North, confronting an invasion from Flanders, could spare no men as reinforcements. That left Carrier with raw recruits from the new levies who barely knew one end of a musket from the other and who seemed utterly incapable of even basic drill. In public he lectured these men about how revolutionary zeal was sure to carry them to victory, but when he lay in his bed at night he dreaded to think what would happen if they had to hold a beachhead against the Grenadier Guards or the Royal Marines. Still, Carrier could at least try to deal with those perfidious, treacherous Bretons who might welcome the English with open arms. There were many such here, in Saint-Malo, which could only be a prime target for William Pitt and all his arse-licking acolytes. And now, into the midst of all this, came the peculiar creature who stood before him. Ludicrous hair plaited into a *queue de cheval*, a ponytail. A sea-captain, or so he said, who had turned up aboard a French privateer in a Swedish harbour and requested passage to France. His antecedents prior to that, unknown. Despite this, a man who had commanded a French crew to victory over an English ship, or so the depositions from the men of *Le Quatorze Juillet* stated. A Breton crew. Jean-Baptiste Carrier was too canny to take the word of mere Bretons, none of whom, after all, had probably ever been within two hundred miles of Paris.

'Items, five,' said Carrier, dictating to his clerk as he continued his examination of the papers taken from the prisoner's room and sea-chest.

Thus far, most of these documents had been either letters of recommendation from assorted admirals, captains and politicians – even, sweet reason, one from an eminent member of the National Convention – or else love letters between a man, presumably this man, and his wife, both sides of the correspondence being conducted in the most childlike French. The wife was clearly not a native speaker and her grasp of the language, even of the forming of individual letters, was rudimentary, to say the least. What sort of man was not content to marry a good healthy French girl but instead sought his conjugal bliss in foreign beds? It beggared belief.

'On vellum, folded. Three in a script unlike any I have seen. Not French, for certain. Suspicious. Possibly code. Two in English, the language of our enemy. Conclusive, I'd say. Most conclusive. Your explanation, Citizen Kermorvant?'

The fellow before him took a deep breath and spoke calmly, slowly, as though speaking to a backward child. The *représentant en mission* of the Committee of Public Safety was displeased by such a tone.

'Citizen,' said Kermorvant, far too confidently for Carrier's liking, 'the two in English are commissions in the rank of lieutenant in the Continental Navy of the United States of America, this one for the *Lexington*, dated 4 March 1782, this one for the *Alliance*, dated 9 November 1782. The other three are in Russian. This one for lieutenant of the *Yedinstvo*, dated 9 October 1787, this for lieutenant of the *Mech*, dated 24 May 1788. The third one as captain of the *Strela*, frigate of twenty-four guns, dated 8 May 1789.'

Carrier turned the commissions this way and that. They might be forgeries, of course, in which case he could throw this strange creature into prison before despatching him to the guillotine following the inevitable righteous verdict of a revolutionary tribunal. But who in their right minds, even the most malintentioned royalist or bloody spawn of fanatic priests, would conceive of such unbelievable documents as these? The American navy? The Russian navy? Carrier was a man of the Auvergne, from Aurillac at the foot of the mountains, and the first time he had ever seen the sea was six weeks before this encounter. No man from Aurillac had ever gone to sea as far as he knew, certainly none who came home to tell tales of ships from America or Russia. Navies were things that existed far away in some alien element, as remote as the man in the moon. But he had worked in Paris for several years, and as every Frenchman knew, Paris was the centre of the world. He had encountered seamen in Paris, captains and *chefs d'escadre* come up to solicit for commands in the navy when old Castries was minister for the marine, or else there were merchant skippers up from Nantes seeking investors in slaving voyages or with cargoes to sell on the exchanges. So seamen were no strangers to Carrier, no indeed. However, the fact that he had never heard any man speak in as peculiar an accent as the fellow before him, even in Paris, gave him pause. He was a lawyer by profession, and lawyers needed all the facts. In this instance, he had far too few. He needed more information, so he took out the remaining papers from the pouch, began to open them in order and returned to reciting the contents for his clerk.

'Item, letter of recommendation and safe conduct, in French, dated 9 April 1793 at Rue de la Planche, Paris, signed by Gouvernour Morris, minister plenipotentiary of the United States of America to the French Republic.'

His confidence returned. This had nothing to do with the sea. This was high politics. This was safe and familiar ground.

'A mere minister plenipotentiary, Citizen,' said Carrier, savouring the words. 'An ambassador would carry much more weight, of course, but there we are, what can one do, eh? These new nations that can't afford a full diplomatic entourage. Ah well, thus so.'

He put down the letter from the American minister and picked up the next paper.

'Item, letter of recommendation and safe conduct, in French, dated 12 July 1792 at 19 Rue de Tournon, Paris, signed by John Paul Jones, sometime captain in the Continental Navy of the United States of America, sometime admiral in the Imperial Navy of All the Russias. Very impressive. A great hero to America, Russia and, yes, France too. Impressive but redundant, I'd say, as my understanding is that the gentleman in question has been dead for a year. Not long after signing this note, in fact. *Quelle dommage*, Citizen Kermorvant, *quelle dommage*. And so we move on. Item, letter of recommendation and safe conduct, in French, dated 13 June 1792 at the Chateau de Chavaniac in Haute-Loire, signed by Citizen Marie-Joseph Paul Yves Roch Gilbert du Motier, called the Marquis de Lafayette, sometime commander-in-chief of the National Guard of the Republic, sometime commander of the armies of the North and of the Centre, sometime major-general of the army of the United States of America, etcetera, etcetera. A great man, the marquis, a very great man. Such a shame that he became a traitor to the Republic, tried to flee from France and now rots in an Austrian prison. Ah well, such is fate. No, Citizen, it will not serve. None of this will serve. I trust you have better credentials to display than the empty words of a nonentity, a dead man and a traitor. None of these prove you to be anything other than a foreigner who has never even set foot in France before. Are you even a citizen? I very much doubt it. As things stand, you are assuredly destined for the guillotine – oh yes, most assuredly!'

Carrier sat back and watched the fellow struggle to make an answer. When he spoke, though, his face was – yes, *smug*, there was no other term for it – and his words had more than a hint of impudence, certainly not the tone to take with a *représentant en mission*.

'Perhaps you should examine my remaining papers, Citizen?' said Kermorvant.

Before Carrier could respond, a boy in the uniform of the National Guard entered, saluted, and placed a paper in front of Carrier's clerk. The fellow unfolded it, frowned, and handed it to Carrier, who struggled to take in the words before him. It was a note dictated by Picon, the notably pungent local man who lost no opportunity to convince the *représentant en mission* of his revolutionary credentials. Carrier read, his frown growing ever tighter. What possible bearing could the identity of this man's father have on the case before him? Then Carrier read the name and understood. Why had no one told him this before? He glowered at his clerk, who merely shrugged. He thought of dismissing the fellow for insolence, but then wondered how easy it would be to find another Breton who could read, write, and was loyal to the Republic rather than to the damned Chouans. Not Picon, for certain. Loyal, yes. Literate, no.

Still, proper form had to be observed. The Republic had to be seen to be systematic and thorough, and of course its very existence was founded upon a rejection of heredity. The old priests always asserted that the sins of the father were not visited upon the son, but there was a corollary: the merits of the father were not necessarily bestowed on the son, either. All that being so, Carrier would treat this Kermorvant's papers as he would those of any other potential traitor. Systematic and thorough, two of the bywords of the French Republic. So Carrier lifted the next paper, then the second, and then the last. As he read, though, the words became ever more unbelievable. He sensed that his eyes were bulging and that his smile was frozen into an astonished rictus. This was impossible. No, it was beyond impossible. It offended against everything he believed in, every instinct in his body. Jean-Baptiste Carrier swallowed hard, drank a long draught from the goblet before him, then glanced over to the clerk to indicate that he was ready to resume.

'Item,' he said, then coughed nervously. 'Item, certificate of citizen-ship of the French Republic, one and indivisible, signed by Citizen Barthélemy de Lesseps, consul of the Republic at Kronstadt in the Russian empire, dated 16 February of this present year. Does a mere consul have the authority to do such a thing?'

Carrier was addressing no one in particular, but his clerk shrugged again. Such a question was very far beyond his competence.

'Citizen de Lesseps is a great admirer of my father's work,' said Philippe.

'Is he? Is he, now? That still doesn't answer my question, Citizen. I shall have to refer the matter to Paris, of course.'

Carrier spoke distractedly, for he knew that he still had to read aloud the contents of this infernal fellow's remaining two papers. The record had to be accurate. The record had to be complete.

'Item,' he said tiredly, 'letter of recommendation and safe conduct, in French, dated 3 April 1791 at Mount Vernon in the state of Virginia, signed by His Excellency General George Washington, President of the United States of America.'

The clerk goggled as he heard the words, but Carrier ignored him and continued.

'Item, passport, together with letter of recommendation and safe conduct, in French, dated 16 February 1793 at the Winter Palace in Saint Petersburg, signed by Her Imperial Majesty Catherine, Empress and Supreme Autocrat of All the Russias.'

Carrier momentarily forgot that he wore the mantle of an ardent republican, an inveterate enemy of hereditary monarchs and all such tyrants and despots.

'Citizen,' said the man standing before him in a level voice that did not quite conceal that insufferable confidence of his, 'the last I heard, France is at war with England, Austria, Prussia, Spain, the Netherlands and Sardinia. My understanding is that we are not at war with Russia, nor with the United States of America. Not yet, at any rate. Now, you may wish to run the risk of bringing yet another two nations into the coalition against us, and if that is indeed your wish, by all means strap me to Madame Guillotine this very day. But, Citizen Carrier, I respectfully suggest that you may wish to consult with Citizens Danton, Robespierre and the rest of the Committee of Public Safety before you steer such a momentous course.'

Bastard. Impudent, arrogant bastard. How dare this mere seaman, this mere fucking Breton, lecture him on the course of action he should take?

Do not respond precipitately, Jean-Baptiste, he told himself. Be calm and think, as your Jesuit teachers taught you to do. Peddlers of superstition who kept the people wallowing in ignorance they may have been. Abusers of young boys some of them undoubtedly were. But the Jesuits were unrivalled at producing men who were at once self-aware and masters of their own feelings. The Republic would need good teachers, so the Jesuits and all the others would need to be *sans-cullotised*, as he termed it, with unimpeachably loyal Jacobins, the party must be committed to true revolutionary ideals, although Carrier suspected that would be easier said than done.

Having considered the issues as his old teachers had instructed him to do, Carrier decided that perhaps high politics was not such safe ground after all. Danton, Robespierre and a few others like Carnot would take this in their stride, the wrath of presidents and empresses being of little concern to them. That had been even more true of poor Marat until the Corday bitch did for him in his bathtub; fearful that history might somehow repeat itself, Carrier hadn't bathed since he heard the news. Even by his own admission, though, Carrier was a lesser star in the constellation of the Republic than all those illustrious colleagues of his, and all things considered, he was content with his lot. He had been sent to Brittany to turn its primitive, recalcitrant, reactionary people into good *sans-cullotes* and Jacobins, even if it meant sending scores of them to the guillotine as an example, and although it pained him to think it, the dilemma presented by the peculiar beast before him was beyond his competence. Yes, he would write to Paris for instructions in the matter. But what to do with the fellow in the meantime? The easiest thing would be to guillotine him as swiftly as possible, of course, or else commit him indefinitely to a cell in the *chateau* of Saint-Malo, but on what grounds? The Republic had to be seen to respect the process of law, for that was one of the things that set it apart from the previous Bourbon tyranny, and even detention on some trumped-up grounds might bring down the wrath of all the great names this Kermorvant could deploy in his cause. Whether the almost mythical Empress Catherine would declare war over the death of this one strange mongrel of a seaman was surely unlikely, but then again, the empress was said to be a highly unpredictable and erratic individual. The thought of English and German troops marching into Paris to overthrow the Republic was bad enough, but the *Russians*? Carrier had read the books and heard the stories about Russians… *mon Dieu.*

On top of that, this man, it now transpired, was the son of Verité, a hero, a legend, almost a god to all those who hated monarchy and religion, one of the men who had laid down the intellectual template for the new republic. His works were known and admired all over the world. Carrier himself had avidly devoured them all and wished there had been more. The Republic needed friends, and its ultimate ambition was to spread its message of liberty, equality and fraternity to all nations, to bring down all crowned tyrants, to plant the fragile sapling of republicanism in every country. Guillotining the son of Verité hardly seemed an obvious means to the end.

Given all the delicacies, therefore, it was possible that an intemperate course of action on Carrier's part might incur the displeasure of the Committee of Public Safety. Carrier had witnessed the wrath of Citizen Maximilien Robespierre being directed at others, and had no wish to experience it first-hand.

Caution, then. Err on the side of leniency, for once.

'Well, Citizen,' said Carrier, 'the men of *Le Quatorze Juillet* plead for you, and they can undoubtedly sway many here in Saint-Malo who waver between the true light of the new liberty and the darkness offered by the priests, the Chouans and the English. That consideration weighs heavily with me. Then there are your credentials, of course, although yes, I will need to refer that element of the case to Paris. That will take time. In the meantime, I am minded to place you in comfortable quarters in Saint-Malo—'

The fellow interrupted him. These days, nobody ever interrupted Jean-Baptiste Carrier. *The sheer unbounded insolence of the man.*

'Citizen, if I may suggest something, with the greatest respect? If you choose to give me my parole, I assure you that I will be in one of only two places. One is Brest, where I hope to take up a command in the navy of the Republic. The other is my family home, although I have never seen it before. It is in the forest near Huelgoat, much less than a day's ride from Brest. I intend to go nowhere else. This is my word of honour, Citizen, as a former captain of the Imperial Russian Navy and, I hope, a future captain of the navy of the French Republic. As such, as a man of honour, I give you my parole.'

'Oh,' said Carrier with as much bluster as he could manage, 'we will make *very* certain that you are in one of those two places, Citizen.'

As if the Republic could spare men to observe just one suspected reactionary. But what did Carrier have to lose? If this Philippe Kermorvant broke his word, went off and joined the Chouans, what difference could just one man possibly make? And if he was an English spy, as Carrier half-suspected – who else could forge such convincing documents but the damned English? – the Republic now knew exactly what he looked like and, more importantly, what he sounded like. The moment he opened his mouth, Kermorvant would betray himself. If this was the best sort of agent that the English and the royalist hell-spawn could muster, Carrier thought, then the triumph of the Republic was undoubtedly assured.

CHAPTER FIVE

Letter of Natasha Kermorvant to her husband, undated but early 1793.

Bulgakov was drunk again yesterday and ranted at me once more. He is my brother and dear to me but I fear him when he is in such a mood. He still cannot forgive me for having married you, a foreigner, despite your noble rank being at least equal to his, nor for our Ivan being born only five months after our marriage in the Trinity Cathedral. This despite all the many bastards he has scattered across Russia, but let that pass. He said many vile things, called Ivan a French bastard and the like, shouted once again that he would go to the patriarch through his friend the tsarevich to get our marriage annulled, and much more besides. Nothing we have not heard before, Philippe my love, but he still smarts from you defeating him when the two of you duelled. So I pray you will be home very soon now that the wars are over and the ships are coming back to port for good. Then we can finally decide whether we stay in Russia, or go to America as I hope, or go to France as you desire. But from what we hear here of recent events in France, I do not think it a place where you and I may live in ease and contentment, and where Ivan and the other children we will have can grow in a land at peace.

As ever you are in my prayers and my heart,

Your very loving Tasha

(Endorsed by Philippe Kermorvant, 'her last letter')

Philippe's return from the chateau stunned Defargues and the other denizens of the Duguay Trouin. A couple of men surreptitiously crossed themselves, even though the practice was frowned upon in the more enlightened age that was Year Two of the Republic. It was evident that the customers had expected to see him next on the steps of the guillotine, and his return with both his head on his shoulders and his freedom seemed more astonishing than the resurrection of Lazarus. Defargues, who had already let Philippe's room anew, gushed over him before scurrying off to remake his arrangements. Very soon, though, shock gave way to whispers. The only reason why the enigmatic half-American had returned at all, and returned so quickly at that, was because he had been recruited to the Jacobin cause by Citizen Carrier and was now to be one of the *représentant en mission*'s many spies in Saint-Malo. Such, at least, seemed to be the new consensus among the customers of the Duguay Trouin. The only man who seemed not to share in this opinion was the old seaman, and Philippe sought him out. The fellow, Etienne Pennec by name, had a glorious fund of stories of the days when he and Philippe's grandfather had sailed out against the English, and Philippe spent hours listening contentedly to the old man talk. He did the same the next day and the day after that, finding himself particularly engrossed in Pennec's tale of how he had served on the ship that got the Scottish prince, the rightful *dauphin* of Britain, off a godforsaken island and away to safety in France after his failed attempt to reclaim the throne nearly fifty years earlier. Nevertheless, during every moment that Philippe sat in the Duguay Trouin he was expecting the door to burst open again, bringing the troops who would haul him before Carrier once more and thence to the guillotine. He looked back on his encounter with the *représentant en mission* with a sense of bafflement that did not diminish over time, but also with gratitude to whichever higher entity was now permitted to exist. Whatever impression Carrier might have had of him, Philippe had spent their interview feeling increasingly anxious, if not terrified. He had placed all his faith in the papers he had gone to so much trouble to obtain, especially in the last few months when the prospect of coming to France began to become more real, but when all was said and done they were merely pieces of paper. They could be thrown in the fire, their bearer sent to the scaffold, and if any of the authors complained – unlikely, Philippe now realised – Carrier and his superiors could wring their hands and apologise for a most unfortunate administrative error. Jean-Baptiste Carrier was surely going to send him to the guillotine, and Philippe spent those few days in Saint-Malo convinced that the *représentant* would either change his mind or that orders would come back from Paris to re-arrest and then execute this strange rootless, homeless beast who had somehow fetched up on France's shore.

But no troops came for him a second time. Indeed, Carrier made no attempt to stop Philippe leaving Saint-Malo. Quite the contrary, in fact, he even provided Philippe with a new *carte du citoyen*, the piece of paper essential to anyone seeking to travel more than a mile or two in France. He was able to hire a horse, make arrangements for his sea-chest, and join a convoy setting off overland for the west of Brittany. The unsettled state of the country and the ongoing war against the Chouans made it advisable for travellers to make their way under escort, and although lone riders often took their chances, Philippe decided that his unfamiliarity with the country made it more advisable to go west with the next substantial land convoy. This consisted of three coaches, half a dozen riders like Philippe, and a similar number of carts carrying valuable cargoes of different sorts, this motley body of civilian traffic being escorted by three score dragoons and National Guardsmen. On the road down to Dinan, Philippe fell into conversation with the dragoon officer, an amiable, curly haired but painfully thin fellow from Normandy named Anquetil who had been in the campaigns in Flanders and Holland earlier in the year, being wounded in the shoulder at the calamitous defeat in the battle of Neerwinden.

'General Dumouriez didn't have his heart in it, even then,' said Anquetil, 'and that was long before he went over to the Austrians. The only thing that saved us up there was that the enemy was just as much of a shambles as we were. I tell you, what'll win this war is one side or the other finding a decent general somewhere – a new Condé or Turenne for us, a new Marlborough or Prince Eugene for them. But I can't see it happening.'

'Maybe you'll be that general.'

Anquetil laughed.

'Look at me,' he said, 'in charge of escorting a gaggle of old ladies, fat merchants and clerks in the arse end of France, looking to fight off brainless peasants who speak a language that sounds like farting, who drag their knuckles on the ground and reckon an eight-year-old boy locked up in the Temple is ordained by God to hold absolute power over them. That's hardly the path to glory, my friend. Besides, I reckon Sergeant Retaillou would make a much better general than me. Better for certain than the *aristo* shitheads we had at Neerwinden, the likes of the Duke of fucking Chartres, who's even younger than me.'

The overweight old sergeant, who had fought in America, grinned.

'General Retaillou,' he said, 'I like the sound of that. Better still, Serge Retaillou, Marshal of France.'

There was more conversation of this sort as they travelled through the Breton countryside. Anquetil and Retaillou were amiable companions, both dedicated to the Republic but not fanatical Jacobins, both career soldiers who were not afraid to criticise either their superiors or the ignorant raw conscripts who made up ever more of the ranks.

'When I was a cadet at the École Militaire, they dragged out old Marshal Biron, the hero of Fontenoy, to address us,' said Anquetil as they rode through a village recently burned by the Chouans. 'He must have been nearly a hundred and was senile; nobody heard a word he said to us, but just to see him there – the oldest living Marshal of France, and a duke to boot! You know he first went to war as a boy when Louis the Fourteenth was still king? But I wonder what he'd have made of the army we have today. What would they all have made of it, eh, Turenne, Saxe, D'Artagnan, all France's great generals?'

'All *aristos*, weren't they?' said Retaillou as he scanned the treeline for any sign of the enemy. 'So they wouldn't get commands today anyway. Their heads would be in baskets, or else they'd be dangling from lampposts. Begging your pardon, Citizen Vicomte.'

It had not taken Retaillou long to discover Philippe's history, and he made the remark with a broad smile creasing his ample features.

'Granted, Sergeant,' said Philippe. 'So you're saying, then, that we'll lose the war?'

'No,' said Anquetil hastily and quietly, perhaps wary in case one of his soldiers had sharp hearing and a fanatical heart. 'They can attack France from the north, the south and the east – the west too, if the English finally find the balls to invade – but we're a big country. And I tell you this, my friend, we French, we French – we're never defeated from outside, only from within. *Always* from within.'

Philippe remembered an old and bibulous colonel in Saint Petersburg who had fought the Turks twenty years earlier. This vodka-drenched veteran once told him much the same thing about Russia, an even larger country. It could only ever be defeated from within, he said, and the Russian serfs were so lumpenly stupid that it would never even occur to them to rebel against their betters. Not so in France.

After an overnight stay in Saint Brieuc, the convoy travelled on to Guincamp, a town surrounded by ancient fortifications. There it divided, two of the coaches and most of the dragoons making due west on the road to Morlaix while Philippe, the third coach, some of the carts and a smaller detachment of dragoons and National Guardsmen commanded by Anquetil and Retaillou set out south-west on a road that ran through Plugonver and then out into the thick, menacing and seemingly endless forest of oak and birch that lay beyond, winding its way through the former province of Finisterre towards distant Quimper and Brest. The Republic had done away with the feudal relic called Brittany and its provinces, instead creating new divisions, the *depart-ments*, but no one in the convoy, not even Anquetil, spoke of anything other than Brittany and Finisterre.

The new horse that Philippe had hired at the inn in Plugonver was a calmer beast than that which he had ridden from Saint-Malo, and west of the town the road surface had evidently been repaired fairly recently, making for a more comfortable ride through the undulating landscape of small fields bounded by high hedges. Once in a while they passed peasant cottages, low, windowless hovels whose roughly dressed, wooden-shoed, hard-faced inhabitants looked upon those in the convoy as if they were citizens of another world. The soldiers were alert, vigilant in case a village or a copse of birch might provide cover for a Chouan ambush, but all was quiet.

It was a warm morning, and conversation soon ceased among both soldiers and civilians alike. Those in the coaches dozed, while even some of those on horseback could allow their thoughts to wander. At first Philippe thought back once again upon his encounter with Jean-Baptiste Carrier, a strange and dangerous man, and wondered if the *représentant en mission* of the Committee of Public Safety really would leave him untroubled from now on. Probably not: the *carte du citoyen* was couched in very specific terms to ensure that Philippe was exactly where Carrier expected him to be, and nowhere else. The sooner he could convince the naval authorities of his credentials, both as an officer and a good republican, and get back out to sea, the likelier it was that he would be able to steer a steady course through the choppy waters of the new France. He still thought upon the young woman he had seen die on the guillotine in Saint-Malo, and knew that the same fate would certainly await him if he put a foot wrong.

–

By noon or thereabouts, the passage of the convoy was almost dream-like. The hot sunshine, the regular clopping of the horses' hooves, the relentless turning of the coaches' wheels, the buzzing of flies and the occasional seductive birdsong from the woods near the road made it hard to stay awake, and more than once Philippe suddenly jerked upright as he felt himself beginning to fall from the saddle.

He did not know why, but his thoughts began to drift to his child-hood and his father, that most elusive character.

Philippe was eleven when he realised his father was not like other men. He was younger still when he first noticed that Edouard Kermor-vant treated and spoke of the slaves and the native Indians of those parts very differently to their neighbours, the plantation owners of the Virginia tidewater; very differently, indeed, to the way his wife, Philippe's mother, regarded them. He recalled frequent arguments over his father's willingness to allow his son to play with boys from the Pamunkey and the other tribes settled in the lands around them. But it was only when he was eleven that Philippe took a proper interest in the books in their library and noticed that many of them were by an author who went under the pen-name of Verité. One day, out of idle curiosity, he took one from its place on the shelf, opened it, and saw his father's name on the title page. His father, the man who dressed in labourer's clothes, who took him fishing, taught him shooting, and told him tales of King Arthur and his knights, was this Verité, or so it seemed. And as Verité, he had written books or pamphlets upon many subjects. He had written upon the natural rights of man, upon the manifest untruth of all religion, upon the errors and evils of the kings of France, upon the rightness of republics as a form of government, and upon a whole host of other subjects from the best methods of breeding cows to the iniquity of slavery, to a history that sought to place those same legends of King Arthur firmly in Brittany, the native land of the Kermorvants. Philippe opened all the books and leafed through a few pages of each but found most of them unutterably boring, the sole exceptions being the books and pamphlets about King Arthur. As he looked through them, though, Philippe noticed a curious thing. Until 1761, the place of publication was always Paris. Then, for two years, it was a variety of places in Europe: some in Amsterdam, some in Copenhagen, some in Zurich, names he had only seen on maps. Suddenly, from 1763 onwards – the year before Philippe was born – the books were in English and were published in Williamsburg. He asked his father about all this, but Edouard Kermorvant was evasive. It had all been a very long time ago, he told his son, and there were now different dispensations. Questions to his mother got even shorter shrift and led to more loud arguments between husband and wife. So Philippe kept his own counsel, but whenever he could, he took down one of his father's works about King Arthur and read it avidly from cover to cover. He swiftly ran out of books on that subject so tried again with some of the more boring ones. He rarely got more than a hundred or so pages into what were usually very lengthy and densely argued treatises, but as the weeks and months passed, he nevertheless absorbed more and more of his father's often unconventional beliefs.

It was a year or more later when the tall, proud and exceptionally elegantly dressed man called Jefferson came to Dunkeld, their family's plantation – in truth, his mother's plantation, a cudgel that she often used to beat her husband – and Philippe managed to sneak unobserved onto the middle landing of the stairs to overhear the conversation they were having in the library.

'We want you to write a polemic,' Jefferson was saying in passable French. 'An essay addressed to the French king and people to convince them of the rightness of our cause, and of the urgent necessity for them to declare war on our side. Your old friend Ben Franklin is most enthusiastic to have such a paper to take with him to France, sir, when he goes there as our ambassador.'

There was much more to the same effect, but Philippe now only remembered the first words he had heard.

'You overestimate me, Mister Jefferson,' said Edouard Kermorvant. 'The present King Louis' grandfather was the man who sent me into exile, and I've had no hint of a return to favour from the grandson. I haven't had a book published in Europe in more than ten years, and in any case, I haven't written a new one in five. Every man in France forgot me years ago.'

'With respect, sir, you underestimate yourself. The works of that great thinker known to all educated men as Verité are in print in many more lands, more languages and more editions than ever they were before you left France. Your word still has weight, very great weight indeed, and it is that truth – yes, that *verité* – that has impelled the Continental Congress to instruct me to make this approach to you.' Philippe heard a silence, but before his father could make any response, Jefferson changed tack. 'I also have their authority to make an additional offer to you. Your valour and success as a soldier in Hesse and Pomerania during the last great war did not go unremarked on this side of the ocean, sir, and it is therefore with both humility and an earnest entreaty that I present you with the offer of a brigadier-general's commission in the Continental Army. I hope and pray that you will accept it, my lord.'

It was the very first time that Philippe had ever heard his father addressed as such, or knew that he had once been a soldier. Later that day, after the visitor had left, he asked both his parents what Jefferson meant by it all. His mother, who was evidently already in ill humour with her husband that day, had him leathered for eavesdropping and impertinence. The next day, though, his father took him out into the woods to hunt deer, and there he told Philippe the truth and of the destiny that lay before him…

The first shot struck the side of the coach just behind him, and Philippe snapped out of his half-sleep. There were shouts from the escort, from the other civilians, and different, more frantic shouts from the country around them. There were two or three more shots, then the first in reply from the Blue soldiers.

The convoy was under attack.

—

'*Vive le roi! Damnation à la République!*'

The cries came from behind the high hedges of the fields to the north of the road. As he dismounted and took cover behind one of the carts, Philippe caught a glimpse of a white banner bearing a bloody red emblem – the sacred heart of the devoutly Catholic Chouan rebels – and the cries swiftly gave way to wild howls. Philippe had his pistol in his hand, but he could see no obvious targets. The Chouans, concealed by the thick hedge, had ample cover, unlike those in the convoy. A couple of the women in the coach were screaming. Anquetil was barking orders to his men, who formed two defensive lines facing the enemy and began volley fire even though they, too, had no real target at which to aim. Philippe reckoned their assailants were very few, probably no more than a score at most, so they were unlikely to be able to flank the convoy. Their fire was ragged and inaccurate, so surely all the Blue troops needed to do was—

The side of Anquetil's head shattered in a sunburst of blood and brains. His sergeant stepped towards him, but the young officer was dead before his body struck the ground. Philippe saw the soldiers looking around, saw one of the young recruits spew at the sight of his dead commander, saw another man fall upon being struck by a Chouan bullet. Sergeant Retaillou was frozen in place at the scene before him. Breaking cover, Philippe ran over to him.

'You have the command now, Sergeant!'

'I know, Citizen. The poor lad, though. The poor, poor lad.'

'No helping him now. But spare me just two men and we'll avenge him between us.'

Philippe rapidly explained his plan to Retaillou. He expected the sergeant to argue, but to his surprise the old soldier agreed at once, even giving Philippe three men rather than two. Philippe took them behind the coach and carts, out of sight of the Chouans, then broke cover at the back of the convoy and ran for a patch of furze, the gorse bushes to the left of the royalist position. As Philippe hoped, the gorse broke up the hedge line, giving access to the field where the Chouans were, but above and behind their force. When he and his three men emerged from the gorse, they had a clear field of fire down onto the enemy.

For men who claimed to be the Whites, the royal army of the rightful king of France, the Chouans were wholly indistinguishable from ordinary Breton peasants. Unlike Retaillou's more or less properly uniformed troops, the Chouans wore rough jackets, baggy breeches, and red caps or broad felt hats. Even though it was summer, some wore goatskins over their jackets. Only one stocky fellow with a purple face, presumably their officer, was better dressed, a gaudy yellow waistcoat apparently the emblem of his rank. All of them were intent on Retaillou's troops ahead of them, and the officer had clearly not obeyed the old military adage to always post a man as a lookout to the rear.

Philippe and his troops kneeled down, took aim, and fired.

Two Chouans fell. The others looked around in confusion, saw the tiny force behind them, and turned to concentrate their aim on their assailants. But at the same time, the main body of Blue soldiers began to advance towards the hedge as Philippe and Retaillou had agreed. Seeing the confusion in the White ranks, Philippe and his men loosed off their second volley. If the Chouans had stood their ground they could have easily slaughtered Philippe and his three companions before the Blue troops were in a position to fire, but the sudden appearance of enemies at their rear and the simultaneous advance of Retaillou's men had alarmed them. The Chouans broke, about half a dozen of them running for the woods off to the north. Their commander screamed oaths at them, but the rebels were not trained and disciplined troops. Retaillou's first rank fired off a volley, and although most if not all the bullets went harmlessly into the hedge, the effect on the Chouans was extraordinary. The entire body of the small rebel force made a break for the woods, the flag of the Sacred Heart still held high.

The Blue troops cheered, but Retaillou ordered silence.

'You think they'll be the only Chouans hereabouts, lads? Might be ten thousand of 'em just over that hill for all you know. So we'll stay quiet as mice until we get these good people to where they want to go, then you can find the nearest tavern, sing as loud as you like and try to drink it dry. First, though, we need to bury the lieutenant and the rest of the boys who've fallen. All due solemnity, my lads, all due solemnity.'

He turned to Philippe.

'You handle yourself pretty well in this sort of fighting, Citizen. You sure you want to waste your talent in the navy? I reckon you'd be a damn handy officer in a line regiment.'

'I've seen both land fighting and sea fighting, Sergeant, and I know which I prefer.'

'Pity. Mind you, I reckon we might all see a bit more fighting before we get to the end of the road – the Chouans are getting bolder by the day because they're imminently expecting the English invasion.'

'In which case it'll be down to the navy to stop them, Sergeant. I just hope I can get a command before they come across *La Manche*.'

But Sergeant Retaillou was wrong. There were constant alarms and frequent reports of Chouan units off to the north or south or west, but the rest of the journey west was untroubled. Philippe stayed with the convoy until Poullaouen, then said his farewells to the sergeant and his fellow travellers and turned off to ride north-west, into the heart of the forest.

CHAPTER SIX

The 14th. To the Chateau de Brechelean, a decaying place but once the home of the notable family of Kermorvant, Vicomtes de Saint-Victor. The previous holder of the title was, of course, the famous Verité, whose reputation every literate man knows. Despite this, he was plainly no great agriculturalist, the fields, hedgerows and woodlands hereabouts having been neglected for many years. The present master of the estate was away when I called, but I had a warm welcome from his young wife. It is said in some of the old books that this was the heart of the land of Arthur and Merlin, which lay in the great forest hereabouts. If there be any truth in this, was there ever a clearer proof of sic transit gloria mundi?

From Arthur Young, Travels in France During the Years 1787, 1788 and 1789

As she grew up in Côte-d'Or in Burgundy, the young Leonore Pothier dreamed of marriage to a man of wealth. An attorney in Dijon, perhaps, or else maybe an army officer, preferably one from an elite regiment like the *Gardes françaises*. In any event, she never dreamed of moving very far away from home. Paris, perhaps – who did not dream of living in Paris? – but no further. She certainly never dreamed that one day she would be mistress of a chateau in Brittany, where on certain especially stormy days the spray from the distant Atlantic crusted her window with salt. Yet a chance encounter with a business connection of her father during a family visit to Paris led in just a matter of weeks to both outcomes. Alexandre was many years older than her, but in those days he had been handsome and worldly, and even though he was both illegitimate and not technically the owner of the estate he managed, he was more than wealthy enough to convince Monsieur Pothier of the merits of the match. So Leonore had come to the Chateau de Brechelean as its new

45

lady, and for six months her life had seemed a paradise on earth. Her new status intoxicated her, servants and peasants alike deferred to her, the *curé* adored her, and her new husband was attentive in all possible ways. Then Alexandre suffered the accident that rendered him less than a man, gored in the groin by a wild boar during a hunt. While he was recovering from his terrible injuries, he caught smallpox, from which he nearly died. He survived this second disaster, too, but his face was left scarred and pitted. Brooding incessantly over the loss of his looks and his manhood, he took consolation more and more in *lambig*, the strong apple brandy beloved of the Bretons. In the days when it was still permissible to do so, Leonore knelt before the altar of their parish church and offered up prayers of thanks that her husband did not take out his anguish upon her. Instead he simply ignored her for most of the time, just as he increasingly ignored everyone and everything else. The estate that he had once managed so diligently fell into decay, despite Leonore's efforts to take on some of the tasks her husband now ignored. Hedgerows were left untended and fields uncultivated, even though wheat prices had been soaring for two years, and that was long before most of the young men from the tenant farms were called up as part of the Republic's desperate levy of three hundred thousand men earlier that year. The chateau's north wing had been in ruins long before Leonore's time, but now the newer quarters and the towers were allowed to crumble too, and pigs, chickens and half-feral dogs roamed free in the courtyard. Her proposals for repairs and economies, especially in the wine cellar, fell on deaf ears. Most of the retainers had drifted away, especially after the revolution began and the wrath of the people was focused on the *aristos* who had lorded it from their chateaux for centuries, or so the vociferous local Jacobins told them. Only the old Penhouets, who had been with the family for half a century, remained, but they were too ancient for any serious work. So more and more of the menial tasks devolved upon Leonore. She proved to be good at most of them and did not resent the burden, especially when her efforts drew very occasional smiles from Alexandre, shared moments when perhaps they both fleetingly remembered what they once had.

That morning she was in the north-west tower in the room which Alexandre laughably called the armoury, musty with hundreds of rusting, likely unusable weapons from the time of the wars of religion and even earlier. She was cleaning a shotgun, preparing to go down to the lake to shoot some game for their dinner, the gamekeeper having disappeared overnight a couple of years before.

A movement on the road, glimpsed through the dirty window, suddenly attracted her attention and that of her husband's ancient and arthritic hunting dog, Lancelot, whose bark, at least, still sounded menacing. A single rider with heavy saddle bags was slowly approaching the chateau, examining with intense interest the overgrown fields on either side of the track and the state of the building before him. A little taller than Alexandre, perhaps, but less broad, his face largely invisible beneath the sort of tricorn hat that officers habitually wore. He was armed, with two pistols in his belt and a sword hanging by his horse's flank. No uniform, so probably not from the Blue army. Maybe a Chouan, then? Thus far, neither the republicans nor the royalists had taken much interest in this ruinous chateau deep in the forest, a long way off any public road. Alexandre paid lip service to the Republic and kept his head down, for those with aristocratic names and a chateau were hardly looked upon with favour in the new France of liberty and equality. But Leonore knew that her husband's true sympathies lay elsewhere, and perhaps the Chouans had finally sent an emissary to persuade him – or order him – to declare publicly for the nominal child-king Louis the Seventeenth.

A robber, then? The rider seemed too well dressed and too brazen for that. Besides, what robber would approach his target in broad daylight by riding up to the front entrance? Moreover, all the thieves in the vicinity knew there was nothing to steal in the Chateau de Brechelean, for all the valuables had been pawned long ago.

With practised movements, Leonore loaded the gun. Then she went down the spiral stairs, Lancelot padding his way before her, and stood in the gate passage between the decayed doors, keeping out of the heavy drizzle that the Bretons called *le crachin*. She waited for the rider to come close enough. Very slowly, she raised the gun to her shoulder, cradled the barrel in her other hand, and took aim.

The rider reined in, considering the unlikely spectacle before him.

'You're trespassing, Citizen,' said Leonore loudly, hoping she sounded more confident than she felt. Lancelot had fallen silent and lain down at her feet, hardly generating the air of menace she required. 'This is the Chateau de Brechelean, and my husband, Citizen Alexandre

47

Kermorvant, is the master here. He is presently arming twenty men of the estate and will be here directly.'

She was suddenly aware that her rough smock and skirt, little better than those of any peasant woman, made her a less than convincing claimant to the title of a chatelaine.

'Forgive me, *madame*,' said the stranger before her, seemingly unfazed by her attire and the large gun pointing directly at him, but probably disbelieving the bare-faced lie she had told. 'I understood that the Vicomte de Saint-Victor was the master here.'

She bridled. She should tell this insolent rogue to begone before Alexandre saw or heard this confrontation at the gate. Her husband might not have twenty men to arm even in his dreams, but if he was drunk enough, God knew what sort of fury he would unleash – perhaps not all of it inflicted upon this unknown rider at the gate. That being so, Leonore resolved to settle the matter herself, and at once. If this fellow did not reply or offered defiance, then Leonore trusted her aim and her willingness to take the life of another. Even in this strange new France where the law sometimes seemed to be upside down, who would gainsay a woman acting in self-defence?

The newcomer removed his hat and bowed his head towards Leonore. The gesture disarmed her, as did the man's firm but not unfriendly expression. There was something about his eyes, too.

She knew she should repeat the command for him to leave. Instead, other words somehow tumbled unbidden from her mouth.

'The old vicomte, my husband's father, the one they called Verité, died many years ago, Citizen. There was talk of a son he'd had by some English wife he found in America, but there's been no word of him for a very long time. Some say he went to Russia and was killed in the wars over there. Others say he's out east with Surcouf. There's an old drunk down in the village who'll tell you the young vicomte lies in the same cave as King Arthur and Merlin the sorcerer, somewhere in the forest out there, awaiting the people's call. Flummery, Citizen, all of it nothing but flummery, so you'd best be on your way before I shoot you.'

But even as she spoke the words, she felt the blood draining from her face. Her knees threatened to buckle. Her left hand shook. For now she could see the resemblance in the features of the man before her, sitting so very confidently upon his horse. He was much younger, the plaited hair much darker. But the eyes were the same, and the nose. The mouth was broader, the chin firmer, the cheeks less fleshy, but despite the strange accent in which he spoke, there was no mistaking it.

'Tell your husband,' my brother, that I am here,' said Philippe Kermorvant, the Vicomte de Saint-Victor.

CHAPTER SEVEN

Extract from letter of Leonore Kermorvant to her sister
Louise in Chinon

*...that he is so different to Alex and yet so similar. Sometimes
he reminds me of how Alex was when I first met him. He has a
kindness to him, but a firmness of spirit too, just as Alex did in
those days. Yet I cannot but wonder at the course he follows. To
come to France of all places now, in these times – but I say no
more, of course. He is confident of his success and is certain that
his experience and recommendations will secure him a command
in our navy. But I fear for him, dear Louise. Does he truly know
what he has come to? Does he understand what has happened
here, and how inflamed so many people are against men like
him? Yet for good or ill, a Vicomte de Saint-Victor rests his head
in the Chateau de Brechelean once again.*

'This is Finisterre, Citizen,' said Leonore to her newly revealed brother-
in-law towards the end of their disastrous first dinner at the Chateau de
Brechelean. '*Finis terra*, the old Romans called it, the end of the world.
Kings and republics come and go, but Finisterre will carry on as it always
has. Bretons see things differently to others. To them it's not *Finis terra*,
but in their own tongue it's—'

'*Penn ar bed*,' said a smiling Philippe in Breton. 'The head of the
world. I know. My father taught me that, long ago.'

Alexandre Kermorvant, sitting in his accustomed position at the
head of the table, made a sound somewhere between a mocking laugh
and a snort of disgust, but said nothing. Instead he drained his glass and
beckoned to old Jacques Penhouet for a refill. Leonore, from her place
at the other end of the table, attempted to catch his eye to make a silent
plea for restraint, but her husband studiously avoided her gaze.

It had been a difficult dinner. Alexandre drank steadily, spoke little and did even less to conceal his resentment of the new situation. He barely looked at his brother, and made at best monosyllabic replies to any questions he was asked. His mood had not been improved by the Penhouets, who could not have been more obviously delighted at the unexpected arrival of the rightful vicomte, the chateau's owner. They insisted on serving at table, proudly proclaiming that they had done this for Philippe's father and grandfather, even though their arthritic hands managed to break three plates and spill an entire jug of wine. In normal times Alexandre would have raged, perhaps even struck one or both of them. Now, though, he remained ominously silent, toying with his food and keeping his eyes fixed on his plate. Leonore kept looking from her husband to his brother, praying that the one did not assault the other. She did her best, of course, and made polite conversation with her brother-in-law. It was merely common courtesy, was it not, the natural duty of a hostess? But she had already had more words out of the vicomte in two hours than she had had out of her husband in two months, and they were *interesting* words, not words about game birds or the contents of the wine cellar or the certainty of France's defeat. Philippe – it was surprisingly easy to think of him as Philippe, rather than the Vicomte de Saint-Victor – talked of distant places that sounded to her like the lands of fable: the icebound archipelagos of the Baltic, the endless plains around the Black Sea, the tidewater of Virginia. He had been in great storms in the Atlantic. He had sailed to the Levant, had gone to Rome and seen the pope. He had talked with native chiefs in the Americas and with Cossacks in the Crimea. He had met the Empress Catherine! Better still, he listened to her and seemed to take seriously her opinions on such supposedly unladylike matters as the management of stock and the likely English threat to Brittany. Alex had listened to her once, but since his injury he had fallen in more and more with the consensus among his lumpen Breton neighbours, namely that the subjects she found so fascinating were not seemly topics of conversation for a woman.

Philippe also talked of his and Alexandre's father, of Verité, and how the American war had reinforced the latter's view about many things, notably about the brotherhood and equality of all men.

'He believed in the cause of independence, of course, and in the republican ideal of the new nation. But the composition of the states troubled him. He saw the inequalities, he saw how one great section of the new republic depended on slavery, which he thought a vicious iniquity, and he couldn't see how the whole could possibly endure as one nation. He thought it inevitable that one day they would fracture into three or four new countries, perhaps more. And the Indians, the way treaties were made but broken with impunity when it suited greedy men to do so... It troubled him, but—'

'How did he die?' Alexandre barked suddenly. 'My father... our father. How did he die? Did you see it?'

They were his first words for nearly an hour. His listless eyes were open and wide with challenge.

'I wasn't with him,' said Philippe, clearly weighing his words very carefully. 'We were both at the siege of Savannah, which is in the territory called the Carolinas, but I was afloat and he was ashore. I was summoned to Admiral d'Estaing's flagship, and he told me of it.'

'And what did he tell you?'

For the first time, Alexandre looked intently at his brother's face.

'It was an interlude between attacks, but there was some sort of skirmish by one of the outer redoubts. Father was alone but for two or three men. It wasn't clear where the shot that killed him came from.'

'And that's how he fell? The great Verité? Not a heroic charge? Not something worthy of legend, like all those tales of King Arthur he wrote about? Those tales he told me when I was a boy? Gawain, all the rest of them? Not some great quest? Not the last man defending a position against all odds? Just some random shot in a skirmish that didn't matter. That didn't matter *at all*.'

Alexandre took another swig of his *lambig*, smiled to himself and looked away. Puzzled, Philippe looked to Leonore, but she could only shrug.

The three spent the rest of the dinner in agonising silence.

—

Later, Alexandre came to Leonore's room. This was a large space, airy in summer but impossible to heat in winter, and sumptuously furnished at first glance. But none of the furnishings would bear close inspection. Leonore often thought that Diane de Poitiers and other great ladies of two hundred years earlier had rooms such as this one. They would certainly have recognised the great oak-pillared bed and the faded tapestries that adorned the walls, for those and other fittings had not moved from the room in all those years.

It was the first time Alexandre had come to her in this way in many months, perhaps even for more than a year. His visits ceased almost completely after his accident, when he lost the ability to perform his marital duties, and he had never been a man who considered his wife deserving of a courtesy visit simply to pass the time of day together. As she heard him approach her door, Leonore feared that he was about to beat her for showing too much favour to her newly discovered brother-in-law. Or rather, to *try* to beat her. He seemed to have learned his lesson the last time, when she gave as good as she got. Alexandre learned the hard way that the wounds in an already terribly damaged groin cannot bear the slightest contact from the knee of even a seemingly feeble and slight woman. He had forgotten that Leonore grew up among brothers and had learned to hold her own against them at a very early age.

He was even more drunk than he had been at the dinner table. She knew he had more bottles of *lambig* in his room, for he made no attempts to conceal them. She had stopped issuing reproofs long ago, and the Penhouets, entrusted with keeping the chateau in some kind of state appropriate for a seigneurial seat, merely shook their heads in mute disapproval.

'I'm the older by twelve years,' said Alexandre, slurring his words. It was at once clear to Leonore that this was not a speech designed for her; this was the speech he had been forming during all the time at the dinner table, the one he had to inflict on some, on *any*, audience. Leonore's misfortune was that she was the only one available. 'He's, what, the son of some English whore my father picked up in America? But because some priest proclaimed them man and wife and there's a piece of paper somewhere that says it was a lawful marriage – under *English* law, I expect, Christ knows if it is under French law – and because he never married my mother... He promised her, you know, promised her he'd marry her when he was allowed back from exile, promised her he'd legitimise me and make me his heir. And now, after all I've done for this estate, the English whore's son turns up here...'

He was speaking so loudly now that even the vicomte, in his new quarters at the other end of the wing, might be able to hear him. Leonore tried to take her husband's hand, but he pulled it away.

After all I've done for this estate. Run it into the ground, if the truth were told, and that even before the revolution, which gave him the perfect excuse to let it decline further while he strayed less and less often from the bottle. Leonore, desperate to calm and quieten her husband, tried to divert him.

'I did not know his mother was English.'

Alexandre squinted at her as though trying to recognise her through a mist.

'Oh yes, his mother was English all right, from some *aristo* family over there. Went out to marry some rich man in America who conveniently died and left the estate to her for her lifetime, then she weaved a spell on my father. As blatant a seduction as you like, or so I heard. Note, Leonore, how he, my half-brother, doesn't trumpet those truths. Not likely to endear him to the Republic, is it? Grounds for suspicion of treason, I'd say.' He struggled to get out the word suspicion. 'He turns up in France now, all of a sudden, when we're at war with his mother's country – he's a spy, if you ask me. And anyway, what proof is there that he is truly my brother? He wears my father's ring, but he could have stolen that. Nobody hereabouts has ever seen him. He grew up in America so the Penhouets don't know him. I expect that's where he got that hair from, that ridiculous *queue de cheval*. Don't the savages out there wear their hair like that? He's no Kermorvant. No true Kermorvant would be seen looking like a savage. No, imposters are everywhere these days, so how can we be sure he is what he says he is, eh? How can we?'

He seemed not to expect her to answer, so she kept her counsel. It occurred to her that no fortune-seeking imposter in his right mind would dare pretend to be an aristocrat in the France of 1793, but she suppressed the thought. Besides, Philippe was no imposter, no matter how desperately Alexandre wanted to prove him so. It was not just the ring, nor even the well-thumbed letters that Verité had sent his heir during the American war and which Philippe carried around with him like holy relics. At dinner Leonore had been able closely to compare their faces and mannerisms. Not only did they look alike, but they also held their forks in the same strange way that she had always thought peculiar to her husband; a trait that both sons of Verité had evidently inherited from their father. Then there was the mute evidence staring out from the dusty Kermorvant portraits on the walls, the similar faces that recurred generation after generation, the faces that betrayed the paternity of both Alexandre and Philippe.

'He will be gone before long, Alex,' she said. 'He'll be off to sea as soon as he can get a command, and things will go back to how they were. Back to you running the estate just as you've always done.'

More's the pity, Leonore thought, even though she recoiled from her disloyalty to her husband.

'And what if he doesn't get a command?' Alexandre paced the floor of her room, barely looking at her. 'Even if he does, this isn't that far from Brest. Most of the ships don't go out for very long, not with the English blockade fleet out there. He'll be here meddling, I'll wager on that. Undermining my authority. Putting into effect all those... yes, those perverse ideas my father had. You heard what he was saying? He swallowed it all, every lunacy my father ever conjured up. If he has his way we'll have every beggar in Brittany turning up here demanding alms. He'll set up schools for the peasants, you mark my words, just like Father tried to do before he wrote one polemic too many attacking Louis Quinze. After all I've done. All I've done, by God!'

Leonore hoped that the expression on her face was sympathetic, but she suspected it was not. Once, Alex's resentments had been nearly invisible, concealed behind a façade of urgency, efficiency and sociability. Then the chance encounter with a boar demolished the façade for ever.

'And you,' said Alexandre. 'You were familiar with him. Too familiar. He's no friend to us, no friend to me, but you treat him like the prodigal son.'

'Husband, it's mere courtesy to any guest, but especially to your own brother – to the vicomte.'

Alexandre's hand came up sharply as though he was about to strike her, but it stopped when it was barely raised to his chest. An invisible force seemed to be holding it down. Just for a fleeting moment, she thought she saw an expression in his eyes that hinted at the kinder, nobler man he had once been. The man who declared and demonstrated his love for his young wife at every opportunity.

'The vicomte,' he said quietly. 'The days of *aristos* and their titles are done in France.'

'You don't believe that.'

'Don't tell me what I believe! You don't know what I believe!' She did, and she knew that in his heart, he wanted nothing more fervently than the return of the old France he pretended to despise. 'But I'm the older, the one our father trusted, the one he chose to run the estate in his absence. I'm twelve years his senior. Twelve years. Yet he turns up here, no warning, no by-your-leave, and I'm expected to defer to him? I'm expected to give him a home and share my table with him? And my wife fawns over him? This stranger, this foreigner? Perhaps they're right, the *sans-culottes*. The lamppost. The guillotine. Perhaps they're right.'

Alex was half shouting his words and his eyes were wide with fury. He would leave her soon, Leonore knew, and all would be quiet until the next time. She did not need to say anything. Much later and with hindsight, she realised she should not have said anything. Her husband's self-pity and rage against the injustices life had imposed on him were everyday occurrences to be ignored like the buzzing of flies. She always ignored such outbursts and let them pass unless they were turned against her.

But this time, fatefully, she answered him.

'We defer to him because he is the vicomte! Think about what that means, Alex. This estate is his. This chateau is his. *We are his.*'

He looked at her, and for a moment he was uncomprehending, then he turned and made his way towards the doorway. As he reached it, he looked back at her, a strange smile on his face.

'Quite so, my dear. All his as long as he is the vicomte.'

CHAPTER EIGHT

...and I may say that I do not know to this very hour how Kermorvant survived the wound he received from the Turk's blade, let alone somehow continuing to command his ship. But he has a strong hide and a fierce spirit, and I always felt that God saved him that day for a purpose. I do not know what that purpose is (I suspect he does not, either) or for which country he will end up fighting, but this letter of mine is a humble supplication on behalf of my old friend, one of the most intrepid warriors I have ever encountered.

I remain your obedient servant

Grigor Petrovich Ustinov

Captain in the Navy of Imperial Russia, from on board the battle-frigate Nepreryvnyy in the harbour of Azov

Philippe paced through the overgrown tangle that still revealed the occasional glimpse of the elaborate formal gardens that had been fashionable in the days of *le roi soleil*, the Sun King. The rigorous mathematical precision of the original *parterre* was long gone, and might even have been in decline before his father was sent into exile nearly thirty years before. What must once have been immaculate roses had run wild wherever they were not completely overwhelmed by brambles. In the weeks since he had first come to Brechelean, though, this chaotic ghost garden had become one of Philippe's favourite places on the entire estate. This was partly because his brother, Alexandre, hated it and never ventured this way at all, preferring either to ride out, ostensibly to meet tenants or neighbours, or else to stay in his rooms. Both activities, Philippe knew, would involve a prodigious amount of drink.

The two brothers had exchanged no more than a few dozen words in the three weeks since Philippe's arrival, despite the vicomte's best efforts to be fraternal and considerate. He made no attempt to interfere in Alexandre's management of the estate, although it was all too easy to see how manifestly incompetent this was, despite Leonore's regular and judicious scrutiny of the rental ledgers. Neighbours who had heard of the mysterious vicomte's return called to pay their respects, all enquiring with varying degrees of subtlety when the true lord of Brechelean would be taking charge of the estate's affairs, but Philippe was always careful to defer to his sibling. One day he would have to take matters in hand; perhaps when the war was over, and he had garnered enough prize money to restore the chateau and its lands and, yes, its garden. For now, he had very different priorities.

And then there was Leonore. Circumstance invariably forced the two of them to dine together, Alexandre choosing to take his meals alone in his rooms instead. In some ways she reminded him of Tasha. They looked nothing alike – Tasha would have been at least a *pied* taller than Leonore – but there was something he could not quite put into words. Yet in many ways Leonore was more than Tasha had ever been. A woman who shot as well as any man, who understood husbandry, who spoke knowledgably about the state of the world – he had encountered women who possessed one of those attributes, not all of them. But she was, of course, his brother's wife, so they both behaved towards each other with the utmost propriety. The very utmost propriety.

As he struggled along a narrow path between grossly overgrown honeysuckle, the dog, Lancelot, going ahead of him, Philippe fretted about the condition of his life. For certain, it was not what he had expected when he left Russia. Shorn of most of its former officers, the French navy was desperate for experienced captains. This was the orthodoxy proclaimed in the messes, drawing rooms and coffee houses of Moscow, Saint Petersburg, Karlskrona and Gothenburg. The French Republic, beleaguered on all sides, would surely welcome him with open arms – not just a man who had served on ships in battle, commanding one of them, but the son of Verité! And where had all this confidence – this arrogance, even – led him? To this morass of weeds and brambles in the remotest corner of the remotest province in France, where all his letters went unanswered and all those who had once promised to intercede for him were utterly silent. The prospect of a command at sea was as remote as the moon. Instead, he whiled away his time walking an estate that was his in name but another's in truth, reading mouldy books in a library with a leaking roof, and avoiding, as much as possible, a brother who hated him and a woman he could not, dare not, touch. He thought back to his last night in Kronstadt and old Kharabadze's words: 'You actually want to sail *for France*? Even after all that's happened – you and Bulgakov, poor dear Tasha, the rest of it? France, Filip? The France that couldn't be content with the hundreds of different ways men have devised to kill each other since Cain slew Abel, so they decide to invent a new one? The France that uses this new killing machine to chop the heads off people with titles like yours, my Lord of Saint-Victor? *That* France? Don't worry, Filip, my friend, I'll make sure the priests sing "Memory Eternal" for you when I hear you're no more.' He could almost hear the old man's laughter, and momentarily thought he heard his dear Tasha's too, joining in the joke at his expense. But as he turned in surprise he realised the laughter could only be Leonore's. He could see her in the distance, over by the brewhouse, playing with one of the dogs. It was strange how her laughter sounded so much like Tasha's.

Of course, it had not taken Leonore long to discover that Philippe once had a wife and son. A discreet question at dinner, a guarded answer, but he knew from his time with Natasha that it would inevitably lead to further discreet but relentlessly probing questions until she uncovered the entire truth. And how much of that truth could Leonore take? His discovery of Tasha's broken body, bloodied from the dozen deep slashes across her flesh? And Ivan's, his little life cut short by a single stab wound to the heart? All that horror inflicted by Tasha's brother, Count Bulgakov, in a vodka-fuelled rage, because in his opinion she had dishonoured the family name by marrying a foreigner? Philippe's noble rank counted for nothing then. After the funeral, he drank himself into a stupor for three days and swore he would be avenged. Then he sobered up, and the realities of the world crowded in on him. Bulgakov had fled to his estate in Siberia, and even if Philippe or the law caught up with him, he was a personal friend of the tsarevich. The empress was old, and one day soon the Tsarevich Paul would ascend the imperial throne. Russia's wars with the Swedes and Turks were over, so Philippe had no prospect of any command. Besides, it was common talk in the inns and salons of Saint Petersburg that if the empress went to war again, it would be to join her fellow monarchs in the grand coalition against the regicidal, atheist Republic of France. If there were to be such a war, Philippe Kermorvant, the Vicomte de Saint-Victor, could fight on only one side.

Philippe reached a corner of the garden and turned, taking another path. He would not succumb to self-pity, he vowed. It would not bring back Tasha and Ivan, and if he were being realistic, he would never be avenged on Bulgakov, who was very far away and probably beyond his reach. Revenge was surely a fantasy, just as wishful and impossible as his father's wild dream that this place, Brechelean, was the heart of King Arthur's Broceliande, the mystical forest where Merlin lay entombed. The past was done with, fantasy was only that and nothing more, and in the bitter reality of the present he knew that his own situation was as nothing to his country's. Rebels were in control of Bordeaux, Saumur, Lyons and any number of other towns and districts. The Sardinians were threatening Savoy and Nice, the Spanish advancing on Perpignan and Bayonne, the English poised to land anywhere along the north-west coasts to support the Chouans and the Vendée. Many commodities were scarce and prices were soaring to unheard-of levels; all this before England's prime minister, William Pitt, imagined by many to be literally the devil incarnate, imposed a blockade on grain, thereby treating the entire population of France as if it was merely a besieged town standing inconveniently in the path of an all-conquering army. The Committee of Public Safety responded by declaring Pitt to be an enemy of the human race. Despite this brave proclamation, there were soon queues, even riots, outside the bread shops. In Paris, the Committee debated endlessly and changed composition constantly: one moment Danton was on, then he was off, then he was on again. To cap it all, there was increasingly confident talk that Marie-Antoinette, the erstwhile queen, was to be put on trial for her life, and if she went to the guillotine then the monarchs of Europe would undoubtedly be even more enraged and determined to wipe out the French Republic. Rumours were also spreading that her son, King Louis the Seventeenth – as far as the royalists were concerned – had died in the Temple prison. Inevitably, conspiracy theories were already rife. The boy had been buggered to death by his gaoler, some said, or else Robespierre himself had suffocated him with a pillow. Not true, said others, who swore that the boy had escaped only to be killed by his evil uncles, the Comtes de Provence and Artois, who wanted the throne for themselves. There was even a rumour that the lad had been spirited away to freedom in one of the much-vaunted new inventions, a balloon, and would return at the head of a crusade of vengeful royalists to destroy the republic. Whatever the truth, the Committee ordered the desecration of the royal tombs in the cathedral of Saint-Denis. Out they all came to be thrown into the common pit instead: the bones of Louis the Thirteenth, Fourteenth and Fifteenth, even good old Henri the Fourth, whom his father, Verité, had venerated, for all his republican bluster. Strangely, Philippe found himself more deeply affected by this news than by many of the woeful tales of what was befalling living Frenchmen. If the test of republican zeal was now a willingness to desecrate the bones of the dead, then was that republic really a worthy cause?

Perhaps, though, he had another course, one that had been an impossible dream when he left Virginia for Russia and then left Russia for France. There was talk, in news brought into Brest, Nantes and Saint-Malo by American ships, that after years of rancorous debate, Congress was finally preparing to act against the depredations of the Algerian corsairs by instituting a new navy for the United States. A proper navy, an ocean-going navy of six sturdy frigates, nothing like the feeble, underfunded and rapidly abolished Continental Navy in which he had served. Perhaps he could—

'You appear to be in a different world, Brother,' said Leonore from behind him. 'I trust it's better than this one?'

'I was trying to imagine how this garden once looked,' Philippe lied.

She smiled with her head slightly cocked to one side, as though she knew his true thoughts but was prepared to indulge him in the lie.

'The Penhouets say it was a splendid sight back in the time of your grandfather, the admiral. I would have it so again, but Alexandre has no interest, there's no money, and I have other calls upon my time.'

'From what I've seen, Sister, you have too many calls upon your time. Calls unworthy of your rank.'

'And if I don't do these things, Brother – if I don't do the work of a steward, and a housekeeper, and a scullion, and a gamekeeper, and all the rest of it – then who will, eh? The Penhouets are willing but they cannot, for the most part. Alexandre will not. We had other servants, but some were taken by the great levy.'

'Not all, from what the Penhouets tell me.'

'No, not all. But my husband has… let's say he has a reputation that makes men reluctant to work for him. And since the war began and so many men went off to the army or to the Chouans, all the estates in Finisterre – probably all the estates in France – are desperate for servants. So the rich ones can offer better wages, and that makes the lot of poor ones like this even worse.'

They began to walk together through the tangled undergrowth, and as they did so, a thought occurred to Philippe.

'I see why it will be hard for the estate to recruit men,' he said, 'but surely there are many women available? Some of the Breton girls I've seen in the villages hereabouts look to be at least as substantial as the strongest topmen I've ever sailed with.'

She laughed, and again it reminded him of Tasha. But then her expression turned more serious.

'Women, too, are reluctant to work here.'

Philippe was puzzled. Surely, in the light of what he had learned about his brother— Uncertain of himself, he stuttered an apology.

'Ah. Forgive me, Sister, I should have been more thoughtful.'

She looked at him, seemingly puzzled, then realised that they were at cross purposes.

'Oh, not for the reason you're thinking of – whatever he may be, Alexandre is certainly no Gilles de Rais.'

Philippe had been far too young when his father first terrified him with the tales of Gilles de Rais, the Breton nobleman of three hundred years before who had tortured, defiled and murdered hundreds of children for his own twisted amusement.

He saw Leonore blush, and knew she was weighing whether to tell him about Alexandre's disability.

'Sister, I know about his accident. When the Cadoudal sisters called to pay their respects, they talked about little else – and for elderly ladies who've never married, they were remarkably graphic in their descriptions.'

They both laughed, Leonore with evident relief but not a little shame. When her laughter was over, she looked up at him. Neither said a word. Philippe began to raise his hand, although his reason told him not to touch her cheek. That was a sure road to disaster, and it was a road he had already travelled in Russia.

Then he heard the singing. At first it was very faint, from somewhere over on the road through the forest, accompanied by the beat of a single drum. As it got louder, it became apparent that the singers were making for the chateau. There had to be dozens of them, perhaps a hundred, and their song was '*Ça Ira*', one of the most popular and scurrilous battle hymns of the revolutionaries.

Ah! ça ira, ça ira, ça ira
les aristocrates à la lanterne!
Ah! ça ira, ça ira, ça ira
les aristocrates on les pendra!
Et quand on les aura tous pendus
On leur fichera la pelle au cul.

(Ah! It'll be fine, It'll be fine, It'll be fine
aristocrats to the lamppost
Ah! It'll be fine, It'll be fine, It'll be fine
the aristocrats, we'll hang them!
And when we'll have hung them all
We'll stick a shovel up their arse.)

The mob barged its way past the furious but impotent Penhouets and made their way towards the garden. The singing and drumming ceased as they came closer to Philippe and Leonore.

The apparent leader stepped forward. He was a small bespectacled fellow with a narrow, unpleasant face and a slight limp. Like most functionaries of the Republic, he wore sashes of red, white and blue around his waist and on his hat. In a loud, feminine voice, he announced himself to be Citizen Roland Quedeville, representative of the revolutionary tribunal – he did not specify whose – and of the Brest Jacobin club.

He studied Philippe neutrally, glanced around as though seeking encouragement from the fellows behind him, then cleared his throat loudly.

'Citizen Philippe Kermorvant, called the Vicomte de Saint-Victor, you have been charged with counter-revolutionary sympathies, of correspondence with the enemies of France, and, in short, with treason against the Republic, one and indivisible!'

Philippe stood stock still, unable to believe what he was hearing. He thought back on all that had happened since he first came to the Chateau de Brechelean, seeking the slightest action or remark that could possibly have been construed as a heinous crime against the state. To the best of his recollection, the only thing that might have caused offence was his recital of the rosary on the anniversary of his father's death, but that had been done in private, and barely aloud. Surely France did not guillotine men for that?

Before he could speak, Leonore stepped forward, looking Citizen Quedeville up and down and failing entirely to conceal her utter contempt.

'I am Citizeness Leonore Kermorvant, sister-in-law to the accused, as you know full well, Citizen Quedeville. What trade did you ply in Loqueffret before the Revolution? Baker, wasn't it? I congratulate you on improving your station in life.' There was some laughter in the mob behind Quedeville, whose face was a mask. 'But by whose authority are these charges brought, Citizen? With what evidence?'

Quedeville frowned. He clearly did not like being challenged by a woman, but there were at least two dozen of the same sex at his back, so he had to take Leonore's demands seriously.

'The man known as the Vicomte de Saint-Victor has been denounced privately by various respectable and trustworthy citizens of these parts, as permitted by the law recently passed by the National Convention. There are sworn depositions, Citizeness.'

'Of course there are. And what are the names of these *worthy* gentlemen?'

Quedeville smiled the sort of smile that men bestow on backward children.

'Citizeness, the names of those who denounce counter-revolutionaries and traitors are, of course, confidential. How else will right-thinking lovers of liberty be free to express their concerns without fear of reprisal?'

The mob behind him growled its approval. Leonore was clearly preparing a response, but Philippe took her arm.

'Hush now, Sister,' he said, as much for the mob's consumption as for hers. 'I will go willingly with these good citizens and citizenesses, and I will clear myself of any charges against me.'

A file of soldiers, commanded by an officer on horseback, emerged from the courtyard of the chateau and marched towards them.

'As you see,' said Quedeville smugly, 'all is done in an orderly way, demonstrating the Republic's belief in the rule of law. And we can't risk such a prisoner being snatched away from the people's justice by a raid from the priest-loving rebel filth, now can we? So a proper escort to take you into custody at Brest, Citizen.'

The officer commanding the troops was a very familiar figure, even if he wore an unfamiliar uniform. Despite the gravity of his predicament, Philippe could not help but smile.

'My congratulations on your promotion, Lieutenant Retaillou.'

'I'll make Marshal of France yet, Monsieur le Vicomte,' said Retaillou, grinning. Then he saw Quedeville's enraged expression and became more serious, but only fractionally so. 'I'm sorry to see you again in such circumstances, Citizen. Sorry, too, that fate has dealt us both this hand.'

'It can't be helped, Lieutenant. At least I'll have good company on the road.'

Quedeville was outraged at the familiarity of the two men but seethed in silence, for there was nothing he could do. His mob might be much larger than Retaillou's detail of only twenty men, but the local *sans-culottes* were armed with nothing more lethal than a pitchfork.

Philippe turned to Leonore, whose eyes were full of tears.

'Be well, Sister,' he said, this time to her alone. 'Be safe. I trust we will see each other again very soon.'

She swayed slightly but regained her composure before he could gather her in his arms.

'Farewell, Brother,' she said formally, her words intended for the audience rather than Philippe. 'I know your innocence, and I will prove it.'

He bowed his head in a slight nod, held her in his eyes for another moment, then turned to join Retaillou's troop.

–

Leonore could not move. She watched the escort take Philippe away and saw the mob disperse, still singing the endless choruses of '*Ça Ira*', damning all the *aristos* to be hanged from lampposts. But lampposts had proved too slow, and besides, there were very few of them here in Finisterre. Now France had a much faster way of disposing of those whose only true crime was to be born with the wrong name.

She felt empty. The Penhouets were running towards her, or rather shuffling as best they could, but she was barely aware of them. She thought she would be sick, but a dry retch brought up nothing. As old Madame Penhouet took her in her arms and pressed her against her formidable bosom, Leonore thought on what had just transpired. Something about it was not right. The mob's anger seemed somehow false, as though it were being acted out. The presence of the soldiers was strange too. Surely few arrests were attended by so many troops? The army was stretched beyond its limits by war on many fronts, and especially here in Brittany by the Chouans. Yet Quedeville knew they would be there. He was not the instigator of this, she was certain, for he was only a jumped-up baker, the sort of insignificant fellow to whom the revolution had suddenly given status and purpose. Who else in the vicinity would have made a formal denunciation of a man who had barely arrived in France, who was wholly unknown to almost everyone?

As she looked through her tears over Madame Penhouet's shoulder, she remembered a detail. She had seen where Quedeville had looked, however briefly, as he turned away from Philippe. He was not seeking affirmation from those behind him; he was seeking it from a window high in the south wing of the chateau. A window in Alexandre's rooms. Brother had denounced brother.

Leonore broke away from Madame Penhouet's embrace and began to stride towards the chateau, intending to confront her husband. Her Chouan sympathiser husband. He probably thought she didn't know that he still prayed for the queen and for the immortal soul of her dead husband, Louis Capet. Or that he wrote secretly to the rebel leaders of the district, promising his support as and when the right moment came to declare himself for the royal cause, which would undoubtedly be when the royal cause looked certain to win and provided him with a sufficiently large bag of English gold. She knew a great deal more about Alexandre Kermorvant than he realised.

But she would not confront her husband yet. He would only rage at her and deny every allegation. It would not save Philippe.

Only one thing might do that.

CHAPTER NINE

As he sits before his log fire in the twilight of his years, an old man's thoughts turn more and more to those he knew in the golden days of his youth. Most of the boys I ran and hollered with back then, down by the Virginia creeks, are long gone. Many, indeed, were gone many years before I first went to our new national capital. The lads who grew up with me were just the right age to fight for our great national cause against Farmer George's Redcoats, and many of them did not last beyond the first fusillade. I wished to go off to sea with my two best friends, Ben and Philippe, but my father would not hear of it. Looking back, he was probably right. Ben Dawkins took an English cannonball in the neck on his seventeenth birthday, or so report had it. As for Philippe Kermorvant, son of a man who had a certain fleeting fame in those days, he had a strange career indeed. I heard tales over the years, some of which were almost believable, and I encountered him once in adult life in the most unexpected of circumstances. What became of him is a matter of historical record, so I shall not waste ink by recording it here.

From The Memoirs of the Honourable Samuel J Arbon
(1762–1850), late United States Senator for the State of Virginia

He was almost within touching distance. He could see the mastheads. He could hear the hammering of treenails into timbers, the grinding sound made by the crane mechanisms, the rasp of the huge saws as they fashioned futtocks and knee timbers. He could smell the myriad smells of a naval dockyard: tar, pitch, wood, damp canvas. Here was purpose. Here was a fleet being made ready for battle. It was frustratingly near. He prayed for one last glimpse of the ocean, that he should see it just one more time before he went to the guillotine. But Retaillou and his men led him through crowded streets where every *pouce* of space was taken up by tall granite-built houses several centuries old, and brought him at last to the ancient fortress that loomed over the innermost part of the town.

As he prepared to transfer Philippe to the custody of the gaoler, Retaillou extended his hand.

'Well, Citizen, I'm sorry it's come to this, that I am. For this to happen to as good a fighter and as amiable a fellow as yourself – well, sir, it fair breaks my heart, it truly does.'

Philippe took the man's hand and shook it vigorously.

'Don't grieve for me, Lieutenant. But when you're Marshal of France, come and stand by my grave awhile and tell me of all the great victories you've won in the name of the Republic. Perhaps my bones will hear you, eh? But don't tell any of your jokes. My condition won't lend itself to shaking with laughter.'

Retaillou, the bluff old regular soldier, nodded and turned away, perhaps hoping that neither Philippe nor his men would see him dab at his eye.

–

The citadel of Brest was even less welcoming than that of Saint-Malo. There, at least, Philippe was not facing any charges, and although regarded with suspicion he was treated, in some ways, as a guest. Here he was a prisoner, and one among many. His quarters were a cell in one of the round towers facing inland, thus again denying him a last glimpse of the sea. The walls ran with damp and there was a hole in the glass of the small window which admitted the wind and rain when the weather turned nor'easterly. It would be a good wind for taking the fleet to sea, Philippe thought, but there was no word of any movement. One of the guards, a fellow named Dujardin, was splendidly indiscreet, and his news about the ships and the doings of the Republic's leaders spread through the cells faster than dysentery.

For some weeks – he swiftly lost count of the days – Philippe shared the cell with a lanky youth named Hauchard, who wept for most of each day, sobbed himself to sleep, and complained incessantly about the unchanging diet of stale bread, salted herring and water. Hauchard was, it seemed, a younger son of an impoverished baron, and almost every conversation with him followed much the same course.

'It's all a mistake, of course,' said Hauchard in his high-pitched nasal voice. 'I'm no Chouan, Citizen, I'm as firm a Jacobin as you'll find anywhere in Brittany. My brothers, now, they're all traitors to a man. I'll tell the tribunal all this, citizen, and I'm sure they'll see the justice of my case and acquit me. It can't be the end of me, you see, I'm only nineteen. What can I have done against the Republic? No, it's definitely a mistake. I could have such a long life ahead of me, could do so many great things, and I'll promise them that I'll be true to the Republic as long as I live. Surely they'll see that?'

Philippe listened patiently and occasionally made soothing replies, not that Hauchard ever really listened. In truth, the vicomte's thoughts were not dissimilar to his cellmate's, albeit with one vital difference. Hauchard blamed everyone else for his predicament, Philippe blamed only himself. The thoughts that had tormented him during his strolls through the derelict garden of Brechelean now dominated every waking moment, and kept him awake long into the night. It had been a mistake. No, worse: it was insanity. Philippe knew almost nobody in France and had no friends here. Those Frenchmen whose recommendation he had called upon to try to procure him a command were largely old friends of his father, so were many years older than him, relics of a different, entirely lost world, and as far as he could see none of them were raising a finger on his behalf. His own friends were either dead or back in Russia − what he would give to drink vodka until dawn in the Chernyy Orel with Kharabadze and Ustinov, putting the world to rights! − or else in America, where Sam Arbon was surely a member of Congress now if he had not been butchered by a jealous husband, and Opechancanough was perhaps a paramount chief among his people, as he deserved to be. He missed good companionship and amiable conversation, and did not know if he would ever find those in a France where everyone was suspicious of strangers, where it seemed that the slightest offence, just one word construed wrongly, could lead to denunciation and the guillotine. Kharabadze and the rest had been right; he was mad to come here, to this land of suspicion, terror and legalised murder. His grief for Tasha and Ivan, and a foolish belief that this is what his father would have wanted him to do, had surely delivered him to his death.

Hauchard was still preaching his usual litany on the morning he was taken to the guillotine. As the realisation dawned, the boy screamed, tore at his clothes, made to attack the guards and even Philippe, but it availed him nothing. Dujardin later reported that the youth had not died well, ranting, roaring and weeping all the way to the guillotine, where he wet himself prodigiously before the blade fell and ended it.

That night Philippe had the cell to himself, but sleep remained elusive.

If he had not come to France, he would not have met Leonore.

A strange thought. She was his sister-in-law, his brother's wife, and he should not be thinking about her in this way. They had come perilously close to indiscretion, a folly that had cost him his liberty and probably his head. What had it cost her, he wondered, at the hands of the damaged, dangerous man with whom he shared a father? He could not help her now, that was for certain.

He hoped he would make a better death than Hauchard. What did it feel like, that moment when the blade severed the neck? He had heard the stories about the heads where the eyes rolled and blinked after being disembodied. There were even legends of heads that had held lucid conversations with the executioner. They were bound to be myths to frighten the credulous. But that did not suppress the morbid curiosity.

The next morning, Dujardin brought him a new cellmate.

'You're honoured, Citizen Vicomte,' said the garrulous guard. 'They've given you somebody really special this time. An English spy, no less!'

There was a growl from behind Dujardin's shoulder as two men struggled with their prisoner, whom they all but flung into the cell. As Dujardin locked the door, the man turned and bawled several choice English obscenities.

He had the look of a spy, in so far as any man ever did. Relatively short, the Englishman walked with a slight but noticeable limp. His face was bland and forgettable but for a fierce scar across his chin. He looked around the cell as though trying to locate an escape route, glowered at Philippe, then sat down heavily on the other pallet bed.

'What brings you here, Citizen?' Philippe asked, hoping his enquiry sounded innocent enough.

'And what's it to you?' the fellow replied, his tone hostile.

'Merely passing the time of day, Citizen.'

'That so? Well pass it some other way, and don't bother me with any more of your citizen this and citizen that horseshit.'

'You speak good French for an Englishman,' Philippe said in English.

The man, clearly startled at being addressed in his own tongue, stared at him as though he were the Second Coming.

'And by the sounds of you, you're a Yank.'

'Born and raised in Virginia, but French by descent. My name is Philippe Kermorvant.'

There was a glimmer of what might have been recognition in the man's eyes, but there was no lessening of his hostility.

'Tell you what, Philippe whatever-you-said, let's come to an understanding. I'll stay over here, and you stay over there, and let's not say another word to each other, shall we?'

'We can do that.'

He returned to his own pallet, lay down, and resumed his scrutiny of the spiders who infested the cell. His cellmate stood, paced back and forth for a few minutes as if he were trying to measure the dimensions of the room, then he too lay down again on his pallet. He began to hum a tune, and to his surprise, Philippe recognised it: 'The British Grenadiers'. It had been a great favourite of the redcoat bands during the American war. So, then, an Englishman in Brest, and an Englishman in Brest could have only one occupation.

An hour or so later, Dujardin brought their midday meal of foul-tasting herring stew and stale bread.

'Jesus,' said the Englishman after his first mouthful. 'Is it always this rank?'

'Generally worse, in my experience.'

The Englishman seemed to see Philippe anew. The outright hostility was gone, although his demeanour was still hardly friendly.

'You sound like an *aristo*. That why you're here, is it? Waiting your turn on the guillotine?'

'I am to be tried before a revolutionary tribunal. Charges were brought against me by means of an anonymous denunciation.'

He maintained the fiction in the words he spoke, but in his thoughts he knew the denunciation had to have been in the handwriting of Alexandre Kermorvant. Who else, after all?

The Englishman laughed, but it was a cold and contemptuous sound. 'And you're expecting to be acquitted, are ye? Don't hear of too many not guilty verdicts from those revolutionary tribunals, as far as I can gather.'

They ate in silence for a little while, but the Englishman evidently found the fare less palatable than Philippe did; but then, Philippe had lived for several years on Russian food.

'How do you find yourself here?' he finally asked, seeking to confirm his suspicions.

The Englishman's lip curled, and the anger returned to his eyes. 'None of your business, Frog or Yank or whatever the hell you are. You don't ask me questions, understood?'

They returned to their pallets and remained in silence for the rest of the day.

The next morning followed a similar pattern, and then the next, but in the middle of the following afternoon Dujardin came and took the Englishman away before returning to bring Philippe a plate of hard cheese.

'So how are you getting on with our English friend, Citizen?' said the guard.

'He has few words. More farts than words, to be truthful.'

Dujardin laughed.

'I always heard that about the English – that they're absolutely ripe, that is. He's probably only the third or fourth of the breed I've ever met so I'll take your word for it. All of 'em have been spies, too. Seems we've known about this one for a while. We've got our men everywhere within the Chouans, so most of the English spies get betrayed to us sooner or later. 'Course, the Chouans are probably saying the same about us. Your man's a captain, though, would you believe? Rough bugger like that. Name's Captain Paul Storr, apparently. They're debating whether he's entitled to a firing squad or whether they'll just hang him. These days in France you need a committee to decide something as simple as that. Either way, Citizen, I guess you'll have another new cellmate before long – still no sign of your tribunal, as far as I can gather. They're taking their time over you, I'll say that. Letters back and forth to Paris, or so I hear.'

The Englishman returned to the cell two or three hours later. His whole demeanour was very different, at once more relaxed and more confident. He was also markedly less hostile towards Philippe.

'You Frenchies do like to talk,' he said as he sat back down on his pallet.

'Some do,' said Philippe, 'but I've observed that the English can be worse. Wouldn't you agree, Captain Storr?'

The Englishman seemed unsurprised that Philippe now knew his name. 'That guard, for one... Dujardin? I wouldn't have a man with a mouth that wide serving under me.'

Philippe smiled. 'I've commanded worse.'

Storr looked up. 'You're an officer? Infantry? Cavalry? You don't look like an artilleryman, that's for sure.'

'Navy, but not the French. Not yet. First the American, then the Russian.'

Storr whistled. 'In that case you're a strange bird indeed. So how does an American Russian who claims to be French end up in the citadel of Brest, then? My story's a simple one, as no doubt you've gathered, but I get a sense that yours is anything but.'

Philippe gave him the bare bones of his life story, omitting such elements as his father – it was doubtful that any Englishman of Paul Storr's rank and condition would know of Verité – and his marriage.

'And that,' said Philippe in conclusion, 'is what brought me to this place. A fool's errand if ever there was one. So whatever crime they settle upon as the justification for sending me to the guillotine, the truth will be that I sent myself there through my own pride and folly.'

Storr was a good listener, but he made no attempt to reciprocate with his own tale. He said that he had fought in America, first in the north with Burgoyne and later in the south, but he was very vague on campaigns and battles. He had not been at Savannah, nor at Yorktown. He claimed to have been inland and named a few places that Philippe had never heard of. Philippe sensed that Storr was learning much about him, but revealing almost nothing about himself in return.

It was the middle of the night when Philippe, who was fully awake, realised that the Englishman was watching him.

'I have two more nights after this one,' said Storr, very quietly. The entire citadel seemed to be silent but for the two of them. 'The following day, they kill me.'

'I envy you the certainty of that knowledge,' said Philippe. 'I think they mean for me to rot here until doomsday. I'd rather the guillotine, and soon.'

It sounded as though Storr was breathing more deeply.

'I don't plan to be here when they come for me. You don't have to be, either.'

The Englishman was speaking very slowly, as though weighing each word with the utmost care.

'Your meaning?' said Philippe.

'I mean Billy Pitt's gold is better than your Citizen Robespierre's gold. It buys the loyalty of more men, for one thing. Of more guards. So tomorrow night, my friend, I'm getting out of here, and you can come with me if you want to. I'm not in the habit of making such offers to men I don't know and have barely met, but if I leave you behind you might raise the alarm. So, what say you, *Citizen?*'

Philippe was silent. He did not trust the Englishman, but the premise of his tale was all too plausible. He remembered Dujardin's offhand remark that the Chouans had agents everywhere, even inside the citadel.

'You've bought Dujardin?'

'Best you don't know who. But half the guards or more have family with the rebels, or else they fear reprisals if they don't do what the Chouans want. Truth be told, it's a miracle that they manage to keep anybody locked up in here at all.'

'And if you get out – if *we* get out – what then?'

'The easy part. We get down the coast to Camaret Bay or somewhere of the sort. Ships from Black Dick Howe's blockade fleet are always sending boats in to land royalist agents or pick them up again. I'll be for England, and you can come with me if you choose. Or you can go inland, join up with the Chouans, then hope they win the war and you can get your chateau back.'

To go inland... Leonore.

'I need to think on it, Captain Storr.'

'Decide by tomorrow's curfew bell. But you make any move to betray me and I'll throttle you with my bare hands. Even if you set them onto me, I'll make sure before I die that one of the men in England's pay does for you. So that's a first certain fate for you, depending on what you decide. The second is that you escape with me tomorrow night. The third is that you stay here and go to the guillotine. Simple choice, Captain, one out of three. Good odds, I reckon. So think about it. Dream about it. And sleep well, Captain Kermorvant.'

—

The next morning, Storr slept until well after Philippe was awake. He only stirred when two guards whom Philippe had not seen before came and took the Englishman away without a word of explanation, before the two men had a chance to discuss Storr's proposition. Storr protested, demanding to know where he was being taken, but to no avail. Philippe lay on his pallet for an hour or so, then he called for Dujardin, ostensibly to get him to send the boy who emptied the pails. The lad, Thibault Coiffic by name, was surprisingly bright for one performing such a menial office. Philippe had spoken to him several times, partly because first Hauchard and then Storr treated him with utter contempt, which he hardly deserved, and learned that the boy's family farmed very close to the estate of the vicomtes de Saint-Victor. Coiffic greeted Philippe like an old friend, and they spoke briefly before Dujardin returned to speed the boy on his way.

'Idle little bugger, that one,' said the guard.

'He seems like a keen lad,' said Philippe. 'Too keen for this job and this place.'

'If he's that keen, he can go off to the army on his next birthday and be cannon fodder. The National Convention's decreed a *levée en masse* – all unmarried men aged eighteen to twenty-five called up for the army. That'll give Pitt and the rest of 'em something to think about, eh?'

Philippe made to reply but was interrupted by the return of Storr, seemingly unaffected by wherever he had been taken and whatever had been done to him. Dujardin welcomed him back with a mock bow.

'Your chamber awaits you, Captain. Purged of your shit-bucket, as you can see. Your guest, the noble lord of Saint-Victor here, has been missing you, so I'll leave the two of you to catch up. Anything you'd like me to do for you before I go, Captain? Some claret, perhaps? A nice ripe *putain*?'

'Fuck off, Dujardin!'

'Really, Captain, that's how you English talk to your friends? Good luck with such a curmudgeon, Citizen Vicomte.'

Dujardin closed and locked the cell door behind him and strode away, laughing to himself. Storr spat on the cell floor and sat on his pallet, looking intently at Philippe, but it was the vicomte who spoke first.

'Where did they take you? For interrogation?'

Storr shrugged. 'You French don't know the meaning of the word. Question after question, always the same, always pointless. If the roles were reversed and I was asking the questions… let's just say my methods would be different. More effective, for sure.'

Storr stood and went to the door to check that no guards were within earshot.

'Well then, *mon capitaine*, have you thought about my proposition?'

'You gave me until the curfew bell, Captain Storr.'

'Damn, you're cool, I'll say that for you. That's your last word?'

'My last until the curfew bell.'

'Freedom or death, that's your choice. Damn long time to think on things when it's between those two, but each to his own.'

Philippe lay down on his pallet, closed his eyes and feigned sleep. He was aware of Storr watching him for some minutes, then the Englishman made a sound that might have been a sigh or a muffled laugh, sat down, and stretched out on his own bed. So the minutes of the afternoon passed and turned into hours, the curfew bell drawing ever nearer.

CHAPTER TEN

...Philippe Kermorvant, Vicomte de Saint-Victor, has written a number of letters to me from Gothenburg, Saint-Malo and his ancestral estate in Brittany. I was glad to receive them, for they put me in mind of happy times when his father and I were young officers in the Regiment de Rouergue, and later when I served with both the father and the son in the American war. I have since followed the young Saint-Victor's career with interest. It was an infinite sadness to me that the late monarchy would not employ the blameless son of a man whose writings had given them great offence, but I trust that in our new and more enlightened dispensation this wrong may finally be righted. Our beloved country needs sea-captains who are both true lovers of liberty and bold warriors. Who better than the son of Verité himself, one of the greatest architects of our new freedom, a son who has been forged in war and hardened by adversity?

D'Estaing

Sometime admiral, sometime general, sometime poet

The two stone-faced soldiers escorted Philippe out through the gate of the citadel. They had come for him at dawn, accompanied by Dujardin. The usually jovial gaoler said nothing as he handed over his charge, just as he said nothing when he came for Storr on the very stroke of the previous night's curfew bell. No more than a minute or two earlier, the Englishman sat up, put his hands on his knees and stared at Philippe.

'It's time, Captain,' he said. 'What's your answer?'

Before Philippe could reply, they heard Dujardin turning the key in the lock and opening the door to reveal the soldiers behind him. Dujardin looked from one prisoner to the other, then beckoned for

Storr to follow him. Philippe thought the Englishman would rage and roar, maybe even rush his guards and die at the end of a bayonet, but he said not a word as they led him away. As he went through the door of the cell, though, the spy turned and gave Philip a strange, contemptuous half-smile, the sort of expression a prisoner in the dock might give the judge who has just condemned him to death.

Now, several hours of sleeplessness later, Philippe had no idea where his escorts were taking him. He thought he would be taken to someone in authority in the citadel, but the two soldiers clearly had orders to take him to another destination. Very few of those who were out and about on the streets of Brest at that time of day, chiefly beggars and shopkeepers getting ready for the day's trade, bothered even to glance in Philippe's direction; in Brest, prisoners under military escort were as common a sight as seagulls. Perhaps they were taking him directly to wherever the revolutionary tribunal sat, maybe the Hotel de Ville. So early in the day, his case would surely be the first on the court's roster and could probably be despatched rapidly. He could be on the guillotine by noon, his head in a basket by a minute past.

The guards took a left turn rather than a right. But that took them away from the centre of the town, where the revolutionary tribunal would surely sit.

It took him a few moments to realise that they were going towards the river.

—

The town and dockyard of Brest stretched along both banks of the River Penfeld, with the civilian houses built on the sometimes steep slopes of the hills on either side. The water's edge was dominated by the dockyard buildings, the long artillery workshops on the right bank, the ropewalk and grand magazine on the left. The largest building was a colossal prison workshop containing, it was said, three thousand convicts, whose sentences were served by providing much of the heavy labour for the dockyard. The river itself was filled with hulls of all shapes and sizes. There were tiny skiffs carrying naval officers or dockyard officials hither and thither, together with larger craft like luggers carrying supplies to and from the yard; Brest sat at the extremity of France, at the end of roads that were uniformly long, poor, and exposed to attack from the

Chouans, so almost all of the dockyard's supplies had to come in by sea. All the craft plying the river had to compete for space, not just with each other but also with the larger vessels that were anchored in the waterway. Some of these were hulks, a few fitted for specific tasks like careening, most with their upper decks planked over to turn them into accommodation for sailors awaiting their final posting, for dockyard labourers, or else for prisoners. A few, though, were men-of-war flying the new Tricolour flag of the Republic, some either ready for sea or just come in. Then there were the others at various stages of being fitted out, and the skeletal new hulls that were still on the stocks. Men swarmed over these, hammering, sawing and painting, filling the entire waterway with a furious cacophony. Just offshore was an ancient dismasted sixty-four, heeling hard to starboard. Philippe nearly looked away without giving her a second glance, but a strange feeling made him look again. He had been on that ship; the unique taffrail gave her away. She was *Jeanne d'Arc*, and Philippe had gone aboard her twelve years earlier when he was still a boy and she was part of De Grasse's fleet, lying at anchor off the Virginia Capes. She was old then, worn out from too many years in Indian waters. Now it sounded as though many men were manning her pumps in a desperate attempt to right her. Shipwrights were at work at her bow, cutting off the old figurehead before installing that of the Republic; it had apparently been decided that she, alone, of all the ships inherited from the old navy, the Marine Royale, could retain the name of a saint, France clearly being in need of the inspirational example provided by the Maid of Orleans. But if the French Republic was depending on ancient wrecks like *Jeanne d'Arc* to go up against the might of the British Royal Navy, then God help the revolution.

The waterside was all bustle. Workmen jostled with soldiers, sailors and the strangest spectacles of all, the well-dressed, elegant men and women who apparently thought that this was a fashionable place to promenade. Hawkers jealously guarded their pitches along the quayside and endeavoured to persuade these refined citizens of the merits of their particular wares. They competed for space with dozens of urchins dressed in rags who were begging for alms.

Philippe asked his guards why they had brought him here, but he got no answer. Perhaps the more likely roads into the centre of town were blocked for some reason – another guillotining, perhaps – and this, despite the throng of people, was the only viable route. But then they turned to the left and took Philippe to the top of a flight of steps which led down to the water's edge. A substantial cutter crewed by six men was secured to the quay, and at the head of the stairs stood a tall, impossibly thin boy with bright red cheeks who looked to be about ten but surely had to be at least fifteen. He was dressed in the uniform of an *aspirant*, the rank that other navies described as midshipmen.

The guards stopped before the child-officer, saluted, then turned away and left Philippe to the boy's custody.

'Citizen the Vicomte de Saint-Victor,' said the youth in a voice that sounded to be only just breaking. 'You will be pleased to accompany me.'

The boy gestured for Philippe to go down into the boat. He knew his mouth was wide open, but he seemed unable to close it. Whatever was happening was impossible. Surely the Republic could not have enacted a new law providing for the drowning of the accused without trial? Or maybe the revolutionary tribunal met in a building on the other side of the river? No, the best case had to be that the authorities had taken note of his status as an erstwhile captain in the Russian navy and had decided that he should be given the honourable death of being shot by a firing squad aboard a man-of-war. It would be better than the guillotine, Philippe thought.

The young *aspirant* followed him onto the boat and gave the orders for the crew to cast off and get under way with exemplary clarity. The boat made its way downstream past moored warships, hulks and cargo tenders, the young officer steering its difficult course capably and without incident. They emerged into the main waterway, the great Rade de Brest, a vast inlet of the Atlantic. There was just as much traffic here as there had been in the river, but the space provided by the broad anchorage was probably ample for all the world's navies with space to spare. The score of large merchantmen anchored just off Brest itself – a substantial fleet that would have crowded out most of the harbours Philippe knew – occupied only a tiny fraction of the capacious Rade: their flags showed them to be neutrals, several of them American, all with papers for the likes of Lisbon and Leghorn in case they were intercepted by the British, but all of which had arrived safely in their true destination.

The weather was relatively calm, little more than a gentle breeze from the south-west, and the boat's crew made no attempt to hoist a sail. Instead they rowed at a steady pace while the *aspirant* gave occasional orders to the man on the tiller.

For some time, Philippe's concern for his fate was forgotten as he took in the spectacle before him. The Rade de Brest was the finest natural harbour he had ever seen, and no less impressive was the spectacle of what lay in its southern arm. There lay France's Atlantic fleet, at anchor in the Baie de Roscanvel to the south-west: three dozen mighty ships of the line and frigates, all proudly flying vast new Tricolours.

Philippe finally turned to the *aspirant*.

'We're bound for the fleet?'

The boy looked surprised.

'Of course, Citizen Vicomte. Where did you think we were bound? You have an appointment aboard the flagship.'

The flagship? Surely no tribunal would be convened aboard a flagship unless it was a court-martial – and he was not an officer of France, so he would not qualify for one.

He could see it now. There it was at the heart of the anchored fleet, by far the largest ship in that company, its sides and masts towering over the waters of the bay. The three-decker *Le Terrible*, 110 guns, the flagship of Admiral Morard de Galles.

As the boat drew alongside, Philippe tried to compose himself. Whatever was about to happen would, at least, happen at sea. If he was fated to die at the hands of the republic he had travelled so far to serve, this was where he wanted it to happen.

—

There was no side party to herald Philippe's arrival on the flagship. There was no reception of any sort. Instead, the *aspirant* led him down to the main gun deck and walked aft, halting before the door through the bulkhead into the admiral's cabin. He knocked twice, heard a peremptory reply, opened the door and led Philippe into the space beyond. Light was shining directly through the huge windows at the stern, and it took Philippe's eyes a moment to adjust.

'Citizen Admiral, Citizen *représentant*,' said the *aspirant*, 'I have brought Citizen Kermorvant, the Vicomte de Saint-Victor, as ordered.'

'Thank you, Barthélemy,' said a man standing away to port, next to a small chart table. The *aspirant* saluted and withdrew.

The man wore the splendid uniform of a vice-admiral, and Philippe recognised his features from the images published in the newspapers. Admiral Morard de Galles was in his mid-fifties, of medium height, and had a shock of entirely white hair, which he wore to his collar. His eyebrows, though, were uniformly black and his nose was slightly hooked, giving him a striking, rather avian appearance. All his movements were very slow and deliberate.

'Philippe Kermorvant,' he said, 'otherwise known as the Vicomte de Saint-Victor. I imagine you expected a visit to the guillotine rather than to *Le Terrible*, eh?'

'I am glad to go wherever France commands, Citizen Admiral, even if that is to the guillotine,' said Philippe, hating his obsequious words as soon as he had spoken them.

The second man in the cabin, who was standing behind the admiral's desk, laughed. 'Wherever France commands, eh? Be careful what you wish for, Citizen.'

The admiral waved his hand towards the other man.

'I present Citizen Jeanbon de Saint-André, *représentant en mission* of the Committee of Public Safety.'

Unlike the dour Jean-Baptiste Carrier at Saint-Malo, this new *représentant en mission* seemed to have a fixed, broad smile on his face. Long-nosed, with bright eyes which darted constantly around the cabin and a shock of curly and utterly unruly grey hair, Jeanbon de Saint-André looked like the sort of fellow who was every man's friend, the life and soul of the village tavern. He wore a shirt with an extravagant white ruff, and on the table in front of him was his hat, which bore both a tricolour sash and a vast tricolour feather, presumably dyed, in red, white and blue. During his time at his chateau, Philippe had heard that the government in Paris was sending down a *représentant* to oversee the setting out of the fleet and secure its loyalty to the Republic. He wondered what Morard de Galles, a career seaman now having to take orders from a politician, thought of that decision.

'We are here because your story interests us, Citizen,' said the admiral. 'Commissions from both the United States and Russia. Experience of war – of several wars, in fact. You carry powerful recommendations, and a number of important persons in the Republic have interceded on your behalf. Most recently Admiral d'Estaing, no less – a friend of your late father, wasn't he?'

So d'Estaing had received his letters after all. Perhaps there was still some hope.

'Admiral d'Estaing's word still counts for something,' said Saint-André offhandedly. 'But probably not for much longer, I regret to say, because I like the old man, I really do. But he spoke in favour of the Capet whore at her trial. Always had a soft spot for her, apparently. Certain to take him to the guillotine sooner or later, I'd say.'

It took Philippe a moment to realise that 'the Capet whore' was the woman previously known as Marie-Antoinette, Queen of France.

'So yes, your story interests us,' said Saint-André. 'But it is our duty to the Republic to be careful, Citizen. Our enemies are everywhere, especially here in Brittany. Priests. Royalists. English spies. So when an unknown captain suddenly arrives in France seeking a command – a man who speaks French like a foreigner… a man with an English mother – well, you can see why the authorities in Paris, like my good friend the Minister of the Marine, might well question the wisdom of employing you.'

'Sir,' said Philippe, trying to conceal his indignation, 'I last saw my mother when I was thirteen; she deserted my father and I—'

'We know all that,' said Saint-André, grinning. 'And truth be told, I'm not the sort of fellow who judges a man based on who his mother was. Nor his father, come to that. Yours wrote a few books and has quite the name, but that doesn't tell me anything about your ability to sail one of our frigates into battle with the English. It doesn't tell me anything about your loyalty to the Republic.'

'I don't see how I can prove my loyalty to the Republic, Citizen, if I'm given no chance to show it!'

'But you've already shown it, in one instance at any rate,' said Morard. 'You denounced an English agent to the authorities in the citadel. By name, one Captain Paul Storr. You revealed his plan to escape, even though it offered you a path to your own freedom and a way of cheating the guillotine. Many would rate that as exemplary loyalty to the Republic.'

'I merely did my duty, Citizen Admiral.'

'Yes, you did,' said Saint-André, 'though not in the way you believe.'

Both the *représentant* and the admiral were smiling, and at last Philippe was able to grasp a thought that had been at the edge of his consciousness while he was sharing the cell with the Englishman.

'He wasn't an English spy,' he said cautiously. 'He was one of ours.'

'And what leads you to that conclusion?' asked Saint-André.

'He claimed to have been a regular officer, but he looked, talked and acted like no English officer I ever saw during the American war. He claimed to have been in some of the campaigns over there, but he seemed to know almost nothing about them. And the way he tried to talk me into going along with his escape plan – it was too sudden. It didn't feel right.'

'So that was why you got the slop boy to carry your message to the governor,' said Morard, thoughtfully.

'I couldn't trust the guards, because if he was telling the truth there was no knowing which of them he'd bribed.'

'And you did that despite knowing it might be your only chance to avoid the guillotine?' asked Saint-André.

'I had reconciled myself to the guillotine, Citizen. Somehow, though, I couldn't reconcile myself to the prospect of a life in England.'

Saint-André and Morard de Galles exchanged glances, and the latter gave Philippe a nod which might have been a form of congratulation. If only they knew the turmoil Storr's offer had bred in his mind...

'So who is Storr?' said Philippe.

'A captain of sorts,' said the admiral, 'although certainly not of a guards regiment, as you rightly surmised. He was a smuggler on their side of *La Manche* – Romney Marsh or some such place, if I recall. Their revenue men got rather too hot for his liking, so he thought he could make more money by serving us. He claims to favour the ideals of the Republic, too, although I think the only ideal our Captain Storr really believes in is his own survival.'

'So you passed one test, Citizen,' said Saint-André, the same fixed smile on his lips, 'but alas, there are always more tests in life – wasn't that something your father wrote? I think it was. I've read all his books, you know, or at least, all the ones I stayed awake for. So, then, let us proceed to a test of my making – I'm expecting a boat to take me back to the dockyard, where the mountain of work awaiting me is truly alpine, so I can't afford to beat around the bush. Now, Citizen, I see from all the papers you have so generously supplied us with that you spent three years on merchant ships plying between England and America, ships owned by a brother of your mother's first husband, a Scot by birth, one Gask. You claim to have sailed to Falmouth, Bristol and London during that time.' Saint-André grinned. 'Now, Captain, I don't know if you know this, but I used to skipper ships to all corners, long before I owned my own hulls and even longer before I fetched up in the National Convention. That's what the Committee of Safety in their wisdom thinks qualifies me to run the fucking Brest fleet, if you'll pardon my English. But you see, Captain, that's what qualifies me to ask you this question. I've sailed to all those ports, so tell me – what are the sailing directions for Bristol, once you've crossed the ocean from Virginia? The outline only, mind you, not every bearing and seamark.'

A test indeed, and for all Saint Andre's jovial demeanour, it was obvious that Philippe's life depended on passing it. He gathered his thoughts, recollected the voyages on the *Julius Caesar* and *Fortune*, then looked the *représentant* of the Committee of Public Safety in the eye.

'Very well, Citizen. You aim to make your landfall between the fiftieth and fifty-first degrees of latitude, preferably more to the latter so you clear the Isles of Scilly. You then steer as close to north-easterly as you can, setting your course by the seamarks on the coasts of Cornwall and Devon. You take special care of the tides, which rise and fall by prodigious amounts in that Channel—'

'Which lighthouses assist you?' demanded Saint-André impatiently.

'There are no lighthouses on those coasts,' said Philippe, 'not until you come to the light in the old chapel at Ilfracombe. May I continue, Citizen?'

Saint-André smiled and waved his hand.

'If the wind strengthens and comes more southerly, or if a storm catches you before you enter the Channel, you take all care not to be pressed into Carmarthen Bay or the cliffs of the Gower, for the coasts there are ship-killers. You leave the island of Lundy well to the south, though, and then make your course due east, looking for the lighthouse on Flatholm—'

Saint-André raised his hand.

'Enough, Citizen, enough! The more you talk, the more you remind me of a hellish voyage when I was nearly wrecked on the Sker rocks on the north coast of that infernal channel. Memories, eh? But good. Very good. You are who you say you are, you have done what you say you have done, your loyalty to the Republic is demonstrated by your informing on Captain Storr, etcetera. I am content, and will report to Paris accordingly.'

'Then I'm no longer under arrest? The charges against me have been dropped?'

'Charges which your brother brought,' said Saint-André. 'Interesting family you have, Monsieur le Vicomte. However, your brother has been denounced in his turn and has already taken your place in the cell in the citadel. You see, the evidence against him is rather firmer than that against you. Treasonable correspondence with the Chouans and known British agents, that sort of thing. Dozens of letters hidden away in that chateau of yours, almost none of them coded. What utter fuckwits these royalists are.'

'Who denounced him?' asked Philippe, assuming it could only have been the Penhouets.

Saint-André rubbed his eyes vigorously, then stood to take his leave.

'His wife, of course. Your sister-in-law.'

'*Leonore?*'

'Leonore, eh? Of course it is. Anyway, plenty of women across France are denouncing their husbands to try to get the bastards beheaded, and who can blame them in many cases, eh? But very few of them can provide chapter and verse in quite such a legally watertight way as your sister-in-law has done. Quite a woman is our Mistress Kermorvant, and that's even without her getting her cousin to intercede on your behalf.'

'She has a cousin? Who?'

'We all have cousins, Citizen, usually far too many for comfort. Some of mine, for instance... When I was young I often thought I had to be a by-blow of the old Dauphin, the one who died back in the sixties, for I was sure I couldn't be related to such a gaggle of imbeciles as my family. But yes, your sister-in-law happens to have a particularly notable cousin. She told you she's from Côte-d'Or, I presume? And that her maiden name was Pothier? But it sounds as though she hasn't told you that her father had a sister, who has a son. His name's Carnot. General Lazare Carnot, recently named to the Committee of Public Safety. Nowadays, the man entrusted with organising of all France's armies. A rising man, Citizen. A very rising man.'

Philippe vaguely remembered a lunch of bread and cheese with Leonore, one day when she was overseeing urgent repairs to the chateau's bakery. She had mentioned in passing a cousin of hers called Lazare who was a member of the National Convention and had acquitted himself well on various missions, but he thought nothing of it at the time.

He was aware that his head was spinning at the enormity of the news, and he barely noticed Saint-André bid him farewell and leave the admiral's cabin. It was only later that he recalled the *représentant*'s final words to him.

'I'll leave the detail to the admiral, but you'd better find yourself some lodgings and a good tailor who can run you up a uniform in no more than a day or two. You're going to need both, Capitaine de Frégate Kermorvant.'

When Saint-André was gone, Morard de Galles reclaimed his chair and his table, inviting Philippe to sit opposite him.

'Not the way you imagined this day would go, eh, Captain?'

'It's true that I'd envisaged... other outcomes, sir.'

The admiral reached for a decanter of red wine, offered Philippe a glass which he accepted, then poured himself an even fuller measure.

'I should think you did. But the truth is you're a considerable rarity in our republic, Citizen Vicomte. A man with experience of command at sea in real wars – do you know how few of our captains have that nowadays? Most of the ones who did have either been guillotined or fled into exile before they could join the queue for the blade. You're a man not tainted by service to the old monarchy, either. Well, there's even fewer of them, that's for certain. All right, you speak French as though there's something wrong with your throat, but we can overlook that. The truth is, cutting your head off would have been a great disservice to the Republic, so let's be thankful your sister-in-law has proved to be a woman of such resource.'

It was one way of putting it. Only a few years before, the priests and civic authorities alike would have had little truck with a wife who betrayed her marriage vows by informing on her husband. Now, of course, matters were very different, although there was still an enormity to it all that made Philippe's thoughts race and his chest feel tight. By denouncing Alexandre, Leonore might very well be sending him – *sending Philippe's own brother* – to the guillotine. The Republic might reward such an act, but what if the king came back? And if, regardless of kings, there was a God after all, would He forgive one of the most heinous sins a woman could commit?

He was aware of the admiral looking at him with some concern. Morard would surely expect him to have one question in mind above all others, and Philippe finally dared to ask it.

'You have a ship for me to command, sir?'

'I do. *Le Zéphyr*,' said the admiral. 'A well-found frigate of twelve, thirty-two guns, twenty-six of them twelve-pounders, the others six-pounder swivels. Three hundred men – that's the nominal complement, at any rate. Quite old now, built fourteen or fifteen years ago down in Rochefort. The crew an unknown quantity at sea but a bloody difficult one in port, as poor Berthomier found to his cost.'

A thirty-two gunner! Much larger than the Russian *Strela*, his only previous command. But his excitement was tempered by Morard's final remark.

'Was he the previous captain?' Philippe asked. The admiral nodded. 'What happened to him?'

Morard de Galles continued to stare out of the window. 'A good officer, was Berthomier – or at least, he had been once. Not the best seaman, perhaps, but old school, one might say. Commanded in the American war, so he knew the proper way of doing things.'

Unlike our current rulers? Philippe wondered. There was a time when he would have asked the question out loud.

'But nowadays, the proper way of doing things offends against the ideals of the Republic. Berthomier thought his crew should actually be obedient to orders and do what he commanded them to do, when he ordered them to do it. A dangerous course in our present day and age, Captain. Contradictory to the doctrine of the Rights of Man. And then, of course, he had the misfortune to be born into an aristocratic family down in Touraine or somewhere like that, I forget exactly where. Fierce for the Republic and the cause of freedom, but that wasn't enough to save him from an anonymous denunciation and the good Doctor Guillotine's machine. And his mind was not what it had been… all in all, a tragedy.'

The Vicomte de Saint-Victor studied the pained expression on the face of his admiral, scion of a noble house in Dauphine, and understood the message. But Philippe had faced the prospect of the guillotine every waking moment for several weeks, and it no longer held any terrors for him.

'The orders, sir?'

Morard sighed.

'Still being finalised by Citizen Saint-André, who I expect will make his usual show of nominally consulting me before he issues them. But in a nutshell, we need more frigates at sea urgently, and *Le Zéphyr* is one of the few we can set out in a matter of days. We need more patrols along the Breton coast, down to the Morbihan and as far as Rhé and Rochelle, to disrupt the rebels bringing in arms and intercept the English spies who come and go with impunity all along those coasts. Admiral Howe's frigates are getting bolder by the day, even running in to Camaret, Douarnenez and other bays that are nearly spitting distance from here. We need to reclaim our coasts, Captain, in part to make Pitt think twice about landing an army in Brittany. So it's going to be unglamorous and dangerous work, I'm afraid. Little chance of prizes, a lee shore at your back, a crew who'll denounce you at the drop of a pin, and bigger British frigates outnumbering us three to one and thinking these seas are their private lake. How does that sound?'

If he answered truthfully, Philippe would have to say that he had hoped for one of the frigates assigned a more offensive role, cruising far out at sea to intercept valuable British and Dutch cargoes as they approached *La Manche*. But considering what his prospects had been only hours earlier, *Le Zéphyr* was a vision of heaven.

He smiled.

'Still preferable to the guillotine, sir.'

Morard raised his glass in a toast.

'Then I wish you joy of your command, Captain Kermorvant of *Le Zéphyr*.'

PART TWO

CHAPTER ELEVEN

As dawn broke over the west of Brittany, Olivier and Roman were already occupying their usual pitches on the Rue Duquesne, close by the ramparts and just down from what had been the Saint Louis church. Most of the other child beggars of Brest preferred the streets closer to the waterside or those around the Hotel de Ville, but the two orphan boys liked it where they were. There was more shelter when the storms rolled in off the ocean, and the inns and lodging houses provided a steady supply of potential marks. This being Brest there were sailors galore, although the various accommodations on this street were more salubrious and generally favoured by officers, who had money – or did, at least, when the Republic deigned to pay them. The same was true of the army and the National Guard, although there were very few of them around the town now; the soldiers were at full stretch dealing with the rebellion and most of them had gone to billets upcountry. But their places had been taken to some extent by the lawyers and officials who seemed to proliferate in the new republic. They tended to have more money than the naval officers, but they were also often sharp-nosed Parisians, accustomed to far more sophisticated street scams and thus more difficult to gull with the boys' stock of sob stories. Olivier could feign a limp so effectively that he could seem to have one leg shorter than the other, while no boy beggar in France could imitate both blindness and deafness better than Roman, or so he liked to believe. Their friend Jean-Claude had been the best, but Jean-Claude would never beg nor breathe again.

The sky was still predominantly dark when a familiarly attired figure emerged from the door of the exotically named Taverne des Indes, formerly the Duc d'Anjou. Roman nudged Olivier, who was still sleepy.

Tricorn hat adorned with the inevitable revolutionary rosette. Dark blue tunic coat with red piping, gold epaulettes and collar. Red culottes, high boots. Leather baldric bearing the anchor emblem of the Marine Nationale, from which hung the officer's sword.

'A *capitaine de frégate*,' whispered Roman. 'A new one, by the looks of him. See the way he keeps adjusting his cuffs? I'll wager he hasn't had that uniform more than a week.'

'He's about early,' replied Olivier. 'No bugger will start stirring down in the dockyard for another hour at least. Maybe he's off for a bout with his mistress.'

'Or his catamite.'

'He don't look like a queer, but then, you can never tell these days. Not with navy men 'specially, like Jean-Claude said, God rest his soul.'

As the captain looked up and down the street, the two boys shuffled out of the shadows, Olivier affecting his limp while holding the supposedly sightless Roman by the arm.

'Alms, Captain!' cried Olivier in his most pathetic voice. 'Charity for a blind and deaf boy and a cripple! Just a *sou* or two, Captain, for mercy's sake!'

The officer saw them and laughed.

'You're out early, lads,' he said.

The response startled Olivier; it was friendly, wholly unlike the curt dismissals or obscene abuse that usually greeted his requests.

'No more than you, Captain.'

The man stepped towards them, and Olivier felt a *frisson* of alarm. No man ever deliberately approached them; invariably they went in the opposite direction as rapidly as they could. The best the boys ever got was a few *sous* thrown in the gutter while their benefactors averted their eyes and walked hurriedly away.

The fellow was now lit properly by the torches that lined the street. He had an old face but was probably younger than he looked. A *queue de cheval* protruded from beneath his tricorn hat; Olivier had never seen anyone other than some of the roughest topmen on the Nantes slavers wearing their hair in such an extraordinary way.

'You're good, the pair of you, I'll grant you that. But I've seen better on the streets of Saint Petersburg.'

'Better, Captain? And where's this Saint Petersburg, then – Alsace?'

'Better. Your friend, for instance. The best in the trade of feigning deafness don't blink every time someone speaks. He needs to work on that.'

Roman maintained his pretence, but Olivier could feel his arm tense.

'So you won't give us any coins?'

'Oh, I will. But not for your act, lads. I need a boat to take me out into the bay. Get me one within the hour and you can have an entire Louis. Half now, the other half when I embark. Interested?'

Roman dropped his pretence.

'You don't sound right,' he said. 'Where you from, Captain?'

'Quite a question, coming from a deaf boy. But I can't deny it, I don't sound right, as you say, but I still need a boat and I need it in less time than it would take me to explain where I'm from. So, do we have an agreement?'

'What's your name?' said Roman.

'I am Capitaine de Frégate, Philippe Kermorvant of *Le Zéphyr*.'

'That the one where the last captain went to the guillotine, ain't it?' said Olivier.

'So I believe.'

'An' you expect to last longer?'

'I certainly hope so. But for now, I still need that boat. I may also need the services of two strong and able lads for other tasks in the future, but we can discuss that another day. So, let's just concern ourselves with the boat today. Are we agreed?'

Roman, who had been seemingly deep in thought since Philippe spoke his name, whispered urgently to Olivier, who shook his head and stepped forward.

'Agreed. Let's see your money, Captain Kermorvant.'

—

The inner harbour of Brest contained dozens of small boats crewed by men who made a living from carrying men, messages, slops and the like out to the warships in the anchorage, or from one side of the river to the other. Olivier and Roman procured one with no difficulty, a sturdy-looking if scruffy skiff manned by two sturdy-looking if scruffy men who appeared so alike they could only be identical twins. They haggled briefly with Philippe before accepting his payment, then cast off and settled to their oars. Roman and Olivier watched the boat pull away from the quayside.

'He's a strange one all right,' said Roman. 'Never met one like him before. Reckon we'll see him again?'

'Hope so. He's the best mark we've made for months, and if he does what he says and takes us on, maybe we could say goodbye once and for all to the streets of Brest.'

'If he does what he says. If he stays alive. *If.*'

'Yeah, well, nothing lost if he doesn't, is there? But I was wondering. He's the new captain of *Le Zéphyr*, right? Should we have told him, d'you reckon? Told him about what happened to Jean-Claude? About that fellow on his ship? Should we have given him the paper?'

'What for? He's an *aristo* and some weird foreigner to boot, maybe Dutch or Chinese. He won't have time to find out, 'cos any crew sailing out of Brest will eat him alive and shit him out. Bet you that if they don't just chuck him over the side, the next time we see him is on the guillotine, and there goes the chance he'll take us on. There goes any chance of justice for Jean-Claude.'

The two boys watched as the boat carrying Captain Kermorvant swung out into the middle of the Penfeld River. Then they turned to make for their morning position outside the gates of the *mairie*, where they continued their argument about whether or not, if they ever saw this peculiar captain again, to tell him what they knew about *Le Zéphyr* and one of her officers in particular.

–

As the rowers edged their craft out into the waterway, the morning gun was fired from the citadel. At once, the dockyard of Brest came to life around them. Where there had been silence just a few minutes before, there was now a rapidly increasing hubbub. The storehouse doors opened and began to disgorge carts and men carrying every kind of naval essential under the sun: cables, sails, timbers, barrels of biscuit and other victuals. The fires in the forges were lit, followed almost immediately by the start of the hammering and sawing that would last all day. The cranes and windlasses, powered by straining convicts, began their operations, hauling masts and yards into place. Others lowered guns and barrels of powder into barges which lay alongside the quays. Astern of them, cutters and pinnaces took up the cables flung from the bows of a sixty-four and began to pull the warship away from the wharf where she had been refitted, the boat captains shouting the strokes for the men under their command.

The boat took Philippe downstream, between the citadel on the Rive Droite and the peculiar conical tower on the Rive Gauche. Dead ahead, the great chain that sealed the inner harbour at night and was its last line of defence *in extremis* was being lowered, admitting the first of the eager coasters from the likes of Cherbourg, Nantes and Lorient. Philippe's boat had to compete for sea room with the oncoming flotilla, but his rowers were skilled men who steered a faultless course through all the traffic. They passed close by *Jeanne d'Arc* and a couple of other ancient ships that were being refitted, a process that seemed to consist largely of giving them a new coat of paint, removing the old royal figureheads and replacing them with republican ones, and putting century-old cannon into them; one fellow in the lodging house where Philippe had taken a room called these obsolete ships 'the drowners' and predicted terrible fates for those assigned to them. Finally, the boat emerged fully into the Rade de Brest. The sun was just rising behind the low hills to the east. The boat steered a different course to that which had taken him to *Le Terrible;* the rowers swung westwards when out of the river, aiming for the three scouting frigates at anchor in the Rade and moored close to the north shore nearer to the Goulet, the narrow passage which provided the only access between the harbour and the ocean beyond. Philippe studied the scene with a keen eye, comparing the sights before him with the charts he had pored over since his appointment to command. Gradually his focus was drawn to the single ship dead ahead, lying at single anchor in the lee of the Fort de Portzic, the innermost defence of the anchorage. The blue-and-gold hull was pristine and presumably newly painted, as this was not a brand-new ship. She still bore her old figurehead from the days of the Marine Royale, a golden lion holding a crowned shield bearing the fleur-de-lis of the Bourbons upon a blue ground. The name at the stern was illuminated by the morning light: *Le Zéphyr*.

As the boat drew closer to the frigate, Philippe realised that all was not as it should be. There was no sign of a side party to greet the wearer of a captain's uniform, not even any sign of an officer of the watch. To be precise, there was almost no sign of life at all. One Marine guard watched from the starboard rail, but his uniform was worn slovenly, his musket was slung carelessly over his shoulder, and he looked bored beyond measure. Once it was clear that the small boat was approaching his ship and none other, though, the guard managed to stir himself enough to take hold of his musket and issue a challenge.

'Identify yourself and s-state your business!' he demanded. But the words were spoken with a mild stutter, and so softly that Philippe had trouble hearing them.

'Kermorvant, captain of *Le Zéphyr* by commission of the Republic, coming aboard to take command!'

'*Putain de merde!*'

The obscenity was louder than the original challenge. As Philippe's rowers brought their vessel alongside and shipped oars, the sentry swung his head one way then the other, desperately seeking someone, anyone, to relieve him of the responsibility of deciding whether or not this self-proclaimed captain should be allowed to board one of the Republic's men-of-war. The Marine seemed to make a decision, stooping down to open the gate set into the rail, then coming to attention as Philippe climbed up and stepped onto the deck. He saluted the colours, then studied the man before him. The Marine could not be more than nineteen or twenty, and he was sweating like a hog. Philippe suspected that the condition was not caused by the warmth of the morning.

'Where are the officers?' he demanded.

'Sir – that is, C-Citizen C-Captain – they're all—'

'At ease, Herbin,' said a man emerging from the aft companionway. He was slight, probably in his forties, markedly tanned, and wore an amused expression. As he came before Philippe, he finished sketchily buttoning the uniform tunic of a Marine gunnery sergeant, then saluted.

'Citizen Captain,' he said, 'I am Garrigues, First Artillery Regiment of the Marine, master gunner of *Le Zéphyr.*'

'Citizen,' said Philippe, bowing his head in acknowledgement and returning the salute. 'I sent word of my joining the ship sometime today or tomorrow. Why is there no side party? Where are the seaman officers? Come to that, where are the men?'

Apart from Philippe, Garrigues, Marine Herbin and two men up by the foremast, who were half-heartedly splicing a cable while watching the scene in the ship's waist with frank incredulity, there was nobody else on the upper deck of *Le Zéphyr.* Indeed, a casual observer might have wondered if anybody had been on the deck for some time. Cordage lay in chaotic piles rammed between the guns. Shrouds and stays hung loose, and Philippe could see one that had come away completely.

'Lieutenant Roissel gave leave to most of the crew,' said Garrigues. 'The duty watch is below decks.'

'Doing what, precisely?'

Garrigues shifted from one foot to the other.

'Sleeping,' he admitted. 'They've just come back from a run ashore.'

Philippe felt the anger rising. Even the Russians had managed a proper side party when he took command of *Strela*. Even the Russians ran a tauter ship than this. And they got less drunk than the crew of *Le Zéphyr* seemed to have done last night.

'So is this Lieutenant Roissel aboard? He's the first, I take it?'

'Lieutenant de Vaisseau Roissel is ashore, Citizen Captain. But yes, he's the first lieutenant. He and the third are ashore, along with the master and others. So the senior officer aboard is—'

A colossal fart came from the after ladder, followed by a succession of drunken expletives. The figure who finally emerged onto the deck was extraordinary. He had no hair at all, a fact swiftly concealed as he placed his tricorn into approximately the correct position. He had obviously once been a huge and immensely powerful man, very tall and with a vast gut that would have strained at his waistcoat. Now he was slightly stooped, and the gut had turned into an unsightly flap of flesh that spilled from his tunic. His nose, which had evidently been broken more than once, was covered in warts. He looked to be eighty or more, which was surely impossible for a man who wore the uniform of an *enseigne de vaisseau*, once a rank that had been almost exclusively the preserve of ambitious young men in their twenties, but he certainly could not be any less than fifty.

He was followed up the ladder by a score of men, all bleary eyed, several in a state of undress.

The ancient officer stepped before Philippe, looked him up and down with a stare of frank suspicion, then came reluctantly to attention and made a salute of sorts.

'Well, you idle rogues,' he bawled at the men behind him, 'don't just stand there scratching your arses, fall in! Form a side party to salute the new captain!'

'Belay that,' said Philippe. 'We shall do this properly, Enseigne – your name?'

'Ugarte, Citizen Captain. Juan Ugarte.'

His name and way of speaking betrayed him as a Basque. Philippe had sailed with two or three before. Good seamen, but contrary beyond belief.

'Very well, Enseigne Ugarte. If and when Lieutenant Roissel deigns to return on board, you'll be pleased to inform him that I shall come aboard again at eight sharp tomorrow morning. I'll expect a proper reception then.'

'He won't like it,' said Ugarte, loudly sniffing back some mucus as he did so.

'*Won't like it?*'

Ugarte smiled, but the gaps in his teeth made him appear ghoulish. 'He said you'd never get to the quayside, let alone to the ship.' Garrigues was nodding at this. 'He said he had it on good authority you'd been arrested as an enemy of the Revolution and a traitor to France. He said you were an *aristo*. He said your head would be in a basket before the end of the week, just like the previous captain we had. He said Citizen Saint-André and the admiral would then have to promote him and give *him* the command of *Le Zéphyr*.'

'Then it seems Lieutenant Roissel was wrong on all counts.'

'Aye, seems so. He's wrong about most things most of the time, if truth be told. But with all due respect I'd say he wasn't wrong on one count, now was he, Monsieur le Vicomte?'

Philippe stared at Ugarte, but he had always known this moment would come. He had hoped it would come only after he'd had a chance to prove himself to the crew, but he should have remembered that dockyard towns were worse cesspits of gossip and rumour than the most degenerate Parisian *salon* in the days of the *Ancien Régime*. Presumably the whole of Brest now knew that the man who called himself Captain Philippe Kermorvant was the Vicomte de Saint-Victor, and those who could read – surely there were men in Brest who could read – would know he was the son of Verité. So be it. He could not change who he was, but perhaps he could change how others saw him. He would start in the morning, and he would have to start with this Lieutenant Roissel.

CHAPTER TWELVE

On the main deck of *Le Zéphyr*, Lieutenant de Vaisseau Martin Roissel paced up and down the ranks of men, fidgeting restlessly with his collar and his cuffs. He kept feeling for his sword hilt as if checking it was still there. He fingered his buttons to ensure that none had silently fallen off. To a greater or lesser extent he did this every day, for the trappings of a commissioned officer were still relatively new. Until six months before he had been a bosun, as he had been for half his thirty years in the navy. Under the old dispensation, when Louis Capet was still known as King Louis the Sixteenth, the navy drew its admirals, captains and lieutenants almost entirely from the ranks of the nobility. Then the revolution came, the Republic was proclaimed, and the Capet was beheaded. Half the navy's officers, or so it seemed to him, were arrested as *aristos*, counter-revolutionaries and potential English agents. The other half resigned their commissions in disgust and either went into exile or retired to their country estates, hoping to avoid the notice and the wrath of the *sans-culottes*. But the ships still needed to go to sea, especially now that France found itself in a war against the greatest navy in the world, and that meant captains and lieutenants had to be found from elsewhere. Many merchant skippers, like the vile Ugarte, were brought in because it was believed they would at least know how to navigate a warship from A to C without running it onto the ship-killing rocks at B. But many warrant officers were promoted from the ranks too, and Roissel, who had long ago reconciled himself to never achieving his ambition of becoming a ship's master, suddenly found himself given a sword and a uniform, was told he was now a *lieutenant de vaisseau*, and was ordered to leave his comfortable shipkeeping berth on an old sixty-four at Toulon, traverse almost the entire breadth of France, and become first officer of a frigate at Brest. His old mother, still unaccountably alive in Rouen and whom he had visited en route, preened herself and told him he could now aim to become a captain, then an admiral. He could certainly dream of the command of *Le Zéphyr*, his new posting. Many frigates of the same size were commanded by *lieutenants de vaisseau*, so did they not need even to go to the trouble of promoting him. The denunciation, arrest and, in short order, execution of Captain Berthomier for counter-revolutionary sympathies seemed to have presented Roissel with his opportunity. But the cruise ordered for *Le Zéphyr* was delayed, then delayed again, until the whispers started to reach the inns and restaurants of Brest of the strange background and doings of one Kermorvant, supposedly the Vicomte de Saint-Victor, a man with no experience and no seniority in the *Marine Nationale* but apparently the son of some famous philosopher.

Roissel, who did not read books of any sort, least of all philosophy, had been overconfident. Ugarte, the mountain of Basque blubber, was undoubtedly right in that. He had convinced himself that Jacobins like Saint-André would never commission a vicomte to a command in the Republic's navy. Even if they did, he reasoned, the *sans-culottes* of Brest would never stand for it. A man who had only days before been languishing in a cell in the citadel, denounced as a counter-revolutionary, who was reportedly not truly French? No, the worthy Jacobins of the town, the *Montagnards* and the *sans-culottes*, the most dedicated revolutionaries, would never tolerate such a thing. Roissel knew them well. On first arriving in Brest, he had assiduously cultivated the town's Jacobin clubs and there loudly proclaimed his impeccably staunch republican opinions. He found himself among friends. The rest of Brittany might be a hornets' nest of inveterate priest-lovers, Chouans, returning royalist exiles, lumpen peasants and all the rest, but Brest sucked in men from all over France to man the ships and work in the dockyard that sustained them. Brest was a shining light of liberty and republicanism amidst a sewer of superstition and rebellion. So Martin Roissel disregarded the notes that had come to the ship and instead spent much of the previous day in the Oiseau-Lyre, a discreet establishment round the back of the citadel, where a discerning man might drink fine wines and indulge in certain other proclivities to his heart's content. Madame Bouvilliers had recruited some new boys from the country, very young and very innocent... But the happy memory faded almost at once. He had returned to the ship very late to be informed by Ugarte of the unexpected appearance of the new captain, contrary to all his expectations. Now that new captain's face was visible as his boat drew ever nearer to the hull of *Le Zéphyr.*

Roissel took his place at the head of the side-party, gave the command of '*Sur le bord!*', and as Bosun Payen piped the still, he drew his still-unfamiliar sword and brought it to his face in salute.

Well, Citizen Captain Philippe Kermorvant, he thought, *let's see how long you last.* Roissel tried but failed to suppress the other thought that entered his mind in the moments before he formally addressed his new captain.

Will you discover my secrets, Monsieur le Vicomte? Or will I have to bring you down, as I did with Berthomier?

—

Philippe returned Roissel's salute and briefly studied the man before him. Sturdily built, as most erstwhile bosuns tended to be. Probably in his middle forties, the eyes still bloodshot from the previous day's debauch. An unimpressive fellow, Philippe judged, but the formalities still had to be undertaken. He presented Roissel with his commission and the supporting letters from Saint-André and the navy minister Dalbarade. Roissel studied them for an inordinate time before returning them and nodding, the signal for Philippe to read his commission to the assembled crewmen. As he spoke, he saw men frowning and glancing at their neighbours. When he finished, he heard the stage whispers somewhere in the rear ranks.

'Fucking *aristo!*'

'Fucking foreigner!'

'Won't last a week, if you ask me.'

'A *queue de cheval*? Bloody hell, they've sent a pirate to command us.'

A milder reception than he had expected.

He passed down the file of commissioned officers, exchanging salutes with each in turn. Ugarte had smartened himself up a little, but still looked as though he were eyeing up one of Philippe's limbs for breakfast. Next to him stood a slight, eager young man with a mop of unruly red hair wearing the uniform of an *enseigne de vaisseau*, so presumably the third lieutenant of *Le Zéphyr*. He could easily have been taken for the remainder of Ugarte's breakfast. Philippe knew his name from the muster book he had received, but had put it down to a transcription error. Surely no Frenchman could have such a strange name as—

'Fingal, Citizen Captain, Enseigne de Vaisseau Claude-Marie Fingal.'

Philippe had a sudden recollection of a man he had met briefly during the siege of Savannah, and had a stroke of inspiration.

'An Irish name, Enseigne?'

'Just so, Citizen Captain. My old pappy's family were Jacobites, driven out of some place called County Clare. But we've been French for three generations now.'

Philippe felt himself grinning, despite his efforts to maintain the stern, aloof face expected of a ship's captain.

'We must talk of County Clare, Enseigne. I've been there even if you haven't – a ship I once sailed on was driven by a storm into a harbour called Kilrush. Perhaps I encountered some of your relations.'

Philippe was aware that all three of his lieutenants were looking at him as though he had gone stark mad. Strictly speaking all four lieutenants, he thought as he exchanged salutes with the commander of the ship's 'garrison', its contingent of gunners and Marine infantrymen. The fellow, technically Master Gunner Garrigues' superior officer, was taller than Philippe, at least as young as Fingal, and had his black hair cropped unfashionably short. He had a cheerful air about him, and Philippe knew from the muster book that his name was Jerome de Machault. He would have a private talk with this man later in the day; the only way Philippe could ultimately guarantee control of the ship was by ensuring the loyalty of the Marine contingent. He could have wished for an older, more experienced man, but at least he might be able to sway the inclinations of a youth like de Machault.

The warrant officers formed a row behind their superiors, and Philippe nodded to each in turn as he passed them. The ship's *maître d'equipage* or sailing master, Yves Guillaumin, was a fellow Breton, an experienced man of forty or thereabouts with more than a quarter-century at sea. His hair had already gone entirely grey and he was starting to run to fat, but he still looked to be a vigorous man. He was another whom Philippe would need to cultivate as a counter-balance to his two senior lieutenants. Guillaumin stood at the head of an elaborate hierarchy, the *maîtres de manoeuvre*, consisting of *contre*-masters, quartermasters, helmsmen and mates, every rank having first, second and sometimes third classes to distinguish experience and seniority, as well as the coxswain and the *bosseman* or bosun. It was already evident to Philippe that several of these men might be a concern: holders of such offices were all meant to be veteran seamen with a minimum level of experience, but several mates and helmsmen and even the bosun, one Guy Payen, could be no older than their mid-twenties. Surely Payen would lack the experience to fill the bosun's traditional role of enforcing discipline on the fo'c'sle in particular. Although he was fairly tall, he was also painfully thin and could not conceivably have the physical strength to pick up a recalcitrant seaman and throw him over the side, as the bearlike bosun of *Strela* had once done. Philippe could even imagine the erstwhile bosun Roissel, no giant, doing such a thing rather more easily than the pale, sticklike Payen. Next came Garrigues, the Provençal master gunner or *maître de cannonage*, now wearing his Marine sergeant's uniform with the buttons properly done up, who had already impressed himself upon Philippe and seemed to be a steady man. Another potential ally, perhaps. The carpenter was a wiry Toulonais named Fouroux. There should have been a surgeon, but he had not yet appeared, nor had the three *aspirants*, midshipmen as the English called them. That left one man, the only man on the deck who remotely approached Enseigne Ugarte's girth. Although Philippe had little eye for such things, it was obvious that this fellow's attire was considerably superior to anything possessed by anyone else aboard *Le Zéphyr*, Philippe included. It was entirely possible that this outfit also outdid anything worn by Admiral Morard de Galles, across the estuary in *Le Terrible*.

'The steward, I presume,' said Philippe.

'*Commis des vivres*, Citizen Captain. Premier steward. I look forward to sailing with you, sir. I was talking to Citizen Saint-André just the other day and he sang your praises to the heights. The son of Verité, no less! I have read every one of your father's books at least three times. What a writer. What a mind.'

'As you say, Citizen. But remind me just what your name is?'

Philippe knew this perfectly well thanks to the muster book, but there was no harm in taking this overstuffed peacock down a peg or two.

'Saint-Jacques,' said the peacock, clearly a little abashed. 'Valery Saint-Jacques.'

'Parisian, Citizen?'

'I have the honour of being so, Citizen Captain.'

Philippe nodded and moved on, but as he did so he wondered why this elegant personage, clearly a devotee of good living and a metropolitan through and through, had fetched up as the mere steward of a small frigate. He also wondered how the said steward of a small frigate still managed to maintain elements of a Parisian lifestyle, but then he recalled Kharabadze's *bon mot* about the strange paucity of thin, poor pursers and stewards in the world.

It was a new republican dawn of equality, but as had been the case since the dawn of time, some evidently remained resolutely more equal than others.

Philippe turned and looked out over the crew. *Le Zéphyr* had a nominal roll of three hundred men, but she was between a fifth and a quarter shy of that. The muster book told him that there was nearly a full complement of sailmakers and caulkers, but both the garrison of artillerymen responsible for the ship's guns and the ranks of the *matelots* who would work its sails were dangerously thin. Matters might have been easier if France followed the pattern of the English navy and made less of a distinction between gunners and seamen, but when had France ever copied anything the English did?

Philippe considered addressing the men, but his words, spoken in an accent they would find strange – if not downright alien – were unlikely to have much impact, and might indeed prove counterproductive. The faces in front of him, regardless of whether they belonged to Marines or *matelots*, bore one of three expressions: sullen, sceptical or hostile. Some contrived to manage all three at once. Only actions would win over this crew, but he had no idea what actions might serve the purpose. It had been easier with Russians, who were used to be being ordered about by men whose first languages were German, French, Danish, Scots, English and God knew what else. Moreover, the Empress Catherine's mariners, many of them former peasants, were perfectly accustomed to being flogged and had no great resentment of such punishment. Philippe suspected it would be different with these men, who had drunk from the well of liberty and imbibed the waters of equality and the rights of man. Waters that his father had done much to channel.

He got Guillaumin to dismiss the men, the master blowing on his *sifflet*, his whistle, to do so, then turned to his officers.

'Citizens, I will inspect the ship. Individual officers to stand by their usual stations, Lieutenant Roissel to accompany me.'

Roissel's face was thunderous, but he could hardly object. This was the expected first duty of a captain taking command of a ship, and even though the tour of inspection was usually escorted by a more junior officer, the choice of the senior lieutenant could be interpreted as a sign of confidence in the man. Roissel clearly did not regard it as such, but nodded and led Philippe aft onto the long quarterdeck, the *gaillard d'arrière*, which stretched for some half the entire length of the ship. It was a generous space, largely uninterrupted but for the *artimon* or mizzen mast, the steering wheel or *roue du gouvernail* immediately abaft the mast and the officers' ladder hood immediately forward of it. A dozen seamen, seemingly engaged in such tasks as coiling and splicing cables or desultory attempts to paint the rail and ensign staff, eyed their new captain with overt curiosity but little apparent respect. Philippe walked slowly up and down the deck, noting the loose, frayed state of some of the rigging and the grubby condition of some of the timbers, a marked contrast to the paintwork on the sides. The wider expanses of open decking showed signs of frequent holystoning, as was only right, but the less accessible spaces, corners and joints looked as though they might not have been cleaned since the ship was built. The guns, though – both the large ones and the swivel guns – were gleaming and could not be faulted. He examined the binnacle, just forward of the steering wheel, by rubbing his finger over the glass. When he lifted it, the finger was black. Roissel witnessed all this, and as they walked forward to the waist he turned to Philippe.

'I'm afraid to say that Captain Berthomier was somewhat lax in his enforcement of the regulations, sir.'

'My understanding is that Captain Berthomier was executed five weeks ago and arrested some weeks before that,' said Philippe, sharply. 'Surely, Lieutenant, more than two months is ample time for an officer in acting command to bring good order to his ship?'

The barb stung Roissel, who glowered.

'I have tried, Citizen Captain, but I have faced obstruction at every turn! Ugarte and Fingal – most of the other officers, in truth – they are idle men, sir. Ugarte is from the merchant service after all, and we all know what that's like.' He lowered his voice. 'I suspect him and some of the others of being counter-revolutionaries as Berthomier was. Traitors to the Republic, in other words. And there are many recalcitrants among the crew, Citizen Captain, the Bretons especially. Half of them are secret Chouan sympathisers, I'm convinced of it.'

Philippe heard out his second-in-command, but merely nodded noncommittally. It was not the time or place to examine such accusations. They went along the gangway on the starboard side, passing the boats stowed in the well that opened to the main gun deck below. This brought them to the fo'c's'le, where three men were greasing the small capstan. Philippe paused to look out over the cathead and bowsprit towards the *Goulet* and the ocean beyond. Could he make this ship and its crew fit to sail on those great waters and face with confidence the dreadful enemy that lay over the horizon?

The bell behind him rang to mark the hour and he turned to go below, Roissel following reluctantly in his wake.

CHAPTER THIRTEEN

Eyes were the difference. On Russian ships, sailors kept their eyes lowered to the deck in the whip-driven deference to which they were accustomed on land. On American ships, and from what he had seen and heard, the same was true of the English too, men looked at their superiors either respectfully or sullenly, but always looked them in the eye. On French ships, though, it seemed as though men thought it entirely reasonable to stare openly at their officers, often with defiance and contempt in their eyes. They responded to orders with shows of reluctance, as if they were doing their nominal superior the greatest favour in the world by complying with what they seemed to regard as an inconvenient request. Had his father ever envisaged that revolutionary freedom and the equality of man would lead directly to indiscipline and downright rudeness? How could a navy function when every man seemed to regard himself as the equal, at least, of the captain? It was a mystery that Philippe would need to solve, and quickly.

The fo'c's'le was dominated by the galley which filled the space immediately abaft the foremast. Enseigne Ugarte stood here, glowering at Roissel and guarding the oven as though it were his private property. Nearby a few members of the off-duty watch lounged in their hammocks, not deigning to come to attention when officers were present and fixing Philippe with the defiant, contemptuous stare that seemed to be ingrained in the French *matelot*.

'The fo'c's'le is your station, Citizen Ugarte?' said Philippe, ignoring the men's disrespect.

'Very much so, Citizen Captain. Guns, men, oven, the lot.'

'An iron oven. I'd heard our navy had them now.'

Our navy. He had to think and speak of it as such, even though it still seemed to him a peculiar shadow world where some elements were familiar, others entirely alien.

'Aye, sir. It takes coal, too, stowed in a store down on the orlop. Makes sense that, here in Brittany where there's enough timber to build entire new navies ten times over, but no coal.'

Philippe saw Roissel scowl at Ugarte, who seemed to have no compunction in criticising such idiocies on the part of their superiors, but the Basque merely smirked.

'And the cook?'

'Ashore, sir, trying to procure more bread, meat and cheese from the storekeepers. Word is there's none left, apart from for the flagship of course, but Croguennec – that's the name of the cook, sir – well, he's a Breton and seems to be related to half the farmers in Finisterre. If any man can get us some decent victuals, it'll be him. That's why it's devolved on him rather than the steward.'

'Very good, Enseigne Ugarte. Carry on.'

'Aye, aye, Citizen Captain!'

Philippe and Roissel went aft on the other side of the ship, passing the ship's boats and hatches again, and walked past the main capstan and the mizzenmast before entering the great cabin. It was an impressive space, dominated by four more guns and the large table at which Philippe would be expected to wine and dine his officers; he suspected that the meals in the company of his brother Alexandre might prove to have been more enjoyable. At the head of the table, standing behind the chair that Philippe would be expected to occupy at dinner, stood a tall, painfully thin man with sunken cheekbones. He looked to be as old as Jacques Penhouet back at the Chateau de Brechelean, but was probably in his late forties. His eyes were green, set in a piercing stare, the eyes of a much younger and livelier man.

'Driaux, Citizen Captain,' said the thin man, 'valet to the captain and officers of *Le Zéphyr*.'

'You are the only officers' orderly, as well as the *maître d'hôtel* for the captain?'

'Alas so, Citizen Captain. The levy...' Driaux shrugged without completing the sentence. The mass levy of France's manpower explained much in the Republic: fields going uncultivated, buildings going unrepaired, men of rank left unattended. 'But a couple of the *mousses* are keen to learn the valet's trade for after the war, so I can call upon them at dinner.'

Mousses were the ship's boys. Every navy had them, for how else would errands be run, messages be delivered, and powder and shot delivered to the guns? Such lads usually dreamed of being captains and having a woman in every port, or of being pirates sailing the seas in galleons of gold. According to Driaux, though, the *mousses* of *Le Zéphyr* wanted to serve undercooked meat to unappreciative diners or help well-heeled citizens to tie their cravats. A strange new world indeed.

'You served Captain Berthomier?' said Philippe.

The question clearly made Driaux uncomfortable, with the valet shooting a nervous glance at Roissel.

'I did, Citizen Captain.'

'You must tell me about him. Another time, though. For now, show me to my cabin if you please, Citizen Driaux.'

Astern of the great cabin, the deck was effectively divided in three, the middle element of which led to the cover for the rudder head beneath the central stern windows and contained a table that was far smaller than the one in the great cabin. This was notionally the council chamber of *Le Zéphyr*. The English gave the captain the entirety of this space, right at the stern of the ship, but even in the days of the monarchy the French navy had been more democratic. Only the starboard side belonged exclusively to Philippe; his tiny cabin was a bare space with no trace of its previous occupant. Philippe's heart sank, for he knew the port side was occupied by Roissel as the next most senior officer. Nevertheless, he turned to Driaux, feigned a smile and nodded with seeming satisfaction.

'Excellent,' he said. 'I'll sleep on board tonight and from now on. My sea-chest and other possessions are in my lodgings ashore, so I'll need a boat's crew to go into the river and retrieve them.'

'Of course, Citizen Captain,' said Roissel.

Philippe returned to the main deck where Garrigues, the gunner, awaited him by the main capstan.

'Gun deck awaiting your inspection, Citizen Captain,' he said.

'Thank you, Master Gunner. Carry on.'

The conditions were calm enough to allow the gunports to be open, bringing welcome light and air into the deck. Despite this, the low, red-painted space stank of gunpowder, damp timber, tobacco and stale piss. It ran the entire length of the ship and accommodated twelve twelve-pounders on either side. Mess tables and hammocks would usually occupy the space between and even above the guns, but these had been stowed to create a more warlike impression. As on the upper deck, the guns were highly polished and appeared to be in good order. Philippe closely inspected two to starboard, then two to port, and was impressed. The tackle was in good order, the cables properly stowed, the guns themselves clearly well looked after. One officer of *Le Zéphyr*, at least, knew his business.

Several dozen men were on the deck, most of them more or less at some semblance of attention. Philippe noticed one, a small, lean fellow of forty or so, whose left eye was a mass of recent scar tissue, a wound which disfigured what was already a markedly ugly face. The one remaining eye somehow conveyed even more disdain for the captain of *Le Zéphyr* than the two eyes of every other man in the crew. Philippe went over to the man, ignoring what seemed to be a warning glance from Garrigues.

'Your name, Citizen?'

'Pierric Korbell, Citizen Captain.'

The reply, delivered in a strong Breton accent, bore no trace of deference or respect.

'*Gabier, matelot* or novice?'

'Novice, Citizen Captain.'

'And how did you come by your wound?'

The sailor mumbled something under his breath, then looked Philippe in the eye.

'The Chouans, Citizen Captain. One of their boats, trying to run in under the lee of the Pointe du Raz when I was in *L'Amethyst*.'

'You did for them, I hope?'

'Sank 'em with all hands, Citizen Captain.'

'Very good,' said Philippe. 'I'll look for more such valour from you when we go to sea, Citizen Korbell.' He began to turn away, but then turned back and spoke in rapid Breton that neither Roissel, Garrigues nor any other Frenchman within earshot could understand. 'But you call me *mab a'r chast*, a son of a bitch, ever again and I'll have every *pouce* of skin flogged off your back, you hear me?'

Korbell's one eye nearly burst from its socket in astonishment, and the mouths of several other men nearby, evidently Bretons too, were agape.

Roissel led Philippe to the nearest ladder and they went down to the *faux pont*, the orlop deck, a dark, rank space where both men had to stoop and which was lit entirely by lanterns. This contained the gunroom, the cockpit and the warrant officers' cabins in the after part of the ship, while further forward were the storerooms for the carpenter, the bosun, the sailmakers, and others. The cockpit, which normally served as the wardroom, would be the surgeon's domain in battle, the place where he could lay out the wounded and the dying, but *Le Zéphyr* still had no surgeon. It also had no sheep, who on longer voyages would occupy pens amidships, between the food hatch into the hold and the main hatch. Saint-Jacques made his obsequious appearance here, asking whether the Citizen Captain would care to inspect the hold compartments in the bottom of the hull, which contained cables, water, oil, vinegar and wine, together with the breadroom and powder magazine lying astern of them, but Philippe had seen enough. *Le Zéphyr* was well designed and well built, but apart from the main guns, the domain of the brisk Garrigues, everything had an air of slovenliness. Worse, the ship was both woefully undermanned and under-provisioned. Saint-Jacques bemoaned the priority given to the flagships and other large ships of the fleet, despite the fact that the frigates went to sea far more often and were more likely to see action against the scouting frigates that the British impudently deployed well inshore. Roissel, who evidently had no love for the steward, concurred with him nonetheless.

As he went through the different spaces in the hull, Philippe assessed the quality of the men he encountered. There were perhaps a few dozen old hands or *gabiers*, the topmen, mostly Bretons but with a smattering of Gascons, Provençals and Basques. They should be the backbone of his crew, the men he could most depend on, but the strange times and his own strangeness in their eyes made it impossible to judge how they would respond in a crisis. The great majority of the crew worried him. France had always recruited men for its navy by a system of compulsory registration, the *inscription maritime*, by which the coastal provinces and communities provided set quotas of skilled seamen. In America he encountered many English sailors – prisoners, deserters and so forth – who had been taken into their navy by the brutal system known as the press gang, yet these same men loudly proclaimed how England was more a land of freedom than France. Whatever the rights and wrongs of that case, it was universally acknowledged that the French system was infinitely superior to the English. But the strains of revolution and war were clearly stretching the system to its limits and beyond if the men of *Le Zéphyr* were anything to go by. There were fishermen galore, mostly Bretons, mostly old men as Larsonneur of *Quatorze Juillet* had been, but some of them seemed unable to comprehend that such a large vessel as the frigate could actually exist and float, let alone that they were serving in it. At least they, even the caulkers and sailmakers, had some idea of life at sea, of sails and ropes, of the words used to describe parts of the ship. But then there was the rest of the crew, perhaps a third to a half of it as far as he could see, who were raw novices, *matelots d'eau douce* or freshwater sailors. As he climbed back up to the gun deck, what seemed to be a typical example of this set of men was staring at him open-mouthed as though he were some sort of apparition.

'Where are you from and what trade did you follow, Citizen?' said Philippe.

'From near Vervins in Picardy,' said the fellow, his voice little more than a whisper. He was very young and terribly thin, his face pock-marked by the unmistakeable souvenirs of smallpox. 'Truth to tell, your honour, I was apprenticed to a tanner—'

Roissel stepped forward and struck the youth hard across the cheek.

'Salute and address the Citizen Captain properly!' he snarled.

Philippe frowned but said nothing. It did not do to contradict one's officers in public, and even if his discipline was brutal, Roissel was undoubtedly correct in principle.

The tanner's apprentice came to attention and saluted, with several of his fellows looking on to see what would play out.

'Sorry, Citizen Captain,' he mumbled. He was one of the few men so far who averted their eyes from Philippe instead of brazenly staring at him.

'Your name, Citizen?'

'Arnaud Lucas, Citizen Captain.'

'And how do you find yourself in the navy, Arnaud Lucas?'

The lad looked perplexed.

'They said our village had to provide ten men for the army and one for the navy, so they drew lots. I was the one who got the navy.'

'You'd been to sea before, or at least in the river trades?'

'Never seen the sea before in my life. Never ventured further than Vervins. Didn't know what a navy was until I got to Brest.'

'Then what are your duties aboard ship?'

Lucas glanced nervously towards Roissel, whose expression was furious.

'Don't rightly know, Citizen Captain. Officers or some among the older men tell me to do this or do that, haul on this rope or that. But they use words I don't understand. Just this morning, one of the mates ordered me to attend to a cat harping. Begging your pardon, Citizen Captain, but just what is one of those? I could see no cat and no harp.'

Roissel swayed forward as though preparing to strike the boy again, but Philippe raised his hand.

'Well, Citizen Arnaud Lucas, we'll have to see if we can make a proper seaman out of you, comfortable with catharpins and everything else about a ship. You've a good heart and want to fight the enemies of France?'

Lucas brightened. 'Nothing more, Citizen Captain. My old ma says the English have horns and tails and roast children on spits.'

There was laughter from some of the others on the deck, but also a few serious nods.

'Well, Citizen Lucas,' said Philippe, 'I'll forgive you your ignorance of the catharpin and the like if you prove to be a good fighter.'

'Aye, aye, Citizen Captain!'

As they moved away, Roissel turned to Philippe.

'With respect, sir, leniency is no good with his sort. We've got scores of men like him aboard from the inland provinces who still don't know one end of the ship from the other. The only things they understand are the fist and the lash.'

'And with respect to you, Lieutenant, I have commanded Russians, men who had been peasants in the remotest Steppes only weeks before and had never seen ships or the sea in their lives. Yet they feared God and loved their empress, and they hated the Swedes and the Turks who were then their enemies. They learned quickly and fought like demons. Are you saying Frenchmen aren't at least their equal? Besides, don't the fist and the lash run counter to the rights of man – to the very principles of the revolution itself?'

Roissel's lips tightened as though he wanted to protest, but he merely inclined his head.

'As you say, Citizen Captain.'

A crew with too many men like Arnaud Lucas and Pierric Korbell, thought Philippe. *Men who don't know the sea. Men who think me an* aristo *and a foreigner. Men who think the revolution gives them the right to question orders and have their say about anything and everything. A first officer who hates me and will seek to bring me down. Oh, Tasha, my love, wait for me, for I'll surely be joining you very soon.*

CHAPTER FOURTEEN

The fleet was sailing. The wind was a strong easterly, bringing unseasonably cold squally rain showers, and Morard was taking the opportunity to slip out of Brest. He was making a show of it, perhaps to impress Saint-André but more likely to give the English and royalist spies in the town something juicy to report back to their masters. So the fleet, bound down the coast for Quiberon where it could better guard against enemy landings in the Vendée, was going out as one. Philippe watched from the quarterdeck of *Le Zéphyr*, still lying at anchor, as the signal guns were fired, the anchors were raised, the sails were set, and the pride of France headed out past him and into the Atlantic on the morning ebb. First were a couple of scouting frigates followed closely by the first of the seventy-fours, *Trajan* and *Superbe*, and a couple more frigates. Next came another brace of seventy-fours, *Audacieux* and *Tigre*, and then the two mightiest ships of all, the *Bretagne* and the flagship *Le Terrible*, both of 110 guns. A band on *Le Terrible* was playing 'Ça Ira', 'La Marseillaise' and all the other war songs of the revolution, proof that the Republic far outdid the old monarchy in tunes that were at once jaunty, eminently singable and quite astonishingly bloody. Morard's command flag flew out proudly on the breeze, and the remaining ships of the fleet fell briskly into the flagship's wake: three eighties, *Juste*, *Auguste* and *Indomptable*, intermingled with a dozen more seventy-fours. Philippe recognised several of them from the American war, when he was serving on sloops and cutters running messages and carrying provisions out to the French fleet, which had come to the aid of the infant United States. Taking their stations between, beside or behind the ships of the line were the remaining nine frigates. The fleet passed through the Goulet and out into the broad ocean beyond. It was unquestionably an impressive sight, although whether the Republic's enemies would think so was quite another matter.

Le Zéphyr should have been sailing with the fleet, but she was still several days away from being ready to put to sea. More bread and wine by the *velte* were arriving on boats coming out from the dockyard, albeit nowhere near enough to fill the ship's hold. A few dozen more barrels of powder arrived, but Garrigues was scathing about its quality. The promised 'new' slop clothes proved to be nothing of the kind, being little more than louse-ridden discards from the prisons. Their distribution triggered more disputes and quarrels among the crew; there was bad blood between some of the landlubbers and a few of the old hands who thought they should have first pick of the slops, while a Breton pulled a knife on a Parisian who apparently thought his hometown made him the ship's arbiter of fashion. Many, whatever their seagoing experience or background, grumbled that they were free citizens of a republic, true-hearted sons of liberty, and as such they deserved better treatment. Above all, there was no sign of the shortfall in the ship's complement being made good. Fouroux, the carpenter, was especially vocal about the difficulties his under-strength crew caused him. It meant that the essential repairs to the rudder and its mechanism were taking far longer than they should have done. Philippe did what he could, going below to encourage the carpenter's men in their work and writing ever more urgent demands to slothful officials in the yard, but it all seemed somehow desultory. Men worked with little urgency, many of them with resentful expressions on their faces. He still heard whispered insults directed at him, although it was never possible to identify the perpetrators. With the single exception of Garrigues, even the officers kept their distance, as though they, too, thought there was no point in becoming too close to their strange beast of a captain who was neither fish nor fowl and was bound to find himself on the guillotine sooner rather than later.

He was thinking such thoughts as he signed manifests at his table in his cabin when one of the *mousses* brought him a letter. It was a note from Leonore. The sight of her handwriting and her name affected him strangely, and he gripped the table to steady himself. But it was not an intimate letter – *why on earth should it have been?* It was not even a courtesy note, but a formal sentence to inform him that his brother, Alexandre, would go before the revolutionary tribunal of Brest the next morning at ten. She had come to town and was lodging with an old widow who was an acquaintance of the

Penhouets. If his duties allowed, perhaps he would care to attend the trial? Philippe considered her request, but he was already reaching for pen and paper to make his request to Saint-André for a brief leave of absence, justified by the excuse that he could use the rest of his time ashore to pursue the reluctant storekeepers of Brest rather more vigorously than Steward Saint-Jacques seemed to be doing. Somewhat to his surprise, the *représentant's* reply came within a couple of hours and was positive. Perhaps Saint-André reasoned that attending such a spectacle might give Philippe an idea of what could await him if he strayed from the path of revolutionary virtue.

The tribunal was held in the Hotel de Ville, a squat, bland building in the style of Louis the Fifteenth's early years. It had four storeys and far too many bays for any pretence at real grandeur, although the ornate railings, gates and guardhouses that fronted it did their best to bestow some sort of dignity and status on the place. It was in the heart of the town, a few streets back from the waterfront, and was decked out in red, white and blue bunting. Before it stood Brest's Tree of Liberty, the obligatory symbol of the new republic, the brothers and sisters of which had supposedly been planted in every town and city in France. At the main gate, the sentry, a National Guardsman, who inspected Philippe's credentials, must have been seventy if he was a day and seemed to be having difficulty staying awake. The loud and excitable child beggars massed around the gates could easily have rushed him and gained admittance, but none seemed to have the slightest interest in any proceedings that might be taking place inside.

Philippe went into the building, hoping for a sighting of Leonore. But there was no sign of her, and it took an enquiry directed to a pale, limping young clerk for him to find his way to the courtroom.

The trial was already under way, so Philippe slipped in at the side and took a seat on the nearest bench. Alexandre stood nearby in a makeshift dock facing the president and his four fellow judges, who sat beneath an overly large Tricolour. He must have registered Philippe's arrival, but did not react if he had. Off to the side of the courtroom sat twelve jurors, an innovation apparently taken from English law. How deliciously ironic our father would have found it, Philippe thought, that the French republic he had craved all his life should denounce England as a blood-soaked tyranny and yet steal the cornerstone of its legal system.

Then he saw her.

She was on the other side of the room, dressed soberly in a purple dress that could have been taken for black in poor light, as though she were already widowed. She looked thinner and paler than when he last saw her, and her eyes were cast down on the floor as if in prayer. Philippe did not know if she had seen him.

He made no attempt to catch her eyes, focusing instead on Alexandre and the public prosecutor, who was holding forth theatrically in the centre of the courtroom. He was a short, sallow fellow with a grating high-pitched voice who sported an oversized revolutionary rosette in his lapel. It was obvious that he was a fellow who longed for advancement to the principal tribunal in Paris, where he could impress the countless lawyers who thronged the National Convention and the Committee of Public Safety.

The prosecutor was evidently part way through the lengthy indictment against Alexandre.

'...and that, by letters found in secret places within the Chateau de Brechelean, it is abundantly apparent that the said Alexandre Kermorvant did conspire and plot treason with known counter-revolutionaries and convicted traitors, and did correspond with the armed forces of the enemies of France who are perfidiously intent upon the destruction of the Republic. It will be further proved that in private, the said Alexandre Kermorvant did express his contempt for the Republic and his favour for the sometime king Louis Capet, and his whore, Marie-Antoinette Capet. It will also be proved that in an attempt to divert suspicion from himself and to conceal his manifest guilt, the said Alexandre Kermorvant falsely denounced his half-brother, Philippe Kermorvant, called the Vicomte de Saint-Victor, now worthily employed as a captain in the navy of the Republic and present in this courtroom today.'

The prosecutor looked towards Philippe and inclined his head respectfully. Alexandre half-turned, this time clearly registering his brother's presence, but showed no emotion. Leonore, though, looked up as though she had been startled in a moment of intense prayer, saw Philippe, blushed violently, and immediately looked downwards once again. He, in turn, lost track of the prosecutor's words, and only realised where he was when a different voice, that of the president of the tribunal, intruded. The judge was reading the summary of charges against Alexandre, then he donned his glasses to look directly at the accused.

'This is what you are accused of Citizen Kermorvant. Grim and heinous charges indeed, the most infamous crimes against the Republic and the common good of the people of France! We turn now to the interrogation of witnesses, although in this case, the written evidence of your crimes is so overwhelming that the Republic calls upon only one witness, other than yourself, to speak here in open court. I, as president of this tribunal, call upon Citizeness Leonore Kermorvant, wife of the accused and denouncer of the same.'

There was a sudden heightening of the tension in the courtroom. This was what the spectators, those unconnected to any of the parties involved, had come to see: a woman accusing her own husband of charges that, if proved, would send him to the guillotine.

Leonore stood and stated her name so quietly that the president had to ask her to speak up.

'Citizeness,' said the public prosecutor, 'you have recorded your deposition for this tribunal in writing. I draw your attention now to only two elements of it. First, you record that you recently discovered your husband's secret correspondence with rebel leaders in Brittany and the Vendée. When was this, precisely?'

Leonore glanced across at both Philippe and Alexandre, took a deep breath, and looked directly at the prosecutor.

'On the first day of August, Citizen.'

'And how did you come to discover them?'

Philippe barely heard her answer. She was lying. The first of August was the day when he and Leonore walked in the lost garden of Brechelean. The day when the revolutionary mob came to arrest him. Surely she would have spoken to him if she had made such a discovery that very day? Perhaps she found them after Quedeville, the erstwhile baker, had taken him into custody and started to escort him along the road to Brest, but that seemed unlikely. The story he could hear her telling the court, that she had been cleaning in the armoury and found the correspondence concealed within an ancient suit of armour, was simply unbelievable to anyone who knew her and knew the ruinous old chateau. That being so, there could only be one truth, and it was not the testimony being given before the revolutionary tribunal of Brest. Leonore had always known where the correspondence was and had always known what it contained. She had always known her husband was a traitor to the Republic. If it emerged that she had concealed such damning evidence for months, she too would surely be bound for the guillotine as an accomplice to treason.

Fortunately the public prosecutor, for all his rhetorical fireworks, had no interest in pursuing the point. He was concerned only with the content of the letters, reading aloud several of the most damning passages before commending Leonore on her public-spiritedness and self-sacrifice in denouncing her husband to save her brother-in-law, an innocent man unjustly accused and who sought only to serve the Republic. It was one version of events, Philippe supposed.

He glanced across at Alexandre. His brother's expression had changed, seemingly not just because of the enforced sobriety he would have endured in prison. Before Leonore began to give her evidence he had seemed confident, arrogant and dismissive of the entire proceedings. Now, though, Philippe saw a change in his brother. Alexandre seemed at once younger, more thoughtful and more solemn. He was looking at Leonore, who could not meet his eyes. Philippe expected rage and hatred from the Alexandre Kermorvant he had come to know at Brechelean. But the older half-brother's expression was the opposite of that.

'Let us move onto the second point in your evidence that the jury should weigh with especial gravity,' said the prosecutor, addressing Leonore again. 'You testify that on or about the thirteenth day of May, you saw the accused greet and entertain three citizens within the Chateau de Brechelean. That you recognised one of them as the Seigneur de Hézec, a near neighbour and a known leader of the counter-revolutionary insurrection. That you heard your husband, the accused, address another man as "Most Reverend Bishop". Tell us about the third man, Citizeness.'

Leonore cleared her throat and blushed again, as if being the centre of attention embarrassed her. But this time when she spoke, her voice was clear, loud and confident.

'I never saw the third man properly,' she said. 'He was shorter than the other two, but younger. I only heard him speak a few words, but I knew at once that he was not French. He spoke poorly, using the wrong words, and could barely string a sentence together. I had heard foreigners trying to speak French in Paris, and thought he had to be from another country.'

'And did you form an opinion as to which other country that might be?'

Leonore was silent for a few seconds, as though she was arranging her thoughts and choosing her words.

'He reminded me of a Dutch merchant who did business with my father,' she said, 'but also of several Englishmen who we knew in those days, men whose attempts to speak French were always atrocious.'

There was knowing laughter among those present in court.

'You are saying, then, that this third man might have been English, an agent of a country with which France is at war, or Dutch, also enemies of the Republic?'

'He could have been, yes.'

'And what did the accused, your husband, and these three visitors discuss?'

'I did not hear most of their conversation – they went through to a different room. But I did hear them make a toast before they retired.'

'What was the toast?'

She hesitated, looking first at the prosecutor, then at the president of the tribunal, and finally at Alexandre. Her response was inaudible.

'Speak up, Citizeness,' said the president, impatiently.

'*Vive le roi*,' she said.

The courtroom erupted. Spectators and jurors alike chattered loudly, several of them gesticulating wildly. Philippe, though, remained fixed in his seat, looking between Leonore and Alexandre. His brother was impassive, with what looked to be a faint smile on his lips. The shock of the forbidden toast was burying deep the obvious lesson of Leonore's words: if she had heard such words being spoken in May, why had she not reported them then? Alexandre would surely know that he could easily drag her down with him. He had failed to destroy his hated sibling, but he could surely destroy this woman whom Philippe could not, dare not, desire.

The president finally obtained a semblance of silence in the courtroom and bade the public prosecutor continue, but he had no further questions for Leonore. Perhaps he was showing mercy to her by not pursuing the obvious problems with her evidence. More likely he was so intent on convicting Alexandre that he had no interest in lessening the impact of Leonore's evidence by questioning her more closely. Or perhaps, thought Philippe, despite his pompous blustering and rhetorical skills, the public prosecutor was simply inept.

The president of the court addressed Alexandre.

'Citizen Kermorvant,' he said, 'you have heard the case against you. I wish now to put to you the two principal instances brought by the public prosecutor, and to hear your response to the charges of having entered into treasonable correspondence with rebels and other traitors to the Republic, and having entertained—'

'I have nothing to say,' said Alexandre, interrupting the president mid-sentence.

'What? This is your chance to convince the jury to acquit you, Citizen. I advise you to take it.'

'I have nothing to say.'

Philippe stared at his brother. Alexandre was a brutal drunk who had tried to destroy him, and if he spoke now he would surely destroy Leonore. Then, as if the elder brother was reading the younger's thoughts, Alexandre turned to look properly at Philippe. He gave him what appeared to be a very slight nod, smiled at Leonore, then turned back to face the president and the public prosecutor.

'Nothing to say but this,' he said, grinning broadly, and cried, '*Vive le roi!*'

He shouted the words as if he were trying to get them to hear him in Paris. Once again chaos reigned in the courtroom, with the president ineffectually hammering his gavel to demand silence. Philippe looked across to Leonore, who was open-mouthed in astonishment at what her husband had done. He, too, looked at his brother anew, and with respect. When it mattered most of all the elder son of Verité had indeed told the truth, or perhaps *a* truth, even at the greatest possible cost to himself.

Gradually, order returned to the courtroom. At last the public prosecutor was able to deliver his peroration to the jury, a piece of flummery so loud and delivered with such false pathos and drama that he might have been on the Paris stage. Most of it was obvious stuff – viperous treason, guilt abundantly evident, wife's heroic devotion to the Republic and so forth – but the lawyer's conclusion still shook Philippe to his core.

'There is one verdict that the law demands, my friends. It is the verdict that the Republic demands, that the people demand, that liberty demands. I venture to say it is the verdict that the shining reputation of this man's father demands! What would the great Verité say if he could come back to us and see how low his son has fallen, how greatly he has betrayed the reputation and the legacy handed down to him?'

Betrayed their father? Philippe had no reason to love his brother, and yes, Verité would probably have been appalled if he knew that a son of his had actively conspired against the Republic. But Alexandre could have condemned Leonore and he had not. Philippe struggled to understand why, but then he remembered something Alex had said, one of the few things of substance he had said to his younger sibling during that dismal first dinner at Brechelean. Verité had read both his sons the tales of King Arthur, so Alex, too, would have listened to the story that made a particularly vivid impression on the young Philippe Kermorvant: Sir Gawain and the Green Knight, the tale of the valiant hero riding out to sacrifice himself so that those close to him might live. Philippe wished he had made more effort to get to know his brother better during his weeks at Brechelean, to reach the man buried within the mutilated drunk, to bring out the boy who, like him, must have been enthralled by the legend of Gawain, but now he would never have that opportunity.

The jury, after barely a minute's deliberation, returned a verdict of guilty, and with gruesome inevitability the president of the tribunal sentenced Alexandre Kermorvant to death.

—

An excited crowd milled around the Hotel de Ville, frustrating Philippe's attempts to reach and speak to Leonore. He saw the beggar boys Olivier and Roman again, seemingly intent on speaking to him but struggling to fight their way through the throng. But he had eyes only for his sister-in-law. She was getting into her hired carriage when he finally caught up with her, but turned when she heard him call her name.

'Leonore!'

'Captain Kermorvant.' She had been crying, but otherwise her expression was cold and remote.

'I... I am sorry, *madame*. Sorry for Alexandre... for all this.'

'I am not,' she said, although her damp red eyes told a different story. She dropped her voice to a whisper. Several of those in the crowd had evidently recognised her and were murmuring among themselves or pointing accusing fingers. 'But it is not appropriate for us to be seen together.'

He wanted to disagree and argue the point, but of course she was right. Philippe did not care for his own reputation, but he cared greatly about Leonore's. If they did not do the right thing now, she would be marked down by the townsfolk of Brest as the brazen *putain* who had sent her husband to the guillotine so she could jump into bed with his brother and maybe make herself a *vicomtesse*.

'I sail within a day or two,' he said tentatively. 'We will be out for weeks, perhaps months. What will you do in that time?'

'I will leave the chateau, of course. It is undoubtedly yours now, Citizen Vicomte.'

He struggled to find the right words for his reply.

'There's no need for it. Brechelean is more your home than mine, and if my career prospers, I will rarely be there. Besides, I need to know the estate is safe in the hands of someone competent, and I can think of no one better than you.'

'It won't be suitable for us to be under the same roof, don't you think? But it doesn't matter, Captain. It won't matter for a long time. The president and prosecutor were talking about Alex being taken to Paris for execution – they say it'll make a stronger impression and a greater example if the son of Verité goes to the guillotine there rather than here, where half the people are secret Chouans. If they take him there, I'll go too. I can appeal for his life to my cousin, General Carnot.'

'Just as you appealed to him for mine.'

She looked away.

'I was... confused.'

'Then you regret what you've done?' he demanded, lowering his voice so the gossips nearby could not hear. 'You regret what you said in there?'

'Alex is my husband,' she said simply. Her eyes were welling up again.

'I owe you my life,' he whispered. 'I cannot begin to thank you enough.'

'Thank me by defending France and winning your battles, Captain Kermorvant.'

'Leonore, I…'

She climbed into the carriage, and struck the roof as a signal to the driver.

'Farewell, Philippe.'

She did not wave from the carriage, did not even look out for a farewell glance. He felt utterly, impossibly cold, as if it were a bitter winter's day in Kronstadt rather than a warm summer afternoon in Brest.

He took one last look at Leonore's carriage before it was swallowed up in the crowd of carts and horsemen thronging the road leading towards the eastern ramparts. Then he turned away, colliding as he did so with Olivier and Roman, who had finally managed to reach him.

Their conversation changed the two boys' lives and, in one key respect, Philippe's too.

CHAPTER FIFTEEN

Le Zéphyr was under orders to sail on the afternoon tide if the wind permitted, which it did. Philippe left his officers to make the final preparations for taking the ship to sea. He would go above later, but in the meantime it did not do for a captain to insist on supervising his subordinates too closely. He needed to show trust in them, even in Roissel, and besides, he had a duty to undertake. He wished he did not, for his thoughts were still filled with Alexandre's trial and his difficult parting from Leonore. But a boat had finally brought out the last three crew members who were to join the ship before she sailed. Philippe wished they included a surgeon and another couple of Marines, or else three more decent *gabiers*. Instead he got three children.

They were an unlikely assortment of youths, thought Philippe as he studied the three *aspirants* assigned to *Le Zéphyr*. They stood stiffly before him as he sat behind the table in the council chamber, two of the three looking as though they wished they were anywhere else, the third seemingly already sizing up the space for his own furnishings. This lad, a remarkably tall specimen with delicate pale skin, immaculately combed hair and what was evidently a brand-new uniform, had the haughty air of, say, the Empress Catherine's perfumed flunkies or General Washington's staff officers. His two companions, though, were all too evidently wearing the cast-offs of men who had been promoted, killed or arrested. One was a stocky, pink-cheeked fellow with unruly sandy hair, who filled a uniform that seemed to be at least a size too small for him. Philippe thought of ordering him to exchange with his silent, mouse-like companion, whose tunic coat was surely two or three sizes too large. He thought better of it. The young men needed to learn responsibility, and that included the responsibility for appearing in public looking utterly ridiculous. The caustic opinions of the lower deck and the townsfolk of Brest would soon make them correct their rig.

'So,' said Philippe, 'three *aspirants*. Your names, Citizens?'

As he expected, the tall, confident and exceedingly elegant youth replied first.

'Fabian Vaquin, Citizen Captain. It is an honour to sail with you, sir.'

'We shall see if the feeling becomes mutual, Aspirant Vaquin. Your father is a lawyer, I take it?'

The lad's self-assured mask slipped just for a moment.

'Why yes, Citizen Captain – an attorney who serves the revolutionary tribunal in Lille. But how could you know?'

'Call it an inspired guess, Aspirant.' Philippe smiled. Although he had not been in France for very long, he had already learned that every other man in the Republic seemed to be a lawyer.

'And you?' he said, his gaze settling on the straw-haired lad in the ludicrously undersized uniform.

'Jean-Jacques Lievremont, Citizen Captain. An honour for me, likewise.'

The youth spoke smoothly, unlike the over-eager Vaquin, and seemed entirely at ease in his surroundings.

'Lievremont. That's a familiar name – I knew a Lievremont in the American war, a *lieutenant de vaisseau* with De Grasse who was often sent ashore on liaison missions.'

'My father, sir. He died in Tasmania during Kermadec's voyage to the Indies.'

'I'm sorry for your loss, Aspirant. I remember him as a good officer and an amiable man.'

Lievremont looked uncomfortable.

'I never really knew him, sir.'

Philippe nodded. It was a story all too common among naval families the world over.

'And you, Aspirant?'

The third youth, the silent mouse, kept his eyes on the deck, blushed furiously, shifted uneasily from one foot to the other, and mumbled something that might have been his name.

'Speak up, Aspirant, whispering and mumbling will get you nowhere on a man-of-war! You'll have to give commands, perhaps dozens of commands a day, and you'll need to be heard.'

The youth lifted his head for the first time and met Philippe's eyes.

'My name is Armand Carabignac, Citizen Captain,' he said, a little more audibly but still in barely more than a whisper.

'Very good, Aspirant Carabignac. And what brings you to sea?'

Carabignac hesitated, and Vaquin immediately spoke up in his place.

'To serve the Republic, sir! To guard it against all enemies for the honour and glory of France—'

'Yes, very good, Vaquin, but I want to hear from Aspirant Carabignac there.'

The little youth looking miserable beyond all measure and far younger than his years. If anything, he looked and acted more like an eight-year-old whose favourite toy had been taken away than as a trainee officer of the French Republic. Nevertheless, he took a deep breath and addressed Philippe with a little more confidence.

'My father ordained it, sir. He's a member of the National Convention and I'm his seventh son. All my brothers are in the army, medicine or the law. I was the one destined for the church, but then the church was brought low.'

Vaquin and Lievremont were looking at their colleague in astonishment. Perhaps they had never heard him speak so many words at once; perhaps the revelation that his father was in the National Convention immediately elevated Carabignac's status in their eyes. Well, Philippe thought, that should make for an interesting *aspirants'* mess.

They were indeed little more than children, but all of them, even Carabignac, were much older than many of the midshipmen in the British navy, whose age was often only barely into double figures when they first donned their king's uniform. Come to that, they were all older than he had been when he first went to sea. It was in the summer of seventy-seven, not long after his mother disappeared, and the thirteen-year-old Philippe Kermorvant badgered his father into allowing him to take a berth with Ben Fairfax, a grizzled old skipper who was about to sail a small man-of-war out of Norfolk with a commission from the newly minted State of Virginia. Verité, clad in the new and wholly unfamiliar blue uniform of a brigadier-general in the Continental Army, probably thought that one cruise would disabuse his foolish son of the notion that the sea was his destiny. For a while, it seemed as though Philippe's father would be proved right. The boy boggled at the strangeness of the frightening element upon which he found himself, wept when Fairfax upbraided him for the countless mistakes he made, and sulked when some of his shipmates mocked him as a Frenchie and a milord with airs and graces. But there was one old seaman, a free black man named John Calvin Smith, who took the young Philippe under his wing and taught him the ropes. And when the *Assistance* sailed into battle against a British brig off Cape May, Philippe stood undaunted on the deck while several of his abusers cowered down below. The shot flew all around him; a man at his side was killed by a cannonball in the guts that sprayed blood and gore all over Philippe, but in that moment he knew that this was what he was born to do. Within five years, John Calvin Smith's pupil was a lieutenant in the Continental Navy, Philippe's greatest regret being that his father had not lived to see the moment. Perhaps one of the three youths before him would take to the sea as quickly and as successfully as he had. He doubted it, but they deserved the chance that had been given to him.

'So, Citizens,' said Philippe, 'you find yourselves as *aspirants* on *Le Zéphyr*. An important responsibility, for you will have men in your charge – their well-being will be your concern, and your orders may be matters of life or death for them. You are here to learn how to discharge these duties and to prove yourself worthy, in due course, of receiving the Republic's commission. For my part, I am responsible for your education both in the ways of the sea and in the knowledge that all men of refinement and education should possess. As you know, the larger ships have schoolmasters dedicated to this task, but *Le Zéphyr* is too small to allow for such an officer. That means I am your teacher as well as your commander. So, *aspirants*, I am devising a programme of training in seamanship, in gunnery, in mathematics and in navigation, the aim being to make you masters of trigonometry, cosmography, algebra and all the other skills essential to an officer's success in the navy.' Vaquin seemed to swallow hard at the word 'trigonometry'. Philippe made to continue, but before he could do so he was interrupted by a knock on the cabin door. 'Yes, come!'

The knock was followed by the entry of a surly-looking seaman who saluted perfunctorily, then handed Philippe two letters. He recognised the admiral's seal and the handwriting of his clerk. He used his paper knife to open the first envelope and read the unwelcome tidings that the note conveyed. The surgeon assigned to *Le Zéphyr*, a keen young man well recommended by the surgeons of Paris, had been caught in a Chouan ambush no more than a league short of Brest and was dead.

Philippe could not mourn a man he had never met, but he certainly grieved for the supplementary news in the note. It was imperative that *Le Zéphyr* put to sea as soon as possible to counter the ever-increasing rebel activity on the coast. That being so, there would not be time to procure a new surgeon for the ship before she sailed. The admiral would do his best, as would the dockyard authorities, and when the ship came back into the Rade for fresh supplies and any new orders, perhaps in four- or five-weeks' time, there should be a surgeon duly appointed and ready to join the crew. Philippe placed little credence on this reassurance. Sea service was hardly an attractive proposition for a good surgeon, and if any were left in Brittany after the larger ships had taken their share then it was a fair bet that the army or the National Guard had taken them. Besides, four or five weeks was ample time for *Le Zéphyr* to encounter an English warship and reap the usual harvest of splinter and gunshot wounds demanding stitching at best, amputation at worst.

Philippe turned to the second letter, and as he opened it he prayed that it contained better news. He slit open the envelope, took out the enclosure, and read the terse message that Morard de Galles had evidently despatched to all his captains.

'Sir?' He was dimly aware of Vaquin speaking to him. 'Citizen Captain? Are you well, sir?'

He had no answer for the young *aspirant*, for he could not claim to be well when the Republic was dying.

Toulon had rebelled, declared for the king, and brought in the English navy.

The French Republic's Mediterranean fleet was no more. The admiral, the Comte de Trogoff de Kerlessey, had delivered it entire – thirty ships of the line, more or less – to the enemies of the Republic. *Tonnant, Languedoc, Triomphante, Tricolore,* all the rest of them. All were gone. *Commerce de Marseille* and *Sans-Culotte,* the Republic's largest warships, were in royalist hands. The Union flag and the fleur-de-lys of the monarchy flew side by side above Toulon.

The tolling of bells, the distant, urgent shouts of men and women in the town, and the endless, defiant but desperate choruses of '*Ça Ira*' told Philippe that the word was out all over Brest. *Ça Ira:* it'll be fine. Never had the optimistic, defiant song sounded more forlorn and pathetic. He could see increased activity over on the flagships and the other big ships of the line. He, Morard de Galles, the hysterical fellows running up and down the streets, and even the three perplexed young *aspirants* before him were surely all having the same thought.

If Toulon had defected to the English and the counter-revolution, would the town and fleet of Brest be next?

CHAPTER SIXTEEN

The bells of Brest tolled long into the night. The songs of the crowds ashore got ever louder and more drunken. From the deck of *Le Zéphyr*, Philippe and his officers, including the three *aspirants*, could see bonfires spring up in all parts of the town and on the hills around about. There were occasional gunshots. The men on some of the small boats who plied the Rade at all hours swore that the enemy was already in the town and attacking the citadel, although others claimed that the news from Toulon was a fiction and that the Mediterranean fleet and its base remained in republican hands. Philippe doubled the lookouts but resisted Roissel's suggestion for de Machault to muster the entire Marine contingent. He had never been to Toulon, but from the charts he had seen he knew it would be much more difficult for a sudden royalist uprising or Chouan assault to seize the ships in the Rade de Brest. The anchorage was too large and the bulk of the fleet lay on the far side of it, well away from the town. True, that meant any attempt to seize any of the warships in the harbour would probably be directed at *Le Zéphyr* and the other frigates lying nearer Brest itself, just offshore on the north coast of the Rade. But massing the Marines on deck when there was no immediate threat seemed excessive and might inflame tempers.

Just past midnight, Philippe realised that tempers below decks were probably already inflamed enough. The sounds of jeers and catcalls from large bodies of men reached the quarterdeck.

Ugarte, at his captain's side, was grinning.

'Sounds as though some of the lads are getting a bit lively,' he said.

'Surely some of the officers are down there to keep things quiet?'

'Aye, first officer's down there all right, but he couldn't keep a Trappist nun silent, that one. Bosun's down there too, but Payen would have much rather been a nun himself, I reckon. Begging pardon, Citizen Captain.'

Ignoring Ugarte's flippancy, Philippe went below, the enormous Basque following close behind.

The gun deck was a battlefield. Mess tables had been overset, leaving the deck covered with plates, food and the spillage from overturned tankards. Descending by the rear ladder, Philippe and Ugarte came down behind what was evidently a party composed chiefly of Bretons. They were swearing and shouting abuse at a roughly equal number of men from other parts of France who were standing much further forward. The space between the two parties contained Payen, blowing his whistle to no effect, and Roissel, whose sword remained sheathed. Vaquin stood just behind him with the other two *aspirants*, Carabignac and Lievremont, standing and staring from a position across the deck alongside one of the starboard midships guns. Just forward of them, two large men, one from each party and both stripped to the waist, were engaged in a no-holds-barred contest that seemed to be a combination of boxing, wrestling and the crudest, most underhand form of street brawling. They were clearly the champions of the two parties, the Bretons and the Frenchmen wildly cheering each blow, kick and attempted eye-gouge.

Philippe attempted to attract Roissel's attention, but the lieutenant seemed utterly engrossed by the combat before him.

'He's enjoying it,' said Philippe.

''Course he is, Citizen Captain. I expect he'd give you some bollocks about men exercising their revolutionary right to free expression. Me, I reckon he just likes to see men's naked flesh and an old-fashioned scrap.'

Philippe chose to ignore the implication of Ugarte's words, which accorded uncomfortably with the information given him by the boys Olivier and Roman. He was listening to the shouts and catcalls, and it was clear from them that the second officer was only partly right. The Parisians, Gascons and others massed for'ard were accusing the Bretons of being papists and pagans, secret Chouans and covert royalists who were plotting to deliver *Le Zéphyr* to the English that very night. The Bretons were replying by calling their shipmates useless lubbers, sodomites and other colourful insults, somehow also ending at the same destination by accusing their adversaries of being traitors to the Republic. There was nothing unfamiliar in such rivalries, of course. He had witnessed would-be sophisticates from the Gulf of Finland coasts of Russia accusing men from the Steppes of being inbreds and the sons of monkeys before having their skulls broken by the latter. He had seen Bostonians slugging it out with men from the Carolinas. In both cases, the baiting and fighting stopped when an officer's whistle blew, or the captain interposed himself between the two sides. But on the gun deck of *Le Zéphyr* that night, the all-too-obviously drunken men of the frigate's crew were entirely ignoring the shrill notes of Payen's whistle while the first lieutenant, a man who surely should have had the authority to stop such rampant indiscipline, instead seemed to be condoning it. Ugarte had given his opinion of Roissel's inaction, but Philippe wondered whether the first officer, a man of low birth, an outspoken Jacobin and *sans-culotte*, had actually absorbed some of the old prejudices of the aristocratic officers of the vanished Marine Royale and thought that physically interposing himself between brawling men was beneath the dignity of a commissioned officer.

Philippe considered for a moment. He could have ordered the Marines forward, of course – he could see de Machault out of the corner of his eye, awaiting his command – but that would only have added another element of conflict and bitter hostility to an already toxic mix. One thing for it, then. Slowly, Philippe began to unbutton his uniform coat.

Ugarte knew at once what was in his captain's mind.

'Ain't proper, sir.'

'Neither's a full-blown riot on one of the Republic's frigates, Enseigne.'

Ugarte nodded.

'Aye, well then.' He began to unbutton his own coat. 'It's a while since I've done this sort of thing, mind. Reckon I've slowed up a lot these last few years.'

The huge Basque grinned. He, unlike Roissel, had served in merchant ships for most of his life, and as Philippe knew from his time sailing with the Gasks in the Atlantic trades, things were done very differently on such vessels.

Philippe pushed his way through the throng of Bretons crowding the after part of the deck. Several men objected to being jostled from behind and turned to confront him, their mouths opening and eyes widening when they saw just who it was.

He reached the front of the crowd, which was growing quieter every moment. Roissel saw him and looked blank, as though unable to comprehend what his captain was doing. Vaquin coloured and looked away as though unable to meet Philippe's eyes. Payen, red-faced from vainly blowing on his whistle, attempted to shout, 'Captain on deck!', the command that would normally bring men to attention, but it came out as little more than an incredulous whisper. The two combatants, entirely oblivious to what was going on around them, continued to tear into each other.

Ugarte, at Philippe's shoulder, bellowed, 'Attention, all hands! Break off, you two!'

The fighting men halted, the scarred, black-haired Parisian in mid-punch. They looked at each other for a moment, then the strapping and hirsute Breton disengaged and ran towards Ugarte, his fists pummelling the Basque's ample chest. The Parisian, howling incoherent obscenities, launched himself at Philippe.

The deck fell entirely silent. Even in the democratic regime of liberty, equality and fraternity, hitting a commissioned officer was a sure-fire road to the firing squad or the gallows, and every man there knew it.

The silence was short-lived. Ugarte gave his assailant a look somewhere between puzzlement and utter contempt, then leaned forward and head-butted the Breton with such force that the man's nose shattered in a radiant corona of blood. He staggered away, his hands clasped to his face and blood streaming through his fingers. The other Bretons gasped.

Philippe barely had time to register the Basque's quick victory before his own attacker was upon him. The Parisian was quick but had no finesse, his fists flailing and his footwork clumsy. Philippe easily weaved out of the way of his first punches and made no attempt to land any blows of his own on the man. The fellow was being egged on by some of the crewmen behind him and launched another attack, this time a little more deliberately but still far too fast, opening his stance too much and putting himself a fraction off balance. Philippe waited until the last possible moment, then ducked low and pushed forward hard, his head and shoulders smashing into the Parisian's torso. Then, using a move that was common to both the Pamunkey and the Cossacks, Philippe brought up his hands to grip his attacker's forearms, drove forward, pushed the man off balance and threw him over his shoulders and back, turning as he did so to slam the Parisian onto the deck. He held the man down, gripping his arms tightly and keeping his knee in the small of his back. Then he looked up at the astonished faces of Roissel, Ugarte, Payen, de Machault, the three *aspirants* and the front ranks of the men in both hostile factions.

'We are one crew,' he shouted. 'One crew, one ship, one France. *Vive la Republique!*'

There were only a few half-hearted response at first, then Ugarte bellowed '*Vive la Republique!*' and both sets of men joined in, Roissel doing so a fraction late.

Payen, looking a little shamefaced, stepped forward to take the fallen Parisian into custody.

'When shall we carry out the punishment, Citizen Captain, and how many lashes do you order?'

'No lashes,' said Philippe. There was a gasp and confused whispers from all quarters of the deck. 'Today has been an exceptional day, Citizen Payen, bringing exceptional news. Terrible news. Heightened passions are understandable. Besides, I think both of these men have suffered more pain tonight than they would from any flogging.' He looked down at the man trapped beneath him. 'What's your name, Citizen?'

'Gaston Mougenot, Citizen Captain. Caulker, from Villennes-sur-Seine.'

The words came out in gasps.

'Gaston Mougenot, eh? Well then, Gaston Mougenot, caulker from Villennes-sur-Seine, I hope you'll abjure assaulting your captain, or *any* senior officer, from now on. Others may not spare you the lash, or even the firing squad.'

'Aye, aye, Citizen Captain.'

Philippe released Mougenot, who scuttled back into the sympathetic but astonished ranks of his messmates. As he rose, Philippe turned and saw Roissel slinking towards the stern ladder and the quarterdeck, Vaquin following in his wake. Ugarte, his hands on his knees, breathing heavily.

'Damn me,' he said. 'Aye, I'm definitely slower than I used to be.'

'Still fast enough to easily defeat your opponent, Enseigne.'

'Silly quarrel anyway,' sniffed Ugarte. 'Bretons, Gascons, Parisians, the lot of them, none can hold a candle to the Basques and the whole world knows that. Begging your pardon, Citizen Captain.'

'Granted, Citizen Ugarte. Granted readily, this once.'

CHAPTER SEVENTEEN

On the command of, '*Lever l'ancre!*' the bower anchor came up, groaning its protest like a dead man being dragged, unwilling, from his grave. Guillaumin blew on his whistle, Roissel bellowed clarifications and additional orders through his voice trumpet, and the *gabiers* responded with brisk cries of '*Commande!*' Headsails, topsails, courses and spritsail were set. Philippe reminded himself once again to set aside the English and Russian names for the individual sails, so familiar to him for so long, in favour of *hunier, perroquet, civadière* and the rest. The wind was largely southerly, veering westerly, and brisk under leaden grey skies. *Le Zéphyr* rode the ebb into the Goulet with Philippe standing impassively in the captain's preserve, the windward side of the quarterdeck, assessing the trim of the sails and the abilities of the men working them. The crew remained seriously short-handed with too few *gabiers* and far too many *matelots d'eau douce*, freshwater sailors or outright landlubbers like Arnaud Lucas, standing in the wrong places, gazing vacantly about them and ignoring orders to carry out tasks they found incomprehensible. It did not matter so much in inshore waters where there were enough experienced men to work the ship, but once they were out in brisk weather in the open sea and the call went out for all hands, God – or His approved republican replacement, Reason – help them. But Philippe knew that no onlooker, especially not the fashionable young ladies promenading on the shore close to the Battery de Leon, would be able to see these deficiencies from a distance. He hoped rather that *Le Zéphyr* was putting on a brave show, a sturdy ship and a valiant crew venturing forth under the Tricolour to fight for the Republic against her countless enemies.

A valiant crew. As far as that went, there had been no repeat of the confrontation between the Bretons and the rest. Even so, he saw a few eyes glancing surreptitiously in his direction, still seemingly unable to comprehend the notion of a captain of the *Marine Nationale* taking part in, and winning, what ashore would have been a common tavern brawl. He heard a few whispers and murmurs from some, chiefly lubbers who had yet to learn the importance of ensuring that any conversations they held were inaudible to the ship's officers. They had expected brutality from Ugarte; the man might be old, but he had obviously been a truly formidable fighter in his younger days and neither age nor fat could entirely take that away. Moreover, he was a Basque and it was a well-known fact that the Basques were all blood-crazed madmen. But that their captain, this *aristo* half-foreigner whose being given command of the ship at all was an incomprehensible mystery – that this oddity should prove to be as brutal a street fighter as any product of the sewers and dosshouses of Brest was entirely beyond all understanding.

Thankfully, there was no sign of English ships. The *rosbifs* often sent sloops or even small frigates right into the mouth of the Goulet, daring a French ship to come out and challenge them, always taking care to stay just out of range of the cannon in the shore batteries on both sides of the channel. They sometimes even kept larger ships, up to and including seventy-fours, on station as an inshore squadron within clear sight of the shore. It was impudent, but there was nothing the French could do to prevent it. With the prevailing wind coming from the south-west, English ships could easily run close inshore, especially on a flood tide when it was more difficult still for any of the ships in the roadstead to beat out to sea to pursue them. Today, though, there were no enemy hulls in sight, although Philippe had no doubt they would be out there somewhere.

Philippe knew that countless Frenchmen detested the English with every breath in their bodies. His half-brother Alexandre was one such, though regardless of Leonore's testimony in court, whether he had actually ever met an Englishman was a moot point. Having witnessed some of the things the British had done in America, Philippe understood that sentiment perfectly. But he could not share it. For one thing, he was half English, his long-dead mother having been a cousin of a peer of King George III's realm. For another, the man he had respected most in the world was John Paul Jones, whom he came to know and admire during the long, frustrating months they had spent at Portsmouth, New Hampshire where Jones was trying and failing to commission America's first ship-of-the-line and the young Vicomte de Saint-Victor was serving as one of his aides. But then, Jones was a Scot who explained to Philippe the difference between Englishmen and Scots in the most forthright terms imaginable. Moreover, the Bretons were descended from the ancient Celts, and his father often said that they, the Welsh and the Cornish could still understand each other's languages. They had been one people, Verité often said, brothers and cousins, the people of King Arthur, the most enduring foes of the English. It was a pleasant dream, but alas, such dreams had no place in war.

The grey cliffs of the Crozon peninsula, off to port, fell away, and Camaret Bay opened up to the south. Guillaumin, the capable old Breton sailing master, set a course that took them well clear of Les Filettes, the Young Girls, the strangely named but deadly rocks that obstructed the Goulet, and pointed out Saint-Mathieu, the ruined abbey and lighthouse upon the headland to the north, which served as superb seamarks for the ships entering and leaving harbour. A dozen or so fishing smacks, on their way back into Brest or the smaller ports upstream, swarmed around *Le Zéphyr*, the crews cheering and waving, before they continued on their way into the anchorage. Then, at last, Philippe and *Le Zéphyr*, her main courses now unreefed, were out into the waters that the Bretons called *Ar Mor Braz*, the huge sea, but which the rest of the world knew as the Atlantic Ocean.

Philippe ordered Guillaumin to set a course for Quiberon, where they would rendezvous with the fleet and see if Morard had newer orders for them, in accordance with the instructions the admiral had given to Philippe before the fleet sailed. Then he turned his attention to the trim of the ship and the thorny question of how to turn this makeshift and obstreperous crew, far too heavy with lubbers for his liking, into a cohort of men who could sail and fight as well as Admiral Howe's crack crews, somewhere out there to the west.

It was quickly clear to him that *Le Zéphyr* sailed well, responding easily to the helm and carrying her press of sail comfortably, although the breeze was strong enough to make topgallants and studdingsails unnecessary. The creaking of the timbers, the familiar sound of every ship afloat, was more a gentle murmuring than the groans of protest he had heard on some of his other ships. France's naval architects and shipbuilders had reputations for designing and building excellent ships, and *Le Zéphyr* seemed to be a prime example of their arts. When they were past the Parquette shoals and crossing Douarnenez Bay, Philippe gave the order to luff up, bringing the head round into the wind as far as she would go. The close-hauled sails and yards squealed in protest, but the bow came further and further round.

'Try her a little further yet, Enseigne Fingal,' he said to the officer of the watch.

'Aye, aye, Citizen Captain!'

Closer... closer still... then, when Philippe judged she was as close to the wind as she could get without going into irons, he gave the order to bear away one point. Not bad at all, he reckoned. They had got close to three points off the wind, much better than the sluggish old *Strela* had ever managed, but the Russians had only the sketchiest notion of the importance of keeping their ships' bottoms clean. *Le Zéphyr*, though, had been careened recently, and it showed. Set against that was the competence of the crew. Even such a simple order as 'Hands to the braces!' generated dozens of blank faces and a shambolic shuffle.

By midday they were approaching the Pointe du Raz, the headland at the end of the peninsula that formed the southern arm of Douarnenez Bay. Off to starboard was the low shape of the Île de Sein, where King Arthur was taken after the fatal battle of Camlann; or so Philippe's father had claimed in one of his many books. The island marked the western limit of the Passage du Raz, the channel that provided a shortcut between Brest and the Bay of Biscay without them having to make a long rounding of the Chaussée de Sein, the vast platform of rock that extended west from the island for many miles. It being almost noon, Philippe made quite a show of having his navigational instruments brought up from his cabin, and had the three *aspirants* fall in around him to make their own noonday observations. He was particularly proud of his sextant, one of the new ones that incorporated a Vernier scale and which he had acquired at considerable expense in Saint Petersburg. He explained its mysteries to the three young men before him: Carabignac eager, Lievremont earnest, Vaquin terrified of something infinitely more difficult than waving his sword and looking gallant.

Objectively, there was no need whatsoever for such a ritual in that place and at that time. Guillaumin had been sailing these waters since he was a babe in arms, and probably knew their location to the very *pouce*. But it was a ritual undertaken by the captain of every ship at sea in the world at noon every day. Omitting it risked a reckoning with the gods and demons of the vasty deep (which many sailors believed in implicitly, no matter how loudly they proclaimed themselves to be good atheist republicans) and, more immediately, with the clerks at the Ministry of Marine who checked every logbook to see that each captain was complying with his instructions. Philippe also had a purpose of his own in making a show of the familiar rites of the observations of the sun, taking bearings on the visible seamarks, and checking the tide and latitude tables. He was unknown to the *aspirants*, to his officers and men, and indeed to France itself. He had to demonstrate very quickly that he was competent to command this trim man-of-war for the Republic. He had in mind Saint-André's words, which made it more or less clear that France was so desperate to find qualified and experienced men to command its ships that it was prepared even to employ him, an *aristo* and an unknown half-foreigner to boot. But he had no doubt that if he was found wanting, or if the crew of *Le Zéphyr* denounced him and sent him to the guillotine as they had with their previous captain, the ingenious Citizen Saint-André would scrape the few remaining dregs at the bottom of the barrel and find someone else to replace him. Perhaps he might even promote Lieutenant de Vaisseau Martin Roissel.

Philippe checked the *aspirants'* calculations. Carabignac surprised him; the mouse might be silent, clearly still resenting being at sea at all and having to undertake self-evidently pointless tasks like this one, but his numbers matched Philippe's own almost exactly.

'Well done, Citizen Aspirant,' said Philippe.

The boy brightened.

'*Merci*, Citizen Captain. I've always had a way with numbers. The old priest who taught me said I could be a new Descartes if I apply myself.'

Vaquin snorted in derision. Philippe fixed him with a fierce stare which abashed even the proud, confident youth, and as punishment he examined Vaquin's navigational workbook next. He frowned, then took Lievremont's book and compared the two. The figures produced by the two youths were very similar, suspiciously so in fact. Philippe had watched them go about their observations and knew at once that Vaquin was copying whatever Lievremont recorded. Well, much good it had done him.

'Why, Citizens,' said Philippe loudly enough for the others on the quarterdeck to hear him, 'who says a republic of reason can't have miracles, eh?'

The two *aspirants* looked at each other, aware that the eyes of every man on the deck were on them. Roissel was scowling, although that was more likely to be in response to his captain's levity.

'Now, let us see,' said Philippe, peering at the two workbooks as if he were remarkably short-sighted. 'Why yes, both of you have decisively established our position as being somewhere due east of Vienna, in the vicinity of Pressburg! I congratulate you, Citizens, but alas, we'll now have to deal with the Austrian emperor's armies as well as the English navy!'

Guillaumin, Fingal, the two helmsmen on the wheel and the master's mates roared with laughter. Even Roissel, standing a little apart, smiled. Lievremont blushed. Vaquin, though, was unable to conceal his fury, and Philippe knew he had made another enemy.

'Sail ho! Broad on the starboard beam!'

The cry from the lookout in the mainmast crow's nest quashed the laughter at once. Philippe raised his telescope to look out to the west, the direction the lookout was pointing.

Yes, there was a sail, hull down on the horizon. Too far out to be a stray coaster heading for Brest, which would have taken this more inshore passage. Too far north to be an Atlantic trader bound for Nantes, too far south to be a big merchantman heading up *La Manche*. There was a chance she was a fellow frigate out of Brest – three were meant to be at sea when Philippe took command of *Le Zéphyr*, although they and a couple of others out of Lorient and Rochefort were entrusted with patrolling the coast and escorting convoys all the way from Calais to Biarritz, so it was probably unlikely to be one of those. That left the probability that she was one of the scouts for the English fleet, lying somewhere beyond the horizon.

Philippe kept his telescope fixed on the distant sail, but it came no closer. Instead, after half an hour or so in sight, it disappeared from view – probably gone to report to Black Dick Howe that another French frigate had come out of Brest and was sailing south.

Damn them. The day would surely come when Morard would take the fleet out and drive the English off France's coast once and for all.

He laid the impossible thought to one side, but it was raised again at dinner in the great cabin an hour later while the ship idled, awaiting slack water in the Passage du Raz – the only state of the tide that allowed ships to pass through it safely. Ugarte had the watch on deck with Guillaumin, so Philippe dined with Roissel, Fingal, de Machault the lieutenant of Marines, and the young *aspirants*, whose nautical education embraced such essential etiquette as knowing which fork to use for which course and not farting when the captain toasted the success of the Republic. Driaux and two eager *mousses* served at table discreetly but, in the case of the boys, with little discernible skill. The fare provided by the cook Croguennec was simple but adequate: beef, cheese and fresh vegetables, washed down with a rough but acceptable claret.

Fingal, who was a bright-eyed and enthusiastic young man, was holding forth on the damnable impudence of the *rosbifs* in lording it over France's coast and bemoaning the Brest fleet's relative inactivity. Philippe thought he might have taken a little too much wine; even implicit criticism of the Republic's rulers could be interpreted as counter-revolutionary, if not worse. His time in the cells of Brest's citadel had taught him greater caution, or so he liked to believe.

Unexpectedly, though, Roissel agreed with the younger lieutenant.

'No matter how many ships the Republic builds,' said Roissel, 'the English are always able to build more, and build them more quickly, too. They've a bigger navy in peacetime and have far more merchant ships than we do, so they'll always have more experienced men.'

'Then what is the point of it all, Citizen Roissel?' said Fingal animatedly. 'Why do we not just lay up the entire navy and send all the men to the army?'

Philippe half-raised his hand, but Roissel was chewing on a particularly tough piece of the cook's roast beef, so Philippe answered in his place.

'The navy defends France by merely existing,' he said. 'While we have a fleet at Brest, Pitt and Howe and the rest of them will think twice about landing an army on our coast. And just because we're the smaller force and will always be so doesn't mean we sit at anchor and dare them to come. Our best chance is to do what the Americans did – to be guileful and sting the mighty Royal Navy whenever and wherever we can. I never once encountered a British warship in the American war when we had the superior force. But handle a smaller ship well, or mass as many ships as possible where the enemy least expects it, and the lesser navy can more than hold its own.'

Fingal weighed the answer carefully, then nodded gravely. Vaquin seemed to want to say something, no doubt to make a protest about the inglorious nature of such a strategy, but with a degree of insight that was evidently rare for him, he thought better of it and kept his mouth shut. The brief silence was broken by an unexpected and ominous change of tack from Philippe's second-in-command.

'Do you still consider yourself to be American, then, Citizen Captain?' said Roissel, taking advantage of the relaxation of deference traditionally permitted when officers talked informally. Fingal, de Machault and the *aspirants* turned to see Philippe's reaction, while Driaux's normally imperturbable features creased.

'I never did. I was brought up as a Frenchman and have always regarded myself as such. I fought for America, but so did many: Lafayette, La Rouërie, all the others. So when I heard that France was at war, I knew where my duty lay.'

It had not been as simple as that, of course, but he saw no reason why the supercilious Roissel should know that Philippe learned of the declaration of war three days after the funeral of Tasha and Ivan. The coincidence of the two events made him forsake the sea of vodka in which he was trying to drown himself and begin to make plans for going to France, the fatherland he had never known.

'Lafayette and La Rouërie, you say, Citizen Captain?' said Roissel. 'Both *aristos*, no? Marquises, in fact. Both traitors to the revolution.'

'Your point being, Lieutenant?'

Roissel smiled thinly. 'Merely that this is a new age, and men's former affiliations are no guide to their loyalty to the cause of liberty. And, begging your pardon, Citizen Captain, who a man's father was is no guarantee of his own beliefs.'

Roissel's expression was smug, and the others seated at the table seemed astonished at what could be taken for an affront to their captain's honour. But Philippe had no desire for a confrontation with his first lieutenant, not yet, at any rate. He had no doubt there would be one in due course – the information that Olivier and Roman had conveyed to him when they finally caught up with him after Alexandre's trial made that certain – but Philippe needed more time to gauge the man properly, to take the measure of his other officers, and to be certain of the loyalties of the crew.

Unexpectedly, it was young Lievremont who defused the tension.

'What was it like, sir?' he asked. 'The American war, I mean.'

Philippe recalled that the young man's father had died in that war, as indeed had his own.

'Bloody, as all wars are,' he said carefully. 'There's an old saying that civil wars are the bloodiest of all, and that's what it was, whatever President Washington and the rest of them say nowadays. The French and the English knew the laws of war and more or less stuck to them, but plenty of the Americans on both sides saw it as a chance to settle old scores. Some of them even recruited the Indians, who have ways of killing a man that aren't best recounted if we all want to keep our food down.'

Lievremont's eyes widened.

'Have you met any Indians, Citizen Captain? Did you learn wrestling from them?'

Philippe reflected upon his answer. This part of his life seemed so very long ago, and yet he recalled it so vividly. But how much of it to reveal in this company of men he barely knew?

'I spent much time among the Pamunkey, long ago, when I was a little younger than you, Aspirant. They're a tribe of Virginia. People in France and Russia and all our civilised countries see them as primitives, no better than cavemen. But the Pamunkey are part of the Powhatan, a great nation of many tribes. They have laws and customs, as do we. They love and laugh, live and die. We could learn much from them – about medicine, about caring for each other, about respect for their elders, about caring for the land they inhabit instead of exploiting it. And, yes, about how to fight, too.'

Roissel, who seemed either not to register what his captain was saying or chose to ignore it, finished chewing his piece of beef.

'Savages, surely? Beneath the notice of a man of your birth, I'd have thought – begging your pardon, Citizen Captain.'

Driaux refilled Philippe's glass, which gave him a moment in which he could consider his answer. He remembered Opechancanough, whom he had once called friend and from whom he had learned so much, and Matoaka, the playful, mocking girl-woman who had been his first lover. He could not reveal such memories. Roissel would probably consider them grounds for sending him to the guillotine.

'Different, certainly. Primitive in many ways, indeed. But the way I see it, Lieutenant, every nation has its savages.' He thought of the guillotine at Saint-Malo and the sight of Tasha's body, butchered by her own brother. 'Individual men become savage for many reasons – power, revenge, money, lust – wouldn't you say so, Lieutenant? But entire peoples only become savages if others make them so. The Indians of Virginia are the most peaceable folk I've ever known, but do them an injustice and they will defend themselves... savagely.'

'Just like France against all our enemies,' said Lievremont.

Roissel looked utterly astonished.

'You dare to compare the Republic to naked primitives? Be careful, Aspirant!'

'Lievremont is correct,' said Philippe. 'We regard ourselves as civilised, but we often behave in the same way as those we call uncivilised. Surely history teaches us that it has always been so.'

'But, Citizen Captain,' said Roissel complacently, 'the Republic has come into being to write a new history. To create a new and higher level of civilisation, founded on liberty, equality and fraternity. Once we've fought off the foreign tyrants and dealt with those inside France who still cling to the old lies, we'll have a new age of peace where all those violent passions you listed will simply wither away. There'll be money for all, the people will have the power, and no man will seek vengeance on any other.'

Philippe raised his glass to his lips and took a sip of his wine. They were fine sentiments – the sort of sentiments that adorned so many of the pages written by his father, in fact – and he knew he should agree with them, but he thought of Tasha and knew if her murderous brother, Count Bulgakov, ever crossed his path again, then no power on earth would stop Philippe from exacting his vengeance on him. But Bulgakov remained well within the borders of the nearly endless Russian empire, very far from the retribution he deserved. With that thought in his mind, Philippe's reply to Roissel was sharper than it should have been.

'And lust, Citizen Roissel? Will the Republic do away with lust, too?'

Roissel made no answer. Lievremont, unaware of the tension in the cabin, asked Philippe more questions about the lives of the Indians. The rest of the dinner passed amiably enough, but only the captain of *Le Zéphyr* noticed the uncharacteristic silence of his first officer.

CHAPTER EIGHTEEN

Leonore packed for Paris with a heavy heart. Once, it would have been inconceivable that the chatelaine of any estate in France, even one as impoverished as Brechelean, should do her own packing; there were maids, footmen and goodness knows who else available to do such menial tasks. But those days were gone, and although old Martha Penhouet still hovered in the corner of the room, occasionally bringing Leonore a kerchief or a fan and advising on which items to pack in which order, the housekeeper's arthritic fingers and bad back ruled out any active involvement in preparing her mistress for such a long journey. Leonore knew it would probably be a wasted one, too. Alexandre was one of many traitors to the Republic, justly condemned and awaiting their fates, so what chance was there that he would be treated differently? What, in any case, did she expect to achieve in Paris? A pardon? That was surely impossible. The forgiveness of the man she had once loved, and who had once loved her? Almost as unlikely. An explanation of his reason for not questioning her in court, potentially exposing the flaws in her evidence? Perhaps. No matter how she weighed it all, though, it was her testimony that had brought him to this. And if by some miracle he was pardoned and returned once again to his position as master of Brechelean, what would that mean for her life? For Philippe's life, too. So perhaps, when all was said and done, the only realistic outcome was that she should be present at his execution, just one face that he knew and had once loved among the crowd. Whether he would welcome her presence was another matter, but that could not be helped now. She was set on going to Paris, and that was an end to it.

She was aware of old Jacques Penhouet shuffling through the door behind her, and turned to face him as he nodded an acknowledgement to his wife.

'Begging pardon, *madame*,' he said, 'there are two boys at the gate, insisting that they speak with you.'

'Boys? What sort of boys?'

'Dirty and ill-dressed, *madame*. Boys from the street, I'd say.'

'Egyptian tinkers, do you think?'

There had been a plague of those mysterious people in Brittany in the last couple of years, as though their wandering breed had finally reached the end of the earth and now had nowhere else to go. Persecuting them and driving them out was one of the few subjects upon which the most ardent Chouans and *sans-culottes* could agree.

'Possibly, *madame*. But—'

'Then get rid of them, Jacques. Threaten them with one of the guns if you have to.'

'But, *madame*, they say they've been sent by the vicomte. They showed me an envelope which they say contains a note from him to you.'

Leonore bridled. She would send these impudent little devils packing, just as soon as she had exposed the supposed note from Philippe for the forgery it was bound to be. She stormed down the corridor, leaving the ageing Jacques Penhouet trailing far behind her, all but ran down the stairs and made her way across the hall, out of the main door of the south wing and across to the gate. She had a sudden and unbidden memory of her first encounter with Philippe in exactly the same place.

She was confronted by two odiferous children, one tall with striking red hair, the other short, squat and dark.

'Be off with you!' said Leonore harshly. 'I've told the steward to fetch a gun.'

The short boy thrust an envelope towards her.

'He told us to give you this, Citizeness.'

The youth was unexpectedly well mannered and well spoken. But the idea that the Vicomte de Saint-Victor would have had any dealings with the likes of these… Nevertheless, she took the envelope and tore it open.

It was Philippe's handwriting and signature, there was no doubt of it. She had seen them often enough during the weeks he was at Brechelean.

Leonore,

I send you these two orphan boys in the hope that you will take them into the service of the estate, as is my wish. They may be poor lads who have begged for their bread, but that condition is no fault of their own. I believe them to be honest, and they have done me what may prove to be a great service entirely of their own volition, with no expectation of immediate reward. You and the Penhouets may train them into good workers, for the chateau certainly needs young, vigorous hands to tend it, and it's not fitting that you should do so much menial work yourself. Their names are Roman – he is the short one – and Olivier. I confess I have no idea what their surnames are.

With my respects, I remain your most affectionate brother and friend,

Philippe

Your most affectionate brother and friend. But then, what else could he write... what else was he to her?

The two boys before her were a rather more immediate concern. If it were her choice, she would have nothing to do with such doubtful-looking creatures, even though there was a certain keenness in their eyes. But the note was effectively the written order of the vicomte de Saint-Victor, owner of the chateau and estate of Brechelean, and how could she possibly deny his command? And there was an undoubted need for more vigorous hands. So as long as these two could somehow avoid the insatiable demands of the army for more and more men...

She turned to Jacques Penhouet, who had finally caught up with her.

'Jacques, these two boys are to be employed as servants of the estate by the vicomte's order. Take them to the servants' hall, get them washed and into clean clothes, find them beds and give them a meal, then start allocating duties for them. I will talk to them later.'

The old man looked as though he had been commanded to personally guillotine his wife, but no matter what the Republic might proclaim, he had been too good a servant for too long to argue with his betters. He led the boys away, both of them grinning like a Pierrot who'd caught his Columbine, and Leonore returned to her preparations for Paris.

–

The tide began to flood through the Passage du Raz, and Guillaumin, with his long experience of the local waters, conned the ship through it with no alarms. Philippe, up on deck following dinner, took in the sights around him, trying to imprint every element on his mind. If he prospered in the Republic's service and commanded more men-of-war flying the Tricolour then he would come to know these waters intimately. He knew from the charts and from Guillaumin's commentary that off to starboard lay Île de Sein, a low island that marked the easternmost extremity of the Chausée de Sein, the vast shelf of rock that extended far out to sea. Ships going south, as they were now, used the Passage du Raz to avoid the long rounding that would otherwise face them, even though winds and tides often combined to make the passage a perilous course to steer. Off to port and no more than half a mile away, waves broke upon the jagged cliffs of the Pointe du Raz and its detached fingers of rock that further narrowed the channel. Small chapels and shrines dotted the clifftops, giving the impression that no revolution had taken place in France. Behind them, smoke rose from the chimneys of the villages that lay just inland.

Carabignac, of all men, was the first to notice the troops. He pointed to a headland just to the east of the Pointe du Raz itself, and Philippe trained his telescope on the band of men. Four, perhaps five hundred, he thought. He could make out individuals and the strange assortment of costumes they wore.

'Local militia, probably,' said Guillaumin.

'Not army or National Guard, for certain,' said Ugarte.

Philippe could see the troops gesticulating at the distant *Le Zéphyr*. They were raising a banner, and he recognised the familiar sight of the sacred red heart upon a white ground.

'Chouans,' said Philippe. 'Impudent, I'll give them that.'

He sent for Garrigues, and the master gunner duly presented himself and saluted.

'We'll exercise the guns when we're clear of the Passage du Raz,' said Philippe. 'It'll be a show for the rebels, and I want to get a sense of our rate of fire.'

'With respect, Captain, it might not be the sort of show you'll applaud. The gun crews are very raw. We practised running out the guns and bringing 'em back inboard when we were anchored in the Rade, of course, and I alternated the watches firing salutes to give 'em a bit of experience, but they've never fired a broadside.'

'Then it's time they did so, Master Gunner, wouldn't you say?'

'Aye, aye, sir.'

Vaquin, who had been listening to the conversation, addressed Philippe.

'Begging your pardon, Citizen Captain, but shouldn't we fire on those fellows? With the number of guns we carry, we can surely wipe out dozens of them!'

'A noble sentiment which does you credit, Aspirant Vaquin,' said Philippe. 'But observe that the rebels are very high up and a fair distance away. Probably at the limit of our range, in fact, if not just beyond it. No gun of ours can be elevated enough to hit anything more than some seabird nests halfway up the cliff.'

Lievremont was trying and failing to suppress a smile, Ugarte shaking his head contemptuously. But Philippe realised immediately that perhaps he should not have been so dismissive of Vaquin's scheme. Yes, they would only hit the cliff, but at least the wall of rock would present *Le Zéphyr*'s gunners with some sort of target. More importantly, though, it would unsettle the Chouans, few or none of whom would have any idea of the capabilities of naval ordnance. Ideally, it would drive them and their damn flag off the headland entirely.

'But now I think on it, there's some merit in what you say, Citizen Vaquin. Very well. Take new orders to Citizen Garrigues. Run out the port battery, guns to maximum elevation! Bosun! Call the men to their quarters, port watch first! On my command, fire in sequence, bow to stern!'

The ship's bell rang, Payen blew his whistle vigorously, and men formed their gun crews along the port side. The gunport lids were pulled open. The gun captains adjusted the elevation. Shot and wadding were rammed home. Men hauled on tackle to run the guns out. The gun captains readied their lighted linstocks.

The reports were bellowed back to the quarterdeck – 'Ready! Ready! Ready!'

Philippe was aware of men's eyes on him, awaiting his command. He looked once more towards the distant rebels, nodded slightly to himself, and turned back to give the order. He placed his hat on his head, the signal for firing, but also called out the command so there would be no misunderstanding.

'*Feu!*' Fire!

Flames erupted from the mouths of the gun barrels. The cannon recoiled, making the entire ship shake. Even with the breeze from the north-west, smoke momentarily shrouded the entire ship like a sudden fog.

Ragged. Very ragged. Guns fired at erratic intervals. Guns fired out of sequence. A report came up from the gun deck that one of the twelve-pounders had somehow jammed. Philippe had witnessed only one worse broadside in his life, and that was when *Yedinstvo* fired on an Ottoman frigate off Ochakov. Captain Antonov had raged at his men, going puce in the face, stamping his feet on the quarterdeck and bellowing abuse at Philippe, his first lieutenant. The day was saved, but only because the Turks proved to be even worse gunners than the Russians. Philippe doubted whether Black Dick Howe's fleet contained any crew who would be as magnanimously inept. But even gun crews of blind men could hardly miss a Breton cliff, and the fall of shot onto the rockface had the desired effect. The Chouans turned tail and ran for cover further inland, little realising that they were more likely to sustain hurt by falling over their own feet than from the broadside of *Le Zéphyr*.

After firing two rounds per gun, Philippe declared himself satisfied and sent for Garrigues.

'A fine showing for beginners, Master Gunner,' Philippe lied; but he had vowed during Antonov's rant that he would never berate a crew of his own in the same way. Garrigues' expression suggested that the lie was recognised, and its concealment appreciated.

Philippe turned to Carabignac.

'Aspirant, convey my order to the steward and cook – an extra ration of wine for the men of the port battery.'

'Aye, aye, Citizen Captain!'

–

Le Zéphyr had left the Île de Groix and Lorient behind her. Several miles off the starboard bow lay Belle-Île, with the low land in the east of the island rising steadily to the much higher terrain in the west.

Philippe knew the British had seized the island and held it for some years in the great war thirty years earlier, just before he was born, and it was undoubtedly the sort of place they might seek to secure as a base from which to harry the coast and aid the royalist rebels; deterring such an attack was one of the reasons Morard had brought the fleet down into these waters. To the north-east of the island, and thus much closer to Philippe's ship, the long, low peninsula of Quiberon stretched out into the Atlantic as though trying to reach across Teigneuse Passage and touch Belle-Île. Behind it, in the bay in its lee, the mastheads of Morard's fleet were plainly visible. But as he trained his telescope on the distant shapes, Philippe felt the hairs on his neck prickle.

Something was wrong. Badly wrong.

He expected to see the Tricolours and the assortment of signal flags. But there was another flag too, one which should not have been flying from a French fleet. They drew nearer to the anchorage, and finally when *Le Zéphyr* swung round to make her own entry into the bay, this flag became more prominent. It flew from the maintopmasts of over half the ships in the fleet, plain red with no cantons or emblems at all. It even flew from the flagship *Le Terrible*, there in the middle of the anchorage. It was a flag whose meaning was well understood the whole world over. Philippe had last seen it flying from *Pobeda* off Izmail, when poor Terekhov and most of his officers were hacked to pieces by their crew.

The red flag was the universal banner of revolt.

CHAPTER NINETEEN

It was an utter catastrophe. The Toulon fleet was already gone and now the Brest fleet had mutinied. France had no navy, and her coasts lay wide open to the enemy.

For two days, *Le Zéphyr* lay slightly apart from the rest of the fleet in the Quiberon roadstead. She was the newest arrival, so Morard's order for Philippe to anchor her at the outer edge of the fleet made sense, but he also hoped that being a little removed from the main body of ships and men might make it less likely for the mutinous spirit to infect the men of *Le Zéphyr*. It was soon apparent, though, that this was an utterly forlorn hope. Boats went from ship to ship carrying messages and transferring stores. The frigate was also within easy hailing distance of a number of the other outermost ships, and these included several that were flying the red flag. The nearest was *Le Revolution*, a seventy-four whose crew seemed determined to live up to her name and were particularly vocal. Even below decks on *Le Zéphyr*, it was still sometimes possible to hear the shouts from across the water. These set out the demands of the mutineers throughout the fleet and invited *Le Zéphyr* to join them.

Of course, it had all been triggered by news of the loss of Toulon. Men took it into their heads that Brest, too, would fall to the enemy if the fleet did not return there at once to protect it. Rumours were sweeping through the ships at Quiberon: a combined counter-revolutionary army of the Chouans and the Vendée was besieging Brest, flying the white flag of the monarchy alongside the Sacred Heart banner; the English had landed a great army in Camaret Bay and taken the town without a shot being fired, and so forth. True, the fleet was also short of supplies and ravaged by illness, the crews badly clothed and unpaid, but those were the everyday conditions of French fleets from the beginning of time. No, for now Brest was the only topic of conversation throughout the fleet, from the lowliest mess table to Admiral Morard's state cabin. Even on *Le Zéphyr*, which had been in Brest most recently and whose crew knew that it was still in loyal hands when they sailed, the whispers and rumours spread as easily as rats in the bilges.

Philippe, convinced that the only way of ensuring the loyalty of *Le Zéphyr* was to get her back to sea as soon as possible, sent several notes to *Le Terrible* requesting to see Morard, but there was no reply to any of them. Admittedly, the admiral had much to occupy him. He had been forced to convene a council of representatives from the lower decks of every ship, and this, unsurprisingly, was deaf to Morard's requests for the fleet to return to its obedience pending new orders from Paris. It soon became apparent that some ships were more obstreperous than others. About half of the hulls under Morard's command were flying the red flag, the rest flew only the Tricolour, but the former included the largest units and the latter more of the frigates. Tensions between the two groups were high. The loyal *Jean Bart*, moored close to *Le Zéphyr*, even had her guns run out, seemingly trained on the mutinous *La Convention*. The crews of the one could be heard shouting across the water to the other, denouncing their erstwhile colleagues as traitors to the Republic. It would take one false word, one misinterpreted action, one trigger-happy sentry, and the fleet would be at war with itself, just as had happened at Toulon.

Philippe's nightmare became real in the morning of the second full day in the Quiberon anchorage. A Marine knocked on his cabin door to inform him that Lieutenant de Machault believed he should come on deck at once. Donning his uniform jacket and sword, Philippe went above to see that a large deputation of forty or fifty men had formed just forward of the quarterdeck, and were being joined by more men all the time. The line of Marines stood firm across the breadth of the ship, preventing the men from rushing aft. Most of *Le Zéphyr's* commissioned and warrant officers and a dozen or so mates and the like stood behind the Marines. Several, like Lievremont and steward Saint-Jacques, looked as though they were about to soil themselves. Ugarte, though, was red-faced with rage and seemed to want to smash a few heads together. Roissel stood a little way apart, inscrutable.

Philippe stepped forward, parted two of the Marines and stood at the quarterdeck breastwork, by the ship's bell. He was facing the mob, which thronged the gangways on either side of the boat well and the fo'c'sle beyond. Philippe's surprise at the identity of this potential ringleader of mutiny did not last. In truth, it was no surprise at all that the man at the head of the delegation should be not a man at all but a mere boy, *Aspirant* Fabian Vaquin. A lawyer's son. Who else could it be when all was said and done?

'Citizen Vaquin,' said Philippe, 'so you're the fellow who seeks to deprive me of the command of *Le Zéphyr*.'

Did Vaquin's eyes betray a flicker of doubt? Philippe thought they might. But the youth quickly collected himself.

'Not so, Citizen Captain,' he said. 'We seek merely to persuade you of your duty.'

'I see. And what is my duty, Citizen Vaquin?'

'Your duty to the revolution, sir. Your duty to the Republic. Your duty to France.'

Philippe tried to keep a straight face. Vaquin was so full of youthful self-importance, drawing strength from the mob behind him. But he should not be underestimated. Philippe had learned that several *aspirants* were among the ringleaders of the mutiny in the main fleet, and in some respects it was hardly surprising. They had the fiery certainty and idealistic zeal of youth – Vaquin certainly had plenty of both – but were also educated, literate and could construct coherent arguments, conditions that applied to very few of those on the lower decks.

Philippe looked at Vaquin levelly. Yes, he was the son of a lawyer all right, making the rhetorical equivalent of going from Paris to Versailles by way of Bordeaux.

'I say again, what *exactly* might that duty be?'

'To go back to Brest with the fleet. We can't allow it to fall as Toulon did, Citizen Captain.'

There were nods and cries of concurrence behind Vaquin, but Philippe could see that the mob was perhaps not quite the united whole it had first seemed. Most of Vaquin's support seemed to lie in the first two or three ranks of men and included several characters whom Philippe had already marked down as troublemakers, the likes of Pierric Korbell. The rear ranks and the men coming up from below to join the rear of the deputation had less certain expressions and were largely silent. Most seemed no more than curious, waiting to see what would happen.

'Well, Aspirant, that's a worthy sentiment. Indeed it is. And I agree with it. I, too, want to keep Brest safe, to prevent another Toulon.'

The answer confused Vaquin, who seemed to be looking over Philippe's shoulder as if in search of reassurance from someone behind the captain.

'But a captain also has a duty to comply with his orders. And until new orders come from the admiral or from Paris, I have no authority to sail this ship back to Brest.'

Vaquin straightened. 'You have the authority of the people, Citizen Captain. The authority given to you by the crew of *Le Zéphyr*. It was the authority of the people that stormed the Bastille, that dragged Louis Capet back from Varennes and sent him to the guillotine. And it is the authority of the people that speaks from the *sans-culotte* crews of this fleet, from this very ship. We must save Brest, sir, and if you will not sail the ship there, then we want a captain who will.'

Once again Vaquin glanced quickly and nervously behind Philippe, and it was now obvious whose eyes he sought. There were genuine mutineers in the crew, and Fabian Vaquin probably believed the words he was declaiming. But the real instigator of all this was surely Lieutenant de Vaisseau Martin Roissel.

Philippe took too long to respond for the liking of those immediately behind Vaquin, who began to press forward. The Marines behind Philippe tightened their grips on the muskets. Out of the corner of his eye he could see de Machault awaiting his orders, although he had no doubt the young Marine officer would use his own initiative if no command came from his captain. That initiative would mean levelled muskets and a bloodbath.

Philippe looked again at the men behind Vaquin. Several waverers seemed to be persuaded by the *aspirant*'s words, while others were murmuring amongst themselves. Several were pointing to the red flag flying from *Le Convention*, and behind her, from the flagship *Le Terrible* itself. The stakes were high, and Philippe had only one roll of the dice left.

'Yes, look around you,' said Philippe, loudly enough to be heard in the rear ranks. 'What do you see? There lies the Atlantic fleet of France, Citizens. The *only* fleet of France after what happened at Toulon. Do you think the enemy doesn't know this? There'll be Chouan agents ashore, over there in Quiberon. The reports will be on Admiral Howe's desk at this very moment. Yes, he might do what you fear and attack Brest while our fleet lies here. But Brest has mighty batteries, strong walls and a stout citadel. It has a large garrison. Brest can withstand a siege from the English for weeks, if not months. Howe will know this. But he also knows our fleet lies here, in a crowded anchorage on a lee shore. A very tempting target, *mes amis*. All that lies between him and the destruction of all the fine ships at anchor over there is having some of our frigates at sea to provide intelligence of his approach. So yes, you can demand that we go back to Brest with all the rest of the fleet, but look at the size of *Le Zéphyr* compared to the rest of them – to *Bretagne, Juste, Côte-d'Or, Terrible*. We would be just a pinprick against the English if they came through the Goulet, but out there at sea, sailing large and alone, we can be what this ship was designed to be: the eyes and ears of the fleet. Yes, *mes amis*, the eyes and ears of France itself!'

'You talk of France?' cried a swarthy, ugly fellow in the throng on the starboard side, his accent the broadest Breton. 'You're not even French! You're an *aristo*, too! We should string you from the yardarm, I say, then sail the ship back to Brest with the rest of the fleet!'

There were at least a half-dozen shouts of approval for that, and rather more heads nodding in agreement. Philippe saw Roissel, standing to his left and slightly behind him, smile faintly to himself.

In normal times, and in a normal navy, such indiscipline and downright insolence, if it occurred at all, would be punished immediately and sharply. But in the French navy of 1793, in a republic forged in revolution and proclaiming the ideals of liberty, equality and fraternity, every man, no matter how lowly, had the right to speak his mind without fear. Or at least, he thought he did. Such men expected frankness from those who sought to lead them. Well, then, thought Philippe – time to be frank.

'It's true I was born an *aristo* and far from France,' said Philippe, raising his hand in an attempt to quieten the prospective mutineers. 'I had no say in either of those conditions. But I took up arms in the cause of liberty when I was thirteen years old. My father was arguing for a republic long before I was born, and suffered exile for it at the hands of the Capets. That was why I didn't come to France when the American war ended. I wouldn't serve a monarchy that I believed to be evil, a monarchy that had treated my father so shamefully. So in time I went to Russia, and when my service there ended, I could have gone anywhere – offered my services to any navy. The Swedes wanted me to take their commission. The Danes made me an offer. And yes, I could have gone back to America, gone back to commanding merchant ships, made far more money than I would ever make from serving any navy on earth. But I chose to come to France, fellow citizens. I chose the Republic. I chose the revolution. You could string me up from the yardarm, my last words will still be *Vive la Republique! Vive la liberte!* You can do that, or you can choose to follow my orders and those the admiral has given us. You can choose to put to sea and fight for France.'

Philippe waited for a response, but there was none. The wind shook the shrouds; the gulls on the yardarms cackled; the tide lapped against the hull, but no man in the crew of *Le Zéphyr* said a word.

Vaquin, still at the head of the mob, was silent and seemed to be shaking slightly. Philippe glanced behind him and saw that Roissel was tense, his hands curled into fists so tightly clenched that they had to be causing him pain. If the first lieutenant was going to formally denounce his captain and order his arrest, this had to be the moment. Philippe had said all he could. The crew knew Roissel better. He had come up from the ranks, he had been one of them. They were bound to side with him...

'*Vive le Capitaine Kermorvant! Hourra! Hourra! Hourra!*'

It was Garrigues. The gunner waved his arms to encourage a response, and enough men joined the shout to make it plain that they were in the majority. There were a few hostile shouts, and a couple of men squared up to each other, but the men on the fo'c's'le, at the back of the crowd, were already beginning to disperse. Vaquin looked around, perhaps hoping to rally the men behind him, but even some of the diehards were starting to drift away. Philippe turned, noting as he did so that Lieutenant Roissel was staring blankly into space.

–

It was a victory, but only a very small one, and it might well prove to be short-lived. The atmosphere aboard *Le Zéphyr* continued to be tense. Roissel did not appear at dinner in the great cabin, pleading a headache. There was jostling and raised voices between some of de Machault's

Marines and a few of the more discontented hands. But Ugarte and Garrigues, the officers whom the men seemed to respect most, were tireless in their perambulations around the messes, settling arguments, quietening troublemakers and slowly damping down the flames of mutiny. The situation in the rest of the fleet remained volatile, though, with Morard continuing to insist on the need to wait for fresh instructions from Paris. Another of the Committee of Public Safety's *représentants en mission* was said to be on his way, but there was no sign of him. Philippe needed to get the ship back to sea, away from the corrupting influences in the fleet, but no fresh orders came from *Le Terrible* until early in the evening, when a boat from the flagship came alongside bearing a packet for Philippe from the admiral.

He went to his cabin, dismissed the over-attentive Driaux, sat down heavily on his sea-bed and opened the new orders. *Le Zéphyr* was being diverted temporarily from her original orders to patrol the coast, and instead was to sail to the latitude of forty-six and there cruise between five and seven degrees west of the Paris meridian. The ship was to maintain this station for ten days, from the twenty-sixth of September to the fifth of October, as that was the designated rendezvous for two East Indiamen which were known to have made landfall in the Azores and were bound for Nantes. Philippe thought this likely to be a hunt for a needle in a haystack, as the English said, and that was before one considered the realities of the situation in which France found itself. To get home, the Indiamen would have to sail through seas filled with ships belonging to enemies of the Republic. France was at war with Portugal, so presumably the Indiamen must have found an anchorage in the Azores remote from the reach of the Portuguese authorities there; she was also at war with Spain, which had a reinvigorated and powerful navy that had played a vital role in the capture of Toulon by the counter-revolutionary forces. Even if the ships avoided the navies of France's Iberian foes, they still had to run the gauntlet of the British fleet, which roamed imperiously, far and wide across the oceans. The Indiamen's chances of reaching the rendezvous seemed like a slim and desperate prospect, but the confidential covering note from Morard explained why *Le Zéphyr* was to be diverted from her important mission and put in harm's way for what might prove to be a chimera.

My dear Citizen Captain,

You will have perused your orders, which I trust are clear enough. Permit me, though, to add an explanation of the importance of this particular mission. Several prominent members of the National Convention and the Committee of Public Safety have invested heavily in these voyages, having been tempted into the East Indies trade since the monopoly of the old Company was abolished. It has been insinuated that I should send out the entire fleet to bring them home, but in the absence of any direct orders to that effect, and uncertain whether all of my command would obey such orders in any case, I choose to allot the task to Le Zéphyr instead. I hope that your crew, having joined the fleet late, is less infected with mutiny than most of the other ships under my command, so I have confidence in your ability to sail promptly and reach the rendezvous within the dates specified in these orders. Yet nothing is more important than defending our own coast, and I do not wish you to be diverted from your original orders for any longer than is strictly necessary. Remain on station until noon on the fifth, Captain Kermorvant, but not one moment longer. Then, as your orders state, return to your originally allocated station.

Morard de Galles

So they were to sail for no better reason than to line the pockets of some of the politicians who strutted around the grand chambers of Paris. Morard was clearly as unhappy at ordering Philippe on such a mission as he himself was to undertake it. He knew that the French East India Company's monopoly had been abolished in the early days of the revolution, brought down so that all Frenchmen could have a chance to take part in the lucrative trade; but by 'all Frenchmen', the enlightened representatives of the people undoubtedly meant themselves, not the peasants around Chateau de Brechelean nor the men on the lower deck of *Le Zéphyr*. It was the same in every country. He remembered his father holding forth about America's fledgling Congress, and he had witnessed it himself at Saint Petersburg, where 'the best interests of Russia' invariably meant the best interests of the Empress and the select circle around her in Tsarskoye Selo or the Winter Palace. But orders were orders, and on the other side of the coin, it would be quite a coup for Philippe if he managed to rendezvous with the incoming ships and escorted them safely into Nantes. If the wind permitted, then, he would take *Le Zéphyr* to sea at first light, leaving the Brest fleet to its quarrels and mutinies.

Not only the wind needed to permit, he thought. Putting to sea would depend above all on whether his words, Garrigues' support and the armed force of de Machault's Marines proved sufficient to sway the crew. Perhaps Roissel, Vaquin and the rest of the devoted *sans-culottes* were winning back the waverers, and by the morning Philippe would find himself under arrest and in irons in the hold.

–

As it was, Philippe slept surprisingly soundly and awoke to find himself still a free man. He went on deck prepared for any eventuality, his sword at his side and two loaded pistols in his belt. He had issued his orders to his officers, and it was time to see if he and they would be obeyed. It was nearly halfway through the morning watch, and the first hint of light in the sky was just apparent to the east, over Vannes and the Morbihan. All three lieutenants were on deck. Even in the semi-darkness it was possible to see that both Roissel and Ugarte were red-faced, and their stances suggested they had been arguing with each other. Guillaumin was examining the binnacle and pointing out something to Carabignac and Lievremont, who stood by his side. There was no sign of Vaquin. Perhaps he was down below at the head of a large deputation of armed mutineers, preparing to take over the ship.

Le Zéphyr seemed to be the only ship in the fleet where there was any sign of activity. Lanterns indicated the positions of the other vessels, but all of them continued to swing gently at anchor. The wind was a moderate westerly breeze, the visibility good. Ideal conditions for taking the fleet to sea and back to Brest, if the rebellious crews got their way. Philippe did not envy Morard the continuing struggle with his own men that would occupy him for yet another day, but perhaps he should not judge until he knew what awaited him, too.

'Very well, Citizens,' said Philippe to the officers nearest to him on the quarterdeck, 'we shall get under way at five bells.'

This was the moment. If Roissel or any of the others were going to object and disobey, it would be now. Philippe hoped his voice sounded confident and did not betray the tension he felt.

'Five bells,' said Roissel, his expression taut. For a moment, Philippe thought his first officer was about to refuse the command and instead denounce him as a traitor to the Republic. But Roissel turned around as though looking for a sign from one of the mutinous ships. Then he stiffened and bowed his head slightly. 'Aye, aye, Citizen Captain.'

CHAPTER TWENTY

Le Zéphyr reached the rendezvous area without incident. The weather remained remarkably benign for the end of September; there were no alarms from enemy warships, and the familiar routines of shipboard life seemed to dampen down the embers of mutiny. Watches changed when they should, men took their meals at their mess tables, they holystoned the decks, they worked the ropes and sails, they joked and argued as seamen had surely done since the cave dwellers of old first ventured onto open waters in hollowed-out logs. No doubt some of them still argued in favour of a return to Brest, or took the side of one of the national factions against another, or argued for the guillotining of Robespierre or the queen or even Philippe Kermorvant, but for now none of it spilled over into open mutiny. Philippe continued with the training of the *aspirants*: Lievremont keen but prone to make errors, Carabignac silent but a quick if reluctant learner, Vaquin aloof, hostile and a complete disaster.

He conversed with his officers, both individually and as a group at dinner. He talked to Driaux, learning more from him about what Captain Berthomier had been like and how Roissel had moved against him. He toured the messes, chatting to men with the informality and sense of equality that citizens of the Republic seemed to expect. Above all, he watched the men go about the hourly business of a man-of-war, and as they did, so he took stock.

At long last, Philippe could take a proper measure of the competence of his crew. The officers and *gabiers*, the old hands, were doing their utmost to train the lubbers, and Roissel, to give him his due for once, had done a creditable job of making up the watch bills and messes to ensure all the green hands were thrown in with *gabiers* and *loups de mer*, the ship's few real veterans. They now handled the ship well enough, although they had yet to be tested in an emergency. The setting, taking in and bracing of the sails still lacked speed and precision, but improved little by little. So, too, did the rate and accuracy of fire. Philippe ordered exercises of the main battery at least once a day, sometimes twice, even though this unheard-of rigour drew protests from Roissel, who considered it un-French, and Garrigues, who objected to the extra-vagant expenditure of the Republic's gunpower. The starboard watch, the *quart de tribord*, improved faster than the port, but the performance of both was now perfectly creditable. Or at least, creditable compared to the likes of the Russians, the Swedes, the Turks and even some of the Americans. Whether it would be so against the English remained to be seen.

Be they seamen or Garrigues' gunners, though, the men of *Le Zéphyr* made too much noise for Philippe's liking. Men shouted or even chatted eagerly to their neighbours as they went about their tasks, but that was apparently the French way. The British and the Americans, who learned their trade from their erstwhile colonial masters, went about such routines in near-silence. But to deny a Frenchman the right to have his say loudly and animatedly on any subject and at any time was evid-ently taken as an affront to his very Frenchness, to the rights of man, and to the ideals of liberty, equality and fraternity. Philippe had no doubt that some, perhaps many, of the men were still disaffected, resentful of this peculiar beast of a captain who had been inflicted on them, and still staunch in the belief that only *Le Zéphyr*, her two hundred and sixty or so men and her thirty-two guns, could save Brest from conquest by the royalist forces of reaction or, worse, by the English. For now, though, enough men accepted orders without audible complaint for the ship to function as it should. Even the most reluctant, obstreperous men in the crew, the likes of Pierric Korbell, seemed to accept that they were defenders of the French Republic and the ideal of liberty against mighty and relentless foes. The simple patriotism that had once driven ordinary French peasants in their thousands to take up arms for the Maid of Orleans still had a powerful effect at the end of the more enlightened eighteenth century. But Philippe was under no illusions that one error, one false or intemperate word spoken in haste, and the red flag might be hoisted to the maintop of *Le Zéphyr*. Philippe still had no doubt that the man giving the order to hoist it would be Lieutenant de Vaisseau Martin Roissel.

Slowly, though, one tell-tale sign of a more united crew was beginning to emerge: singing. At first it was only groups of three or four,
but as lubbers slowly became familiar with the tunes and words, more
and more joined in. With only a few exceptions the songs were alien to
Philippe, and very different from the mournful, deep-throated dirges of
the Russians or the jaunty, irreverent drinking songs of the Americans.
The men of *Le Zéphyr* sang the songs of the revolution – 'Ça Ira', 'La
Marseillaise' and the rest – but many of the old hands knew the older
songs from the time of the Bourbon navy, the words of some of them
suggesting that they had been sung by the crews of French men-of-war
since at least the time of Joan of Arc.

Qui portera la nouvelle à Audierne,
Que la flotte est perdue excepté un navire
Un navire appelé le Mouton Blanc
Qui tint au vent de la Torche.

'Who will take the news to Audierne,' sang some of the Breton contingent, 'that the fleet is lost except one ship, one ship called the White
Sheep, keeping to windward of La Torche…' Some of the Provençals,
led by Garrigues, came back with a newer song, which some of the
men from inland provinces seemed to know too.

Le premier bord quails ont tiré
Ils nous ont bien tout démâté
Ont cassé le mat d'artimon
Avec toutes ses cordes
Les pauvres matelots, hélas,
Criaient miséricorde.

Philippe was not sure that a song about the mizzen being smashed by
the enemy's first broadside, causing the poor sailors to cry out for mercy,
was conducive to morale, but he let it pass. A competition began, the
Bretons pitching themselves against the rest. Roissel wanted it stopped,
but Philippe allowed it to continue. He had seen something like this on
the *Lexington*, where the Virginians had been joined by a large, unruly
contingent from New England. Initially as suspicious of each other as
cats, a united crew had been born out of shared drink and shared songs,

many of them directed against the English. It was different on *Le Zéphyr*, where the Bretons were the most numerous part of the crew and also far better singers than most of those drawn from elsewhere. But men were smiling, and in Philippe's experience, smiling men did not mutiny, and they did not fight each other on the gun deck. Smiling men sailed willingly into battle, risking their lives for their shipmates and their country.

–

Without incident, or, at any rate, without one that found its way into the log book that Philippe wrote up every night in his cabin, *Le Zéphyr* reached the cruising station specified in Morard's orders. On the following day, the crew was exercising the guns once again, with the captain in his usual place on the quarterdeck, watching proceedings, giving orders as necessary, and timing the speed of fire with the watch that Tasha had bought for him as a wedding gift.

The scream came from below, down on the gun deck. It silenced every man within earshot, including those on the upper deck. Leaving Fingal with the watch, Philippe all but threw himself down the nearby officers' ladder and ran two-thirds of the way down the gun deck to where a score or more men were craning their necks for a view of what had happened at Gun Five on the port side. The crowd was contrary to all naval discipline, and it exuded sympathy and morbid curiosity in equal measure. Philippe pushed his way through and saw the gun captain, with Garrigues behind him, propping up one of the lubbers, who was weeping profusely. Philippe did not know the man's name but recognised him as a fairly young, short and bespectacled Breton, one of the mutinous coterie around the one-eyed Pierric Korbell, who now stood a few feet away looking on in undisguised horror. Philippe looked down and saw that the landsman's right arm was bloody and horribly mangled, protruding out from the elbow at an impossible angle.

'What happened here?' Philippe demanded.

'His spectacles slipped off his face just before the gun fired,' said the gun captain, a square-jawed, broad-shouldered Breton Marine, 'just as I was putting the linstock to the powder. He tried to reach in to get them, but the recoil took his arm.'

'What's his name?'

'Launay, Citizen Captain,' said Korbell, his voice hesitant and broken. 'Morgan Launay.'

Men were looking at each other and murmuring. Every single one of them stepped back from the bleeding, screaming figure of Morgan Launay, his shattered arm surely as certain a death sentence as any verdict of a revolutionary tribunal. Aspirant Lievremont, who had been assigned to this section of the main battery, went to the gunport and vomited through it. Philippe knelt down by the injured man, although he had not the slightest idea what he could do. It was obvious that with no surgeon aboard ship, the man would die.

The intervention came from the least expected quarter.

Aspirant Carabignac pushed his way through the men, and as Philippe looked at him in astonishment, the boy pointed to three of the burliest topmen in turn.

'You,' he ordered, 'get clean rags; you, fetch boiling water from the galley; you, help me to raise him and get something to prop him against! A barrel, a box, anything of that sort.' They stared at the mere child who was giving them orders. '*Now!*'

Philippe looked at the boy, looked at the men, and knew what he had to do.

'Do what the *aspirant* commands!' he ordered. The men turned and hurried to their tasks. 'The rest of you, back to your posts! Give us space!'

Carabignac knelt down, rapidly studied Launay's arm, then looked up at Philippe and Garrigues.

'I want a good length of clean cloth – I'm going to bind the arm tight, just down from the shoulder. That should stem the bleeding. Then I want a knife, a clean one. You!' He gestured to the nearest man, who happened to be the prickly Pierric Korbell. 'Get a bottle of spirits from the steward's store. Brandy, preferably.'

'On my authority,' added Philippe, reckoning that the haughty ship's steward Saint-Jacques might object to receiving orders from a mere *aspirant*.

Korbell looked utterly stupefied and seemed not to have registered Philippe's or Carabignac's words. But he looked down again at his friend, then saluted his captain and ran off in search of the steward.

'My father serves in the National Convention,' said Carabignac urgently to no one in particular, as though he was speaking to himself, 'but he's a surgeon by profession. My two eldest brothers followed him, but I think he had no interest in another of his sons taking the same path. Especially not the youngest, the runt of the litter, the one who was going to be sent off to be a priest in some stinking country parish and forgotten about.'

Philippe sensed that there had been a powerful undercurrent of tension and resentment in the Carabignac family, but he could hardly air the thought. Instead he handed Carabignac his own knife, and the youth immediately began to cut away the torn fragments of Launay's sleeve, speaking soothingly to the injured man as he did so. Flaps of bloody flesh hung down, exposing raw bone. The young *aspirant* was handed a piece of clean cloth by Garrigues and bound the arm tightly, eliciting howls of pain from Launay. Korbell returned with the bottle of brandy and an irate Steward Saint-Jacques, who took one look at the ugly sight on the deck, turned pale and withdrew at once without making any protest to Philippe.

Garrigues held the bottle to Launay's lips and the injured man drank greedily. Carabignac seized his opportunity and gently touched his patient's elbow, then applied light pressure to the arm just above and below it. Launay screamed and bucked like a bull in a field, but three men took hold of his undamaged limbs and held him down.

The *aspirant* stood and beckoned for Philippe to follow him a little way away, where Launay could not hear them.

'The arm has to be taken off, Citizen Captain. It's the only hope he has.'

'You can do it?'

Carabignac's face fell, and he looked and sounded once again like the youth he was rather than the Parisian surgeon he could have been.

'I saw my father do it often – he let us watch his operations, y'see – but no, I'm not sure I can, sir, I can stitch him up, but I don't think I can saw…'

The boy had turned white simply at the thought of sawing through flesh, bone and tendon.

Garrigues stepped forward to approach Philippe and Carabignac.

'Begging pardon, Citizen Captain, Citizen Aspirant, but my pa was a butcher, my ma a midwife. I reckon I can chop or sew any meat or flesh you want, and blood's as second nature to me as my own piss.'

Philippe made his decision.

'Very well. We'll take him down to the cockpit, get together the necessary implements, then you can carry out the amputation, Master Gunner, under the direction of Aspirant Carabignac. Aspirant, what will you need to mend Citizen Launay?'

'Brandy, sir. As much brandy as the stores can provide. I wish we had a proper surgeon's chest – I need salves and ointments to ease the pain he'll be in, but brandy will have to do.'

An idea came to Philippe.

'Korbell,' he said, 'go to the carpenter, ask him if there's any willow bark in his stores or anywhere on the ship.'

Korbell seemed stunned and opened his mouth as if to form a reply, but thought better of it and went off to follow his orders.

'Willow bark, sir?' enquired Carabignac, his curiosity undisguised.

'When I was a boy I sometimes visited the Pamunkey, an Indian tribe of Virginia. Their medicine men used what they found in the forests – herbs, berries, all kinds of treatments unknown to Europeans. Once, I got an arrow in my shoulder by accident during a hunt. I was told to rub willow bark into the wound... I was in so little pain, I thought it was a miracle. When a Turkish sword cut my side open a few years ago, I craved willow bark as it healed wounds so well. But it was Russia, Aspirant, so there was only vodka.'

'Plenty of willow in France, sir,' said Garrigues, 'even if Fouroux and the carpenter's crew don't have any. We can cut down a few trees when we next go ashore.'

Korbell returned with the news that, as expected, *Le Zéphyr*'s carpenter had no willow bark anywhere aboard ship. Philippe nodded, then watched as four men, Korbell being one, carried Launay down to the orlop deck under the direction of Carabignac and Garrigues. He did not watch the operation, instead returning to the quarterdeck to scan the horizon in the forlorn hope of sighting the incoming Indiamen, but the wounded man's screams could be heard even from there. It took over an hour, but word finally came that the limb had been severed and the wound cauterised. Launay was in great pain but was calmer, conscious, extremely drunk from Saint-Jacques' brandy, and singing the praises of Aspirant Armand Carabignac as the finest surgeon in the whole of France.

That night, as he sat in his cabin writing up the log, Philippe reflected on the day's turn of events. *Le Zéphyr* might be the only ship with no surgeon in the entire Brest fleet, but surely no other could have done such a good job with Launay's terrible injury. Carabignac had been a revelation, Garrigues only slightly less so, and perhaps Philippe had been able to make some little contribution of his own thanks to the esoteric knowledge he had learned from Opechancanough and the wise men and women of the Pamunkey. Once *Le Zéphyr* returned to coastal waters, he would indeed send a boat ashore with orders to seek out a copse of willow trees.

The effect of all this was not quite what he expected, as Driaux informed him shortly before he took to his sea-bed.

'Men are saying Aspirant Carabignac is the king's old surgeon, run away to sea in disguise to escape the guillotine. That, Citizen Captain, would be a good story if only Carabignac were thirty or forty years older.'

Philippe laughed.

'Nonetheless,' he said, 'I think our young *aspirant* needs to reconsider his vocation.'

'With respect, Citizen Captain, perhaps you do too, if you listen to half the talk down on the gun deck.'

'And why is that, Driaux?'

'There's an argument, sir. Men are closer to blows than they were over the mutiny at Quiberon, even. There's one side says you were a medicine man among the Indians, while others say you were their principal chief. Then there's a third faction who misheard what you said about the wound in your side. They believe you were a headman among the Cossacks, Citizen Captain.'

Philippe laughed again. Everyone in France – everyone, perhaps, except Leonore – thought him an outsider. Did it matter, therefore, if his own crew thought him stranger still?

CHAPTER TWENTY-ONE

The sails of the enemy ship were sighted in the middle of the night. She was off to the north, sailing close-hauled in a stiff westerly breeze, and by dawn her hull was clearly visible through the telescope, perhaps five miles from *Le Zéphyr*. She had clearly seen the French ship and, on the starboard tack, she was on a course to intercept. She was a small two-decker, and as far as Philippe could make out she carried somewhere between forty and forty-four guns. He knew that the British preferred single-decked frigates of around thirty to thirty-eight guns, and they seemed to have an infinite number of these; but they had built forties and forty-fours for the American war, and he had seen several of them off the Virginia and North Carolina seaboards. She would be more heavily armed than *Le Zéphyr*, albeit not by much, so a contest between them would not be particularly uneven. But a battle at sea was always an uncertain business. The Englishman would almost certainly have a larger and more experienced crew than *Le Zéphyr*, and Philippe's orders were clear. He was to put the safe return of the Indiaman above all else, and any sort of encounter with this British man-of-war was bound to imperil that. Moreover, he needed to get the enemy ship away from the area, and to do that he would need to convince his opposite number that *Le Zéphyr* had no obvious reason for holding this position, cruising this particular line of latitude. The British ship was surely somewhere around the southernmost limit of the patrol area allocated to her by Admiral Howe, so dragging her further south and east, towards the coast of France, was Philippe's favoured strategy.

He put down his telescope and turned to his assembled officers.

'We'll wear ship, make our course east-south-east and outrun him,' he said. 'He'll probably think we're heading back to Rochefort or Rochelle, and I'll wager he won't want to come so far south nor to risk being trapped on our coast. Once we lose him, we can beat back up and return to this station.'

'And if we can't outrun him, Citizen Captain?' said Roissel sharply.

Philippe smiled. 'Since I first went to sea, I've heard nothing but praise for how well French frigates sail and how they can outrun any damned English slug. Are you telling me that isn't true, Lieutenant?'

Roissel made no reply, merely inclining his head slightly.

The Englishman hoisted a private signal in case *Le Zéphyr* proved to be one of the many French prizes that had been taken into King George's navy over the years. Philippe ignored it, instead giving the orders to bear away and put on more sail. He gave the orders for topgallants, as well as ordering men to ready the stern chase guns. The Englishman responded in kind, but there was no sign of her closing the distance between them. He felt the enemy ship was straining to her limit, although there was no obvious evidence of this. But old hands who he'd sailed with over the years often talked about the sixth sense that good seamen needed: that instinct that sometimes told them when the weather was about to turn, or when a submerged rock lay dead ahead. Philippe fancied that he felt it now. There was also something in the air which seemed to presage a storm, though as yet the barometer gave no evidence of it. The wind had a damp tang to it; the clouds to the west were a little thicker, a little greyer. He exchanged a glance with Guillaumin, who had sailed this sea more often than any of them, and the old Breton sailing master's eyes told him he was thinking the same thing.

One turn of the *ampoulette*, the sand glass. Two. Three. Four.

Philippe stayed on deck the whole time, Driaux bringing him strong and vile-tasting tankards of coffee. At different times Guillaumin, Ugarte and Fingal all discussed their course and speed with him, their attention focused above all on what the weather might or might not do. The three *aspirants* expected their daily lesson from the captain to fall victim to the exigencies of the sea-chase, but Philippe got them to join him on the quarterdeck. Even Carabignac, with no urgent cases to occupy him, came up on deck for the first time since he had assumed the role of acting surgeon. The three youths were set the task of taking bearings on the enemy and assessing the distance between them, in addition to checking the barometer at frequent intervals, Vaquin displaying his usual resentment at being set any task whatsoever. Meanwhile, men went about their duties on deck and up in the shrouds and yards, all the while casting glances towards the English ship, its red ensign sometimes visible as the wind swirled and gusted.

Still the ships maintained their relative positions. Surely it would be apparent to the British captain that if all things remained the same, he would never catch *Le Zéphyr*? In a chase, with all other things being equal, a two-deck forty-four could never hope to catch a single-deck thirty-two. But not only did seamen have a sixth sense, Philippe knew, they also had a stubbornness that could persist beyond all reason. He put himself in the position of his opposite number and knew that if he was on the quarterdeck of the British warship, he would be giving the same orders and thinking the same thoughts as his counterpart. The closer the two ships got to the coast of France, the greater the risk for the Englishman of encountering other French warships. But set against that, there was the chance that something would go wrong aboard his target. Perhaps a sail would tear, or the press of canvas would prove too much for a spar or a topmast or a stay. Perhaps *Le Zéphyr*'s captain would make an error in a command or a misconceived change of course. Perhaps the officers and men of the French frigate would have a miraculous conversion, realise the errors and heinous crimes of the Republic, heave to and surrender gratefully. The Englishman would clutch at such desperate thoughts because he would want the honour and glory of taking one of the first prizes of the war – Philippe had heard the English were giving out knighthoods for such feats. Then too, of course, the pursuing captain would only reluctantly give up the chance to make a fortune in prize money. Above all, though, whoever stood on the quarterdeck of the British ship would crave a large dose of the powerful, irresistibly addictive but elusive drug that all warriors sought: victory.

The Englishman held his course. All the while the barometer fell, the sky in the west darkened and the wind strengthened. The grey-green waves grew choppier; the ship's pitching, rolling, rising, falling and creaking increased; the sheets sang and howled, and the first flurries of rain fell.

'Surely we need to shorten sail, sir?' said Roissel.

'Not yet.' Philippe's telescope was trained on the English ship. The older, larger hull was rolling more than *Le Zéphyr*. He remembered from America that these two-deck frigates had been built especially for the coastal waters there, so the hulls were rounder and flatter in the bottom than the likes of *Le Zéphyr* and most of the smaller frigates in the British navy. The enemy's bows were rising and falling sharply with the swell as the strengthening wind formed the waters into ever higher peaks and ever deeper troughs. The hull spilled the waves clumsily from the cutwater like a man who chose to batter his way through a closed door rather than simply opening it and walking through. If he were on the enemy ship's quarterdeck, Philippe thought, he would already have given the orders to start reducing the canvas she had aloft.

'Sir...' said Roissel once more.

'Not yet.'

The eyes of the others on the quarterdeck were all on Philippe now. The *aspirants* were struggling to keep their footing as the ship's rolling and pitching became more pronounced; Vaquin had already spewed over the side, and both of the others looked green and thoroughly miserable, their uniforms already dripping.

There was a movement on the English ship, with men hauling on halyards and edging out along the yards. The main and fore courses were being hauled up ready to be secured.

Philippe turned to his officers.

'*Serrer les voiles!*' Take in the sails. 'Double reefed topsails alone.'

Through voice trumpets and by the shrill notes of the bosun's and mates' whistles, the commands were repeated to the hands, the response of, '*Commande!*' coming more swiftly and from more mouths than had been the case at the start of the voyage. Men went aloft while those on deck hauled on halyards. They were a different crew now: better trained and more experienced for one thing, but the imminence of what threatened to be a ferocious storm was also driving the rawest human instinct of all, the urge to survive. Now there were no *sans-culottes* and secret counter-revolutionaries, no Bretons and Provençals. There were only men upon an angry sea, subject to the full fury of wind and wave, their only protection against sure and terrible death by drowning the small, fragile wooden hull and the decisions of its captain.

The first fork of lightning lanced across the blackening sky like a bullwhip. The colossal thunderclap that followed seemed to shake *Le Zéphyr* from topmast to keel. The *aspirants* and the few lubbers who were out on deck looked utterly terrified, as if they had suddenly found themselves living through the end of the world. Philippe took pity on his three young charges and sent them below, leaving only himself,

Fingal, two of the master's mates, the helmsmen and several *matelots* on the quarterdeck. The ship was rearing and bucking like the wild stallion he had once tried to tame, much to the amusement of his Pamunkey friends. It was amusing to him, too, until he broke an arm and three ribs.

The men on the quarterdeck were all secured by lifelines. Even so, Philippe lost his footing several times as great waves lashed high and hard over the side, and several times he was certain he was about to be swept overboard until the rope securing him to the mizzen snapped taut. One of the mates was caught by a huge wave and smashed against one of the port guns. The man proclaimed himself perfectly well – he shouted above the storm that he was from the Île de Batz where men were not born but forged, and the citizen captain should not worry about him – but nonetheless Philippe ordered him to attend Carabignac in the cockpit.

The thunder and lightning was interminable. The old prophets spoke of the rending of the heavens, and to Philippe it seemed as if the ferocious black sky was truly breaking apart. The huge seas rose up to embrace the falling clouds. It was as if the elements were having their own revolution to outdo France's earthly example.

Through the depths of the storm, the drowning spray breaking incessantly over Le Zéphyr, and the crazy movements of the ship, Philippe concentrated on the position of the British frigate. Two or three times, when lightning lit the scene like a theatre stage, he thought he caught sight of her. As far as he could judge she was falling further astern, but he could not be certain. If he really was glimpsing the enemy vessel then the Englishman could evidently see Le Zéphyr too, and that would surely strengthen his resolve to continue the pursuit.

'We should change course, Citizen Captain,' shouted Roissel. The first officer had relieved Fingal and somehow managed to stagger through the spray, rocking with the movement of the ship, before reaching Philippe.

'We can't be sure he won't see it and follow,' bellowed Philippe, spitting seawater from his mouth as he replied.

If he could speak more than a handful of words at a time, Philippe would have told Roissel that he had considered ordering a change of course every few minutes during the storm. But the change could only be made from the helm alone, it being impossible to put more canvas aloft than the reefed topsails that were already set, so *Le Zéphyr*'s freedom of manoeuvre was very limited. A change of course might negate their advantage of speed – they would be more side on to the wind and the waves – if the Englishman spotted their move he might be able to close some or all of the gap – these and a score of other calculations had driven almost all else out of Philippe's mind for hours.

'Holding our course makes it easier for him,' shouted Roissel.

Philippe did not respond. He still believed that the English ship was coping less well than *Le Zéphyr* with the surging, seething waters. He had not seen any sight of the enemy for perhaps half a glass. If the storm died away that very moment, he might be proved wrong. Even a brief lull might bring the unmistakeable, ominous hull of the two-decker back into sight. But the sky was still black and the sea tumultuous. Nothing manmade lay within sight of *Le Zéphyr*, only the wrath and power of nature. They had lost the English ship. He was sure of it; he could sense it. Philippe's body was soaked and screaming for rest, but he would stay at his post until he was proved right or wrong.

—

The storm continued for the rest of the day and the first part of the night, although the thunder and lightning died away in the afternoon. The driving rain continued unabated and the sea remained a cauldron, testing the sea legs and stomachs of even the most experienced *loups de mer* on the ship. Philippe, who was usually unaffected by seasickness, had lost count of the number of times he had vomited or, when there was nothing left to bring up, retched like the greenest lubber. It remained impossible to take any bearings, forcing Philippe and his officers to rely on dead reckoning alone. But there was also no sign of the British ship. Roissel continued to advocate a change of course, and just before night set in, Philippe finally concurred. It was not a great change, only five points to port, but if the Englishman was still out there somewhere, invisible beyond the horizon, it should finally throw him off the scent.

The storm blew itself out in the early hours. Philippe gave the orders to make more sail and men emerged from below, many of them pale and unsteady. Some gulped greedily at the fresh air, or looked in apparent wonder at the sky as though it was the first time they had ever seen it.

Slowly, though, men recalled their duties, went to their stations, and obeyed the command signals issuing from Guillaumin's whistle.

Philippe wiped crusted sea-spray from his telescope and scanned the horizon. There was no sign of the Englishman, nor of any other ship. *Le Zéphyr* seemed to be alone on the broad ocean.

'The course, Citizen Captain?' asked Guillaumin.

'We return to our previous station, in accordance with our orders. Lay a course to achieve that object, Citizen Guillaumin.'

'Aye, aye, sir.'

Ugarte, who had relieved Roissel, scratched his chin with his meaty hand.

'Begging pardon, Citizen Captain,' he said, 'but might not that take us back towards the Englishman?'

'That's a risk whatever course we make, Enseigne. But if we do encounter him again we'll be expecting him, and if he carried on sou'easterly, thinking we were still running for the coast, then we should have the wind of him this time.'

Ugarte nodded, although he still looked doubtful. He was a good officer, Philippe thought, but he still had a merchantman's instincts – if an enemy warship was lurking in the same waters, the merchant skipper would want to run for the nearest port. But the captain of *Le Zéphyr* had to do his utmost to obey his admiral's orders.

Philippe's eyesight seemed to break into a thousand swirling shards. He swayed, and it was only the quick reactions of Ugarte that stopped him falling to the deck.

'Sir?' said the Basque, full of concern.

'You have the ship,' said Philippe, suddenly aware that he must have been on deck for something like thirty hours without food or sleep. 'Call for me if there are any likely sightings.'

Unsteadily, he made his way below and went to his cabin, where he found Driaux with the complexion of a walking corpse. But the valet was alert enough to take one look at his captain, then wordlessly prepare a makeshift meal of coffee, cheese and cold salt pork. By the time the valet brought it back to the cabin, Philippe, still wearing his sodden clothes and boots, was sound asleep on his sea-bed.

CHAPTER TWENTY-TWO

Lieutenant Martin Roissel loved taking the watch in the hours between midnight and dawn, especially on perfect moonlit nights like this. There were relatively few men on deck and they were usually silent, or as silent as Frenchmen ever were. Roissel could listen without interruption to the waves lapping against the hull, the wind in the sails and shrouds and the flapping of the Tricolour ensign, ghostly in the light of the moon and the stern lanterns. He would go to the binnacle to check the course, compare that with what the stars told him, make desultory conversation with whichever of Guillaumin's mates and helmsmen had the watch, then go back to scanning the eastern horizon for the first, nearly imperceptible signs of light. There on the quarterdeck, with no Ugarte, no Fingal and above all no Kermorvant, he felt as though it was truly his ship.

A day had passed since the end of the storm, and *Le Zéphyr* had spent it returning to her station in the hope of encountering the returning Indiamen. There was no sign of the British ship that had pursued them, and for much of the day there was no sign of the captain, either. Roissel privately hoped that Kermorvant had caught a fatal fever, but in mid-afternoon the infernal man came up on deck, seemingly in a rude state of health. He took observations but then did not do what Roissel would have done, namely busy himself with complex calculations. Like Ugarte the man was evidently a follower of the abominable Delague, whose writings were the vogue among the seamen of the day and who held that intuition was more important in navigation than systematic workings on paper. Roissel, who had spent years struggling to master trigonometry, found this philosophy almost as repugnant as royalism. At dinner, too, Kermorvant was in cursedly good spirits, regaling his officers with yet more tales of America's war against the English and Russia's wars against the Swedes and Turks. As if such experiences were of any worth in the French Republic's fight against the tyrants of the earth, a righteous struggle for truth without parallel in the history of mankind. Roissel, who had spent the American war in the skeleton harbour crew of a laid-up seventy-four in Toulon, could not understand how the *aspirants* and even the other lieutenants could possibly be impressed by their captain's stories. In the new age of the Republic, the only thing that mattered was pure revolutionary virtue.

The middle watch, during the blackest hours of the night, was the perfect time for thinking, and Roissel had much to think about. He was still set on denouncing the half-American as he had denounced his predecessor, Berthomier, but timing was all. To have done it when they were just out of Brest or at Quiberon would have been too soon. Bringing accusations against a second captain of the same ship in such a short period would surely be too blatant even for a revolutionary tribunal, so Roissel had to bide his time. But the danger was that if he left it too long, there was a chance that Kermorvant might win over the crew despite his foreignness and aristocratic birth. Garrigues clearly favoured him, but Provençals were never to be trusted. Ugarte, that vile heap of ugly flesh, would support the captain simply to spite Roissel. The rest of the officers would surely sway in whichever direction they thought the breeze was blowing, so the moment had to be chosen to perfection. As for the crew: they were sheep, of course, but they were surely certain to obey and respect a man who had come up from the ranks as opposed to some stranger whose only qualification to command was having an eminent author as a father. The men, most of whom were too ignorant to read and write, would care nothing for that, nor for the strange and inappropriate ways Kermorvant had learned from the Indian savages and the Russians, but they would certainly defer to a committed republican, a dedicated *sans-culotte*, who had many influential friends in the Jacobin clubs. But the grounds for moving against this captain were as yet uncertain. There was no evidence of incompetence. In navigation he favoured the school of Delague, but so did most captains in the fleet. He sometimes forgot the French words for ropes or parts of the ship – 'stanchion' had caused him a particular problem – but the men seemed to like the way he made a joke of it and asked whoever stood nearest him, no matter how lowly, for the correct term. The man hadn't mastered every intricacy of the signal book, but that was true of many officers who had spent their entire lives in the navy. In any case the fleet was full of incompetent captains, especially if they had connections to members of the National Convention. Kermorvant, though, was obviously an accomplished seaman, quick thinking and decisive, as he had shown in the chase and storm. His endurance on deck for all those hours, not eating, drinking only rainwater, and pissing where he stood – Roissel had overheard talk among some of the men which suggested they were impressed by that. Worryingly and unaccountably, Kermorvant seemed to be the sort of leader men liked to have over them. No, any charge against Kermorvant would have to be on purely political grounds, but proving him to be a counter-revolutionary and traitor was more difficult than Roissel had anticipated. Yes, the man was an *aristo* and a foreigner to all intents and purposes, but Citizen Saint-André knew all that perfectly well when he placed him in this command. And as yet, the captain had shown impeccable loyalty to the Republic. Roissel agreed wholeheartedly with the demands of the mutineers at Quiberon and had put up Vaquin, that promising young fellow – promising in so many ways – to see if he could win over the crew. But Kermorvant's response was undoubtedly what the men of power in Paris would want it to be; no man was ever guillotined for following the orders of the Republic to the letter. Not yet, at any rate. So no, Roissel would have to wait for his moment and he would have to be subtle.

A large seabird swooped low over the deck. To the east, the sky was becoming just a little lighter. Soon the bell would ring for the end of the watch. Timing was all…

–

Le Zéphyr stayed on station for three more days, cruising back and forth in the increasingly forlorn hope that the East Indiamen would make the rendezvous. There were glimpses of distant sails several times a day, and Philippe gave orders to close some of them until it was obvious that their size or course ruled them out. The danger was that one or more of them would prove to be English men-of-war, perhaps even the one that had chased *Le Zéphyr*, but for once the sea was mercifully free of ships flying the peculiar, ugly hotch-potch of a flag that represented Great Britain. The time specified in Morard's orders was nearly up, and Philippe had already decided on his next course, which would be to return closer inshore where they would have a better chance of intercepting traffic to or from the rebels.

The lookout's call came late in the morning, only an hour or so before Philippe would give the order to bear away. There was a distant sail on the horizon, off to the south-west. Philippe levelled his telescope, although it was difficult to keep it steady against the buffeting from the fresh, gusty breeze and choppy sea. One hull only, that was certain, so not the two Indiamen. Surely too little sail aloft for her to be one of the two?

'Your orders, Citizen Captain?' said Ugarte. 'Do we alter course to close her?'

'I don't think so, Enseigne. Getting to her would take too long, even if she holds her course and doesn't try to run westward. Besides, I reckon she's too small to be an Indiaman. So we hold our present case for another hour, then—'

The lookout in the mainmast crow's nest shouted again, but his words were carried away by a gust. He repeated them, and this time Philippe caught his message.

'Three master, low in the water! Only foremast standing, jury rigs otherwise!'

Philippe raised his telescope again. Yes, the lookout was right – there was something familiar about the lookout's voice – and the distant ship was larger than it seemed to be at first sight. She was making little headway with the small amount of canvas she had aloft, most of it billowing much too loosely from the foremast. The jury masts that had replaced the main and mizzen were now just visible. The hull was indeed lower in the water than it should be, even for a fully laden merchantman. It was wallowing clumsily through the waves, which broke high, white and angry over its bows.

'Correction, Enseigne Ugarte,' said Philippe, 'we shall close her. And after he's been relieved, I'll see that lookout in my cabin. He deserves a coin, I think.'

'Deserves it indeed, sir. Never known one like him – day, night, doesn't matter. Has the eyes of a hawk, that Lucas.'

'Lucas? The lubber? A tanner's apprentice, wasn't he?'

Ugarte grinned. 'By day, but a poacher by night. Eyes that can see in the dark, he says. Can spot a rabbit at half a mile. And he's no lubber any more, Citizen Captain. Once he'd learned points of the compass and relative bearing, which was faster than any other *matelot d'eau douce*, it was obvious there was no better lookout on the ship. Maybe not in the whole navy.'

Le Zéphyr beat up into the wind, steadily closing the damaged hull. From her size and decoration, she had to be one of the two Indiamen, but she was little more than a wreck. As well as the damage to her masts and rigging, the ship's sides bore unmistakeable scars of battle, repairs with fresh timber showing where enemy cannonballs had smashed into the hull. She was listing to starboard and very low in the water. None of that was strange of itself, but what was strange beyond all sense was that there was no sign of life anywhere on the ship. That explained the slovenly trim of the topsails and staysails – no courses were set – and the erratic course; there was no one steering the ship, no one aloft. The Indiaman seemed to be an empty hull, driven along her course by wind and tide alone. *Le Zéphyr* was closing a ghost ship.

'No one, sir,' said Fingal, who had relieved Ugarte at the bell and was studying the Indiaman intently. 'No one at all.'

'Perhaps they're all below,' said Lievremont.

'Unlikely,' said Philippe. 'But we need to secure her. Enseigne Fingal, take *the chaloupe* and a dozen men. Carpenter Fouroux, too, with a couple of his crew. Question any survivors and search for any papers in the cabins. The carpenter to inspect the hull, judge whether she'll bear a tow, and make any necessary repairs.'

'Aye, aye, Citizen Captain!'

Fingal assembled his boarding party, the ship's *chaloupe*, its longboat, was swung outboard, and Philippe watched as the boat's crew rowed through the lively sea to the shattered Indiaman. He hoped Fingal and Fouroux would work swiftly, for *Le Zéphyr* was dangerously exposed, lying-to in waters where an enemy man-of-war might appear at any moment.

Fingal took little more than an hour, and as the *chaloupe* drew nearer, Philippe saw that the young *enseigne* was bringing what seemed to be a package wrapped in rags. Fingal got back aboard with difficulty, although the swell seemed to have moderated a little since about noon. He came before Philippe and saluted, also acknowledging Roissel who had come on deck.

'She's the *Patrie*, Citizen Captain, one hundred and twenty-four days out of Pondicherry, by her journal, most of that time sailing in company with *Le Chameau*. Captain, Robert Janot. Cargo of pepper, sugar and dyewood. The wheel's been lashed to keep her roughly on her dead reckoning, but all seems intact, sir. Crew of one hundred and twenty-five, according to her muster. Number of crew accounted for, none. No ship's boats, so the crew must have abandoned ship for whatever reason. No sign of life other than a cat, seven chickens and this.'

He turned and indicated the bundle, which was being manhandled onto the frigate's deck by the crew of the *chaloupe*. Philippe went down with Fingal and Roissel, who had come on watch.

The bundle was moving, and it had eyes. Fingal pulled back the cloths a little further, exposing a small, terrified face.

'Who are you?' said Philippe, then repeated the question in English, much to Roissel's disgust.

The boy – a boy it plainly was – made no reply. Instead, he stared at Philippe and Fingal with wide, frightened brown eyes.

'He hasn't made a sound,' said Fingal. 'Don't know if he can't understand or if he's too afraid to speak. But he's the only human being on the ship, Citizen Captain. There's some blood on the decks, so that and the damage tells us she's been in a fight. But unless we can find some way to get the boy to talk, we don't know what happened to the crew or the other ship, *Le Chameau*.'

'Maybe there'll be someone in Nantes who speaks a tongue he'll understand,' said Philippe. 'If we can get the ship there. What's the carpenter's opinion?'

'Says she's holed twice below the waterline, sir, but nothing that he and his crew can't patch. Pumps are intact, so we should be able to keep her afloat unless the weather worsens and swamps her.'

'Very well. Citizen Roissel!' The first officer of *Le Zéphyr* stepped before Philippe and saluted. 'Select a prize crew – thirty should be sufficient, I think. Adjust the watch lists and stations for *Le Zéphyr* accordingly. Citizen Fingal, you will be in command of the prize crew with Aspirant Lievremont as your second in command. Select two mates who can stand watches.'

'And the boy, sir?' Fingal asked.

'Send him below to Citizen Carabignac, who can examine him for disease.'

With the boy gone, Philippe and his officers concentrated on assembling the prize crew. *Le Zéphyr* had a clear-cut mission, as laid down in

Morard's orders: the frigate would escort *Patrie* to the nearest friendly port as the wind permitted. That, Philippe deduced from his chart, had to be Saint-Nazaire, a small port at the mouth of the Loire estuary. They would escort the Indiaman there, hand her over to the authorities, and resume cruising the coasts of Brittany and Vendée. By late afternoon Fingal and his prize crew had *Patrie* under way under her makeshift jury rig, Fouroux also staying aboard for the time being to establish whether she would need a tow after all, and *Le Zéphyr* made sail to escort its charge to safety. In previous times Philippe would have thanked God that there was no sign of the English, but now he whispered thanks to Reason, to Leonore, to the shades of Tasha and Ivan, to his father and to his long-dead friend, Ben Dawkins.

Leaving the watch to Ugarte, Philippe went down to the orlop to get Carabignac's opinion on the health of the boy from *Patrie*. He expected the young *aspirant* to be alone with his patient, or else only in the company of one or two of the unofficial orderlies that Carabignac had recruited from among the lubbers and *mousses*. Instead, there was an unexpected visitor to the makeshift surgeon's cockpit.

'Driaux? Why in—'

'*Eze! Eze?*' said the boy, recoiling and staring at Philippe as he did so.

'He is calling you a king, Citizen Captain,' said the valet. '*Mba. Onye ndu.* I have told him you are not a king, but that you are a leader.'

'You can understand him?' said Philippe. 'You can speak his language?'

'As I explained to Aspirant Carabignac,' said Driaux, a little proudly, 'before the revolution I was a footman at a chateau in Touraine. The Dowager Duchesse de Roannais, whose estate it was, had a great liking for young black boys – I was one of the few servants who wasn't a slave. A few of them still spoke the tongue of their homelands, or at least knew a few words, and they taught me. When I heard of this mysterious child, I wondered if I might be of some help.'

'Perhaps you can, Driaux. Well done. Have you been able to discover what happened to the crew?'

'*Abughi m onye amoosu!*' said the boy loudly, pointing to himself. '*Abughi m ekwensu!*'

'He is saying he is not a witch nor a devil, Citizen Captain. That is what the crew of *Patrie* thought he was. That was why they abandoned the ship.'

Philippe looked at the small, frightened boy before him. It was hard to conceive of an entire crew fleeing a sturdy ocean-going vessel and chancing their fate on the ocean because of irrational, wildly superstitious fears of a mere child.

'Why? Why in the name of... in the name of the Republic would they imagine this boy to be a witch?'

Driaux shrugged. 'As far as I could make out from the babble of words that poured out after I first spoke to him, the crew became suspicious of him almost as soon as the captain bought him in Senegal. They had a priest on board, a diehard of the old faith who was returning home from India. This fellow somehow convinced himself and then the crew that the boy was a servant of the Devil. There was unexplained sickness on the ship – strange accidents – I could not make out everything he told me, but it seems the crew blamed him for every misfortune on the voyage. And there were many misfortunes, even before they encountered an enemy ship – Spanish, I think, from what he says – and a great storm immediately afterwards. Only half the crew was alive by that time. Then the captain went mad and shot himself.'

'Why didn't they just throw the boy overboard?' said Carabignac.

'It sounds as though the priest went mad, too. He seems to have believed by then that the lad was not just a servant of the Devil but the Devil himself, Satan incarnate. The only chance the crew had, he said, was to get away as quickly as they could.'

'So they abandoned the ship and its cargo out of superstition, nothing more,' said Philippe.

'Superstition is a powerful force, Captain,' said Carabignac. 'That's why the Chouans and the Vendée march under the banner of the Sacred Heart.'

'A surgeon and a philosopher,' said Philippe, smiling. 'You continue to surprise me, Aspirant.' He turned back to Driaux. 'Does he answer to a name?'

'He is called Ama, Citizen Captain. Short for Amandi. So what are we going to do with him, sir?' said Driaux.

'We land him at Saint-Nazaire,' said Philippe. 'He can be another man's problem. Until then, we three speak not a word of his story. You can diagnose him with a virulent sickness, Aspirant Carabignac, which means we can keep him isolated down here.'

'There's nothing wrong with him, sir,' said Carabignac.

'No, young Ama here has a most virulent sickness. Highly infectious, I'd say, although my medical knowledge doesn't approach yours, Citizen.'

The young *aspirant* caught Philippe's meaning and smiled.

'As you say, sir. Most infectious. Most virulent.'

'Driaux,' said Philippe, 'tell Ama that no man on this ship thinks him a witch or a devil. Tell him that he is bound for France, the fount of liberty, and that when he sets foot ashore he will be free.'

'Will he, sir?' asked the valet.

Philippe looked at the boy's wide, questioning eyes.

'Possibly. Probably not. But he must not know that.'

Saint-Nazaire was a small port on the north bank of the Loire estuary, at the point where the river broadened out into a wide bay and became a part of the sea. Here ships going up to Nantes waited for pilots if going upstream, or landed them if making for the open waters of the ocean, but otherwise the town had little to distinguish it. Several fishing boats were drawn up on its beach, but most of them appeared to be derelict. It had a small church right on the water's edge with a few old houses clustered around it, a fort flying a large Tricolour, and very little else. Philippe intended to spend as little time as possible here. They would take on water and fresh vegetables, hand over *Patrie* and its crew of one to the authorities, and get back to sea as soon as possible to resume *Le Zéphyr*'s original mission.

But as he stood on the quarterdeck to oversee the revictualling of the ship and its return to sea, Philippe realised that his plan was in danger. A boat was coming out from the quay of Saint-Nazaire. From its ensign staff flew a Tricolour that was easily as large as the hull itself. The red, white and blue colours swirled in the breeze, sometimes wrapping themselves around a cloaked man who had evidently insisted on standing throughout the passage, despite the considerable risk of toppling over the side.

As the boat drew nearer to *Le Zéphyr*'s side, Philippe realised that there was something familiar about the figure. The face was hidden by a tricorn that somehow stayed on in the wind, but he knew he had seen this person before.

The man looked up, saw Philippe, and nearly fell into the Loire. Philippe's reaction to the identity of his visitor was similar.

It was Représentant en Mission Jean-Baptiste Carrier.

CHAPTER TWENTY-THREE

'Philippe Kermorvant, Vicomte de Saint-Victor,' said the high representative of the Republic, a cold smile on his lips. 'Captain of a fine frigate, no less. Somebody believed all those scraps of paper you had on you at Saint-Malo, then. All those mighty names. So many men with titles like yours languish in prison or their heads have already tumbled into baskets, eh? Yet here you are, free and prospering, wearing the Republic's uniform. Strange how the world turns, is it not?'

They were in Philippe's cabin. Through the windows the Indiaman was in plain view astern of *Le Zéphyr.*

'I count myself fortunate to be able to serve the Republic, Citizen.'

'So you should, Captain, so you should.' Carrier nodded towards the *Patrie.* 'There are a good few very influential men in Paris who won't be able to thank you enough for bringing that ship safely home. I had money invested in this voyage myself, so I hope there's enough profit still floating over there to make up for the losses I made in the one the English took. If there is, I'll be the first to tell the Committee of Public Safety that Citizen Captain Kermorvant is an asset to the Republic, not yet another worthless *aristo* traitor like your brother. Oh yes, I heard about all that. Remember I told you at Saint-Malo that I'd keep my eye on you? So I did, Captain, for the Republic has eyes and ears everywhere, you see.'

Even when Jean-Baptiste Carrier seemed to be in good temper, he had an air of menace about him. He was a little man to whom the revolution had brought great power, Philippe realised, and he knew from America that such men were dangerous and unpredictable.

'I hope you're not being detained from your duties at Nantes, Citizen,' said Philippe.

The newspapers had spoken of the *représentant*'s transfer from Saint-Malo. The need there for a vigorous man of action was greater, or so the

Republic's army of servile scribblers claimed in their cheap newssheets. Nantes was much closer to the rebel front line in the Vendée, so that was where Carrier had been sent.

'Want to be rid of me, eh?'

'My orders from Admiral Morard de Galles—'

'I know about your orders from the esteemed admiral. But I have another scheme in mind. A more pressing scheme. I want you to escort the *Patrie* upstream to Nantes.'

Philippe could barely register the man's words. Abandon his orders and sail far inland, through territory infested with rebels? No. It was inconceivable. Whatever authority Carrier had from the Committee of Public Safety, it could not possibly extend this far.

'With the greatest of respect, Citizen, that's impossible! My orders are to keep *Le Zéphyr* at sea, to patrol the coasts of Brittany and La Vendée. I've heard Nantes is a long and difficult passage with much warping and towing. The time it would take to get up there, then to come back down again—'

Carrier waved his hand impatiently. 'I'll put all the boats and men you need at your disposal. No ship will ever have come up the Loire and then gone back down again faster than yours, Citizen Captain. But the country hereabouts is full of malcontents, and I wouldn't put it past the rebel scum to make an attempt on *Patrie*. A cargo like that could buy them several entire arsenals of weapons – enough to equip an entire rebel army, I'd say. They'll think twice, though, if they see that the cargo's guarded by the guns and men of your ship, as well as the cavalry and infantry I'll order to patrol the banks.'

'With respect again, Citizen, it still contravenes my orders from Admiral Morard and Citizen Saint-André.'

'I shall take full responsibility with my esteemed colleague and your admiral, and I've no doubt that Paris will second me. So we're agreed?'

Philippe felt a coldness in his chest. The man was rushing him, bullying him into agreeing to something that directly contradicted his orders. But deep down, he had no doubt that Carrier was right. If this cargo was so important to so many great men then Paris would undoubtedly sanction anything, no matter how irregular. And what choice did he have? For all his compliments to Philippe, Carrier would probably take refusal as mutiny or treason and send Philippe to the guillotine, as he had obviously wished to do in Saint-Malo, in which case the ship would still go upriver under the more pliable Roissel. Carrier somehow reminded Philippe of Tasha's murderous brother, Count Bulgakov. There was the same utter certainty, the same arrogant confidence in his own view of the world, the same switchback changes of mood from calm, persuasive rationality to the almost manic suspicion that Carrier had displayed at Saint-Malo and Bulgakov... And Bulgakov... Philippe had refused to comply with his deranged brother-in-law, and it had put Tasha in her grave. He still dreamed that one day, if they were ever in the same orbit for even a moment, he would be avenged on Bulgakov. One day, perhaps, he would kill him as brutally as Bulgakov had killed Tasha. But until then, until that impossible day came, he would bend the knee to the Bulgakovs and Carriers of the world. That meant taking *Le Zéphyr* to Nantes.

–

For the first few miles, the Loire presented no difficulties. *Le Zéphyr* took on a local pilot at Saint-Nazaire and initially made good progress on a flood tide and a beneficent breeze from the south-west. The leadsman's regular cries told Philippe that there were ample *toises* beneath *Le Zéphyr*'s keel. The estuary was broad, the land on both sides low lying and largely given over to small, partially flooded fields where cattle grazed and large birds waded. Small boats made their passages up and down the river or moored just offshore so the men and boys on them could fish. The few villages of sandy-brown, red-roofed cottages and other signs of settlement were set back from the river, where the fields gave way to forest and the land was presumably less susceptible to flooding. Tricolours flew loyally from a few houses and church towers, although there were occasional signs of recent warfare: buildings shattered by artillery fire, an ancient abbey reduced to a charred ruin. He sketched much of what he saw, as John Calvin Smith had taught him to do so many years before. Charts told a man so much, but his own drawings told him so much more.

Substantial river traffic was sparse, although one large outward-bound merchantman passed *Le Zéphyr* and *Patrie* when they were off the town of Cordemais and the tide had just begun to ebb, favouring the vessel going downstream. Her crew massed at their ship's side, clearly astonished at the sight of a warship and a shattered Indiaman proceeding up the Loire. Philippe ordered her to be challenged, which probably annoyed her captain, but the ship responded smartly enough. *L'Hercule*, for Senegal and then Saint-Domingue. A slaver, then, part of the trade that was the mainstay of Nantes' prosperity. He waved to wish her *bon voyage*, but not without bitterness. He recalled his father's frequent outbursts on the subject of slavery and the raging arguments they caused with Philippe's mother, who had inherited ownership of the slaves on their plantation from her first husband. Philippe also remembered Agricola, the slave boy who became his friend: the most cheerful, good-natured soul it was possible to know until the day Philippe's mother had him flogged for theft, a crime it was later proved he did not commit. The two boys never spoke after that, and for all Philippe knew Agricola was still there, toiling in the fields for whichever of his mother's relatives now owned the Dunkeld plantation.

Philippe and de Machault had placed Marines in the tops and along *Le Zéphyr*'s sides. The deck swivel guns were manned, as were four cannon on each side of the main gun deck. The Vendée rebels were unlikely to be stupid enough to present themselves to partial broadsides of twelve-pounders that could not train to any extent, but Philippe hoped, as Carrier had done, that the very sight of *Le Zéphyr*'s powerful battery in the middle of the Loire would deter any attempt to capture *Patrie*. The Indiaman was being towed behind the warship once again and manned by a large, heavily armed contingent under Fingal. In any case, it was doubtful whether the rebels could approach the river in any numbers, in daylight at any rate, without being detected at once as they tried to cross the wide-open country on both banks. Carrier had been true to his word, too, with patrols from the Blue army sometimes visible on the few roads and tracks that came close to the shore.

The *représentant en mission* also carried out his promise to expedite *Le Zéphyr*'s passage up to Nantes. A few miles short of the city, where the river narrowed just by the inland port of Le Pellerin, a flotilla of well-manned pinnaces and other towing craft came down to meet the incoming warship and the Indiaman. This enabled *Le Zéphyr* and her charge to make the final passage into Nantes on the ebb as easily as if she were being carried on a full flood. The frigate anchored in the broadest of the several channels into which the Loire divided, while *Patrie* was towed up to one of the wharves. A large crowd assembled along the banks to gawp at the unexpected sights of a battle-damaged wreck and a trim warship of the Republic.

Verité had sometimes spoken of Nantes, and Philippe weighed his father's descriptions against the reality before him. The city had some impressive buildings: a decent Gothic cathedral, now thankfully stripped of the superstitious trappings that had deluded the people for so long, and a large chateau that had been home to the Dukes of Brittany in the long-ago days of the duchy's independence. There was clear evidence of Nantes' prosperity derived chiefly from the slave trade, with substantial, busy warehouses lining the quays and grand houses visible a little further inland. But on the fringes of the city there were also pockmarked walls, shattered roofs and burned-out shells of buildings, evidence of the siege earlier in the summer when the royalist army had attacked it.

A small boat was coming out towards *Le Zéphyr*. In its stern was a man who had all the hallmarks of a bureaucrat: the spectacles, the leather case, the elegant clothing, the large Tricolour cockade in his hat.

'Who's this peacock, then?' said Ugarte, surely loud enough for the fellow to hear it.

'The man who'll detain us here for days, I expect,' said Philippe. 'He'll want depositions, inventories, mountains of paper. We'll be lucky to sail from Nantes this side of the new year.'

Ugarte raised his eyes to the heavens, but then, he had longer experience than his captain of the Republic's insistence on the most minute and voluminous record-keeping. He, like Philippe, had a clear line of sight to *Patrie*, which appeared to be already overrun by a legion of clerks and other functionaries.

The peacock climbed aboard, stepped onto the deck of *Le Zéphyr*, and then did the strangest thing. He looked up at the masts and rigging, then his gaze swept over the great guns and the ship's boats. Finally he grinned broadly, stood to attention and raised his hat to salute the ensign at the stern, exactly as every officer of the Marine Nationale would.

Philippe stepped forward and opened his mouth, but the peacock reached forward, grabbed his hand and shook it enthusiastically.

'Captain Kermorvant! An honour, sir, an honour indeed to meet you and be aboard your ship! Such a fine vessel! Such a splendid battery! But I forget myself. I am Yves-Pierre Mercier, agent acting on behalf of Citizen Dalbarade, the Minister of the Marine, and the Committee of Public Safety. You'll want to see my credentials, of course.'

Without waiting for a reply, Mercier opened his leather case, reached within and produced a set of papers, which he handed to Philippe, who scanned them rapidly. One signed by Dalbarade, a second by Carrier, both in order. While he read, he was aware of Mercier continuing to look around the ship with undisguised glee.

'If you'll permit me to say so, Captain,' he said as Philippe returned the papers to him, 'I had the honour once to serve as an *aspirant* in the navy, back in the days of the *Royale* – I was on the old *Triomphant* under Vaudreuil and Cheyron du Pavillon until my leg got shot off in the Saintes fight. So I clutch at every chance I get to go aboard a man-of-war. A reminder of what might have been, if you take my meaning.'

'Citizen Mercier, you're welcome aboard *Le Zéphyr*,' said Philippe, trying and failing not to stare at the man's awkward gait and now all too obviously false leg. 'My officers and I will do everything in our power to assist you.'

'As long as I don't delay your return to sea, eh?' said Mercier, grinning once again. 'Don't worry, Captain, I'll interfere with your work and the business of the ship as little as I can. I need your journal and those of your other watchkeeping officers for the day you came upon the *Patrie* – nothing more than that, I assure you. Once I have fair copies of all the entries, and the custody of the slave boy from *Patrie*, I shall leave you in peace. You'll want to sail on the morning ebb, I expect?'

'Citizen, I hadn't expected to be able to leave Nantes that soon. But if possible, yes, tomorrow morning's ebb.'

'As I say, I'll do all I can to expedite matters. But in the meantime, you may enjoy a little entertainment that Citizen Carrier is putting on this afternoon. He asked me specifically to invite you, along with as many officers of *Le Zéphyr* as you think you can spare.'

'I don't think any of us can spare any time for entertainment, Citizen.'

'Citizen Carrier is most averse to refusals. Besides, no good republican would want to miss what he proposes to stage. There's never been anything like it, Captain. Tell you what, I'll accompany you. Give me an hour to do my work, no more, so you have an assurance I'll be off your ship in such a short space of time. Then we can go together to see what he's planned. It'll be the talk of Paris, I assure you – of the whole of France, come to that.'

It took Mercier longer than he had expected to complete his work, so by the time Philippe, Roissel, Fingal, de Machault, the three *aspirants*, the child Ama from *Patrie* and the one-legged clerk were rowed across to the quayside, Jean-Baptiste Carrier's mysterious entertainment was already under way, judging by the commotion coming from the other side of the Île de Nantes. If the officers from *Le Zéphyr* had not been wearing their uniforms it would probably have been impossible for them to make any progress down the packed streets and alleyways. But their appearance caused many to move aside deferentially, and National Guardsmen cleared a path for them through those parts where the crowd was at its thickest.

The Loire at Nantes divided into several channels. Philippe and his companions emerged onto a quayside on the south bank of the northern channel, where a large crowd seemed to fill every *vouce* of space. There was a palpable sense of anticipation: men puffed on their pipes and shuffled impatiently, women murmured animatedly to each other, children played in the gutters or else ran between their elders, whooping and shrieking like wild animals. Every adult, it seemed, sported a Tricolour cockade or rosette to demonstrate their loyalty to the Republic.

Mercier, who had chattered incessantly, amiably but inconsequentially all the way from the ship, led them through to the water's edge. Philippe could see Carrier, who was standing on a cart pressed into service as a makeshift stage. This was surrounded not by soldiers but by a phalanx of tough-looking men with cudgels. The *représentant* was haranguing the people nearest him, but the words did not reach as far as the party from *Le Zéphyr*: the sounds from the crowd and of the many boats moored alongside the quays and wharves drowned him out. Then for some reason the spectators nearest the channel began to boo and shout, and Carrier pointed animatedly towards the river. Philippe craned his neck and saw two barges being moored in the middle of the stream. These were clearly the objects of Carrier's tirade and the mob's wrath. The upper decks of the barges were full of men and women, packed tightly together and all chained to each other, perhaps a hundred or so on each vessel. They were of all ages, although there were more old than young. They were all naked.

'"Revolutionary marriages", Citizen Carrier calls them,' said Mercier. 'The *sans-culottes* call them underwater marriages, though. Splendid, isn't it?'

Splendid would not have been the word Philippe chose to describe the scene before him. Many of the prisoners were looking to the heavens as though hoping some miracle, some sudden act of divine intervention, would save them. Some of them were singing tunes that Philippe recognised as psalms, others mumbling the words of the old prayers over and over.

'What is this?' he said to Mercier. 'Who are they and what have they done?'

'Oh, monks and nuns, mostly,' said the one-legged clerk in an offhand manner. 'A few priests who refused the oath to the constitution – those sorts of deluded scum. Citizen Carrier takes the view that the guillotine might be a wonderful machine, but it's far too slow for proper revolutionary justice. Too few of them in the whole of France, he says, and they can only kill one traitor at a time. So he devised these *noyades* instead. He calls the Loire the national bathtub, you know? Real wit, I call that.'

Philippe now knew what was about to happen. The men crewing the barges came up on deck, elbowed their ways past the doomed prisoners, and swiftly climbed down into the small boats tied to the barges' sides. As the boats pulled away, the barges began perceptibly to settle lower in the water. The scuttles had been opened, and they were sinking. The psalms and prayers got louder, as did the shouts and cheers from the crowds ashore. The water began to lap onto the decks of the barges. A few of the nuns screamed and called out for mercy. But mercy was the last thing on the minds of Jean-Baptiste Carrier and the mob he was inciting. Many in the crowd were jeering, women and children being the worst. Carrier himself was leaping up and down in excitement like a small boy seeing the circus for the first time. The *représentant*, member of the National Convention, the Committee of Public Safety and the high representative of the French Republic in Nantes, was screaming ever more lurid and obscene insults at the dying prisoners on the barges. Alongside Philippe, Mercier's face was flushed and he was grinning broadly. Philippe realised that the sometime *aspirant*, who had seemed so friendly and reasonable, was not just relishing the spectacle before them, he was in true ecstasies. Roissel, on the other side of him, seemed entirely rapt, but the direction of his gaze and the expression in his eyes suggested to Philippe that the lieutenant was moved less by republican zeal than the nakedness of those who were dying in the waters of the Loire. Lievremont and Carabignac were silent, expressionless and very still, as though they had suddenly been transformed into statues by some evil deity. Unexpectedly, Vaquin was in tears, but it was impossible for Philippe to tell whether they were tears of joy or grief. Only two of the company from *Le Zéphyr* seemed unquestionably to share Philippe's feelings. Fingal's face was even paler than usual and displaying open revulsion at what was being played out on the river, while Ama, the silent, frightened slave boy from *Patrie*, had his mouth open and was staring in horror at the spectacle before him.

Philippe hoped that his own feelings were not so transparent.

Father, he thought. *Verité. Is this what you wanted from the republic you idealised?*

The barges sank ever lower, the crowd accompanying them into the dark waters of the Loire with an ever-louder and more frenzied cacophony of abuse.

Is this the dream I came to France to pursue – the cause I came to serve?

For a moment, Philippe contemplated throwing away his sword and uniform coat, running as far as he could from the waterfront of Nantes, getting out of France, returning to Virginia and there running free and wild with the Pamunkey once again. It was just one moment, one fleeting and terrible thought, but as the last heads of the tallest men disappeared beneath the Loire and the last words of the last prayer were cut off, Philippe felt his faith in the French Republic shaken to its very core.

CHAPTER TWENTY-FOUR

Timing was all.

He was in the company of a *représentant en mission*, a member of both the National Convention and the Committee of Public Safety. In former times, Martin Roissel would have thanked God for such an unambiguous sign of His blessing. He had never been at such an elegant *soirée* as that given by the wife of one of the most prominent Jacobins of Nantes to celebrate the events of the day. The glittering ballroom was full of the most important people wearing the latest fashions, toasting each other from delicate flutes of fine wine. The *représentant* was at the centre of it, receiving the congratulations of one and all like a Roman emperor receiving the homage of his grateful subjects. Kermorvant was one of the first to be presented to him, curse the man; but even in the new age of liberty that detested *aristos* and cut off their heads with gusto, it seemed that a noble title still conveyed a certain precedence on such an occasion. Roissel turned away. It would be the last time that the title of Vicomte de Saint-Victor would count for anything, so the lieutenant of *Le Zéphyr* sought out a footman to recharge his glass.

If he could have chosen, he would have wanted to do this more discreetly. The occasion was too public, but he had no choice. Kermorvant was insistent on them getting back to sea as quickly as possible, and if Roissel were honest with himself, he would be taking exactly the same view if he were in command of *Le Zéphyr*. In any case, the *représentant en mission* was a very busy man, and access to him would be difficult for any man of Roissel's rank. So this was his only chance.

All around him, young men and women smiled, laughed and danced while their elders indulged them. Roissel engaged in conversation with a pair of merchants who had large investments in the Caribbean and were prominent in the local Jacobin clubs, then moved on to a lawyer who served the revolutionary tribunal and a tall, refined lady whose husband was a colonel in the Army of the North. All the while, Roissel worked his way closer to Jean-Baptiste Carrier. As he did so he occasionally caught sight of Captain Kermorvant, who looked distant, miserable, and was either alone or else engaged in desultory conversation with people of no consequence. The intolerable man even spent an age talking with Ugarte, who was also clearly uncomfortable in the surroundings. Roissel, though, was in his element, regaling his audiences with tales of the sea and the perils of the deep. If he could make such an impression as a mere *lieutenant de vaisseau*, how much better would he fare as a captain? He drew near to the *représentant* at last and prepared to address this titan of republican virtue and integrity, the man who had turned the Loire, the very lifeblood of France, into the baptismal font of revolution. Martin Roissel reached inside his uniform jacket and drew out the envelope. All he had to do was give it to the great man before him and his life would be transformed.

Just as he was about to make his bow, Carrier stood and called for silence. The audience turned to him, everyone eager to hear what the *représentant en mission* had to say.

'Citizens,' said Carrier. 'Friends of liberty, friends of the Republic. I thank you for your attendance here tonight, and for witnessing this afternoon's events. Now, I suppose it's possible that some of you have misgivings about what you saw today. I understand that. I am a husband and a father. I do not have a heart of stone, nor do I relish watching the suffering of others. But this is a time of revolution, and the truth of the revolution sweeps away all such sentimental weakness. So I have unleashed the revolutionary thunderbolts from my hands, *mes amis.*'

There was enthusiastic applause at this, and Roissel joined in. Such clarity of language, such sincerity of purpose. Yes, the *représentant* was a very great man.

'Those who died today were not innocent. Far from it, my friends. Let me tell you who they were. They were the agents of darkness who concealed the truth from the people for centuries. They were the peddlers of superstition and falsehood, seducing every rank of society from princes to peasants simply to line their own pockets. Their days are done in the France of liberty and reason. These just and lawful executions, these *noyades*, demonstrate this to the whole world. But what has happened here today is but the start, good citizens of Nantes!

From here, we will purge France of all error, all wrong thinking, all crime of any sort!'

Carrier signalled for the music to restart, and the end of his speech triggered louder applause and cheering. Roissel joined in, and as he did so he happened to see his captain, standing with Ugarte just a little to Roissel's right. Kermorvant was not clapping, and his face was grim. *Oh, I see you now, Monsieur le Vicomte,* thought Roissel. *I will see you to the guillotine, or into the dark waters of the Loire.*

His moment had come. He inclined his head respectfully to the *représentant en mission*, who acknowledged the gesture with an almost regal wave of his hand.

'Roissel, Citizen, Lieutenant de Vaisseau of *Le Zéphyr*. My congratulations on an inspiring address and on a day of glory for the Republic.'

'*Merci*, Citizen. Second-in-command of the frigate, eh? Yes, I thought I recognised you. You hold a responsible position, Citizen. A worthy defender of the Republic against her foes, eh?'

'As you say, Citizen.' Roissel lowered his voice. 'And this concerns one of those foes.'

He handed Carrier the letter, but the *représentant* made no move to open it, instead studying Roissel's features intently. Then he did the unthinkable. He beckoned to Philippe Kermorvant, who came forward to join them. Those nearby, aware that something strange was playing out, fell silent.

'I imagine, Lieutenant,' said Carrier, 'that this is a denunciation of Captain Kermorvant, here, for being an *aristo* and a traitor to the Republic. Or am I wrong?'

This was not how Martin Roissel had expected it to play out. The *représentant* would surely open the letter at his leisure after the *soirée*, and the troops would come and arrest Kermorvant when they were all back on the ship. But if it had to be done in public, so be it. Roissel had no reason not to be proud of the blow he was striking for the revolution.

'You are not wrong, Citizen. This man is the Vicomte de Saint-Victor, so by birth alone he is an enemy of the people, of liberty, of—'

'I'm aware who he is, Citizen.'

'And I have proof of counter-revolutionary conspiracy on his part, also witnessed by others on *Le Zéphyr*!'

'Well,' said Carrier. 'Well, well, well. Serious, this. What d'you say to it, Captain Kermorvant?'

'You have the evidence, Citizen Carrier. It speaks for itself.'

'Yes, I remember from Saint-Malo. A great man for pieces of paper, aren't you, Monsieur le Vicomte? All those letters on your behalf. All those mighty names you trot out.'

They knew each other. Somehow, Kermorvant and Carrier knew each other from Saint-Malo. Roissel swallowed. He had not expected this. But perhaps it changed nothing – the *représentant* seemed hostile to the vile foreign *aristo*.

'So in the one hand,' said Carrier, 'I hold Lieutenant Roissel's denunciation of his captain as a traitor. The lieutenant says many of the officers and crew concur in this but provides no proof of that. You, Citizen,' he said, gesturing to Ugarte, 'you are the next in command of *Le Zéphyr*, I recall. Do you or any men you know support the charge brought by Lieutenant Roissel?'

The Basque seemed tongue-tied at being addressed directly by such a great man of the Republic, but then he looked directly at Roissel.

'I agreed when he denounced Captain Berthomier,' said Ugarte. 'Many of the crew did. But treason didn't enter into it, Citizen. Berthomier didn't know his business any more, he was mad or senile or both. His punishments were harsh and his orders made no sense; the crew hated him, and we reckoned he'd end up losing the ship and drowning us all. But Captain Kermorvant, he's a true seaman, the men can see that and respect him for listening to them, and I'd reckon there isn't an officer in the navy as loyal to the Republic as him. Maybe some of the malcontents in the crew agree with Citizen Roissel, but only a fraction of them at most, and no officers, that's the very truth, Citizen.'

Carrier nodded, but Roissel stared furiously at Ugarte. The Basque was beneath contempt. Surely the *représentant* would see that.

'But I am become Solomon,' said Carrier, 'for in my other hand I have papers passed to me by Captain Kermorvant. Shall I tell you what they are, Citizen Roissel? Shall I tell you so all these people around us can hear?'

This was not part of Roissel's plan. No, this was certainly not how he had imagined the unfolding of events.

Carrier scowled. 'Item, sworn deposition by Fabian Vaquin, *aspirant* aboard the Republic's frigate *Le Zéphyr*, accusing Lieutenant de Vaisseau Martin Roissel of committing buggery with him.'

Vaquin, that little weasel – that ungrateful turncoat…

'And then there is this,' said Carrier, unfolding a badly crumpled, torn piece of paper. 'A deposition sworn before a *notaire* of the city of Brest, witnessed by a respectable physician of that place, made by a boy called Jean-Claude Sinquin shortly before his death, testifying that his fatal injuries had been sustained in a building called L'Oiseau-Lyre. Sustained at your hands, Lieutenant Roissel, as the climax of what I can only describe as the most depraved and perverted kind of orgy that evil men can devise.'

Sinquin? He had never heard of a Sinquin. But the name Jean-Claude was familiar... That one. It had to be that one. Surely the boy was dead when he left him – but there had been those other two boys, down at the far end of the street, the ones who had run when he levelled his pistol at them. They must have come back; the lad could not have been dead, and one among them must have had the presence of mind to summon both a doctor and a lawyer.

'I have far greater concerns than spending my time on such unspeakable perversions,' said Carrier, and Roissel sighed at the glimmer of hope. 'But as I said to this audience, I am a father. Even in a republic at war, even as we seek out and destroy the enemies of liberty, crime is still crime, murder is still murder, and it will be judged. Lieutenant Martin Roissel, in the name of the French Republic, one and indivisible, I order your arrest.'

Roissel was bewildered. This was not what should have happened, not how he wanted matters to conclude. This could not be happening to him – not at the posthumous behest of a worthless child, a mere scraping from the gutters of Brest. Surely Représentant Carrier, a worthy representative of the power of the Republic, could not think the so-called evidence of such an insignificant creature outweighed Martin Roissel's word and revolutionary zeal? He looked about for support, for sympathetic faces, for a man with the authority to stop this farce, but found none. The worst thing, the very worst thing of all, was the expression on the face of a man who had always hated him.

'Properly fucked this time, Roissel,' said Ugarte, the new first lieutenant of *Le Zéphyr*, as two of Carrier's guards led his predecessor away.

At Ugarte's side, Captain Philippe Kermorvant remained silent.

CHAPTER TWENTY-FIVE

It took *Le Zéphyr* three days to return to sea.

The passage downstream was uneventful, perhaps in part because of the cold, miserable, foggy weather. The royalist rebels were either unwilling to risk an attack on a warship of the Republic or they preferred to warm themselves before their hearths. Once the ship was clear of the mouth of the Loire, Philippe gave orders to sail north and then west, past Lorient, the Île de Groix and the Glénan archipelago to Penmarch. There was no sign of enemy activity, perhaps because there were still two frigates from the Lorient squadron at Quiberon, perhaps because the campaigning season was largely over and there was little prospect of the British attempting a landing so late in the year. *Le Zéphyr* then set her course out into the open sea, cruising south-westerly before turning south-east towards La Rochelle. Philippe ordered the chase of several distant sails, but none merited close attention; there were a couple of neutrals making for Nantes, one American and a Lubecker, a friendly exchange with the new frigate *Beveziers* returning to Lorient from the Americas, and several far distant ships that changed course and disappeared before *Le Zéphyr* could close them. There was no sign of the English navy, which presumably meant they were concerned for now only to blockade Brest and bottle up Morard with the main fleet. The weather, although bitterly cold, was relatively settled for October, with nothing more alarming than a few sharp but short-lived squalls, some of which bore snow.

Philippe gave orders, took his bearings, made his journal entries, ordered punishments, inspected stores and messes, and carried out all the other duties expected of the captain of a man-of-war, but it was as though he was somehow detached from the man carrying out those tasks. He could not clear his mind of what he had seen at Nantes. No matter how Carrier, Mercier and the rest of them dressed it up, no matter what fine words they spoke to justify the drownings, Philippe knew that what he had witnessed was mass murder, pure and simple. Surely not even the Russians would contemplate such a thing, yet here was France, the epitome of civilisation, a republic devoted to freedom, reason and the rights of man, committing atrocities beyond anything he had seen from the Turks, Russians, Indians or English.

He should not think about it.

–

In overcast weather, *Le Zéphyr* made a leisurely cruise along the coast from the Île de Ré towards the Île de Yeu, aiming to pass between the latter and the mainland. The shore consisted chiefly of long sandy beaches, very different to the more rugged terrain around Brest and, indeed, the whole coast of Finisterre. This was largely rebel-held territory; although the Republic held Nantes, troops venturing from there exercised only sketchy control over the hinterland and even less over the coast, where the Vendée rebels predominated. Even so, this was hardly a propitious shore for the sorts of operations Philippe was under orders to undertake, notably the interception of vessels carrying guns or other supplies to the rebels. There were no creeks or harbours, so it would be nearly impossible to land a substantial cargo for many miles. On the other hand, it would be very easy indeed for a small ship to run in under cover of darkness and use small boats to land or take off a few men, be they English spies or rebel generals. *Le Zéphyr* might get lucky and stumble across one of these, but it was unlikely. Philippe dare not risk her too far inshore on what was usually a lee shore, and the smaller craft sent out of Brest or Lorient to carry out such missions were almost all concentrated further north, cruising the much more complex coast of Finisterre where there were countless cliff-bound inlets and small fishing harbours. In truth, the sight of *Le Zéphyr* making her stately way north along the coast served principally as a deterrent and a reminder to any rebels watching her from the sand dunes of the all-seeing presence and power of the Republic.

The calculations changed as Philippe saw the Île de Yeu fall away to port. Ahead was the much longer, thinner and flatter island of Noirmoutier, beyond which lay the arm of the wide Bay of Biscay that stretched up to Belle-Île and Quiberon. As well as forming the approach to Nantes, the coastline here became less regular and was indented by many more coves. The Île de Noirmoutier itself was held by the rebels, as were many of the villages on the mainland. From time to time Philippe saw the enemy: horsemen, usually, riding along the shore, sometimes pausing to study *Le Zéphyr* through their telescopes. Twice he saw men riding under the banner of the Sacred Heart. Yet there was no sign of any vessel that might be construed as suspicious, only fishing boats venturing out of the tiny coastal villages. Off Belle-Île, Philippe ordered Fingal to hail a group of a dozen such boats and offer the hospitality of *Le Zéphyr* to their masters. The fishermen accepted with alacrity. They gawped as they boarded the frigate and looked around nervously as Philippe and his officers entertained them in the great cabin. Most of them responded to questions with single words that were usually little more than grunts; Philippe suspected that in this part of the world a fair proportion of any random dozen men would be open or secret royalists who would see their invitation aboard the frigate as an opportunity to report on its condition to the local rebel leadership ashore. But there was one man who stood a little apart from the others drinking a prodigious amount of wine and brandy, and who responded to Philippe's toast to the Republic rather more fervently than any of his fellows. A couple of hours later, when the other fishermen were returning unsteadily to their craft, this fellow requested a private audience with the captain, so Driaux showed him to Philippe's cabin. There, with Ugarte also present, the fisherman – Gilbert Gendron by name – proclaimed himself to be one of the most loyal Jacobins on the entire coast of Poitou. Moreover, he was a man possessed of secret intelligence that would undoubtedly be of value to the Republic and the most honourable Citizen Captain of *Le Zéphyr*. Times were hard, though, and he had a wife and six children to feed...

Philippe listened to his tale with considerable scepticism, but, with Ugarte's concurrence, he calculated that he had nothing to lose by taking Gendron at his word. So he gave the fisherman a small purse of coins, saw him off the ship, then gave orders for *Le Zéphyr* to drop anchor off the citadel of Belle-Île to await the early hours and the flood tide running into the Loire. The frigate sailed south-east in darkness, all lights extinguished and the crew under strict orders to maintain silence throughout the ship. A half-moon showed itself intermittently through the clouds. Philippe ordered Arnaud Lucas to serve as the principal lookout, but in the event the poacher's keen eyesight was not needed. Philippe, standing on the quarterdeck with his telescope in constant use, saw the ship in nearly the same moment that Lucas's urgent call came from above. Its sails were glimpses of white against the black shore of Noirmoutier to the south, its hull barely distinguishable from the coast behind it. Like *Le Zéphyr*, it showed no lights.

The frigate rapidly closed the distance to the sluggish but suspicious vessel, and its characteristics became more apparent. The ship was a Dutch *fluyt*, a type that Philippe knew well from his time in the Baltic. With a shallow draught, a broad beam and a large hold, it was ideal for carrying large cargoes into coastal waters and small harbours. Any other officer of the Marine Nationale might have looked at it and not given it a second glance. Just another coaster going up to Nantes, what of it? But as Ugarte, the veteran of merchant ships, said, the *fluyt* was an ancient design, long outmoded and superseded by faster and sleeker craft. They were hardly used any more in the confined and gentler waters of the Baltic, so why should one have braved the feared Bay of Biscay when every merchant of Nantes, rich from the proceeds of the slave trade, could easily afford to have their cargoes shipped in something newer and better? In its heyday, Ugarte said, the *fluyt* had apparently been everywhere, in the service of skippers and merchants of all nations. But the design had been employed principally by its original creators, the Dutch, and now, in the last flickerings of its twilight, the *fluyt* was still used above all by conservative Dutch shipowners. And the United Provinces of the Netherlands was one of the many nations at war with the French Republic.

Moreover, it was night and the ship was darkened. Why would a merchant skipper risk the navigation of this coast and the estuary of the Loire at night time? Why not take in sail further out to sea and wait for morning?

Philippe knew they were very tenuous suspicions on which to build a case for stopping and boarding what might prove to be a neutral hull, or worse, a French ship with an owner who had powerful friends in the National Convention. But something he could not explain made him look and look again at the ungainly hull. She was too close to Noirmoutier to be making for the estuary. Surely she was making instead for the eastern side of the island… the rebel-held island? Finally, he made his decision and turned to Ugarte.

'Hail her once we're in range, Enseigne. "Heave to. Prepare to be boarded." If she doesn't respond, we'll put a shot across her bows. Then get the *chaloupe* outboard and muster a boarding party of twenty men, half and half of seamen and Marines.'

'Aye, aye, Citizen Captain! And the commander of the boarding party, sir? Myself or Fingal?'

Philippe looked again at the dark hull. Leonore would have scoffed at him — Tasha always did — but he had a feeling about this. Verité, the arch-rationalist, had a superstitious streak that he had passed on to his son. Merlin's sense, he called it.

'No, Citizen. I'll command it myself.'

Between them, Merlin and Verité had much to answer for.

—

Philippe climbed onto the deck of the *fluyt* with Fingal, Lievremont and two Marines at his back, followed by the rest of the boarding party. They were confronted immediately by the skipper, a bear of a man with a vast matted beard who made even Ugarte's proportions seem modest. He was brandishing papers in his hand and proclaiming loudly that he was a Dunkirker and as French as the Citizen Captain, even though his accent placed him rather further north than Dunkirk; somewhat closer to Amsterdam, Philippe reckoned. A couple of seamen stood behind their skipper, glancing at him and each other, fidgeting, and occasionally looking behind them. The men from *Le Zéphyr* were moving to secure all parts of the ship, a couple of the seamen taking the wheel, Fingal and the Marines leading the way below decks. It all seemed perfectly normal, and if the Dunkirk skipper's papers proved to be legitimate then—

A shot was fired somewhere down below, followed immediately by the sound of frenzied, desperate shouts and commands. The two seamen drew daggers and cudgels and rushed Philippe, who drew his sword and pistol. But Lievremont, with the quick reactions of the young, was already ahead of his captain, and the first stab from one of the rebels went for him rather than Philippe. Lievremont took the blow in his waist and gasped, but his own thrust at his assailant pierced the man's throat, bringing forth a jet of blood.

It sounded as though there was bloody chaos below decks, but Philippe had no time to react to it. The skipper of the *fluyt* had two pistols drawn and was raising them, but Philippe fired first, opening a hole in the big man's chest. The skipper looked at him in astonishment, then fell to the deck. The Marines were overcoming the other two men and Lievremont, though wounded, was still conscious and upright, so Philippe ran to the hatchway and went below. There was almost no light, but there were clearly many men battling each other in the confined space. The *fluyt* was carrying more men than would be needed to crew a legitimate trader, and no legitimate trader's crew would resist the French navy or cry '*Vive le roi!*' as these men did.

As Philippe's eyes adjusted to the darkness, he recognised two of his men standing close by. The Marines were making a determined push forward against the rebels ahead of them, so the sailors behind them momentarily had no opponents to fight.

'You two,' cried Philippe, 'with me!'

He turned and went towards the stern of the *fluyt*. The master's cabin was generous, larger than Philippe's own on *Le Zéphyr*, and well lit, no doubt because the skipper had closed the shutters of his stern windows. There were two men in the cabin, although one was little more than a boy. The youth was dead on the deck, thick red blood oozing from the wide and livid cut across his neck.

The other man in the cabin was Philippe's erstwhile cellmate, Captain Paul Storr.

The Englishman recovered from his surprise first. 'My lord of Saint-Victor,' he said calmly. 'Your condition has improved from when I last saw you.'

Philippe levelled his pistol at Storr. 'Yours, I think, has worsened.'

Fingal came into the cabin behind Philippe, looked in bewilderment at the scene before him, but remembered his duty at once and reported to his captain.

'Ship's secure, sir. The hold contains large quantities of muskets, cannon and other weaponry. A substantial inventory, I'd say.'

'Thank you, Enseigne.'

'Is all well here, sir?'

'Well enough while I have a gun on that man, but you'd better send in a Marine so I can rest my arm. It would be a tragedy if my pistol were to go off accidentally. Oh, and, Fingal – until I'm free of my responsibilities here, you have this ship.'

'Aye, aye, sir!'

Fingal's place was taken by a Marine – Herbin, the man who had been on duty when Philippe first attempted to take command of *Le Zéphyr*. Herbin levelled his musket at Storr, enabling Philippe to lower his own gun.

'I'm interested to hear your explanation,' said Philippe, nodding towards the dead boy, 'if you're going to dare to offer one.'

Storr spread his hands innocently. 'You have a suspicious mind, Citizen Captain.'

'You're standing over a dead boy with his throat cut, aboard a ship with a cargo of arms clearly bound for the rebels. I hope you're not going to try to deny that you cut it, or that the arms are intended for somewhere more innocent than the Vendée revolt.'

The Englishman nodded.

'I won't insult your intelligence, my lord. Of course I cut his throat, and of course the arms are destined for the royalists.'

Philippe could barely register the enormity of the crime and the lies he knew he was being told.

'I was told you were an agent of the Republic against your own country,' he said, 'yet I find you aboard a ship carrying weapons to the enemies of France and confessing to killing a youth barely out of his childhood. So let me tell you what I think, Captain Storr, if you truly deserve to be called by that rank. I think you've only pretended to be a lover of the Republic. I think you're an English double agent and always have been.'

'Not very imaginative,' said Storr casually, 'although I can see why you'd think that. It's the obvious thing for you to think – yes, I can see that. But I tell you what, Captain – what do you call yourself now? Kermorvant, or your title? No matter. If I was still true to England I could be back on Romney Marsh plying my old trade, 'cos now the war's on I reckon my old friends'll be coining it from all those fine gentlemen who won't be deprived of their French brandy, whatever old Billy Pitt says. Whereas me? Your precious republic barely pays me enough to afford a bed in a lousy shared garret in Nantes, but I still put myself in harm's way on its behalf so that one day, those lads on the Marsh can live in liberty under a free republic too. Not that they'll thank me for it.'

'You said you wouldn't insult my intelligence, Captain Storr, but I think you just did.'

'Maybe, then. Maybe, too, that boy there had more wit than you, my lord. He found me in here and reckoned I was using the shutter to signal to your ship. He was going to call out and bring 'em down on me, so I had to shut him up. Nothing else to it, Citizen Captain.'

Philippe considered the dead boy, studied Storr's complacent expression, and finally looked at the shutters enclosing the stern windows of the *fluyt*. One of them was a little ajar, as was the pane behind it. But they could have been open for a reason other than that which Storr had just given.

'*Nothing else to it*. Or else, perhaps, he found you doing something else from the window? Say, throwing weighted papers overboard?'

Storr chuckled to himself.

'Whatever the state of your intelligence, my friend, there's plainly nothing wrong with your imagination.' He sighed. 'Well, then, here's the truth. I report to the *représentant en mission* at Nantes, Citizen Carrier – I heard you've had dealings with him? He ordered me to ingratiate myself into the Vendée army hereabouts, so I got close to its general, fellow called d'Elbée, and he gave me the mission of bringing in this shipment. But as far as Citizen Carrier and the Committee of Public Safety are concerned, there's a much bigger fish to fry. They know the Comte d'Artois is mad keen to come to the Vendée to take command of the royalist army. You know about Artois? Yes, well, who doesn't? Artois wants to lead the rebels into Paris and oversee the slaughter of every man, woman and child who's ever so much as read a republican placard. It'll make Madame Guillotine's busiest days seem like quiet holidays in the country. So that's what I'm doing here, Citizen Captain. I'm one of the agents the Republic's sent out to try to learn when and where Artois will land, and if I can prove myself to d'Elbée and the rest of them, I'll be well placed to betray him to Citizen Carrier.'

Philippe opened his mouth to speak but thought better of it. He stared at Storr, not wanting to believe the man but bemused by the tale he had spun. If it was a lie, it was a lie so huge, so utterly implausible, that it might perhaps be true. Philippe certainly did know of the reputation of the Comte d'Artois, which had reached even Russia. The guillotined

Louis Capet had two younger brothers who had escaped the same fate and now lived in exile. The elder, the Comte de Provence, nominally the regent to his young and imprisoned nephew, was said to be fat, amiable and pragmatic. The younger, Charles, Comte d'Artois, was the exact opposite. Mystical, austere and utterly fanatical, he sought the overthrow of the Republic and restoration of the monarchy by the bloodiest means possible. It was perfectly believable that Artois wished to be there in the Vendée, just as Storr claimed. Having encountered the man, thought Philippe, it was also perfectly believable that Jean-Baptiste Carrier would devise an intricate strategy to capture the ferocious, feared prince. What a feather in Carrier's cap it would be if he could send to the guillotine the most hated and dangerous of all the members of the royal House of Bourbon!

A gust of wind blew the open shutter a little wider, and Philippe saw that it was getting lighter. He had to get the prize and *Le Zéphyr* herself to a safer position as soon as possible in case there were rebel artillery batteries of Noirmoutier with the range to hit them. Therefore, he needed to make a decision about Storr, and he had to make it immediately.

'Very well, Captain Storr, you say you report to Citizen Carrier. I propose we should do exactly that. He can then confirm or deny your story and decide on your fate if you've lied to me and to the Republic.'

Storr's eyes widened momentarily, but his expression retained its fixed smugness as Philippe instructed the Marine to bind the Englishman's hands and take him to *Le Zéphyr's chaloupe*. Philippe recalled the Blue-held fort held at Saint-Nazaire from their earlier transit of the Loire, so both Storr and the *fluyt* could be handed over to the army there. Lievremont, who was sitting on deck drinking brandy to dull the pain from the wound, could also be landed and taken to Nantes for more qualified treatment than he might receive from his mess-mate Carabignac. Lievremont had become the best seaman of *Le Zéphyr's* intake of *aspirants*, and his loss, following that of a hated but competent watch-keeping officer in Roissel, would heavily weaken the resources at Philippe's command. To set against that, a substantial shipment of weapons would now be denied to the royalist rebels of the Vendée, and perhaps the schemes of the vengeful and bloodthirsty Comte d'Artois would be thwarted, even if only temporarily, by *Le Zéphyr's* little victory off the Île de Noirmoutier.

CHAPTER TWENTY-SIX

It was the day France was going to cut the head off its queen.

Leonore had been in Paris for almost a month by then. She spent almost all her waking hours at the doors of the National Convention and the Committee of Public Safety, hoping to talk to one of the great men of the Republic, hoping to plead the cause of her husband, Alexandre. But the town was seething with anticipation of the execution of Marie-Antoinette, and nobody had time to hear or had any interest in the case of a convicted minor traitor from France's most distant and backward province. In any case, she was merely one out of hundreds of desperate solicitants who thronged the same locations every day; she now knew many of the faces, and was on speaking terms with several. Her hopes of reaching her cousin, General Lazare Carnot, proved illusory. He was away at the northern front, fully engaged in the frantic reorganisation of the Republic's armies, and was not expected to return to Paris for some time, perhaps not even until the spring. The minor functionaries of the National Convention and War Ministry who told her this initially expressed some sympathy for her, but that usually vanished once they knew that this woman pleading for mercy for her husband had also denounced him to the revolutionary tribunal. Officially, republican France commended wives who put their loyalty to the revolution above their marital vows; but the old anathemas proclaimed by the priests for centuries were proving difficult to budge, and even many of the most dedicated Jacobins were privately horrified by the very idea of a woman betraying her husband and then inexplicably seeking to make amends by saving him from the guillotine. She did not blame them or resent the strange looks she received and the critical words she heard from the mouths of some of those to whom she told her story. She understood the incredulity. If she found it difficult to explain and justify her actions to herself, how could others be expected to understand?

In spite of everything, she persevered and refused to lose hope. Having proclaimed terror to be the official policy of the state, the Committee of Safety was accelerating the rate of executions. But it was also greatly increasing the number of arrests, leading to a backlog of cases, so Alexandre's execution was delayed and delayed again. Moreover, the attentions of the authorities in Paris seemingly focused entirely on the imminent execution of the former queen. More troops had been drafted into the city as a precaution against counter-revolutionary disturbances, and those walking the streets on perfectly innocent business were sometimes challenged and asked for their papers several times on the same street. There were rumours that the Emperor of Austria had sent a cadre of his finest troops into Paris in secret to rescue his aunt from the very steps to the guillotine, and alleged sightings of these men – all blond giants at least seven feet tall, it was said, each with the strength of ten – were frequent, sending entire neighbourhoods into hysterical panics. Almost none seemed to make the obvious deduction that such a force, if it existed, would be the most conspicuous covert rescue mission in history. Paris, Leonore reflected, had truly become the capital city of credulity.

For days beforehand, Leonore told herself that she had no desire to see the execution of the queen. She had no love for the woman – if only a small fraction of the stories about her were true then she thoroughly deserved her fate – but neither did she hate her with the venom spat out by the rich widow who had the adjacent room in the lodging house on the Left Bank. Madame Guitard had come from Arras especially for the event and flaunted overlarge red, white and blue feathers in her hat as she set out alongside Leonore, insisting that it would be far too dangerous for either of them to walk through Paris alone. As far as Leonore could see, Madame Guitard was built more powerfully than any National Guardsman they had encountered and could probably have given a good account of herself against one of Emperor Francis's mythical giants.

They were in lodgings near the vast Hôpital de la Pitié-Salpêtrière on the Left Bank, so had to cross the Seine to get to the Place de la Révolution where the execution would take place. They walked along the river and crossed the bridge onto Île de la Citie, the crowds increasing with every pace they took. Troops stood sentry on the street corners while others moved through the throng, checking papers and acting arbitrarily against those they judged suspicious. But Leonore and her companion attracted nothing more than curious glances, most of them directed at Madame Guitard's astonishing hat.

'Don't mourn your husband for too long, dear,' said the widow as they waited for the huge press of people on the bridge to start moving forward again. 'I waited perhaps four days before I discarded the black weeds. Too long, I'd say now. Vincent was as good a husband as a woman could expect to have, I suppose, and at least he didn't make much of a fuss about dying. Fell ill on the Thursday, dead on the Saturday, in the ground on the Monday. I was back at the *salon* on the following Friday. Admirable dispatch, I'd call it.'

'Madame, you know I'm not a widow. We've talked of it many times. But if Alexandre does go to the guillotine then I'll mourn him appropriately.'

'Of course you will, dear, although I suppose it's different in your case. I mean, well, it was the typhus that did for Vincent, not me. Same thing in the end, though, yours will be gone just like mine is gone, and then you'll be free to dally with that sea-captain brother-in-law, eh? I envy you, my dear. We know all about the reputation of sailors in Arras, even if they're as rare as chaste nuns around there.'

Leonore bitterly regretted having told Madame Guitard about Philippe during their second meeting, when the widow had invited her to a *soirée* in her room and Leonore had drunk far too much claret. The discovery that Philippe was both a naval officer and a vicomte hugely impressed Madame Guitard, whose revolutionary vehemence did not preclude an almost fawning obsession with blue blood and titles. The widow's breezy attitude to Leonore's situation did nothing to improve her mood. Every day, every hour, she swung between the most intense feelings of guilt and a conviction that she had done the right thing, the *only* thing. One morning she was full of optimism that Alexandre might yet be spared, by afternoon convinced again that it was for the best if he went to the guillotine as quickly as possible. One moment she looked forward to running and improving the estate of Brechelean alone and entirely as she wished (she had *so many ideas!*), the next she wanted Philippe permanently ashore, installed as the *seigneur* of his ancestral home, playing a part in her life that she dare not think about. Leonore had always regarded herself as a strong woman, confident in her chosen path, independent in her thinking, capable of aiming and firing a gun, making up accurate accounts, and knowledgeable about both politics and religion. She contrasted herself with other women she had known over the years, family, friends and neighbours alike, whose greatest intellectual challenge seemed to be finding new superlatives to describe their invariably mediocre husbands and children. Yet here she was, as doubt-laden as any of her sisters, as uncertain and retiring as her mother, as childless as her bitter spinster aunt, unsure of her feelings about anything. Perhaps witnessing something as shocking as the execution of the queen would bring her to an understanding of it all, to the place of certainty that she craved.

–

Leonore and Madame Guitard shuffled with the rest of the crowd past the towering façade of Notre-Dame, now empty of the priests and the pathetic kneeling ranks of the deluded, muttering their superstitious prayers to a god that had been deemed not to exist by the more enlightened atheist leaders of the Republic.

'I hear they're going to put on a festival of Reason in there,' said Madame Guitard, 'whatever such a thing may be. With the old Church, there were plenty of things to show off to the people: relics, crucifixes, all the rest of it. Amiens had the head of John the Baptist, you know? I saw it many times, and always thought how odd it was that Salome should have left it in Amiens of all places. But what can you display for Reason, I ask you? I suppose you could dig up Voltaire and put his bones on show. Not really the same as John the Baptist, though, in my opinion.'

Leonore wished that her companion would be silent, but there was probably more chance of the queen being reprieved. So she let her thoughts drift, and although she tried not to, she found herself thinking once again of Philippe. There had been no letter from him, but then, why should there be? For one thing, what did he think of her for denouncing his brother? She recalled what they had said to each other in Brest, when they were both overwhelmed by the situation. But out at sea, alone on his deck or in his cabin – he had told her about the lonely state of a sea-captain – what was he thinking? Perhaps there had been letters, though. He would not know she had come to Paris, after all. But even if he did, if say he had been in correspondence with the Penhouets, why should he even think of her? He bore the heavy responsibilities of command, and even though there had been no further mutinies in the fleet she knew that the state of the war was desperately precarious. The Republic was still under siege, and at séa its navy was hugely inferior to the countless wooden castles that England could set out. What was happening today in Paris was bound to further inflame the enemy powers, especially the Austrian emperor, and make them more determined than ever to destroy this upstart revolutionary government. Philippe knew more of such things than she did, and he would also have to think of his men and his ship. He would have no time to consider her and how she fared in her lonely condition. No time at all.

Leonore and Madame Guitard followed the singing, laughing crowd along the troop-lined riverbank, past the Louvre, and finally reached Place de la Révolution, where the spectacle would be played out. The obstreperous widow had no qualms about pushing her way through the throng, Leonore trailing in her wake, in order to reach a decent viewing position near the wall of the Tuilleries. From there they had an uninterrupted view of the scaffold, the dreadful contraption that stood upon it, and the headgear and bayonets of the rows of National Guardsmen who surrounded the place of execution. The crowd was vast, but by now there was surprisingly little noise from it. Only a few shouted and cheered; most spoke in low voices, as though they were in church in the previous times. Even the loud Madame Guitard lowered her voice and spoke little. It was as though even the most ardent republicans were struck dumb by the enormity of what was about to happen. Leonore, who certainly had no love for the queen and her vanities, felt a tightness in her chest and a vague feeling of sickness.

Around eleven, the talk in the crowd grew louder and an excited hubbub broke out in the ranks nearest the Louvre and the river. The sometime queen was being brought from the prison of the Conciergerie on Île-de-Cite, close to Notre-Dame, and the first they knew of her approach was the appearance of a troop of cavalry, their swords drawn. Now it was possible to hear bawled insults and obscenities as the most hated woman in France finally appeared. She stood on a mere tumbrel, an ordinary unadorned cart, being pulled very slowly by a single horse. Another cavalry escort rode behind her, watchful for any attempt to rescue her. She was dressed simply, all in white, and her hands were tied behind her back. Leonore marvelled that one frail woman could inspire such venom. Even though they were too far away for the prisoner to hear them, most of the people around her were shouting abuse at the woman they had once been told to pray for. But she had no urge at all to castigate the frail, thin figure in the distance, and to her surprise Madame Guitard was silent too.

The tumbrel stopped before the scaffold and the torrent of vitriol reached a crescendo as Marie-Antoinette climbed the few steps onto the stage. She carried herself like a queen, Leonore thought, not turning her head but only looking straight ahead. There was no sign of fear. She bowed her head before a black-clad priest, presumably one of the constitutional priests still permitted by the Republic to minister to the irredeemably superstitious, and the man made the sign of the cross. *That would be the granting of absolution*, thought Leonore. *It is a long time since I last received that. I need it now more than ever, but I will never receive it again.*

The queen was helped to lie face down on the hurdle, her head beneath the blade. On three, perhaps four, dozen drums, a terrifying, almost unworldly, roll began. A distant church bell, one of few left in Paris, tolled for noon. Then, without warning, the blade suddenly fell, and a great roar went up from the crowd. Madame Guitard joined it, but although Leonore opened her mouth, no sound emerged. On the scaffold, the executioner raised the severed head and showed it to the four corners of the Place de la Révolution, shouting, '*Vive la Republique!*' as he did so. There was more cheering, but Leonore saw more than a few men as well as women wiping away tears. Suddenly three young women broke through the ranks of troops surrounding the scaffold and stooped to go under the stage.

'Stupid girls,' said Madame Guitard, 'what d'they think they're doing?'

Leonore recalled a book she had once read in the library of the Chateau de Brechelean. It described the history of the civil war in England during the previous century, and she read with both fascination and revulsion the account of the execution of that country's King Charles. Thanks to that, she knew exactly what the girls beneath the scaffold were doing.

'They have gone to dip their kerchiefs in her blood.'

Madame Guitard turned and looked at her in astonishment.

'*What?* Stupid girls! That's a sure way to get their pretty little heads lopped off!'

Indeed, several soldiers were already going under the scaffold to arrest the young women. Up above, meanwhile, the queen's corpse was untied from the hurdle and thrown into a cheap coffin. A well-dressed man with the look of a lawyer to him, who was standing close to Leonore, spoke with authority to the woman next to him.

'They're going to bury the whore down at La Madeleine, where they put her husband. A plain grave filled with quicklime so the recidivists won't be able to dig up relics. Better than she deserves, if you ask me – they should have just fed her to the dogs.'

The crowd began to disperse, and Leonore turned to Madame Guitard. The widow from Arras, the vociferous foe of the Bourbons, was surreptitiously wiping away a tear.

'You are affected, *madame*?' asked Leonore.

'No, dear, of course not. A fly in my eye, nothing more.'

It was strange, thought Leonore, that for every two men and women who were loudly cheering the demise of the former queen, there seemed to be at least one who also had flies in their eyes. Leonore's own eyes were dry, but as they began to make their way back towards their lodging house, she could not get out of her head the words of the forbidden old prayer.

Requiem aeternam dona eis, Domine.
Et lux perpetua luceat eis.
Grant them eternal rest, oh Lord,
And may light perpetual shine upon them.

CHAPTER TWENTY-SEVEN

1 Novembre 1793

Philippe wrote the date automatically at the head of his daily journal entry, looked at it, cursed, took up his quill once again and crossed it through with two bold strokes. Then he dipped the pen in the ink, consulted the single sheet of printed paper newly arrived on *Le Zéphyr* among the despatches brought out of Brest by a fast ketch, and applied his pen once again.

11 Brumaire II

So there it was. The new date. The new calendar. The new truth. Not content with bringing down the monarchy and the church, or slaughtering thousands in the name of liberty, the rulers of the Republic now decreed that time itself would bend to their revolutionary fervour. So out went the old years dated from the birth of Christ – after all, who or what was Christ but a myth created to gull the superstitious? – and the old names for the months and days of the week, most of them also derived from names of fictitious so-called gods whom Reason had consigned to the dung heap. Now the date of the proclamation of the Republic was the first day of Year One, there were new months with names drawn from nature and appropriate to the season – Brumaire, which was principally the old November, meant 'fog' – and seven-day weeks had given way to ten-day 'decades', three of which formed a month. To accommodate the quirks of the old calendar there were five additional or supplementary days every year with a sixth, a *'Jour de la Révolution'*, every leap year. The starry-eyed poets who named the new elements of the calendar had even come up with names for every day of the year. He checked down the list and saw that today, the day formerly known as Friday 1 November, was now *Salsifis*, the *primidi* – Oneday, or first day – of the middle decade of Brumaire.

Philippe smiled to himself. His father would have been delighted at such a triumph of logic and reason over the old superstitious ways. But here and now, in the real world, Philippe wondered how this incredibly elaborate confection, devised and ordered by committees of earnest lawyers, poets and pen-pushers meeting in rarefied chambers in Paris, would be understood by the peasants on the lands around Brechelean or by the illiterate hands dicing and swearing as they sat at their mess tables on the gun deck of *Le Zéphyr*. He still told himself that he believed in the ideal of the Republic, despite all that had happened and all he had witnessed at Nantes. But that perfect republic, and even the imperfect homicidal one that had actually been created, surely needed rulers who understood there were more important things for them and their citizens to do than learn to call the eighth day of Nivôse by its new name of *Fumier*, dung. At least none of the days were named *merde*.

His sense of disillusionment was exacerbated by other items in the packet brought from Brest. An official notification from there under the name of Jeanbon de Saint-André brought the news that Morard had stood down as admiral. Even the bland wording of the communique made it clear that this had not been quite as voluntary as was claimed. It seemed that Morard had ventured out with the fleet but turned tail on sighting Howe's blockading armada and scuttled back into Quiberon. Finding this unacceptably pusillanimous, Saint-André replaced him with one Rear-Admiral Villaret de Joyeuse. Philippe had met the new commander-in-chief briefly at the tailors in Brest where they were both being fitted for new uniforms before Philippe took command of *Le Zéphyr*. A perfectly amiable fellow with a pronounced pointed nose, Villaret was a Gascon from an undistinguished bourgeois background with lofty pretensions of noble status. More pertinently, he had been no more than a *lieutenant de vaisseau* only a year earlier. He had little more seniority than Ugarte or Fingal and little more battle experience than Philippe.

The next item he took up was a letter from Lievremont, who, it seemed, was recovering well at Nantes and hoped to be ready to return to duty within a month if he could find a way of getting back to the ship. He had become friendly with the clerk Mercier, and it was from him that he learned some news he knew he had to transmit to his captain as quickly as possible. Lieutenant Martin Roissel had not been executed or imprisoned. He had not even been arraigned. Instead, he had been acquitted and released. The judge who heard his case was damning of the evidence from a dead catamite, 'a mere child of the worst, most corrupted and most sordid kind' as he had put it, and the sworn statement of a priest, even a constitutional priest who was supposedly loyal to the Republic, had been set aside, for who could trust the word of any so-called priest in the new France of the Year II? Whereas Citizen Roissel, the judge opined, was known to be an upstanding member of the Jacobin clubs of Brest, an ardent stalwart of the cause of liberty and the Republic... and so it had gone on, according to Lievremont's second-hand account. No doubt the worthy citizens who frequented those clubs, and whose notice and favour Roissel had done so much to cultivate, were responsible for his freedom. Perhaps, thought Philippe bitterly, some of them even shared in the same sordid perversions in the same building. Degeneracy and decadence, the charges always levelled at the old aristocracy of France, had not perished in the triumph of the revolution. They had merely donned different suits cut from slightly cheaper cloth.

Lievremont continued with the relation of more bad news. Before the wounded *aspirant* left *Le Zéphyr*, Philippe had instructed him to report if he could on the fate of Captain Paul Storr. The execution of a British spy would surely be reported widely in Nantes. The more he had thought about it, the more Philippe disbelieved the story Storr had spun to try to save his own skin. Jean-Baptiste Carrier would surely expose the man's lies. But Lievremont claimed there was no word at all of the English smuggler. His friend Mercier, who was a trusted confidant of the *représentant en mission*, had never even heard the name. Philippe frowned at this. Perhaps Carrier had simply sent Storr straight to Paris to be dealt with directly by the Committee of Public Safety. But there would be far more important Englishmen in the pay of France, men far more worthy of the personal attention of Citizen Robespierre and his comrades. Philippe could not bring himself to believe the most likely alternative, that Storr was actually telling the truth aboard the captured *fluyt*. It was not his problem, but for some unaccountable reason he found it difficult to put the turncoat smuggler from his mind. 'Merlin's sense' whispered that he had not seen the last of Storr, nor, indeed, of Martin Roissel.

Lievremont had also asked Mercier about the fate of Ama, the slave boy from *Patrie*. It seemed that the lad was causing some of the finest lawyers in Nantes to have sleepless nights. He had been the personal property of Robert Janot, the ship's captain, but Janot was dead and had left no will. His wife and two young sons had died of consumption during the previous winter. Janot had no other family apart from a brother who was with the royalists and was said to be in England. While the lawyers took their time to resolve the matter, which might take for ever as Lievremont said, Mercier had taken the lad under his wing and was teaching him French. Ama learned quickly, it seemed, and was particularly adept at arithmetic. Perhaps a better fate awaited him than that of some uncaring rich man's slave or rich woman's plaything. But this news was no real consolation after the disheartening reports about Roissel and Storr.

There were no more letters in the package. There was none from Leonore, although he did not know why he should expect any. He went to his stern window, looked out at the surging grey waves, then called for Driaux.

'Citizen Captain?'

'I want a haircut, Driaux.'

'Certainly, sir. A little shorter at the front and sides, perhaps?'

'No. Cut it off. The whole damn *queue de cheval*. The rest as close cropped as you like.'

'You're sure, Citizen Captain?'

'Are haircuts yet another arena for revolutionary debate now? Get rid of it.'

'As you say, sir.'

As Driaux worked, Philippe remembered how much Tasha had loved the *queue de cheval*. Her Indian chief, she called him. Her pirate king. An eternity ago.

Driaux was nearly finished when a shout came down from above. Philippe donned his jacket and sword, picked up his telescope and went up on deck, where the officers on the quarterdeck, Ugarte, Guillaumin and Vaquin, had their telescopes trained on the western horizon.

'Well, there they are,' said Ugarte, raising an eyebrow at his captain's new appearance as he turned to speak to him. 'The *rosbifs*. Black Dick himself.'

Philippe raised his own telescope. There were many sails spread over a broad sea area, and out here, well to the north-west of Ushant, that could only be one thing. Ugarte was right. It was the British blockade fleet, and somewhere in there would be the admiral, Earl Howe, the man with his fingers on France's throat. It was a clear day with a moderate swell, not conditions to alarm any seaman, yet there was something terrible about the distant spectacle. There lay the reason why Morard, and now Villaret de Joyeuse, could not deploy his fleet precisely as he wished in France's own waters. There lay a clear, tangible threat to the Republic's very existence. The British were so very confident, so utterly arrogant, that they were not even deigning to detach a ship to mount a token pursuit of *Le Zéphyr*. Both Philippe and Lord Howe knew that any such pursuit would be a mere gesture, for the French ship was so far away that it would easily be able to get back into the Iroise channel or the Rade de Brest itself long before any British vessel could reach it. No, it would suit Howe's purpose for any French ships that came within range to see his mighty fleet and report back to Brest, thence to Paris. The Republic should know of the vast wooden monster lying off its coast and fear it.

'One day we will drive them from our shores,' said Vaquin, seething.

'One day,' said Philippe.

He did not speak aloud the other words in his mind: *but perhaps not in our lifetimes.*

–

Leonore Kermorvant sat at the head of the long table in the ancient hall of the Chateau de Brechelean. Apart from Lancelot, who was snoring loudly in front of the feeble fire, she was alone, as she had been every night since Alexandre's arrest. She looked at the plate in front of her and the meal she had been picking at for the last half hour. Salted lamb, Madame Penhouet had said, and even if that was true, it was far more saline than ovine. The dish would not disappear if she continued to stare at it, so she looked around the room instead. The patch of damp on the west wall was larger, and it was only the start of November – or rather, the middle of *Brumaire*. Some plaster had fallen from the ceiling over by the fireplace, exposing the floorboards in the floor of the room above. Fortunately that room was never used, so there was no immediate urgency. Next she looked at the paintings on the walls, as she did every night. With only one exception they were family portraits of the Kermorvants. They had been an ugly bunch, she thought, or else Brittany had been poorly served by artists; she suspected both. She tried to avoid the portrait of the old admiral, the grandfather of both Alexandre and Philippe. He was the ugliest of them all, it could not be denied, but it was not that which made her avert her gaze. She always imagined the old man was reproving her, just as she knew the entire country roundabout did. She heard the whispers whenever she rode out. More than whispers in those places where the more brazen or more drunken lived. She was the bitch who had sent her husband to the guillotine so she could whore with his brother, the mysterious vicomte who had turned up out of nowhere and had now vanished again. Strangely, this opinion seemed to be the only one shared by the district's Chouans and *sans-culottes* alike; yet Alexandre was not even dead.

The one exception to the gloomy ranks of dead Breton noblemen was a strange, almost garish painting that adorned the south wall. Philippe told her it represented the legend of the Arthurian knight Tristan and his forbidden love Isolde, a tale that ended tragically for the two of them. She always tried to avoid it, but somehow her eyes always wandered to the unsettling canvas. For reasons best known to himself the artist had included a spectral, half-invisible ship in one corner, just behind the ethereal, weeping figure of Isolde. The ship carried one sail, which was black and was meant to signify the death of one of the would-be lovers. The sight of it often made her shiver.

One or other of the new attendants, Roman and Olivier, looked in every few minutes to see if she had finished, then slipped out again without a word. Philippe had been right about them. They were good lads who learned quickly. Even Jacques Penhouet seemed satisfied with them, and it was a joy to have young faces and willing workers in the ancient, crumbling chateau. The boys' good humour and open gratitude for the chance they had been given were the only cheerful things left in Leonore's life.

Her stay in Paris had been entirely fruitless. Her cousin Lazare remained unreachable, and no one else in the government had the slightest interest in the case of a peculiar woman from the remotest part of France who had denounced her husband, proving him without any shadow of doubt to be a traitor to the Republic, yet who now campaigned for his life with astonishing but entirely misplaced persistence. She could not afford the rent of her Parisian lodgings any longer, while Madame Guitard, who had been overpowering but tolerable company, went back to Arras soon after the execution of the queen. The woman who took her place was a shrivelled, unpleasant widow from Perpignan who took an immediate dislike to Leonore. So she returned to Brechelean, defeated. Cold, damp, empty Brechelean.

Every night as she lay her head on her pillow, she wondered whether she would see the dawn. She fully expected the Chouans to come for her in the small hours to avenge themselves on the woman who had betrayed one of their own. She did not fear death, and there was a part of her that believed she would thoroughly deserve such a fate, but the uncertainty lay oppressively on her heart. If they were going to come for her, she wished they would come immediately and be done with it. But night after night passed without incident, until at last Leonore was forced to conclude that either she was too insignificant for the self-styled royal army to bother about, or else someone among them had the insight to understand that her tormented, guilt-ridden thoughts were the most effective punishment that the mistress of Brechelean could suffer. That and the judgement of her neighbours.

The elder Cadoudal sister called one day, the one purpose of her visit seemingly being to tell Leonore that she was damned to spend all eternity in hellfire – in truth, not a warning that carried much weight in the France of 1793 – and that she should at least show some guilt for sending her husband to his death, even though Alexandre was not dead. This was unfair, for as the Chouans perhaps understood, Leonore did feel guilt. But it was not the sort of guilt that Sandrine Cadoudal and the rest of them wanted her to suffer, the guilt for betraying her marital vows and informing on her husband. Instead, she felt it for the loss of the Alexandre Kermorvant she had married, that vigorous, impressive man for whom she had transplanted herself the entire breadth of France. But that Alexandre died the day he was gored by the boar in the forest. The one who would go to the guillotine was a pale, drunken shadow of that man, and only his conviction for treason could have saved her brother-in-law Philippe, a man who truly deserved saving. She thought all this in a purely disinterested way, or so she reasoned. She tried to convince herself of this at every solitary mealtime and in those small hours of the morning when sleep eluded her. Philippe was a man of action and integrity. He would put the estate to rights better than she could, for society would take him, a man, more seriously than her. He would serve the Republic valiantly and bring yet more glory and honour to the name of Kermorvant. He might do the great things that were far beyond her late husband. These, she convinced herself, were her true thoughts about her brother-in-law.

She dared not confront her other thoughts about him.

–

It was well past midnight when Philippe finished writing up his journal and completing the last of his letters to Saint-André, the new admiral, the Minister of the Marine and half-a-dozen lesser functionaries. He needed air, he decided, so he would take a turn on deck. Ugarte, who had just come off watch, was already snoring loudly in what had formerly been Roissel's cabin and which was barely large enough to contain the vast Basque. As Philippe emerged onto the quarterdeck, Fingal, the officer of the watch, saluted and reported their position, course and speed. Philippe nodded and went to take his accustomed position on the windward side, but as he did so he saw a familiar but unexpected figure leaning on the rail further forward. It was Fabian Vaquin, seemingly lost in thought. Since the departure of Roissel and the loss of Lievremont, Vaquin had been nominally a watch-keeping officer, and no watch-keeping officer in any navy should have been so idle at any given moment. Philippe was about to go forward to reprimand him, but then it occurred to him that to do so would be to undermine Fingal, who was plainly condoning Vaquin's laxity. He also recalled that since they left Nantes, he had not found the opportunity to talk to Vaquin about all that had transpired there and, indeed, since they first sailed from Brest. So when he went forward to stand beside the young man, his words were very different to the ones in his mind only moments earlier.

'Aspirant,' he said.

Vaquin started, but immediately came to attention.

'Sir.'

'You'll take a glass of wine with me?'

'Sir? I'm on watch, Citizen Captain.'

'And a captain's invitation overrides the watch list. I wish to speak with you privately.'

'Sir.'

They went below, Vaquin all too obviously ill at ease as he entered the stern cabin. The sound of Ugarte's snoring brought a smile, though, and the young man accepted the proffered wine gratefully.

'I should have thanked you before now for your part in denouncing Lieutenant Roissel,' said Philippe.

'Thank me, sir? I don't understand.'

'You did a brave thing, Aspirant. Not all men would admit to such a thing.'

Vaquin took a sip of wine. His reply was spoken very slowly, as though he was choosing each word very carefully indeed.

'My father brought me up to exalt the law before all else, sir. For a little while, Citizen Roissel's fervour for the revolution blinded me to what else he was, and what he was trying to do on this ship. To denounce you, Citizen Captain. To send you to the guillotine and take command himself. So yes, for a time, I believed all that he told me. But as time went on, it became clearer to me that what he was trying to do went against both the law and the principles of the Republic. In the previous times, I seem to remember that such men were called false prophets.' Vaquin smiled weakly, and Philippe nodded in silent agreement. 'Then there was the evidence about the boy he killed...'

Vaquin trailed off, and he seemed to have returned to that far-off place he had appeared to be staring at on deck.

'It's behind you now, Aspirant,' said Philippe.

'Is it though, sir? The men snigger at me. I hear the things they say, the insults, the jokes, all of it. I'll never make a good officer, you know that; I can't master navigation, I don't know sea-words the way the likes of you and the *enseignes* do – Lievremont too – and even moderate seas make me spew, sir. And then there's the glory.'

'The *glory*, Vaquin? What glory?'

'That's it, sir. What glory is there in what we do? Cruising along the coast, then out to sea, then back again? Looking for skulking fishing boats that might or might not have Chouans or English spies on them? Shepherding fat merchantmen into harbour? I came into the navy to fight the English, to make a name for myself. The only name I've made is as a mere lieutenant's catamite.'

'You're better than that, Fabian Vaquin. You can still learn all the skills you lack. You're brave – I'd say it took real bravery to turn on Roissel – and you'll learn to close your ears to what men say about you. I did, long ago. You know some of the things men on this ship have said about me, Aspirant. I expect you've said many of those things yourself.' Vaquin blushed and look away. 'As for glory, it may come your way yet. It's an elusive prize, though, and a dangerous one. Glory, like victory, often comes with a price.'

'Perhaps, sir. But I know now I'd prefer to seek it ashore, in the army. When we return to Brest I'll apply to my uncle, who's colonel of a regiment in the Army of the North. He always wanted me to go soldiering with him, but I'd read a story about Jean Bart when I was ten or so and from that day forward, I loved the notion of a life at sea. It's not like the books, though, is it, sir?'

Philippe put down his wine and looked hard at the young man before him.

'No, Citizen Vaquin, it's not like the books.'

CHAPTER TWENTY-EIGHT

The cliffs and lighthouse of Ushant, off to the south-east, were just visible through the ugly waves and squally rain. *Le Zéphyr* had been meant to cover a convoy of four ships returning from Guadeloupe and Saint-Domingue by escorting them into Le Havre, but intelligence from fishing boats and an American vessel outbound from Antwerp to Philadelphia confirmed that the convoy had already made safe landfall, taking advantage of one of the British blockade fleet's retirals to Torbay to revictual. Consequently, *Le Zéphyr* was bound for Brest to take on fresh supplies herself. Philippe, standing at the port rail of the quarterdeck to check his bearing on Ushant, hoped that a brief stay in harbour would bring him a fresh draft of men to bring the ship up to approximately its full complement. He had misgivings about this wish, though. The crew was now much more united and more capable than it had been only a few weeks before, the removal of Roissel having cut out a malignant influence. A large influx of new men might contain more lubbers and, worse, even more extreme Jacobins and *sans-culotte* troublemakers, although there was also a chance it might include solid, experienced men. It was the season when autumn turned into winter, no matter what the months might be named, and unless the authorities in Paris took it into their heads to launch a perilous winter expedition, perhaps to Ireland, the largest ships of the fleet would not go to sea until the spring, freeing some of their men for service on the smaller vessels that stayed out over the winter on cruising and convoy duties. Philippe also hoped a qualified surgeon awaited him at Brest, although Carabignac had done wonders in the unexpected role, treating those common hazards of the seaman's trade, ruptures and fractures, as though he had spent many years in the medical schools. It was clear to Philippe, and perhaps now to the lad himself, that the young *aspirant* would be far better suited to following his father's profession than to a career at sea, just as Vaquin might make a better soldier than a sailor and would almost certainly be happier in the army. Then there was the other hope, the one he dared not entertain, which was that their stay in harbour might be long enough to permit him some leave and a brief return to Brechelean. He would resolve matters with Leonore, he vowed. What that resolution would entail was unclear, although as he went to the starboard rail and raised his telescope, scouring the horizon for another sighting of the English fleet, he knew in his heart what he wished it to be.

'Sail ho! Abaft the starboard beam!'

The lookout's sudden call plucked him rudely from his reverie. He reached for his telescope again, but even before the lookout called a more precise bearing, Philippe could see her with his naked eye, there in the north-west quarter. A warship, obviously, with all sail set, coming down upon a quartering wind. They should have seen her earlier, but in the squalls and choppy seas the other ship must somehow have seen *Le Zéphyr* well before they saw her in turn. It was an hour or so before sunrise, although off the coast of Brittany in the middle of November there was precious little prospect of any sun.

Philippe summoned Guillaumin and the two remaining lieutenants, who levelled their own telescopes at the oncoming vessel.

'Two-decker,' said Ugarte. 'Maybe even the same one that chased us before.'

'Well, Citizen Guillaumin,' said Philippe, 'can we outrun her into the Iroise?'

'She'll be up with us long before, and we can't sail further inshore without the risk of running onto the Ponants. If we can get as far south as Béniguet, though, I can take us through the channel between there and Morgol, which no *rosbif* will dare take. There's foul ground all round those islands, right down to the Black Rocks, but I know the safe channels.'

Philippe nodded. He had expected the answer, which accorded with his own instincts. A few weeks earlier he had seen the ribs of a substantial merchantman wrecked on the shore of La Molène, the largest of the Ponant islands that stretched north-west to south-east between Ushant and the mainland. The channels between the small islands were narrow, shallow, ferociously tidal and full of submerged rocks. It would be a tremendous risk, but to have the slightest chance of taking it they had to get that far to begin with.

'Very well,' he said, then brought up his voice trumpet to address the crew. 'Call for drummers! All hands to their quarters! Clear for action! Haul up the foresail, lower topgallants!'

The officers repeated the commands throughout the ship. All hands to quarters: *tout la monde à son poste*, the whole world to your place, a delicious quirk of the French language. The Marine drummers, two eager lads who were younger than any of the *aspirants*, fell into their positions and began an urgent beat. Men ran up from below, some making immediately for the shrouds to begin the climb to the yards, others readying the guns on the upper deck. Some of the Marines went to the tops to act as sharpshooters. From below came the sounds of bulkheads being taken down to create an uninterrupted gun deck. Driaux came on deck with Philippe's best uniform coat. After all, it was unthinkable for a captain, and even less so for any true Frenchman, to go into battle and perhaps to his death in anything other than his best clothes. All the while the two-decker came on, and Philippe could now make out the English ensign flying stiffly in the strong breeze. She had the weather gage and thus the advantage, but *Le Zéphyr* was closer to her own shore and her safe harbour. If they could hold off the enemy in a running fight, edging south-east and thus ever closer to the safety of the Iroise passage...

Vaquin was within earshot, exhorting the starboard gun crews to exert themselves for the glory of the Republic. Victory would be theirs, he was shouting. The English were devils; the Republic was just; the Zéphyrs were bound to triumph. The *aspirant*'s eyes briefly met those of his captain, and Philippe smiled and nodded. Yes, Vaquin had changed from the arrogant youth who had first boarded *Le Zéphyr* only weeks before. As he himself had effectively admitted, he would never be as good a seaman as Lievremont, never as natural a leader of men as Carabignac. But Vaquin was the best and most fearless warrior of the ship's *aspirants*, and now, perhaps, the prize of glory would be his after all. Philippe envied him his certainty and fighting spirit. He had felt the same in his first battle, an encounter with an English brig off Cape Hatteras, and had been bewildered when their tiny cutter failed to take the larger vessel. He felt the same, too, when *Strela* sailed into action against a larger Ottoman frigate off the Wallachian coast. They had won that day with an even rawer crew than this one, so what was to say that Vaquin was not right? The two ships were not mismatched. *Le Zéphyr* was newer, faster, nimbler, but the Englishman had the larger battery and would undoubtedly carry more men, perhaps many more. It was likely that the enemy crew was more experienced, better trained. But war was never played out as a copy book.

The enemy continued to close, bearing in towards the starboard quarter of *Le Zéphyr*. The drummers maintained their warlike beat, echoed now by their English counterparts on the oncoming hull. Ugarte had gone to his old station for'ard, leaving Fingal alongside Philippe on the quarterdeck. De Machault was prowling the deck, checking his men; Garrigues below, readying the gun crews on the main gun deck. It would be impossible to fight both sides of the ship, Philippe knew, but the Englishman, who would have no one with the local knowledge of Guillaumin and charts that were probably less accurate than those in the captain's cabin of *Le Zéphyr*, was hardly likely to attempt to get inshore of them, losing the advantage of the wind by doing so. The English advantage in numbers of men would surely only count if it came to boarding.

He could see individual faces on the Englishman now. There was an *aspirant*, or a midshipman as the enemy called them, on the fo'c'sle waving a sword that seemed to be rather too large for him. The lad looked to be no more than eight years old and was even smaller than Carabignac, although Philippe knew enough of British practice to know the boy had to be at least twelve. There were the Marines in their bright red coats and stiff black hats. That had to be a lieutenant midships, directing the men aloft as they took in sail. And there, on the quarterdeck – that had to be Philippe's opposite number, wearing a tricorn hat and a blue uniform coat with two epaulettes. A sturdy-looking fellow much the same size as himself, although he looked to be older. Philippe studied him through the telescope, and at one point the Englishman did the same in return. Then he lowered the instrument and raised his hand in what might have been taken for a wave.

They were in hailing distance now, and the enemy was the first to take up his voice trumpet. A gust of wind carried away whatever he said, but the intent was clear enough; it would be a summons to surrender. The captain's words were greeted by loud cheers from his crew, followed by shouts of, 'God save King George!' Philippe grinned, brought up his voice trumpet, and made his reply.

'*Vive la Republique!*'

The Zéphyrs took their turn to cheer. Most of them echoed Philippe's words, but Vaquin, who was red-faced with fury, shouted a war cry of his own.

'Death to all kings! Tyrants to the lamppost! King George to the guillotine!'

Philippe smiled, even though the bowsprit of the Englishman was now level with the stern of *Le Zéphyr* and her figurehead was clearly visible: a bearded Roman wearing a soldier's helmet.

Le Zéphyr fired from the rearmost guns in the starboard battery. The range was not quite point blank but was still well within hailing distance. A cannonball struck home just abaft the enemy's cutwater, bringing a cheer from the gun crew on the deck below. But the shot was too low – Philippe had ordered them to aim for the masts. More guns fired, this time with grapeshot. Once again Philippe felt the entire hull shudder and wiped his eyes against the gunsmoke. Better this time, much higher, slicing through some of the sheets and halyards of the enemy's foremast and tearing holes in his sails. Still the Englishman had not fired. With her two gun decks, the enemy surely had at least six guns that could now bear. They looked to be long guns, not carronades.

There were four flashes from the other ship's gunports. Philippe saw them a moment before he heard the dreadful roar and saw the cloud of smoke obscure the hull of the Englishman. He felt the impact of at least two balls striking the hull, heard screams from the gun deck. The enemy's upper deck guns had fired high with grapeshot. A hole had been torn in the Tricolour flying from the ensign staff and sheets, clewlines and buntlines hung in shreds. The British usually fired for the hull of their opponents, but two gun decks against one gave the enemy captain the luxury of also being able to fire at the upper deck and rigging of *Le Zéphyr* if he wished.

'Enseigne Fingal, call down to Gunner Garrigues – round shot, fire on the downroll!'

But the master gunner already understood the situation and was adjusting accordingly. The next shots from *Le Zéphyr* struck the hull of the Englishman, more and more of which was now drawing alongside the French ship. Against a two-decker, it was more difficult to fire high as the French navy was wont to do. Firing into the hull made it less likely that they would disable the enemy and make their escape, but it also presented an easier target for the inexperienced gun crews.

The enemy ship fired again. Philippe heard a loud crack above his head, looked up and saw the crossjack yard nearly cut in half. A man fell dead from the mizzen top, presumably killed by a shot from the Marine riflemen in the tops of the English warship. De Machault's men were replying in kind, and Philippe saw the boy-midshipman in the enemy's fo'c'sle spin around and fall out of sight.

Le Zéphyr fired once more. Garrigues and his gun crews were almost able to keep up with the English rate of fire, and Philippe sent Fingal below with congratulations and words of encouragement. Guillaumin, meanwhile, was over at the port rail, judging their position in relation to the low, rocky Ponant isles and giving orders to the leadsman who called out the depth of water beneath their keel.

The Englishman fired again, this time on the uproll and only with his upper battery. More rigging torn, more shots through the sails – grapeshot, but too high to hurt the men on *Le Zéphyr*'s upper deck.

The enemy's lower deck battery fired on the downroll. Round shot this time, smashing into the hull. But now Philippe's own upper deck guns were reloaded and ready.

'Steady lads! On my command! Steady now... *fire!*'

The broadside was more ragged than that of their enemy, but for such raw crews the accuracy was impressive. One shot even struck the foremast of the British ship, tearing a large splinter of wood from it. If that mast fell...

'There's the waves breaking on Ar Serrou, Captain!'

In response to Guillaumin's cry, Philippe went to join him at the port rail. A narrow island lay to the east; Trielen, if he recalled his charts correctly. Wisps of smoke rose from the few visible cottages, and it was just possible to make out men, women and children standing on the rocky shore, watching the fight play out before them. To the south of the westernmost point of Trielen, about half a mile from it, was the reef that Guillaumin called by its Breton name, Ar Serrou.

'Give me the signal when you're confident we're clear of it, Citizen.'

Guillaumin nodded, and Philippe went back to the starboard side just as Vaquin – *Vaquin!* – gave the order to fire again.

The upper deck battery of the English ship fired once more. Philippe saw the flames erupt from the muzzles. Then the heat seemed to reach out to him across the water, scorching his left temple with a slashing, burning pain. Philippe's legs no longer seemed to belong to him. He staggered, reached out with his right hand to steady himself on the nearest cleat, and raised his left to wipe away the blood that seemed to be pouring into his left eye. Vaquin rushed to his side and grabbed his arm to stop him falling.

Philippe pushed the *aspirant* away.

'Get an order to the fo'c'sle,' he gasped as the full force of the pain in his head struck him. 'Tell Lieutenant Ugarte to come aft. For now, he has the ship.'

Philippe knew that this wound was as nothing to the terrible cut in his side made by an Ottoman scimitar, so it irked him to relinquish command. He told himself it would only be briefly until his wound could be bandaged, but he retained enough presence of mind to know that as it was, he was in no state to make decisions and give clear orders. He was dimly aware of another broadside from *Le Zéphyr* and another two from the Englishman. She was almost exactly level with them now and was taking some of the wind out of *Le Zéphyr*'s sails. Where were they in relation to the Ar Serrou reef? When would Guillaumin give him the word that it was time for the order to change course? He had to explain his plan to Ugarte – Philippe suddenly felt faint and began to fall forward. Someone caught him and he thought it must be Ugarte, but then he saw the huge Basque still striding towards the quarterdeck. Philippe's saviour was an ordinary seaman, a fellow whose face he could not recall ever seeing before.

The acting first officer of *Le Zéphyr* came up and took one look at his captain.

'We need to get you down to the surgeon, Citizen Captain.'

'No – I can't leave the quarterdeck. He must... he must—'

'He must stay at his post attending to the other wounded. Help the captain below, Nicolazic.'

Philippe wanted to protest again, but the deck and the masts were spinning before his eyes. He could feel that blood was still running, and the pain in his head felt as though someone were tearing his brain out of his skull. So he put his arm round the shoulders of the seaman, Nicolazic, a sturdy fellow with the look of a Breton fisherman about him, and let himself be led down. He caught a glimpse of the main deck just as the broadside fired again, saw and heard the great guns recoil, heard the crews cheer a hit, and saw Garrigues' concerned expression as *Le Zéphyr*'s captain was led down to the deck below.

The cockpit was lit by a handful of lanterns, and filled with the stench of sweat, blood, shit and the bilges. Several men were laid out on trestles on the deck. One man had lost a hand, and Carabignac, looking the part of the ship's surgeon, was bandaging the stump while the fellow screamed. Another man seemed to have taken a large splinter in the stomach, which was a bloody mess. As Philippe watched, one of the seamen assisting Carabignac covered the wound with an already blood-soaked sheet. The makeshift surgeon of *Le Zéphyr* had evidently overcome his squeamishness towards blood and the cutting of flesh. It was just as well, for the little *aspirant* would undoubtedly have more patients very soon.

The hull shuddered from more English shots striking the ship's side. One of the carpenter's crew rushed up to him with a report from Fouroux. There was one hit below the waterline, but so far the pumps were coping and the carpenter was confident of repairing the damage within minutes. Philippe nodded, ordered the man to take his compliments and gratitude to Fouroux, then staggered as his head spun again.

Carabignac got Philippe to sit down on an empty cask, wiped blood from his captain's head and studied the wound intently.

'Glancing blow, Citizen Captain,' he said. 'You've been lucky, but you'll still need stitching up.'

'No, Citizen. I need to be back on the quarterdeck, and you've got more important work here. How many wounded have you got?'

'Fourteen at present, sir,' the youth whispered, 'although those two over there – they won't last out the hour. Ten dead so far. We're putting the bodies down in the breadroom for now.'

Philippe's senses were returning, his vision was no longer spinning, and he knew he needed to get above urgently. Would Ugarte and Guillaumin have the initiative to order the change of course that might be their only chance of survival? Would Ugarte know what to do if the enemy made an unexpected move? They were both good, steady men, but they had never been in battle before. Ugarte knew how to con a ship but not to fight it. No, he could not take the chance. He was the captain, and there was only one place for him.

'Just position the bandage over the wound for now, Aspirant, and I'll wind it into place. Then get back to your other patients!'

Carabignac nodded gravely; he seemed to have aged twenty years in the same number of minutes.

Bandaged but still with a terrible pain in his head, Philippe returned to the quarterdeck and exchanged salutes with Ugarte, who returned to his station in the fo'c'sle. The positions of the two ships were still essentially the same, although the Englishman, with his advantage of the wind, was now edging a little ahead of *Le Zéphyr*. A broadside from her greeted Philippe's resumption of fire, followed almost at once by his own guns blazing their reply. Both ships had taken more damage: *Le Zéphyr's chaloupe* had been shattered and a large chunk torn out of the mainmast, while the enemy ship had taken more shots in both hull and rigging. Not enough to cripple her, unfortunately, which was probably the only way Philippe could defeat the larger ship. If it came to boarding, the British had the larger crew. The men of *Le Zéphyr* would fight like demons, he was certain of that, but that was unlikely to be enough against such odds.

Philippe went to the port rail and saw they were now almost level with the Ar Serrou reefs, visible only as waves breaking on the rocks just beneath the surface. The island of Béniguet lay to the south-east, blocking the direct course into the Iroise channel and thence to Brest. But if Guillaumin's bold scheme worked, they could run through the channel between Ar Serrou and Béniguet, then get into the safe harbour of Le Conquet, from where they could easily sail round to Brest once the Englishman gave up and went away. If it was no longer safe, though – if the Chouans had captured it since *Le Zéphyr* last had intelligence from Brest… No, Philippe knew he dare not think such thoughts.

He turned to the ship's master. 'Now, Citizen?'

Guillaumin stared at the reef, then at the torn ensign to judge the precise direction and speed of the wind. Then he nodded.

'Now, Citizen Captain.'

'Very good. *Babord la barre*! Port the helm, four points!'

The answering call came from one of the two helmsmen at the ship's wheel. *Le Zéphyr's* bows began to turn to the east, the yards began to swing in response to the hauling on the braces. Now was the moment of supreme danger. Philippe was deliberately presenting his ship's vulnerable stern to the Englishman, allowing him to rake *Le Zéphyr* with impunity. He was gambling that the move would take the enemy captain by surprise, but even if it did not, the enemy could almost certainly get off no more than one broadside before their respective courses separated the two ships. The Englishman was larger and less nimble, would take longer to turn, and would then have to steer to the north-east to try to follow *Le Zéphyr* through the channel. If they had no local pilot, the captain would surely be unlikely to risk his ship in waters full of lethal reefs and rocks. Philippe knew he was relying on a dangerous set of assumptions. But just a few moments more, that was all they needed. Then the Englishman would not be able to bring guns to bear any longer...

The broadside from the enemy ship fired almost in unison, the batteries of both decks firing on the uproll, roundshot from both. Philippe heard a terrible tearing sound and thought Guillaumin must have misjudged the course, that they had run onto Ar Serrou. He turned and saw at once that he was wrong. The mizzen mast, severed by the Englishman's fire, was falling onto the starboard quarter. Rigging snapped and lashed out like a score of deadly whips. Men ran to avoid the mass of timber and canvas, but Philippe was unable to move. The sail seemed to be falling directly onto him, followed by the mizzen itself. But somehow it struck just feet in front of him, most of the mast and its sails lying over the side. He knew they would act as a brake, slowing the ship and changing her course, so he had to get men to the quarterdeck at once to cut away the wreckage.

Then he saw it would be pointless. The falling mast had destroyed the ship's wheel and killed the helmsmen. *Le Zéphyr* could no longer steer, and the tide was already starting to push her bow around, back towards the British warship.

CHAPTER TWENTY-NINE

Chester.

Philippe caught a glimpse of her name as the Englishman began to come round and *Le Zéphyr*, now entirely at the mercy of wind and tide, slowly swung back towards her.

Well then, HMS Chester, he thought, *you think you've finished us, but I still have one throw of the dice.*

'Lieutenants Ugarte and de Machault to the quarterdeck!'

The Marine officer, who was midships, was on his way immediately, followed closely by Ugarte. They saluted.

'It's bad,' said Philippe, 'but he has to close us now to make the kill. So, Lieutenant Ugarte, mass the hands for'ard. De Machault, your Marines to be in the front rank. All hands to arm for boarding.'

As the officers of *Le Zéphyr* issued their orders, the two ships continued to close. There was no helm to command now, so, leaving Fingal and Guillaumin on the quarterdeck with some of the mates, Philippe went for'ard into the mass of men assembling there. He saw Driaux of all people, armed with a dagger and a cudgel, standing close to Arnaud Lucas, the sometime tanner's apprentice, poacher and lubber, now looking as ferocious and capable as the most battle-hardened *loup de mer.* Not far away was Gaston Mougenot, the caulker who had attempted to attack Philippe in the altercation on the night when news of the fall of Toulon reached Brest. Alongside them *Chester* seemed huge, and Philippe could see the English officers directing their own men to ready themselves either to board or to repel boarders. The enemy crew seemed innumerable. They would have a larger complement anyway, even if *Le Zéphyr* was not undermanned, and it was likely that more of them were experienced hands. But did they have the fighting spirit of Frenchmen, and of Bretons above all?

A dreadful crash, then grinding and tearing as the jib-boom of *Le Zéphyr* smashed into the side of *Chester.* Philippe felt the bow ride up as the two ships became entangled, the jib-boom lodging between the fore- and mainmasts of the English ship. He could see that the enemy's mainmast was terribly shattered. Perhaps the impact of the collision or the pressure the jib-boom would be exerting on its standing rigging would bring it down. But then the jib-boom suddenly came away, saving the mainmast of the *Chester*. Philippe bawled encouragement at his men, who were screaming and firing their muskets at the English, but he was impotent to do anything more. *Le Zéphyr* swung slowly into the side of the enemy ship, and now a studdingsail boom-iron became entangled in the leech rope of the *Chester*'s main topsail. The two hulls were side by side, and some British sailors were already clambering over the stays and netting. Marines of both ships were firing down from the tops, and with such large numbers of both crews amassed for boarding, even the worst aim easily hit a target. Two men fell into the gap between the hulls and must have been crushed as the waves pushed the ships together again. Philippe saw de Machault's sword raised above his head and heard the young officer's cry:

'*Pour le gloire de la France! Vive la Republique!*'

The Zéphyrs cheered as they followed him, and men pressed tightly to follow their comrades into battle. Philippe found himself in a throng of sailors and Marines and drew his sword with difficulty, but once it was unsheathed he waved it as a command to the men around him to follow him into battle. The Zéphyrs pressed forward, clambering over the entwined rigging of the two ships, trying to reach the deck of the *Chester*. But the British ship was a two-decker, so her hull was higher than that of Philippe's command. He had a strange image of an ancient castle on a high hill, with attackers battling up the slope to attack it. All the advantage was with the defenders, and so it was with the men of *Chester*. A party of them had surged forward to try to board *Le Zéphyr*, but now they fell back. Why abandon the advantage of their higher position?

De Machault was still shouting encouragement and waving men forward. Philippe saw the young officer haul himself onto the *Chester*, fire his pistol with his left hand, engage an English officer with the sword in his right, then disappear from sight. A score or more of Zéphyrs followed him, and a similar number of others followed Ugarte, who was not far behind. The Basque bellowed an order for grenades and the men behind him threw perhaps three or four into the packed ranks of the enemy, breaking their tight formation. Philippe found himself being pushed from behind as more and more men tried to get into the fray and to pour into the gaps that had opened up before them. He hauled and scrambled his way up, but as he stepped onto the deck of *Chester*, an Englishman to his right thrust at him with a half-pike while a young officer, a midshipman by the looks of him, came at his left side brandishing a cutlass. Philippe deflected the half-pike with his sword and swung back to parry the midshipman's blade. The midshipman could be no more than thirteen or fourteen but he fought like a veteran, cutting, thrusting and parrying in a frenzied attack that drove Philippe back against the rail. He could feel the old wound in his side pulling and prayed that it did not reopen. The boy against him kept up his assault, his eyes wide with bloodlust. But he was very young and had no patience. He came in wildly, screaming with fury but overextending his sword arm as he did so. Philippe cut down sharply, feeling the sharp pain from his side, and severed the boy's hand above the wrist. The midshipman fell away, screaming and clutching his bleeding stump.

Another Englishman stepped forward to attack Philippe. This one looked to be a common seaman, but he was a huge fellow, brandishing a cutlass at his right shoulder. A tight press of Zéphyrs on his right constricted Philippe's sword arm so he raised the pistol in his left hand and, with the enemy seemingly only inches away, he fired full into the enemy's face. The man still somehow took two more steps forward as though the shot had missed him entirely, then fell heavily to the deck.

Philippe pushed forward once more and saw that de Machault was down. The young officer was on his knees, speared by the bayonet on a musket wielded by a British Marine. Ugarte was kneeling by his side and Philippe tried to cut his way through to them, but Ugarte saw him and shook his head. De Machault was beyond help. All around, the fragile foothold on the enemy ship established by the Zéphyrs was under attack. The British seemed to have an infinite supply of fresh men to throw into the battle, and now their own grenades were wreaking havoc among the Frenchmen. Amid the gunshots and the screams of wounded men, Philippe could make out the voices of enemy officers bawling their orders. But none of his fellow officers from *Le Zéphyr* were within earshot. The nearest, Ugarte, bellowing Basque obscenities, was already swallowed up in the midst of a throng of Englishmen.

Two more seamen rushed Philippe. One brandished a dirk, the other what looked to be a grappling hook. The man with the hook raised it a fraction too high and Philippe thrust his cutlass deep into his belly, but the one with the dirk slashed it across his left arm before he could bring his sword back round to dispatch him. Philippe saw the blood and felt lashing pain from both the new wound and the old one in his side. He barely saw the English cutlass slicing towards his neck.

A blade came up and took the impact of the enemy's weapon. Philippe glanced behind him and saw that his saviour was Aspirant Fabian Vaquin. The young man smiled, then gasped with shock as his chest was shattered by a pistol ball at point-blank range. Philippe turned at once but could not identify Vaquin's killer. He had to be somewhere in the press of screaming Englishmen who were pushing forward, forcing the much smaller force of Zéphyrs back towards the side of *Chester*. *Poor Vaquin*, thought Philippe. He had obtained his share of glory after all.

It was hopeless. The throng of Englishmen was inexorable. The Zéphyrs stood no chance of taking the English ship. The only hope was to get back aboard their own vessel, somehow separate her from *Chester*, then somehow flee the scene of battle. But *Le Zéphyr* had no mizzen and no helm.

Philippe ran to the side, hoping to shout some orders down to Fingal, who was on the quarterdeck in temporary command of the ship. Or he had been. Philippe could see the young part-Irishman lying on the deck, tended by Carabignac. But the red stain on Fingal's chest suggested he was beyond the care of the finest surgeon in France, let alone the boy *aspirant*.

Philippe waved his sword to the few dozen surviving Zéphyrs who had made it onto the deck of *Chester*.

'Fall back!' he cried in French, then in Breton, 'Fall back to the ship!'

If they could cut themselves free from *Chester* – if they could man the battery – if they could somehow hold the ship against the far greater numbers the British were massing for their counter-attack...

He saw Ugarte falling back towards him, having somehow freed himself from the English horde. The old Basque must have realised Philippe's intent, for he immediately shouted down to the men still massed in the fo'c's'le of *Le Zéphyr* waiting to board to man the side instead and open a covering fire, so the boarders could withdraw. As the first volley went off, Philippe hauled himself over the side of *Chester* and climbed back down onto *Le Zéphyr*.

Ugarte, gasping for breath and sweating profusely, came to stand before him.

'Your orders, Citizen Captain?'

Philippe looked back at *Chester*. The guns of her lower gun deck were run out, ready to fire a shattering broadside into *Le Zéphyr* at a range closer than point blank. The English had more than enough men both to man the entire battery and send a boarding party onto *Le Zéphyr* that would outnumber her entire crew.

'We must cut the rigging!' cried Philippe. 'We must break away from the Englishman!'

Then the gates of hell opened. *Chester*'s broadside fired, and *Le Zéphyr* seemed to be driven across the ocean. Philippe felt the cannon-balls striking the hull, heard the ones that smashed through the timber, saw the shards blown in all directions, heard the screams of the men down on the gun deck. He looked back and saw the enemy boarders spilling over the side of their own ship. That was the moment when hope died.

'Nothing else will serve, Lieutenant Ugarte. Nothing else at all.' Philippe had not been aware of the pains in his arm, head and side when he was on the deck of *Chester*, but suddenly it felt as though they were tearing him in half. He felt a hundred years old. He wanted to lie down on the deck and die, as so many good men had done that day. The pain was too great. He wanted to join Fingal, De Machault, Vaquin. Then the pain would stop, and he would prevent the even greater pain of the three words he knew he had to utter.

'*Amener le pavillon.*' Strike the colours.

CHAPTER THIRTY

Philippe stepped once again onto the main deck of HMS *Chester*. This time there was no fighting, no bodies and almost no blood, which seemed to have been scrubbed off the planks in remarkably short order. The red-coated side party of Royal Marines snapped to attention, the men's movements impressively precise. Poor de Machault and his troops could have equalled them, but the young lieutenant and most of those poor men would never salute anyone again. For the crew of *Chester*, though, 'attention' seemed to be a word they might once have heard but then largely forgotten. Many bore signs of wounds and utter exhaustion, so perhaps they could be forgiven a little slovenliness. Their officers were a different case. There were two lieutenants visible on deck, one of whom had a bandage around his head while the other had his right arm in a sling. Before them stood an extraordinary figure whose torn and bloodstained uniform bore the epaulettes that proclaimed him to be the captain, unlikely though that seemed from his appearance. His face was a mask of black congealed blood, enormous bruises had closed his right eye, and most of the hair on the left side of his head seemed to have been burned off.

He and Philippe exchanged salutes.

'I am the Honourable John Wyndham Prentice,' said the Englishman in good French. 'Captain of the frigate *Chester* in the service of His Britannic Majesty King George the Third. Who do I have the honour of addressing?'

The voice, so very refined and precise, was entirely at odds with his bloody appearance. An 'Honourable', though. The English did love their titles.

'Philippe Kermorvant, captain of *Le Zéphyr* in the service of the French Republic, one and indivisible,' replied Philippe, also in French. 'I congratulate you on your victory, Captain, and surrender my ship and myself to you.'

With a heavy heart, Philippe drew his sword and presented it to Prentice, hilt first. The English captain and his lieutenants exchanged glances, then Prentice smiled.

'I understand that you also go by another name, do you not? The Vicomte de Saint-Victor.' The surprise must have shown on Philippe's face. 'I have to tell you, my lord, that there is very little which happens in your navy that is not known at once to our agents. It is one of the many reasons why we English will win this war.' Prentice raised his hand and touched the hilt. 'Pray keep your sword, my lord. You and your men fought valiantly. I regret that Lieutenant Ingamells, there, will need to take a prize party across to secure your ship, but in the meantime, I trust you'll take a little refreshment with me? Lieutenant Strang will entertain your, ah, other officers.'

Both Prentice and the officer named Strang were glancing with undisguised bewilderment at the extraordinary figure of Juan Ugarte, who was standing a little behind Philippe and looked, as he always did, like a man who had stolen a uniform off a corpse and then found it was a little too tight for him.

Captain John Wyndham Prentice's cabin occupied the whole breadth of *Chester* and was in marked contrast to Philippe's much more confined space on *Le Zéphyr*. The English were a source of endless amusement to the seafarers of other nations for many reasons, and one of them was the exalted, godlike status they bestowed on the captains of their ships. Let it matter not that the other officers were herded into spaces so tiny they had to take turns to breathe and fart, just so long as the captain had enough space to accommodate himself, his mistress, their children, and a string quartet.

Prentice began by pouring wine for the two of them and toasting a hoped-for return of peace. Then, astonishingly, he begged Philippe's pardon, turned, removed his uniform coat and shirt, went to his wash basin and proceeded to scrub caked blood off his face and torso. All the while, he talked as though the two of them were still face to face.

'If you'll forgive me saying so, my lord,' said Prentice, casually picking a large bloody scab off his arm, 'you speak English more like an American than a Frenchman.'

Philippe was still dwelling on the dishonour of surrendering to the enemy and the sure end of his short-lived career as a captain of the French Republic. The last thing he wanted to do was make conversation with his conqueror. If anything, he would rather be chained to one of Jean-Baptiste Carrier's barges, drowning in one of the sickening *noyades* at Nantes. But convention proved too strong, and he briefly sketched out his early life for Prentice.

'Remarkable,' said the Englishman, who now looked somewhat less like a stag being savaged by a wolf and was in the process of donning a clean shirt. 'Quite remarkable. Yet despite your birth and your service under foreign flags, you somehow secure a command in the French navy. I'm intrigued to learn how, my lord.'

'I prefer not to be referred to as such, Captain Prentice. These days, I choose to be called Captain Kermorvant.'

'Really? Good God. Forgive me, Captain, but if I didn't have four older brothers and seven nephews between me and my father's title… What I'm saying is that I can't think of any circumstances in which I'd disown my rank. But then, I suppose we Prentices don't live in the shadow of the guillotine. Forgive me if that offends you, my lo— Captain Kermorvant.'

'Not at all, Captain. I realise that an Englishman might consider the present condition of France a little exceptional, shall we say, but with all due respect, it was your country that taught the world it was possible to cut the heads off kings.'

Prentice smiled. '*Touché*, Captain. I'll look forward to a longer conversation with you during our voyage to Spithead. You'll dine with my officers and myself a little later, I trust?'

'I'm your prisoner, Captain Prentice,' said Philippe with a heavy heart. 'I think I have little choice in the matter.'

–

The voyage to England was purgatory. Prentice was a generous and attentive host, entertaining Philippe and Ugarte most amply and giving them the run of the upper deck. But Philippe's eyes always turned to *Le Zéphyr*, astern of and keeping close to *Chester*, with the humiliating evidence of his dishonour flaunted before him: the colours of England flying above the torn and dirty Tricolour from the ensign staff. He wondered how his men were faring under the watchful eyes of Prentice's prize crew.

The other almost unbearable aspect of his condition was dinner. Prentice was obviously putting on a show to impress, but the quality of the officers' table was exceptional: perfectly cooked fresh meat, a seemingly unlimited supply of fresh vegetables, and, of all things, French wine that was substantially superior to anything on *Le Zéphyr* and perhaps to anything provided to the Republic's navy. The fare was in marked contrast to the conversation. Prentice and his officers evidently found Philippe and Ugarte great curiosities. The war was less than a year old so they had probably not encountered any other French officers, but the garrulous Ugarte was a welcome guest at any table and Philippe's title and the fame of his father went before him. So Philippe spent almost all his time fielding questions from Prentice and his officers, especially the lieutenant named Ingamells who announced himself to be an avid reader of the works of Verité and was unduly proud of the fact that he had read them in French, not in translation. It was all wheedled out of him: his service in the American war and Russia's wars with Sweden and the Turks, his anecdotes of John Paul Jones and the Empress Catherine, all the rest of it. They tactfully steered clear of his and Ugarte's opinions on the state of the Republic, although one of the midshipmen, who had clearly imbibed too well for a boy of his tender age, expressed outrage at the executions of the sometime king and queen. Prentice dismissed him from the table for his incivility. Philippe was careful in how much he drank and what he said, all the while longing for the humiliating voyage to come to an end.

On the fifth morning after *Le Zéphyr*'s surrender, Philippe stood on the quarterdeck of *Chester* watching the distant shore of the Isle of Wight to port. The British frigate was giving the island a wide berth as she bore round on the strong south-westerly breeze to pass through Saint Helen's Bay. He had anchored there a few years before when he was skippering a Gask ship bound for London, so the coast was familiar to him. He took a greater interest in the way in which the officers and men of HMS *Chester* worked their ship. There was far less noise than there had been on *Le Zéphyr*, far less confusion, far more brisk efficiency. These men evidently knew their duties to such a degree that they could probably execute them in their sleep. They seemed barely to need commands at all, moving about the decks, the yards and the rigging with a quiet competence. Of course they would want to impress their French prisoners, but Philippe imagined that this was very much the normal way of doing things on the frigate.

In the early afternoon *Chester* entered the Solent. This was a spacious anchorage, broader than the Rade de Brest but more open to the sea. It was much fuller with shipping than Philippe's home port. Prentice, who had donned his best uniform, was nearly bursting with pride as he pointed out the different landmarks on the Isle of Wight, now to the south-west of them, and the mainland to the north, but Philippe ignored these. His attention was fixed on what first seemed to be a black and amber fortress filling the middle of the broad roadstead. The strange illusion lasted only a few moments before Philippe was able to make out individual hulls and knew that he was looking at a fleet at anchor. A vast fleet.

'A treat for you, my lord,' said Prentice. 'The blockade fleet usually goes into Torbay, of course, but sometimes the admiral brings it back up here. Quite the sight, ain't it?'

Philippe said nothing, for he was busy counting hulls and estimating sizes. There had to be twenty or more of the largest sizes, what the English called the First to Third Rates, together with a dozen frigates and half-a-dozen sloops. Luggers, hoys, cutters and other small craft weaved their way between the great ships, no doubt bringing out supplies and carrying men to and from the shore.

'See that one?' said Prentice excitedly, pointing to one of the nearer hulls; a seventy-four, by the looks of her. 'That's *Ramillies*. I was second on her. Feels like yesterday, but it must have been years ago. See astern of her? That's the good old Billy Ruffian. Real name's *Bellerophon*, of course, but your English tar mangles these classical names to glory. *Polyphemus*, which I served on in the Cape Spartel fight, they call the Polly Infamous. *Agamemnon*, which the last I heard was still out in the Mediterranean under Hood, they somehow make into Eggs and Bacon. I guess you must have the same with your French names, eh?'

'As you say, Captain,' said Philippe, who had no idea what his countrymen did to the names of their men-of-war. If he spent the rest of the war in an English prison, perhaps he never would.

As they drew nearer still, Prentice began to reel off the names of the largest ships. Perhaps he wanted to impress Philippe with his ability to identify vessels from the slightest differences in the configuration of their gunports or the figureheads they bore, perhaps he was trying to awe his prisoner with the might and pedigree of England's wooden walls. Whatever the reason, Philippe listened intently. If he somehow got back to France, Citizen Saint-André and whichever admiral now commanded the Brest fleet might welcome such intelligence. Otherwise, perhaps, one or more of these giants might be his next opponent.

'Most of what you see over there are Thirds. There's *Cumberland, Brunswick*, that's *Ganges* behind her – then *Vanguard, Tremendous, Invincible* – oh, and that's a Second, looks like *London* – and now do you see just coming into sight behind those two Thirds? That's *Royal Sovereign*, the vice-admiral's flagship. First Rate, of course, of a hundred guns. Same goes for the rear-admiral's ship, *Royal George* – the rear-admiral's t'other Hood, y'know, Alex, brother of Sam who commands in the Mediterranean.' *And who would now be lording it over Toulon*, thought Philippe, bitterly. 'And there, behind *Royal George* – well, I expect I don't have to point out the flagship to you, my lord.'

HMS *Queen Charlotte* was only a little larger than her immediate neighbours, *Royal Sovereign* and *Royal George*. But as with Morard de Galles's *Le Terrible*, she seemed to be a colossus, two or three times the size of anything else, such was the aura that attended a fleet flagship. In the case of *Queen Charlotte*, the amount of activity around her was far more than for any other ship in the fleet. Most of the small boats seemed to be making for her, like bees flocking around their queen. But the most striking evidence of the huge ship's special status was the enormous Union flag at the maintop, the unique honour borne by the admiral in command of a British fleet.

As *Chester* and her prize made their slow and careful progress through the anchored ships, the reception for them grew louder and louder. Seamen manned the sides and clung to the rigging of each British ship, cheering wildly and waving as the successful frigate and the proof of her victory made their way through the anchorage. As they neared the flagship, Philippe heard the unexpected and incongruous sound of music. Presumably *Queen Charlotte* carried a band, and it was playing a medley of tunes that he recognised from the time of the American war. 'Rule Britannia' gave way to 'Hearts of Oak', then 'See the Conqu'ring Hero Comes' and 'Britons Strike Home', before seemingly endless choruses of 'God Save the King'. When they were very nearly on *Queen Charlotte*'s quarter, a flag signal broke out from the flagship's mizzenmast.

'"Well done and all honour to *Chester*",' said Prentice. 'Damn generous of Black Dick, that. Mister Stimpson, there! Reply to the flag, "Thank you. God save—" well damn my eyes, there's the man himself, by God!'

Just visible on the quarterdeck of the English warship was a slight and seemingly ancient man standing slightly in front of a dozen or so officers of various ranks. This fellow raised his black tricorn hat to reveal a head of thick, curling white hair. Prentice came to attention and returned the salute of Admiral Richard, Earl Howe. Philippe glimpsed the commander of the blockade fleet for only a few moments, but committed the face to memory.

Chester sailed on, taking advantage of the gentle to moderate south-westerly to make her approach to the entrance to Portsmouth harbour. This, thought Philippe, made the Goulet at Brest seem like an entire ocean. At first it seemed impossible that even *Chester* and *Le Zéphyr* could pass through such a narrow opening; surely the likes of *Queen Charlotte* would stand no chance of getting in and out? But Prentice gave a handful of orders, his first lieutenant and sailing master gave more, whistles blew, and *Chester* came around onto a new course nearly parallel to the shore. Now the harbour mouth seemed wider, and Philippe glimpsed a broad expanse of water beyond it. There was an old castle on the shore ('from old Harry Eight's day,' said Prentice) with newer batteries flanking it, then a long shingle beach on which small fishing boats were grounded, and then the low ramparts and bastions of Portsmouth's outer defences. There were other batteries on the far shore, which Prentice said was a place called Gosport. Red-tunicked soldiers cheered from the ramparts, and a few ladies with parasols, taking the air upon the beach, waved demurely as *Chester* sailed past.

'Can't usually do it this easily,' said Prentice. 'When I was on the good old *Namur*, we once spent a week out at Spithead waiting to come into harbour. It was the very depth of winter and a nor'westerly was blowing as if it wanted to freeze the earth, bringing blizzards every hour or two. In the end we had to be towed and warped in. But this time we've got the tide, the wind couldn't be more favourable, and there's nothing better than making a proper entrance into old Pompey – especially with a prize in tow! Begging your pardon that is, my lord.'

Chester passed two ancient towers on the Portsmouth shore, then a strange spit of land where every available foot of space seemed to be taken up by a building – here a storehouse, there a tavern, there a brothel. Drinkers raised tankards to the victorious English frigate as she passed, then booed loudly as *Le Zéphyr* came into harbour in her wake, the red ensign with the Union canton flying above the Tricolour at her stern.

The harbour broadened out. At the far end, to the north, a long chalk ridge towered above the ramparts of an old castle. To the east, to starboard, lay the dockyard itself: a gunwharf, a mast pond and its attendant buildings, red-bricked storehouses, a ropehouse on an astonishing scale, dry and wet docks, building slips on which stood the wooden skeletons of new men-of-war in various stages of construction. There were glimpses of fires blazing in foundries and the sounds of hammers striking anvils, two-man saws shaping timber and cranes swinging loads onto hulls. The smells of pitch, tar, cordage and timber wafted across to *Chester*. It was reminiscent of Brest, but then it was also reminiscent of Karlskrona and Kronstadt. When all was said and done, every dockyard in every nation had the same characteristics. But this was on an altogether different scale, far larger than anything Philippe had ever known. Quite apart from the ships in dock or moored at the wharves, what seemed to be another entire fleet lay at anchor in the broad upper reaches of the harbour and over towards the western shore, where a small town and yet more storehouses were surrounded by impressive fortifications. This was the maritime might of Britain on full display, and Philippe knew that this land, France's most inveterate enemy, had another four dockyards at its disposal to service the scores more men-of-war which existed for only one purpose: to destroy the republic that Philippe served.

This was Portsmouth, this was England, and this was captivity.

CHAPTER THIRTY-ONE

Two weeks of *Agincourt* were an eternity. The ancient prison hulk, moored on the Gosport shore across from Portsmouth dockyard, was damp and stinking. The mastless, black-hulled three-decker was so old it had fought both with and against the navy of Louis *le Grand*, the Sun King Louis XIV, over a century before. Toadstools sprouted from its decks. It was battered by the westerly gales that blew almost as frequently as they did in Brittany, and now, in December, those gales were blizzards. The men crammed into the venerable hull struggled not to freeze. One poor fellow from *Poursuivante*, which had been captured early in the summer and whose crew shared the hulk with the men from *Le Zéphyr*, had already succumbed. Philippe, assigned his own tiny and rudimentary cabin at the stern of what had been the lower gun deck, struggled to keep warm. The officers huddled around a weak brazier, a privilege conceded to their rank, but the deck was windowless and the confined smoke almost as vicious an enemy as the cold. There were fewer men sitting there now, vainly trying to warm their hands, than there had been when he first came to the hulk. One of the lieutenants of *Poursuivante* had died of a fever, while Ugarte had given his parole, supposedly preferring the more comfortable chains of his word of honour to the squalor of *Agincourt*. Philippe could hardly blame the old man. He, too, had only to say the word to his captors and he could live out the rest of the war in a comfortable billet in some pleasant inland English town, just as Ugarte would if he adhered to his word of honour.

'Thing is, Citizen Captain,' the Basque had said just before he left the hulk, 'I haven't got a word of honour. I'm just a peasant's brat from the Pyrenees. So I'll spend a few weeks in some nice town somewhere in the country, then just walk out, get myself to a port and find a ship that's got a Basque or two on it. Maybe one day I'll see you in Brest or

Paris or wherever and we can raise a glass to the old times on *Le Zéphyr*, eh, sir?'

Ugarte's casual attitude to honour offended the sensibilities of the Vicomte de Saint-Victor, but the more he thought about it, the more Philippe realised he would not condemn his lieutenant for his proposed course of action. He would certainly not betray Ugarte to the English. That decided, and with Ugarte on his way to some place called Tenterden, Philippe returned to contemplating his own situation.

Giving his parole was what Captain Prentice had advised him to do, but for now, he was stubborn. If he gave his parole then he, unlike Ugarte, was bound by the shackles of honour. Once he gave his word to the British, he could not go back on it. This intangible dungeon built out of ancient aristocratic scruples ruled out any prospect of attempting to escape, even though Boyer, captain of *Poursuivante*, told him that escape was a mad dream in any case. Boyer was still on *Agincourt* because he had thought the same way back in the summer, but six months of the hulk and now the bitter chill of winter changed a man's thinking, Boyer said. There was no way to escape. The gunports and windows of the old ship were sealed, and the only entries and exits, as well as the adjacent shore, were guarded by Marines. Boyer said he had struggled for months to reconcile his sense of his duty to his men and to France with his own needs, but now he knew any other course of action was hopeless. Besides, he said to Philippe in a whisper, the war would end soon. France's enemies were too many and too strong, while all the Republic's leaders seemed to do was squabble amongst themselves and denounce each other in attempts to send their foes to the guillotine. The royalist rebels would win the day, and a king would reign again at Versailles. Boyer had been as staunch a man for the Republic as any, he said, but it was a lost cause. Better to accept the inevitable, take up the British offer of parole, and live in comfort for however long the war lasted.

Although *Agincourt* had not been to sea for perhaps thirty years and would never set sail again, the English maintained the fiction that she was a commissioned warship exactly the same as any other. Therefore, she possessed not only sufficient Marines to guard and cow the prisoners but a proper naval crew, albeit a small one, who carried out maintenance and repairs. These were mostly old men, unfit for further service at sea but deemed worthy of a sinecure to reward them for long service, thereby freeing up younger men for the fleet. The same was very much true of the commanding officer. *Agincourt*, so one of the friendlier English sailors said, had once been commanded by the likes of Russell, Anson and Hawke, great admirals all whose fame had reached even to the Virginia tidewater. Now, though, she was commanded by Lieutenant Humphrey Bloodworth. Gone sixty, Bloodworth had held the rank of lieutenant for over thirty years without, it seemed, ever having any realistic prospect of rising further. As he had freely admitted to Philippe, the garrulous captain the Honourable John Wyndham Prentice, youngest son of the Earl of Falcondale, possessed privileged birth, family connections and luck, with the war beginning just as he obtained his first post-captain's commission. Within six months he had his second, *Chester*. By contrast, Bloodworth came from middling stock in some obscure place called Bolton. He had no connections, no luck and, as far as Philippe could see, no competence beyond overseeing a few hundred prisoners on an ancient, immobile hulk lying in a forgotten corner of the harbour. Even that relative sinecure seemed to test him to his limits, or so he complained to his literally captive audience.

The day after Boyer departed, bound it seemed for a comfortable existence in a place called, ludicrously, Abergavenny, Bloodworth approached Philippe when he was on the upper deck, enjoying the hour's fresh air and exercise permitted to the prisoners. The blizzards had ceased temporarily, but the stumps of *Agincourt*'s masts, the cordage and the deck itself were all thick with frost. A bitter north-easterly was blowing, and Philippe found himself thinking of Russia. The wind would have come from there, from the Steppes by way of Saint Petersburg, down the frozen Neva, rattling the branches of the trees near the graves of poor Tasha and Ivan, before sweeping across the plains of northern Germany to bring this evil, biting weather to Portsmouth. Even in this weather, though, the dockyard across the harbour was full of activity. Philippe was watching with professional fascination as a big ship – seventy-four or eighty by the looks of it – was tugged and warped out of dry dock. He was barely aware of a cough behind him, and turned to see the *Agincourt*'s superannuated commanding officer. Bloodworth looked even older than his years. His hair was thin and white, although thick black tufts emerged from his ears. His grey eyes were sunken into dark sockets set in an ashen face that made him look like a cadaver. He looked too feeble even to be a village priest.

'Begging pardon, Captain Kermorvant,' he said in his almost inaudible whisper, 'but new orders have come down from London. Orders concerning you.'

This was unexpected; Philippe thought that if Bloodworth wished to speak to him about anything, it would concern his becoming the senior French officer aboard the hulk now that Boyer had gone.

'Orders, Lieutenant?'

'You are to be taken there. London, that is. Tomorrow. You are to take sufficient possessions for two or three overnight stays there, leaving the rest here. A Marine escort will be coming for you at seven.'

'Do you have any idea why?'

'None. It's a damnable inconvenience, I can tell you. I'd only just made out new papers with your name rather than Boyer's, now I'll need to make up new ones even if you're only away a day or two. I presume one of the lieutenants from *Poursuivante* will now become the senior, seeing as none of your lieutenants are left.'

He pronounced that noble and distinguished ship's name as 'Poor swerve ant'.

The Marine contingent arrived precisely as the church bells of Portsmouth were tolling for seven the next morning. Two privates were commanded by a diminutive and largely silent Scottish sergeant named MacCaughan, who ordered Philippe to accompany him into a skiff which took them across the harbour, landing at stairs just under the stern of an eighty that bore the name *Boyne* below its stern windows. The dockyard gate was only a short distance away, and a carriage was waiting just outside it. As they passed through the still sleepy streets of the town that surrounded the dockyard (dirtier than Brest), Philippe asked several questions of MacCaughan but got few answers, and they were largely unintelligible. Philippe had sailed with Scots on old Alex Gask's ships and thought he understood them, but the Marine officer seemed possessed of a dialect and accent all his own.

Portsmouth was on an island, and Philippe had heard from Verité that his grandfather, Admiral de Saint-Victor, had once been involved in a scheme for France to seize it, fortify it and make it into a French Gibraltar, a perpetual stronghold within the enemy's territory. Nothing came of it, of course – the French were renowned the world over for making grand plans that then disappeared into bottomless whirlpools of argument, delay and apathy – and looking out of the carriage at the lie of the land, Philippe could readily understand why. It might have been possible to take Portsmouth, just as the mutineers at Quiberon had been alarmed at the prospect of the English seizing Brest, but it would be quite another matter to hold it. The flat, swampy island was surrounded on three sides by open water, and the channel separating it from the mainland was far too narrow to present any sort of an obstacle to determined attackers. Even if this could be widened and deepened, the great chalk ridge that rose almost immediately beyond it on the landward side presented an ideal position of strength for an army. It might even be possible for artillery positioned on the slopes to hit the town and dockyard itself, rendering it unusable.

The road from Portsmouth ran through a small fort at the creek's edge and out onto an ancient-looking stone bridge that carried traffic over to the mainland. The post-chaise then took a route roughly north-easterly, through towns whose names meant nothing to Philippe: Petersfield, Godalming, and God knew where else. Traffic was heavy, with coaches, carts and individual riders going in both directions; there were frequent delays while other road users struggled to get round slow and heavily laden carts. The countryside was of little interest, lusher than Brittany even in December, not as pleasant as Virginia. The only incident came at a place called Haslemere during a change of horses at one of the town's many inns. Word evidently got out that there was a French officer in the yard, and a dozen men, all roughly dressed and plainly the worse for drink, stumbled out of the back door of the inn just as Philippe returned from the rudimentary water closet with his escort, the shorter of the two Marine privates.

'So that's what a fucking Frog officer looks like, my boys,' said a red-faced fellow with a vast, carbuncled nose.

'Bloody king-killing filth!' shouted another. 'An' the poor queen too, God rest her soul!'

'We should string 'im up from the gibbet!' barked a third man who had a tankard in his hand and was swaying as he spoke. There were loud growls of support from his companions, four or five of whom began drunkenly to sing 'God save the King'.

The other Marine guard, who had been sitting on a barrel by the carriage, came forward to join his colleague in front of Philippe. They levelled their muskets at the mob.

'Prisoner under the protection of the Admiralty!' snapped the taller Marine. 'No man takes another step, you hear?'

'Ah come on now, lads,' said the florid man, evidently the leader of the mob, who took a step forward despite the soldier's command. 'You're good Englishmen like ourselves. What say you go inside and get yourselves a nice refreshing drink in the taproom, eh, while we look after your man here?'

The two Marines looked at each other as though the offer was tempting, and the mob began to inch forward again.

'The Admiralty's orders!' bawled the taller Marine as he took aim at the leader.

The issue still seemed to be in the balance. The Englishmen had the advantage of numbers and could easily rush Philippe's guards, even if they lost one or two of their number in doing so. Philippe wished he still had his sword, for he was confident he could have evened the odds even more; but if he started killing Englishmen, was there any guarantee that his guards would still remain true to their orders?

The men in the mob looked from one to another as though willing one of them to make the first move. Tentatively, the florid man drew out a cudgel from the length of rope that served him as a belt.

The shot made several in the mob jump and caused the pigeons perched on the inn's roof and outbuildings to scatter noisily. The Englishmen turned almost as one and saw MacCaughan framed in the door from the taproom, where he had seemingly been refreshing himself. His left hand was holding a pistol in the air, the smoke from the shot still clearing, while the Scot drew his sword with his right.

'Well, my brave lads,' he said, his voice slower, louder and clearer than when talking to Philippe, 'what's it to be? A musket ball from my boys, there, or my blade through yer innards? Tell you what, though, if ye're so keen to fight the Frogs I can put you the way of a recruiting officer or two. Second of Foot in these parts, isna that right? Out in Jamaica and parts like that they are these days, I hear tell. Full o' the yellow fever in those parts, my lads. A terrible place for the mortality without a Frenchman in sight. Still, it'll earn a decent pension for yer widows!'

The mob dispersed without another word, shamefacedly retreating past MacCaughan back into the taproom. The Marine sergeant sheathed his blade and strolled towards Philippe, nodding approval to his men as he did so.

'My thanks, Sergeant,' said Philippe. 'I thought they were too driven by bloodlust to see sense.'

'Aye, well, so did I,' said MacCaughan, 'an' if I hadna been wearing this uniform, I'd have been in there with them for the stramash. My brother was killed in Flanders in June under the Duke of York, so I've no love for you Frenchies, *Mon Sewer lee Viscount*.'

—

As Philippe's carriage drew nearer to London, the weather turned. The bitter north-easterly gave way to a mild, gentle south-western breeze which brought torrential rain. This joined with the melting snow and ice to turn the Portsmouth road into a quagmire, conditions that were exacerbated by the increasing traffic. By the time they crossed the broad stretches of common land between Tooting and Clapham, Philippe was able to smell London, even though it was downwind. They went through a few more small villages and then Kennington, where he could see the tops of some of the larger buildings, especially church towers and spires. At a place called Newington and with darkness falling, the carriage turned to the left, passed through Lambeth and then moved out onto a broad and relatively new bridge that crossed the Thames into Westminster. It was ironic, Philippe thought, that this was his second visit to London; he had been there seven years before when the Gasks' ship *Julius Caesar* came up to one of the wharves near the Tower. He had crossed this very bridge and seen this very scene: the great abbey church of Westminster with the Parliament buildings under its lee, where William Pitt and his minions plotted the destruction of the French Republic. His second time in London, yet he, a nobleman and sea-captain of France, had never been to Paris in his life.

The post-chaise turned onto Whitehall, which he recognised, and stopped outside a building close to the top of the road. There MacCaughan turned him over to a fussy, bespectacled official and walked away with no more than a curt nod. The man had probably saved Philippe's life at the inn in Haslemere, but Phillippe knew he would almost certainly never see the Scot again.

The official, who did not give his name, summoned a Marine guard to ensure that Philippe did not escape, then led him to a side door into what he knew to be the Admiralty building. A number of men in officers' uniforms, milling around a gloomy candlelit ante-chamber, fell silent as he entered and eyed him with frank curiosity and hostility as he was led to a door in the far corner of the room. This led to an ill-lit and seemingly little-frequented staircase, which went up to what seemed to be the garrets, which consisted of a cramped and winding corridor with small rooms on either side. A few of these contained clerks, but most seemed to be filled from floor to ceiling with rolled up documents, bundles of envelopes bound together by string, and huge, musty leather-bound volumes, all in a state of hopeless confusion. Close to the end of the corridor, one of the doors on the left was closed. The official knocked on this. There was a muffled response, the official walked away without a word taking the Marine with him, and Philippe was to all intents and purposes left alone in the garret of the British Admiralty. For a moment he toyed with the idea of escape, which would surely be easy; all he had to do was to find an officer on his own, preferably his size or thereabouts, overpower the man, change into his uniform, and simply walk out of the building. It was now wholly dark, afternoon having given way to a long December evening, and the conditions were bound to aid him. If he was challenged, he could surely speak English well enough to convince any guard that he was, say, an American loyalist officer; he knew of several who went to the mother country after their side's defeat and now held commands in the Royal Navy.

The fancy flew higher. Perhaps he could seek out the First Lord of the Admiralty and kill him. Or he could stroll down Whitehall, into Downing Street and assassinate Pitt. That would prove his loyalty to the Republic perhaps even to the likes of Citizen Jean-Baptiste Carrier—

'Come.'

He did none of those things. Instead he went into the tiny office behind the door, just as the invisible voice commanded. The room was largely filled by an oak desk, much of the surface of which was taken up by precarious mounds of papers, mainly letters, as far as he could see. Every inch of wall was taken up by bookcases which contained musty leather-bound volumes seemingly indistinguishable from those abandoned back down the corridor.

A small man of roughly Philippe's age, perhaps a little younger, sat behind the desk. He was very pale and very thin, with badly cut yellow hair and several days of wispy stubble struggling to coalesce into a grossly unfashionable beard on his chin and cheeks. Heavy spectacles were perched on his aquiline nose. His clothes were drab, his jacket a faded brown with holes in the elbows. By the light of a single candle he was writing what appeared to be a long but nearly illegible marginal note on a tightly folded letter. Some sort of clerk, then, Philippe assumed. England seemed to be an entire nation of clerks. God alone knew how they found enough men to do the fighting.

Philippe began to hum '*La Marseillaise*'. It would pass the time and it might annoy the little English clerk.

The fellow finished his note, laid down his quill, removed his spectacles, and focused entirely upon Philippe. Perhaps '*La Marseillaise*' had done the trick.

'Captain Philippe Kermorvant of the frigate *Le Zéphyr*,' said the little man in perfect French and a surprisingly deep voice. 'Otherwise known as the Vicomte de Saint-Victor.'

The clerk rose, stepped out from behind the desk, and took a few paces towards Philippe.

'You have the advantage of me, sir,' Philippe replied in English.

Unexpectedly, the little man extended his hand.

'I am Wilden,' he said. 'Edward, Lord Wilden. I am your cousin.'

Philippe was so astonished that it took him a few moments to raise his own hand and shake that of his new-found relation.

CHAPTER THIRTY-TWO

During the relatively short time he had spent at the Chateau de Brechelean, Philippe, Vicomte de Saint-Victor, took a keen interest in the lists of the British government that appeared from time to time in the Paris newspapers, which belatedly arrived in Brittany a few days after publication.

(Similarly, he tried to keep up with the unfathomable and vicious politics of the land of his birth, which now called itself the United States of America.)

So he knew from memory the names of the enemy's rulers, who changed rather less frequently than the incessantly transient members of the Committee of Public Safety.

First Lord of the Treasury, Chancellor of the Exchequer and Prime Minister, William Pitt, esquire. Secretary of State for Foreign Affairs, Lord Grenville. Secretary of State for Home Affairs, Henry Dundas, esquire. Master General of the Ordnance, the Duke of Richmond. First Lord of the Admiralty, the Earl of Chatham – Pitt's brother, of course, for that was the way the English did things. And so on, down the ranks of the ever more obscure – for instance, what form of exotic potentate could a Lord Privy Seal possibly be – until there, in the list of junior lords of the Admiralty, was a name he knew for other reasons. *Edward, Lord Wilden.*

His mother was not proud of her family and talked little of it. But before she disappeared and he went off to sea, he gleaned the essential elements from snatches of conversation with her, or from unguarded overheard remarks. The family of Pardew, Lords Wilden, descended from charcoal burners in a place called Wyre Forest in the county of Worcester. One of them eventually made a respectable fortune from coal and iron, enough to buy an army commission for his son, who rose to become a general in the long wars between England and France over the succession to the crown of Spain at the beginning of the century. The general was ennobled for modest success in battle. Philippe's mother was a granddaughter of the second lord and thus cousin to the fourth Lord Wilden, but her headstrong nature caused a great falling out with her family, the immediate cause being her insistence on going to the Americas in search of a better husband than the inbred gentry of Worcestershire could provide. The thin, scruffily dressed clerk who showed Philippe into a large, well-furnished room on the floor beneath the Admiralty garrets had to be the fifth lord. Philippe studied his cousin's features in an attempt to find similarities with the image he saw in mirrors, but it was hard to see any. This was especially true of Lord Wilden's eyes. The man's appearance was innocuous, even slovenly. It would be easy to overlook him in company and to assume he was a man of no significance. But the eyes told a very different story. They were a striking green, fierce and piercing, their unsettling strangeness exaggerated by the weak candlelight. Even when he was talking about the weather, there was an unnerving sense of a wild animal waiting its moment to strike.

'I have never not been Lord Wilden,' said Philippe's cousin, after a few minutes of polite conversation. 'My father died three months before I was born – his horse reared and threw him, breaking his neck. My birth, gender and survival greatly disappointed my uncle, a miserable old rector who had banked on the inheritance clearing his debts. He shot himself when I was eight. Bloody business, I'll tell you, which drove my aunt wholly mad. But also good riddance, I have to say. I may have been very young, but I recall that he was an intolerable man.'

'I was the opposite,' said Philippe as an attendant arrived with a tray bearing two glasses of wine, a plate of confectionery, and a sealed letter, presumably a despatch for the attention of the lord of the Admiralty. 'My father never spoke of his title and estates, nor did my mother. The first I knew of the title was when a visitor addressed him as "my lord". At first I thought he was joking.'

'And you never saw your estates, nor even France itself, until a few months ago. I have undoubtedly spent more time there than you have. Curious, no? But then you have lived a curious life, Cousin Philippe.'

'I'm flattered that you have taken an interest in it.'

'In some respects, I know more about your life than you do.'

It was an astounding remark, and Philippe knew he was gawping at his cousin. 'How can that be?'

Lord Wilden chewed one corner of a biscuit, swallowed, and washed it down with a sip of wine.

'You mentioned your mother,' said the Admiralty lord. 'My father's first cousin. What do you know about what befell her?'

Philippe thought it a strange question. But then Wilden had grown up knowing hardly any close family, as had Philippe. It was surely only natural for him to seek information on the relations he had heard about.

'After the revolution began – what you would still call the war for the thirteen colonies, I suppose—'

'Something of the sort,' said Wilden, smiling.

'My father and mother had long argued about politics,' said Philippe, weighing his words carefully. These were some of his most painful memories, and he needed to give full justice to both of his parents. 'My father, of course, favoured the cause of those who sought independence. How could he not, when he had been exiled from France for advocating a republic and liberty? So he became a friend of Adams, Hancock, Jefferson, all those sorts of men. He was always suspicious of Washington, but remember that Washington was a near neighbour, we knew him quite well, we knew what sort of man he was. My mother, though, was a passionate loyalist. She believed in the Crown, and England's rule over America. When the fighting started, the quarrels between them got louder and longer. More violent, too. I remember sitting on the stairs, night after night, as they harangued each other. I was twelve or thirteen at the time, and like all boys, I favoured my father's beliefs. But I loved my mother, too…'

Wilden nodded and gave a slight wave of his hand, encouraging Philippe to continue.

'Looking back, I see now that they were trying to persuade me to one side or other – my father to the cause of the Americans and my French blood, my mother to England.'

'To choose between him and her,' said Wilden.

'Yes, I understand that now. I remember sleepless nights, and tears… but I think that in my heart, my choice was already made. The American cause was young and exciting. My friends were enthusiastic for it. In truth, too, perhaps I was always closer to my father. As it was, I announced one day that I wished to go to sea, to serve on a ship fighting the British. My father was astonished, but my mother – she screamed, she struck me, she wept, and that went on for days on end. But I stood firm, my father and her first husband's family supported me, and in the end she seemed to calm down and accept my decision.'

Philippe drank a little wine. He had never spoken of any of this to anyone except Tasha. Somehow, though, it felt as though Edward, Lord Wilden, was a friend he had known for his entire life.

'Then one day my father and I went fishing at dawn, out on the banks of the Chesapeake, and when we got home my mother had gone. She'd taken her personal maid and many of her possessions, but none of the other servants knew where she went. Some months later, my father got word that she was in New York, which was the British headquarters, of course, in those days. Apparently she was telling anybody who'd listen that she was loyal to King George, whatever her husband's opinion might be. A few weeks after that, we heard she had died of a fever. It was high summer; the city was crammed full of soldiers, sailors and other loyalists who'd fled the independent states. Disease was rife, so there was no reason to doubt the report. Does that accord with your family's understanding of what happened to her, Cousin?'

Lord Wilden took off his spectacles and laid them on the table. He lifted his glass, drained it, returned it to the table, then stared at Philippe.

'No,' he said softly. 'No, it does not.'

The Englishman picked up the letter from the tray and handed it to his cousin. Puzzled, Philippe examined the wax seal, which bore a crest he knew very well indeed from the old armorial in the library at Dunkeld Plantation: the arms of the Pardew family, Lords Wilden. He broke the seal, unfolded the letter, and registered the address and date: *Bath, the sixth day of December 1793.* It was a day that did not exist in France, of course, and the almost forgotten but still familiar handwriting belonged to a writer who, likewise, did not exist.

The handwriting belonged to Philippe's mother.

'What is this?' he demanded.

'She is alive, Philippe,' said Lord Wilden. 'She did not die in New York. She went north from there, into Canada, then returned to England when it became clear the rebels were going to win the war. She became a part of my family again. She lives, Cousin. Your mother lives.'

Philippe's chest was tight, and he was aware that he was breathing rapidly. He seemed to see a dozen Wildens and a dozen letters, all swirling in front of his eyes.

'This isn't so,' he said, aware that his voice was no more than a broken whisper. 'This can't be so.'

'Read the letter, Cousin.'

Philippe took a sip of wine to quieten his racing heart. His eyesight steadied, and he read the words of the woman he had believed dead for fifteen years.

Bath, the sixth day of December 1793

My dearest son Philippe,

I do not deserve your forgiveness. I do not seek it. I ask only that you to try to understand why I did what I did. I pray you will consent to meet me — your cousin Wilden will tell you how that may happen. Then I can tell you my story, and perhaps you will be willing to listen to it. You will say I deserted you, but to my mind it was you who deserted me, at your father's behest.

No. Let us not rake over the past, not until we can meet and I can explain myself. Fate has brought you to England, your true home, and I pray that you will be guided by Wilden as to the ways and means by which we may be reunited. I long to see you, my dear son, to see how you have grown and hear the story of your life from your own lips.

I will not damn your father. I loved him once. But before we meet, there are things you need to know about him, Philippe. He was a walking contradiction. A rationalist and a free thinker renowned throughout Europe, yet he was obsessed with the legends of Merlin and King Arthur. An atheist who insisted on having you brought up in the Catholic faith, though to say it was difficult to persuade priests to cross the water from Maryland — one of them drowned just off our jetty, Philippe, do you remember that? I'll also tell you this about your father, Philippe. He was a vehement opponent of the hegemony of kings who yet insisted upon the absolute hegemony of a husband over his wife. He was a believer in peace and the brotherhood of all living beings yet hunted every animal and bird that drew breath on our lands and flogged his wife until her skin had more welts than unsullied flesh. Verité, the world called him. I tell you this, Philippe, Hypocrisie would have been a better name.

But no, I will not damn him. I have written enough, for these days I find holding a pen to be difficult and painful. I pray you will agree to what Wilden proposes, and that we may be reunited very soon. I am at Bath for my health and fear I am not long for this world. It is my dearest wish that I should see my beloved son before I die, that he may learn the truth about
Your very loving and remorseful mother

Bridgetta, Vicomtesse de Saint-Victor

It was as though she was standing before him, speaking the words herself. He could hear her voice and see her face as clearly as if she were standing in the portico of Dunkeld, scolding him for some misdemeanour.

He was empty. He had no thoughts, no emotions. His mother was not dead. He should have been elated, but memories that had been buried for twenty years were flooding back. With them came a torrent of other thoughts: the guillotine, the *noyades* of Nantes, the deaths of good men in the battle of *Le Zéphyr* against *Chester*, Leonore, the butchering of Tasha and Ivan. He knew he lived and breathed, but it was as though his spirit was dead.

Wilden made no attempt to question him or to resume their conversation. He seemed content to sit opposite his cousin, chewing on biscuits and sipping wine, as the ticking of the clock and the distant street noise from Whitehall provided the only sounds in the room. Philippe had no idea how long the silence lasted, but in the end it was he who broke it.

'She says you can arrange for us to meet. How can that be so when I'm a prisoner of England?'

Wilden seemed to contemplate the question for the first time, although he must surely have discussed it with Philippe's mother.

'There are two ways,' said Wilden. 'One will be known to you, for many of your brothers-in-arms have taken it.'

'Parole.'

'Quite so. Give your parole, and I can arrange for you to spend the rest of the war in a town that your mother can easily reach, even in her condition. Chippenham would be ideal, I think. Parole is a comfortable

life, I'm told, although perhaps a little lacking in action for a man with
your history.'

'And if I don't give my parole, I'll spend the rest of the war on a hulk
or in one of your prison camps.'

'Life need not be so... what term can I use... black and white.'

Lord Wilden leaned forward. 'Cousin,' he said. 'Philippe. You bear
a noble name, you possess a noble title. You may choose to call yourself
Captain Kermorvant, just as I could decide to call myself Mister Pardew,
but that cannot bury the truth, which is that I am Baron Wilden and
you are the Vicomte de Saint-Victor. You've seen what deeds are done
in the name of the French Republic, what horrors, what atrocities...
Even if they don't come for you, my lord vicomte, and send you off to
the guillotine like so many other worthy men and women of our rank
– and every other rank, too – I ask you if that is a cause you really wish
to serve?'

Wilden's words were so uncomfortably close to some of Philippe's
own thoughts that he wondered for a moment if his cousin might be
some kind of sorcerer, a man who could read minds. The small, sickly
looking fellow sitting just a few feet from him was no Merlin, but he
was persistent and his words contained uncomfortable truths.

'You were not born and raised in France,' said Wilden, maintaining
his relentless line of argument. 'You have only been in the country for
a few months – less than a year. What is it to you, Philippe? You have
more to connect you to Russia: your wife and son are buried there.' *So
he knew. But he was a lord of the Admiralty and an intelligencer. Of course he
knew.* 'England is your mother's country, your motherland if you will.
You may not consider yourself English, but we share many of the same
ancestors, you and I. They were not great lords who came over with the
Conqueror, they were common people, charcoal burners in the forests
of Worcestershire, drawn from and part of the soil of England. That is
our shared blood, Philippe.'

'Ancient history,' said Philippe, who still clutched his mother's letter
in his hand and was barely able to focus on his cousin's words. 'I am a
loyal Frenchman.'

'*Our* ancient history, Cousin. But you claim to be a loyal Frenchman.
Very well, what does that mean, mm? I could take you out of here,
across the road, down a lane, and into a tavern full of loyal Frenchmen.'

'Exiles. Royalists. Traitors.'

'Men who are more French than you, Cousin,' said Wilden with sudden venom. 'Men who were born and lived all their lives in France. Men who have lost everything in the revolution, or at least, everything but their heads, unlike so many of their friends and kin. Men who despite all that are still loyal to France, to the *true* France, not to that coterie of deranged murderers around the madman Robespierre.'

Philippe made no reply. He looked again at the letter, then set it down.

'Why are you telling me this, Cousin?' he said.

'You can be a free man very easily, Philippe. One oath and you can walk from this building into the open air, as free as every other man and woman you see on the street out there. An oath to serve Louis the Seventeenth, King of France, sincerely and loyally.'

'And then?'

Wilden smiled, his strange eyes fixed on Philippe's own.

'And then, Cousin, there are two possibilities. One, you can join the royalist forces preparing to return to France and liberate their homeland alongside the heroic armies who are already fighting there.'

The Chouans. The Vendée. The Comte d'Artois.

'The second possibility?' said Philippe.

'The second possibility is my personal preference,' said Wilden, smiling again, 'as you may expect. Not that I would seek to influence you unduly, of course. The second possibility is that you can return to France, where I have little doubt that your heroics in the battle against *Chester* will bring you another command before very long. You take command of that ship, you sail it and if necessary you take it into battle against the navy that I serve. You resume your career, Cousin, exactly as though you had never been taken prisoner.'

There would be a price, Philippe thought, and he could see it clearly.

'You want me to become a spy for you,' he said. 'You want me to be an English agent.'

'Not at all. I want you to be a French agent, serving the true and rightful King of France.'

In his father's library, the young Philippe Kermorvant once read a book that told the story of Faust and his pact with the devil. Edward, Lord Wilden, was an unlikely Mephistopheles, but the bargain he was proposing would surely have done credit to the lord of the underworld.

The clock ticked. Wilden sat still, seemingly quite content to wait as the minutes passed. Philippe had to give an answer. He remembered his cousin's words and all that had happened to him – all that he had seen in France, all that had been said – since he sailed *Le Quatorze Juillet* into Saint-Malo. Then he looked once more at his mother's letter, and he knew what his answer would be.

HISTORICAL NOTE

The French Revolutionary and Napoleonic Wars form the 'classic age' of naval historical fiction, at least as far as British (and to a considerable extent, American) readers are concerned. C. S. Forester and Patrick O'Brian are, of course, the undisputed titans of the genre, have spawned countless imitators (many of them hugely impressive in their own right) and are the benchmarks against which any new work in a hugely crowded field are measured – new authors, myself included, are often promoted with a strapline along the lines of 'For readers of C. S. Forester and Patrick O'Brian'. (As the saying goes: no pressure.) Inevitably, the field is overwhelmingly slanted towards the British angle. There are some novels written from the French perspective, unsurprisingly by French authors, but they are relatively few and none of them have made it into translation. By contrast and vice-versa, translated versions of Forester and O'Brian have a huge following in France, which may or may not tell us something about respective national prejudices. This is strange, because fiction set from the point of view of the enemy has a long, respectable and very successful pedigree: consider among many others *All Quiet on the Western Front, The Blue Max, The Eagle Has Landed, Das Boot* and my own favourite novels in the naval historical fiction genre, the four 'Sailor of Austria' titles by John Biggins. So when it was suggested that I should write something set in what is often known as the 'classic age' of sailing warfare, I knew I didn't want to produce yet another clone of Aubrey or Hornblower, Bolitho or Kydd. Instead, my mind went back to a throwaway remark made at a historical fiction conference (in Cumbernauld, of all places) a few years ago, where a group of naval writers congregated in the bar to put the world to rights. One of our number remarked in passing that it was a shame there was nothing in English from the French side. (I forget who said this – we'd been in the bar for a while by then – but my thanks to whoever it was!) I thought then that it was an interesting idea, but believed that my relative lack of grounding in French naval history of the period and above all my absolutely dire command of the language would rule me out. Since taking on the task regardless of these shortcomings, several friends (you know who you are) have intimated that I must be mad. Maybe they'll be proved right!

There was no frigate named *Le Zéphyr* in the French navy of this period, but I have based my fictional ship closely on *L'Hermione*, built in 1779 and which subsequently carried the Marquis de Lafayette to America. Between 1997 and 2012, a replica of *L'Hermione* was built at Rochefort, and this made its first voyage to the United States in 2015; indeed, it's possible that the first subconscious seeds of this book were sown during a visit to the *L'Hermione* under construction at Rochefort in 2004. If you want to know exactly what my *Le Zéphyr* looked like, therefore, go to the ship's website, fregate-hermione.com/, visit its splendid YouTube channel, www.youtube.com/user/HERMIONE17300, or better still, go and visit the ship itself.

The action between *Le Zéphyr* and HMS *Chester* is based loosely on that between the French *Cleopatre* and HMS *Nymphe*, which actually took place a few months earlier than my fictional encounter and was the first major naval engagement of the Revolutionary War. The captain of *Nymphe* was the Cornishman Edward Pellew, who was knighted for his victory and was thus set on the course to fame as perhaps the greatest British frigate captain of the war (as well as becoming, in fiction, the mentor of Horatio Hornblower). *Chester*, like *Le Zéphyr*, is based on a real ship, or rather a class of real ships: the *Roebuck* class of two-deck Fifth Rate frigates, built between 1776 and 1783 primarily for service in north America. The most famous unit of this class was HMS *Serapis*, which in 1779 was captured off Flamborough Head by the American privateer *Bonhomme Richard* commanded by John Paul Jones. For comprehensive detail on the warships of both the British and French navies during this period, readers are referred to the relevant volumes in the magisterial series by Rif Winfield: *British Warships in the Age of Sail, 1714–1792* and *British Warships in the Age of Sail, 1792–1817*. A companion volume co-written by Rif and Stephen Roberts, *French Warships in the Age of Sail, 1786–1861*, provided detail on both many of the historical ships referred to in this story and the entirely fictional ones that I invented for the purposes of the narrative. Some of the many other sources I consulted while researching this book might be of interest to anyone seeking further information about the French navy during this period. Two titles from the splendid Osprey Publishing proved invaluable, namely *French Warship Crews 1789–1805* by Terry Crowdy and *British Frigate vs French Frigate* by Mark Lardas. For the political and strategic background, see William S. Cormack *Revolution and Political Conflict in the French Navy 1789–94*. Several memoirs of those who served in the French navy during this period have appeared in English editions over the years, notably those of Seaman Garneray and the Marine Moreau de Jonnes. Among many books on the history and topography of Brittany, the most useful was probably *Brittany 1750–1950* by Sharif Gemie. Lescallier's priceless contemporary Anglo–French nautical dictionary, *Vocabulaire des termes de marine Anglois et François*, is easily findable online. Naturally I used many French works too (thank you, Google Translate), perhaps the most valuable being *Brest: un port en Révolution 1789–99* by Philippe Henwood and Edmond Monange, a superb source for the history and politics of the town but more especially for its detail on the layout and features of the town and dockyard during this exact period.

Philippe Kermorvant is a wholly fictitious character, although many of the people and incidents he refers to are reasonably true to the historical record. His mentor John Paul Jones did go on from mythic deeds during the American Revolutionary war to serve as an admiral in the Russian navy of Empress Catherine the Great. Otherwise, some of the characters who feature in *Sailor of Liberty* were also real historical figures: these include Jean-Paul Carrier, Jeanbon de Saint André and Admiral Morard de Galles. The Comte d'Artois was essentially just as Paul Storr describes him in Chapter 24; in 1824 he succeeded his elder brother to become King Charles X of France, but his high-handedness, inflexibility and religious fanaticism led to his overthrow within six years. Similarly, many of the events referred to in this book actually happened: for instance, the revolts of the Chouans and the Vendée, the fall of Toulon, the mutinies in the Brest fleet at Quiberon, and of course 'The Terror', epitomised by the extensive use of the guillotine, although I have presented some elements of this as beginning a little earlier than they did in reality. For example, Jeanbon Saint-André did not arrive in Brest until later in 1793 than I have presented it here; the revolutionary tribunal at Brest was not set up until the early months of 1794, some months after Philippe narrowly avoids its clutches and Alexandre is condemned by it; and Morard de Galles took the Brest fleet to sea piecemeal over the summer of 1793, not as one unit in early September as I have presented it. Jean-Baptiste Carrier's *noyades*, the mass drownings carried out at Nantes, began a few weeks after I have placed them in the story, and it has been suggested that the shackling together of naked male and female prisoners in 'republican marriages' was actually an invented royalist 'atrocity story' or, if you prefer, fake news. Carrier really did describe the River Loire as 'the national bathtub', though. I have deliberately introduced a few other anachronisms for dramatic licence. For instance, the use of hulks at Portsmouth to accommodate French prisoners of war did not begin until the summer of 1794, but it suited my purpose to have Philippe incarcerated on one a few months earlier. I also invented an entirely fictitious passage from a real book, Arthur Young's *Travels Through France*, as the epigraph for Chapter Six. Often, though, truth is stranger than anything dramatic licence can conjure. I needed the name of a French official in Russia in 1792–3 who could have approved Philippe's citizenship. Although there was no ambassador in Russia at the time (Catherine the Great had taken umbrage at the previous one), there certainly was a French consul at Kronstadt, Philippe's home port, and his name was Barthélemy de Lesseps. He was the uncle of the man who designed the Suez Canal.

Acknowledgements

A number of people helped and supported me during the writing of *Sailor of Liberty*. My old friend Dr Ann Coats, chair of the inestimable Naval Dockyards Society, generously shared her unrivalled knowledge of eighteenth-century Portsmouth. Dr Alan James of King's College London provided me with crash courses in various aspects of French naval history. Dr Olivier Aranda of the Sorbonne generously responded to my queries and steered me away from a number of 'howlers' that I would otherwise have made. I expect I've still made many others, but he certainly isn't responsible for them! My thanks, too, to the staffs of the National Archives, the National Maritime Museum and the British Library, where I found many of the secondary materials that enabled me to write this story, and some primary ones too, such as logs, muster books and other sources from ships captured in battle.

This book was conceived and largely written during the Covid-19 pandemic, and the circumstances of that extraordinary period impacted adversely on its writing. For example, it proved impossible to visit the area of Brittany where much of the action ashore is set, and it was also impossible for me to visit the replica of *L'Hermione*, on which Philippe's *Le Zéphyr* is closely based. Fortunately, my cousin Colin Bancroft had been heavily involved in the twinning of Llandovery in west Wales and Plougonvelin in Brittany, and partly compensated for my lack of first-hand knowledge by providing me with some of his reminiscences of the area.

Michael Bhaskar and Kit Nevile of Canelo, and my ever-patient agent, Peter Buckman, responded positively to the proposal for this book and have provided constant encouragement. Indeed, Kit went the extra mile by displaying unstinting enthusiasm for the idea and providing forensic and invariably positive editorial input. Finally and as always, a huge thank you to Wendy, 'Beta Reader One' and principal cheerleader!

David Davies
Bedfordshire
August 2022